A.J. SCUDIERE

NIGHTSHADE

FORENSIC FBI FILES ✦ BOOK 6

GARDEN OF BONE

NightShade Forensic FBI Files: Salvage

FIRST EDITION

"There are really just 2 types of readers—those who are fans of AJ Scudiere, and those who will be."

-Bill Salina, Reviewer, Amazon

For *The Shadow Constant*:

"The Shadow Constant by A.J. Scudiere was one of those novels I got wrapped up in quickly and had a hard time putting down."

-Thomas Duff, Reviewer, Amazon

For *Phoenix*:

"It's not a book you read and forget; this is a book you read and think about, again and again . . . everything that has happened in this book could be true. That's why it sticks in your mind and keeps coming back for rethought."

-Jo Ann Hakola, The Book Faerie

For *God's Eye*:

"I highly recommend it to anyone who enjoys reading - it's well-written and brilliantly characterized. I've read all of A.J.'s books and they just keep getting better."

-Katy Sozaeva, Reviewer, Amazon

For *Vengeance*:

"Vengeance is an attention-grabbing story that lovers of action-driven novels will fall hard for. I hightly recommend it."

-Melissa Levine, Professional Reviewer

For *Resonance*:

"Resonance is an action-packed thriller, highly recommended. 5 stars."

-Midwest Book Review

DEDICATION

This one is dedicated to all the Renegades out there.
Thank you for joining me on this journey. I know you've been waiting to find out what happened to Emmaline ... well, it's here at last. But in typical fashion, I won't leave you there. Donovan has a whole new complicated future opening up. And for those of you who are here for all of it,
THANK YOU.
You are why I do what I do.
A special thank you to the Renegades who have been here since the beginning.

DEDICATION

ACKNOWLEDGMENTS

A book is the dream of the author. The author works hard to bring that dream into the world, but it's never a lone effort.

The book you hold is the work of me, my sister (the management and publication side of things), my Beta-Readers (Victoria, Dana and Laura), my cover designer (JB Schroeder), and more.

People help with information—like the shops I went into on my trip to New Orleans two years ago. Editors point out typos and continuity issues. Even the ARC readers help with anything that slips through.

Thank you to everyone who helped.

1

Eleri stepped gingerly into the tiny shop on Royal Street, though the sign above the door almost too French-ly declared the address as "Rue Royal." She was grateful for the smack of air conditioning. She hadn't yet acclimated to the New Orleans heat and humidity.

Eleri had made a subconscious decision to drive to Louisiana. Consciously, she'd argued with herself that she hadn't wanted to fly and get stuck without a car or deal with the hassle getting a rental at the airport. Also, maybe—she now admitted to herself—she'd wanted to slow her progress into the city and toward the task before her.

Though she was hopeful for closure, there was no way this task would be a pleasant one. She was quite convinced it would not be a quick one, either. So she'd been breathing heavily, drawing in deep lungful of thick air since she'd finally pulled into town, several hours earlier. Like the task, the air felt oppressive and overwhelming any moment she stepped outside into the heat.

The little shop was not only cool, it was dark, and she'd ducked inside on a whim. Something whispered at the back of her brain to push the door open and come inside—although whether it was some kind of soul-deep psychic impulse or merely the need for air conditioning to escape the sun and heat, she couldn't have said.

A woman materialized from the back room, her dark hair twisted into neat, tiny knots all over her head. Her beautiful face smiled convincingly as her hands clasped together in a more elegant version of a classic shopkeeper's pose.

"Welcome to my store. Let me know if there is anything I can help you with." She said it with an accent Eleri couldn't quite place. It was both French and Cajun—straight-up New Orleans—and maybe, a little more.

Something flared in the woman's eyes as Eleri turned to face her. But then, just as quickly, it disappeared. The brief shock felt like recognition, and Eleri was left wondering if maybe she'd imagined it.

The woman left her then, seeming to dissolve into the woodwork as quickly as she'd appeared. Still, Eleri had no doubt of her ability as a shopkeeper to re-materialize the moment Eleri needed anything, or perhaps suddenly came up with a question. So far, she didn't have any.

Despite a hip and welcoming setting inside the store, which was both open and cozy, it was still just a typical voodoo shop in New Orleans—as best Eleri could tell. Mystic Vudu's interior looked like a converted home. How they had managed that, Eleri wasn't quite sure, but it was something she remembered from previous trips to New Orleans.

The shop was divided into tiny rooms, each with a theme. The small front room was lined with books; a separate room a little further back held ribbon-tied fabric bags of various scents and potions. Another shelf in that room displayed lines of incense sticks bearing various labels for the scent and the associated magic. There were also candles, bowls, crystals, and every other thing someone might need for casting simple spells. Another cozy-feeling room held dolls and tchotchkes—pieces that supposedly already held the right portion of magic, just waiting for the buyer to pick them up and take them home.

Grandmere would scoff at these dolls, Eleri thought. Then again, Grandmere never would have set foot in this place. Regardless of the skills of the owner, Mystic Vudu was clearly set up for tourists and—at this moment—Eleri felt like one. On one shelf, nearly identical dolls, though all handmade, lined row after row, staring out at her through painted white eyes with big black centers. Tiny white dots represented the sparkle of light in the eye.

On a whim, she reached out to touch one. Each of the foot-high dolls wore a wrapped-on dress of cut fabric that had never been stitched or seen a needle. Twine held the cloth around the doll's waist, as though it were a belt, and surely it held the whole doll together.

Though she had intended to pick one up and examine it, Eleri was shocked at the slight zing she received just from her initial touch. Instantly, she dropped it. Luckily, she'd barely lifted it and it fell back into place on the shelf, teetering first one way, then the other, before settling flat and staring at her with its cold, dark eyes once more.

Eleri stepped to the side, looking now at smaller versions of the dolls. These were only about five inches tall, with a tag attached to each one. In some cases, the tags were larger than the dolls, with the thick paper bearing the words of some old voodoo spell that Eleri did not recognize.

It bothered her—the feeling she had gotten from the doll—and she analyzed it, as Eleri was wont to do. It was easier to stay in here and breathe filtered, cool air and think about dolls and shelves, rather than think about the task that had brought her to New Orleans.

Did these dolls actually have some kind of magic in them? It wasn't impossible. She'd seen her great-grandmother do far more than add a zing to a poppet. Grandmere had given people things... tokens, spells, candles and more. In fact, that was how her grandmother mostly made her living: selling off pieces of voodoo to help people. Infertile couples, people whose homes needed protection, protection for a lost pet or person, things like that.

But, Eleri thought, Grandmere's spells were one-off items. People came to her and requested specific magic. It was up to Grandmere to decide if she should sell it to them or not. Here, in the shop, the items were already on the shelves, already imbued with their magic. Light or dark, Eleri wasn't sure—, and she also wasn't quite ready to pick up another doll, heft its weight, and test its power.

Could just anyone come in here, grab a doll, and take it home—having no idea what they'd actually put on their bookshelf? She knew it was more than possible.

There'd been a time when she would have easily told you that she didn't believe, but that time had long since passed. Though her mother had raised her without any of her own religion, it hadn't changed the outcome. What she was ran through her blood. Despite its power, it still hadn't saved her sister Emmaline, but it had left Eleri with her own skills.

For a moment, as Eleri stared at the tiny dolls lined up on smaller shelves, staring out at her in repetitive rows that formed eye-opening patterns and soul-catching fear, she thought of her mother. Did Nathalie have skills that she suppressed? Did she have skills that she didn't suppress yet had never shown her daughters? Eleri thought she might never know what powers her mother possessed.

She was reaching out to touch one of the smaller dolls, when she heard the sound behind her.

"Makinde," it whispered.

Eleri froze. Turning, she saw the woman again, though it didn't appear she'd said anything.

At Eleri's look, she asked, "May I help you?"

Eleri shook her head. The woman did not act as though she had just whispered the ancient word.

At that moment, she heard the chimes at the front door, followed by footsteps. At least two other people had come in. The woman smiled, nodded at Eleri, and turned toward her new customers. Maybe she had finally decided that Eleri had come merely to browse and not to buy.

But the word whispered at the back of her head.

Makinde.

Had it really been said? Or had she heard it because she was thinking of Grandmere, and of her mother Nathalie, and wondering just what she might find in New Orleans?

Spotting an archway to her left, Eleri wandered though it, anxious to leave behind all the little dolls. This room held dried herbs, hung upside down, tied with ribbons that clipped to twine strung all along the wall. Had they dried here? It looked like they had, though the perfect state of each bundle of herbs spoke of a shop again—and not an actual witchcraft operation.

Though clearly the herbs had been treated and dried properly, it had happened elsewhere. The herbs here were not in process, but on display.

In another area—again off to her left, as the house seemed to wind around and around on itself—she spotted a countertop. Despite the value of the pieces displayed, there were no glass cases here. Looking up, she was surprised to see no cameras, although many of the pieces on the shelf in front her of bore tags with three- and even four-figure prices.

Again, though her fingers twitched, she didn't reach out and touch. Instead, she looked around the room for anything hinting of a security system. Thinking like an FBI agent, if this were her shop, and these were her price tags, she would have had them in a glass case, or, at the very least, had security cameras to watch the patrons.

Then again, the zing from the doll left her thinking that maybe the shop was protected by something a little bit stronger.

This time, when she turned back to the counter, a knife with a bone handle caught her attention. Reaching out, she picked it up to heft its weight, but she was not able to make any assessment—the jolt that shot through her and the images that assailed her were sharp and petrifying.

She dropped the knife with a clatter and ran from the store.

2

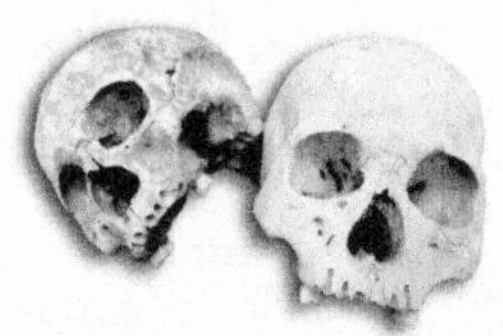

Donovan's cell rang, and he pulled it out of his pocket, placing the phone to his ear before he saw who was calling. He expected it to be Walter, and he caught just a glimpse of her face on his screen before he answered with a smiling, "Hey."

Unfortunately, her response was entirely no-nonsense. "Donovan, we have a problem."

Well, shit, he thought. Eleri had left two days prior, planning to go to New Orleans and look for the remains of her sister. She had what she thought was her first solid lead. Westerfield had not yet given him an assignment, and he'd returned home, hopeful he wouldn't get one. Crossing his fingers, he made a wish that Lucy could follow closely behind.

Though even his phone still said her name was Walter Reed, he was starting to think of her more and more as *Lucy*—her given name —during the time they shared together. It seemed more of who she was then. However, the voice on the phone, while clearly that of Lucy Fisher, was her ex-Marine, MARSOC, Special Forces, Walter Reed voice.

"What's going on?" he asked, his own tone now tersely matching hers. No friendly greeting, no wondering when she was going to come and visit him or when they might get to spend time together again. All his softer ideas had fled with her initial words.

"GJ and I are clearing out her grandfather's basement lab."

He'd known as much, thinking she might make it to him in another few days. He hadn't expected to be cleared so early. There were too many unclaimed skeletons and human bones in the lab. But Walter wasn't a forensic scientist; Donovan expected GJ to do most of the heavy lifting. The good news was that the lab was basically a museum, so at least this shouldn't involve anybody getting shot at. Whatever they were dealing with was likely already well dead.

Walter confirmed that in a moment. "There's a body in the kettle, Donovan."

Shit, he thought again. *Just what they needed.* He was certain—or he wanted to believe, maybe—that once GJ's grandfather was in custody, his "work" would have stopped. The lab would have remained static, and GJ and Walter would merely clean up what was there. Instead, it sounded as though new body parts were showing up.

Donovan remembered that they still hadn't found Shray Menon's body. Walter had declared the man dead during a gunfight, and Walter generally knew what she was doing. Still, given the scenario she'd described to him, it was entirely possible that Menon had somehow gotten carried away by his own people or by the family that owned the land Marks and Menon had raided.

There was also the slight possibility that Walter's assessment had been wrong and Menon was still alive. And if he was, he might still be making use of GJ's lab. Although they knew the lab contained a way to bring a full human body in and out without being noticed, they hadn't found the passage yet. The body in the kettle that Walter referred to was solid evidence that the path existed. The FBI had kept the lab under close surveillance. No one should have been able to get a body in.

"Tell me about it," he said, even as he wondered if the corpse could be Menon himself. He didn't say that, not wanting to sway other investigators if they hadn't thought of that possibility on their own.

"Well, we found it a few hours ago. GJ opened it up. It's already been de-fleshed, so any evidence we might have had is likely gone. *—Wait, what?*"

He could tell she was no longer speaking to him. Somewhere in the distance, he heard GJ Janson's voice. "The DNA would be boiled. Our only hope is that we get lucky with the teeth. Chances are, forensic ID is going to be our best bet."

"Did you hear that?" Walter asked. Before he even had a chance to reply, she said, "*That,* like GJ said."

It wasn't likely she was going to repeat scientific standards to him.

"Did you notify Westerfield?" he asked. Westerfield, his own special agent in charge of the NightShade division of the FBI, had very recently become Walter's boss as well.

"No." Donovan could practically hear her shaking her head. Walter had lived on the LA streets with homeless vets for a while, and Donovan always thought her simultaneous answer and nod or shake of her head was a remnant from being around so many people who'd had their eardrums blasted in war. It wasn't a happy thought, but it was pure Walter. She was still talking. "We looked at it and we wanted to see if we could get some information to report in, other than just 'we found this thing in the kettle'—*Oh, Jesus!*"

The tone in Walter's voice almost made Donovan smile. GJ had a knack for putting Lucy on edge. "What's going on now?" he asked.

"She's got tongs and she's pulling the bones out and shaking the water off."

"Well, how else is she supposed to get them out of the kettle?" Donovan asked. He was familiar with body kettles—large vats, much like pressure cookers, that one could use to de-flesh a skeleton. GJ's grandfather had one of the nicest, newest ones he'd seen. It was a recent model, in better condition and a bigger size than they'd had at the forensic center he'd worked at in South Carolina when he'd been the medical examiner, just a few short years ago.

"Do you need me to come examine it?" he asked.

"Do we need Donovan?" he heard Walter ask GJ.

Next, he heard GJ's reply from a distance. "I don't think so. Not yet. But I wanted him to have a heads-up, in case we might."

"There you have it," Walter said, her voice turning softer. "I miss you."

"Eew," GJ commented in the background, clearly not wanting to be the third-wheel overhearing a phone conversation between two lovers.

Donovan wanted to tell her there were no worries. He and Walter rarely got mushy, even when they were alone. It wasn't part of either of their DNA. "Well, call me back if you need me," he said. "But—a word to the wise. Don't wait more than a day to call Westerfield. Seriously. If nothing else, leave him a message tonight before you go to sleep. Anything longer than that will just piss him off. You want to get a nice balance between delivering feasible information and getting the information to him sooner rather than later."

"Got it," Walter replied. "We're going to see what we can do for this ID."

"Oh, it's definitely one of them," GJ called out from across the room.

Donovan cringed, wondering what word GJ might come up with for *them*. She'd taken to calling him a *werewolf*, no matter how many times he told her that the term was absolutely inappropriate. Unfortunately, the only other real word he'd ever heard to describe his type was *Lobomau*, and the Lobomau were *not* him. They were a very specific group of creatures and much more dangerous than most. However, that identification would not be possible from the bones alone.

"Well," he said, "unless you guys or her grandfather have some secret resource that I don't know about, you're going to need to tell Westerfield to start combing through dental records for a match. So I don't see how you can wait until you have a positive ID on the body before telling him what you have."

They spoke a little longer as he gave the two women tips and hints about how to deal with the boss the three of them now shared. And he hated to admit it, though he desperately wanted to see Lucy, a case was not the way he wanted to do it. He was still hopeful he wouldn't get called in on this one.

As soon as he hung up with Walter, his phone pinged again.

I've arrived.

It was Eleri. She'd made it, although whether that meant she'd arrived in New Orleans, at her great-grandmother's house, or somewhere else, he didn't know. The text didn't warrant a return. She'd simply promised to check in at least daily and give him some general idea of her whereabouts. He'd demanded the promise as she set off on her own. There was no FBI backup for this one, though they both were relatively certain she wouldn't need it.

Settling back into the chair in his living room, Donovan stared out the window. A tall wooden fence ringed his backyard. A gate at the far edge allowed him access to the National Forest land behind him. He thought about going for a run, and then, in the next moment, he stood up to make it happen. It had been far too long since he'd run at all, let alone in his own woods.

Piece by piece, he shed his clothing as he moved toward the back door. He was an investigator. He understood what it would mean if anything happened to him and anyone came in and found this. Still, he didn't let it stop him. He was fully naked by the time he reached the back gate and reached up, undid the latch near the top, and let himself out into the woods.

Turning, he stretched one hand over the high top of the fence and closed the latch behind him. For a moment, he looked up and around. *This is a new world,* he thought. He hadn't worried about these things when he was a child, but as he'd gotten older, technology had become more advanced, too. What he'd seen in the Ozarks had made him even more worried. Now he'd taken to looking for drones every time before he changed. The last thing any of them needed was someone catching a glimpse.

Unlike Wade and the de Gottardi and Little families in the Ozarks, Donovan had had no one to teach him or watch out for him. No groups were here scanning the area for technology, bugs, cameras, and even wolf hunters.

He hadn't known until the Ozarks that such hunters existed. Now, he stopped and checked for them far more cautiously. This run would be the first run where he wondered whether he would truly enjoy his freedom in the woods. Still, he figured, if he didn't do it now, when would he?

Stepping under the cover of trees, making it harder, at least, for someone to spy on him, he rolled his shoulders, popped his jaw, and felt the bones shift and move against each other. He felt tendons snap into a new position and the goose-pimpling of his flesh as the hair on his arms and legs and back rose. When he was finally down on all fours, he stretched long and low in a full run into the woods.

3

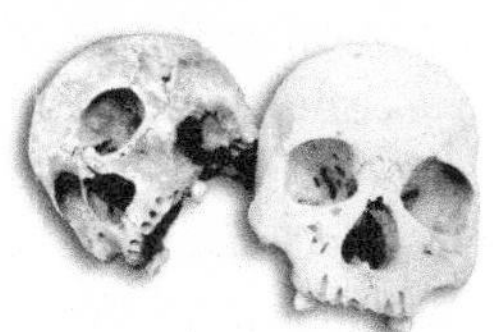

"Grandmere! I'm here," Eleri called out as she entered through the front door of her great-grandmother's house.

She needn't have hollered, and she knew it. Grandmere always knew who was at the door, just as she knew who was on the phone, and even when it would ring. She'd never seen the need to replace her old phone that still hung on the wall and rang with sounds that gave no sense of digital tone. The rotary dial used to drive Eleri crazy, but now it made her smile. Grandmere had no use for such frivolities as push-button dialing.

Grandmere didn't reply to Eleri's announcement. She merely turned the corner from the kitchen into the small living space. Everything in this house was small. "Cozy," Grandmere would call it. It suited her perfectly, though it had been far too small for Eleri's mother, Nathalie. Nathalie had fled Grandmere's home as soon as she had turned seventeen. She'd run off and married a man who owned multiple homes, any of which would allow Grandmere's whole house to fit inside a single bedroom.

That was how Eleri had been raised. However, there was something about Grandmere's shotgun house in the Lower Ninth Ward that none of her own family's homes could ever duplicate.

Grandmere wiped her hands on the towel she had tucked into the sash of the apron tied around her waist. Despite the fact that she was wearing the apron, as well as flour and possible other baking foods, she engulfed Eleri in a huge hug. Only then did Eleri finally begin to calm down from her encounter at the shop in the French quarter.

"Makinde!" Grandmere held her back by the shoulders and looked in her face. "What has you so strung up?"

Knowing that lying was useless, Eleri told her Grandmere at least a portion of the truth. "I drove into town and headed straight for the French Quarter. Thought I would walk a bit and wander some of the shops. It was a mistake."

"Did you go into those voodoo shops?" Grandmere admonished her, snapping the towel as she turned and headed back into the kitchen.

Of course. I went to the French quarter. What else would I do there? Eleri thought. That provided the entire answer to everything that had worked Eleri up.

"Yes," she said. "It looked like a cute little tourist shop."

"Did you find some real voodoo in there?"

"I did," Eleri replied as she followed her great-grandmother into the tiny kitchen. She was still trying to forget the zing that she'd felt when she picked up the bone-handled knife. Images had assaulted her —violent, scary, overwhelming scenes. But now, she was ashamed at the way she had dropped the knife and run from the shop.

She'd caught a brief glimpse of the shopkeeper's dark skin and wide smile as she spoke to the other patrons in the store. But the woman's eyebrows had frowned as she watched Eleri flee. Eleri wondered if the woman knew what she had in the shop. Still, she didn't tell Grandmere.

"Go set yourself up in your room," Grandmere said, and Eleri obliged.

Heading back toward the other side of the house, she stepped toward the small bedrooms tucked back there. The house was long and narrow with the short side facing the street. Eleri's bedroom—at the far back end of the house—was snugged in beside Grandmere's. Both were the same size. The house had no master bedroom set up.

One bathroom afforded all the residents of the home the opportunity to brush their teeth and use the toilet, taking turns in the same small space. *Her room,* as Grandmere called it, had been hers and Emmaline's when they had come to visit as children. The room still had the same two twin beds shoved into the corners. Just enough wall space remained for the door to the hall and another for the tiny closet.

The home was old enough that the closet door looked like another door opening to a room, yet the space was barely deep enough to hang clothes. Somewhere along the way, possibly a decade ago, Eleri had finally begun to use Emmaline's bed as a place for her suitcase. Grandmere had said nothing about it, though surely she'd noticed the change.

Before then, Eleri had been continuing to put her pieces into the closet, leaving the bed empty. She felt, perhaps as Grandmere did, that one day Emmaline would return and demand her space in the room.

Eleri now knew that was never going to happen. She suspected Grandmere knew it, too. They didn't talk about it. However, Grandmere still loved the bed. Surely, it had become purely symbolic.

When Eleri returned to visit Grandmere, she managed to ignore the signs of Emmaline that were still around. She saw them, but they usually didn't burn her heart the way they once had. This time, though, they did.

A tiny table sat, against the wall, taking up the gap between the beds. On the table stood a framed picture of Eleri and Emmaline.

Eleri must have been no more than ten, given that Emmaline was in the photo with her. They had their arms slung around each other and mud smeared on their hands and their pale dresses. They had obviously been playing in the yard. Grandmere had offered their mother a copy of the picture, but Nathalie refused it. The pictures that hung in Eleri's other homes included those of the two girls in their riding gear, dressed for Sunday best, or in their mother's arms at family portrait time. Grandmere's picture showed them playing. *This might be the only photo of its kind in existence,* Eleri thought.

Eleri had been named for her grandmother on her father's side of the family, but Emmaline, Eleri's little sister, had been named for Grandmere's daughter and their mother Nathalie's mother. The first Emmaline had disappeared young, too. However, she'd come back with baby Nathalie on her hip, and then once again disappeared—mostly likely into her addictions to booze and drugs. Grandmere had never seen her daughter again. She'd raised Nathalie on her own.

Nathalie had envisioned a bigger life for herself than this tiny house in this poor section of the wild town could offer, but Eleri loved it here. As she stood in the bedroom, looking out the back window, she could see through the spaces between the houses that backed up to Grandmere's home. Those houses faced the other street, which ran behind the one Grandmere lived on. The lack of fencing created a kind of backyard alley that ran the length of the block. Eleri saw empty lots, a few fresh-colored homes, and several that had faded to a dull brown-gray. Spray paint marked the sides of some houses. Plywood covering the windows still bore the marks "Gas X," Letting the search-and-rescue people know the gas had been shut off and the house would not explode.

The remnants of Hurricane Katrina still showed here in the Lower Ninth Ward, where Grandmere lived. Grandmere had refused to move, although she'd had the option to do so after the devastation had swept through. Her house, once a bright red, had been washed out a bit in the flood. Still, it had survived with less damage than most. She claimed it was the sandbags that she'd stacked around the base of the building, and the fact that it was ever-so-slightly elevated off the ground. Eleri knew otherwise. Similarly constructed houses had been washed out, deluged with four to five feet of water. Most of the owners on the street had fled during the storm—but not Grandmere. Although the water had washed into her house, the same as all the others, her water had washed right back out again, leaving no muddy residues or black, moldy patches.

As a child, Eleri had always wondered if her Grandmere had real magic. Now, as an adult, she knew it. And she wondered if she'd need it.

4

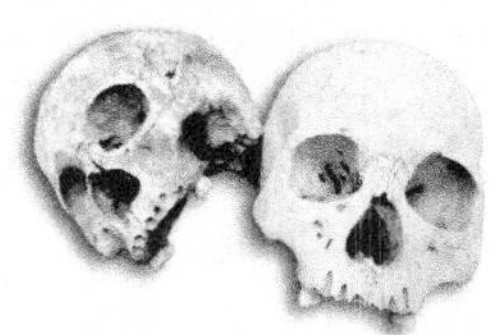

Eleri woke from the nap that Grandmere had practically insisted she take while Grandmere made dinner. She woke to the smells of home cooking and the sounds of frogs in the backyard awakening in the dusk outside. Given that it was New Orleans, Eleri almost expected to be able to look out the back window onto a bayou—but she couldn't. The back window gave only views of the backs of small houses, broken houses, or the empty lots where houses had been razed but never rebuilt.

Her drive through New Orleans on her way here had reminded her that the original neighborhoods had weathered the decade-plus old storm very differently. In town, most homes had been fully rebuilt, although you might find an occasional, well-tended space between houses where another home had stood before the hurricane. Those neighborhoods barely showed scars at all.

Here, many of the lots still had standing structures full of mold. The abandoned homes were broken down and boarded up. It was clear that this neighborhood had changed dramatically, and although the neighbors had been poor, now they were poorer. Eleri wondered about this. Grandmere, it seemed, could have made more money by moving to a more prosperous area any time she wanted, but she refused to leave the little red house.

It wasn't until she was an adult that Eleri understood this decision better—the sense of home Grandmere had here and her need for roots. The older Eleri got, the more she realized her Grandmere's roots ran deeper than she ever could have fathomed.

Donovan had pointed out, only recently, that Grandmere was a Remy. The Remy family had been in New Orleans for generations—possibly centuries.

Looking out the back window, Eleri smelled that dinner was almost ready. As she walked the short distance from the room to the kitchen, she recited a prayer to Aida Weddo under her breath. It seemed appropriate now. She would need strength in the days to come. She would need it to find Emmaline. She would need it to deal with what had happened to her sister. Possibly the hardest thing facing her was that she would need to confront Grandmere about why the old woman had not done anything.

Pushing those harsh thoughts aside, she headed into the fragrant kitchen, greeted by smiles from her grandmother. A guest sat at the table. An older woman, someone Eleri did not recognize—but then again, the time she spent here with her Grandmere, she spent mostly with only Grandmere. The old woman's clients had only seen the girls every once in a while, when they stopped by. Grandmere had mostly separated Eleri and Emmaline from her business, which explained why Eleri had not known about it until she was well into adulthood.

There was a reason Grandmere cooked stews for some of the people, and a reason she batted the girls away from it, telling them that, despite the wonderful smells, they were not allowed to eat it. Now, Eleri understood.

Almost as though she were a child of eight or nine again, Eleri watched as Grandmere thanked her guest and bade her to leave. The guest, in turn, thanked Grandmere profusely and clutched a tiny bag of fabric, drawn tight with thin twine, much like the ones Eleri had seen in the voodoo shop in the French Quarter. It seemed her Grandmere had more in common with the small store than she'd previously thought. Even the fabric resembled the old flour-sack fabrics that she'd seen on the Mystic Vudu shelves.

A thought flashed to her of the word *Makinde*, whispered to her from somewhere in the shop's shadows. Was the woman in the store a relative of hers? She was a Remy, after all, and New Orleans was crawling with Remys. Was it perhaps simply a more common term than she'd ever thought? Maybe it was as simple as "sweetheart" or "darling." Perhaps it had been spoken to the shop keeper by someone Eleri had not seen. Looking back, there were so many options that didn't involve a mysterious whisper of the pet name her grandmother had called her.

Grandmere let the guest show herself out, and Eleri heard the screen slap on the front door.

"Sit. Let us have dinner," Grandmere told her.

The last time she'd been here, she'd been sitting at this table with Donovan. Grandmere had fed them both. But Donovan had seen far more than Eleri did, and now, as she sat and ate her biscuits and stew, she tried to look around with fresh, open eyes. When she was three to five bites in, Grandmere looked at her with a frown on her face.

"That voodoo shop spooked you more than you wish to admit." The words were low, flat, and clear.

Eleri nodded. It was no use lying to Grandmere. "They had dolls, Grandmere. They were selling them to the public."

"But they were real?" A hint of suspicion showed in her tone, but it was partly a statement, as though Grandmere already knew. When Eleri nodded, Grandmere asked, "Which shop?"

"Mystic Vudu," Eleri replied, remembering the name lettered so beautifully in gold on the wood plaque over the door. "On Rue Royal."

Grandmere shook her head. "I do not know them."

Eleri laughed. "Do you propose to know all the voodoo shops in the French Quarter, Grandmere?"

"I know many," Grandmere said, and she didn't laugh in return. "Two are owned by Remys. One by a distant relation, but your Cousin Frederic has a hand in the other one. At least four are owned by the Dauphine family."

Eleri had not heard of them before, so she listened and absorbed.

"Several are owned by white folk who came and studied and decided to open a shop."

Eleri nodded. "White folk" referred not so much to the color of skin, but more to heritage. It meant these shop owners were new to the city. They had learned the craft from books, not from their ancestors—and Eleri understood what that meant to Grandmere. She didn't disavow it. It didn't mean these newcomers were bad or even not good, but it meant they lacked an element of blood that could not be replaced.

"Did they have poppets and pink candles and love spells?"

Eleri understood that such items were showy "finger-snapping"—but still not a trifle, and not to be sold to the public on a whim. She nodded.

Grandmere clicked her tongue, tsk-ed, and went back to eating her stew. She had feelings about this but there was nothing she could do.

Eleri changed the subject. "I saw that you gave something to the woman who came here. Can I ask what it was?"

"Fertility treatment," Grandmere replied.

Though Eleri wanted to ask exactly what that entailed, she kept silent—and, as she ate, she wondered. She pondered things in her past and began to put old pieces together in new ways. She thought of Donovan's words about what it meant to be a Remy and re-evaluated Grandmere's tiny garden in the back lot, where she grew vegetables and herbs. Eleri had noticed that many of the plants had no purpose in the kitchen, and she hadn't understood. Now she was beginning to stitch together a story of her Grandmere's true life—not just the one her granddaughters had seen.

Fabric scraps sat in bags in the bottom of the closet, in the room that she and Emmaline always shared. Again, those began to make more sense, as did the small, white cotton squares that Grandmere had always used if they cut or hurt themselves. Eleri began to wonder now just how much Remy blood was worth.

5

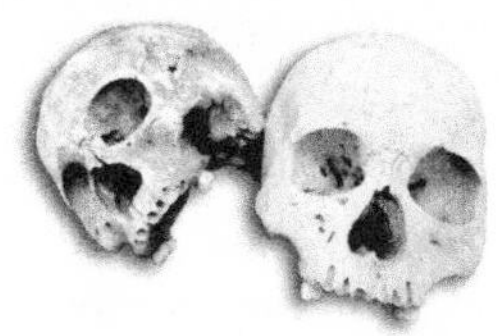

Donovan was restless. The run through the forest had done him some good, but what benefits it had conferred had worn off far too quickly.

Later that night, he'd gone for another run. As the pads of four feet hit the dirt and pushed free for a moment, his mind wandered. Would Westerfield assign him to anything without Eleri at his side? She'd been his senior partner the entire time he'd been in the FBI, and now she was on leave.

She could afford to be on leave. Donovan couldn't. So, technically, he was still on active duty, even if he didn't currently have a partner. He would have taken leave if he could. The job was too strange to just meet up with new agents and work a case. He'd grown to depend on the soul-deep trust the two of them had built. He didn't have that with anyone else. However, he also didn't have a trust fund and generations of money behind his family, or even that much in savings account.

He was *okay,* but hardly ready to use the word the rich always used: *comfortable.* To make matters worse, Walter wasn't coming to visit as he'd hoped. They grabbed time wherever they could. Often, Walter showed up at his door, stiff, stern, and ramrod straight, then smiling as she transformed into Lucy. But tonight there would be no Lucy Fisher and no Walter Reed. His girlfriend, as it were, was stuck at GJ's grandfather's, sorting out the mess that had been left behind.

Walter had called back the night before, letting him know they'd gleaned some preliminary information from the newest body. She talked about how GJ had made her take a wooden box and measure the length of the bones. Walter could handle that, Donovan thought, even as she'd said she had no idea what she was measuring for. She'd then told him she was surprised when GJ pulled out a calculator and grabbed a chart from a book off a shelf and started calculating what she had presumed was the height of the skeleton. Together, the women came up with a relatively narrow range for their body when alive.

"What we found," Walter told him, "means the skeleton can't be Shray Menon."

That had been their first and most obvious guess. Somehow, the body of the man they knew was dead had made its way back to the laboratory, where he'd most likely spent a lot of time working.

GJ's grandfather, and perhaps his people, would have wanted to save Menon—wouldn't they? Then again, maybe they wouldn't.

As far as Donovan knew, there was nothing special about Shray Menon, and that was the point of many of the people in the organization. They didn't like *special*. Not like Donovan. Not like Wade. Not the de Gottardi and Little families in the Ozarks.

Walter had also relayed something that GJ said about the back of the corpse's teeth. Though her wording was unclear, Donovan figured it out. Shray Menon was of Indian ancestry, which meant the front teeth should have been "shoveled"—or scooped out a little bit—on the backs, where the tongue hit. The teeth in this skeleton were not. Lastly, the bones belonged to someone like Donovan and Wade—and GJ had been relatively certain Menon was not one of those people. Still, that information alone was not enough to come close to confirming the identity of the skeleton.

GJ and Walter had called Westerfield, as Donovan suggested, and let their SAC know about the body they found. Walter had grumbled a little bit about Donovan's demand that they call sooner rather than later, and said Westerfield had been of very little help. He'd offered to find them dental records once they had an idea who the body might belong to. But as of yet, they hadn't even found a direction to aim.

Then Walter had called him back again, much later that same night, from her own room. He remembered that GJ's grandfather's home was much, much larger than his own. He sometimes thought of

GJ as coming from a background akin to Eleri's. However, after he sorted it out, he realized that wasn't the case. GJ's monetary background included only her grandfather's ill-gotten gains, like the large house that he lived in.

Her family had not grown up wealthy. GJ herself had not. She had grown up over-educated, though. Now Walter had her own small suite of rooms in the mansion that GJ's grandfather had left behind. Doctor Murray Marks had built a home on top of that sick laboratory, and Walter was now living in it. There were things she hadn't wanted to say in front of GJ that had prompted the late night call—including the fact that the place "gave her the willies."

Donovan understood, though he assumed it wouldn't have done the same for him. He was used to working in morgues. Walter, though accustomed to being around death, was not used to doing anything with the bodies afterward, other than dragging them back to her military base for a proper burial.

GJ, on the other hand, poked and prodded bodies, something Walter wasn't quite ready to deal with. Donovan had laughed until she'd shushed him.

That was new—Walter offering a well-placed, "Shhh!" and talking. The tone of her voice had given him pause, and he waited while she explained her fears.

The measurements on the skeleton, and the Anglo-Caucasian origins that the teeth indicated—at least as far as GJ had told her—led Walter to believe it was possible the skeleton belonged to GJ's grandfather. That, Donovan agreed, also seemed like a reasonable possibility.

"There's no reason to believe her grandfather is dead, though," Walter said in her hushed voice.

The existence of his skeleton would be definitive proof of it, Donovan thought.

Walter continued, "But the size is right, the origin's right." She listed a handful of other matching elements.

"I thought you said the bones belonged to someone who changed. Like me."

"It does. But this wouldn't be the first time somebody who was the head of a hate group was actually one of the hated people. Self-loathing can be a powerful motivator."

Donovan hadn't thought about Walter's ideas on that before. That night, he couldn't stop wondering about it. He had called Westerfield the next day, trying to follow up on Doctor Marks, but had only been assured that the man remained "in custody." No charges had been filed against him. Donovan still wasn't certain how the NightShade Division handled the legal complexities of a case like this.

There was no way to press charges against a man for killing people he believed were werewolves and removing what he thought were threats caused by people deeply encased in the dark arts. In the same regard, there was no way to run a trial for people like Donovan —no way for him to testify under oath about what he had seen, or believed, or had done.

So he'd shed his clothes once again, not quite dropping them in a line toward the back door. This time, with a little less psychosis and a little more reason, he'd gone out for another run. This time, he'd changed indoors and emerged from under the vine-covered pergola on his back porch and headed through the gate into the woods. He hadn't closed it. The last run, though not satisfying, had given him a little more sense of home, and a little more sense of security.

He fielded texts from Eleri the next day, saying she was settling in with Grandmere. Though it didn't sound like she was getting much of anything done, she'd brought along the files that she'd shown him before she left. A few interesting pieces of evidence had led her to believe there was information about her sister in New Orleans. But that was it. Eleri wasn't updating him on her "case," she was merely checking in and letting him know she was still alive.

So he was sitting at home reviewing files from other agents on other cases he wasn't a part of when the call came in at seven p.m. He knew as soon as he flipped the phone over that he wasn't going to like it, even though he'd been waiting for exactly this call.

The picture he used for SAC Westerfield appeared on his phone, though it wasn't even a photo of the man's face. Donovan did not have a relationship with his boss where he could stop and take a photo for his contacts.

There were no formalities. "I have a case for you," Westerfield said.

"Okay, where am I going?" He was always going somewhere.

"Montana. The family that got burned out? The Littles. I want you to examine the house. Pines will be going with you. And de Gottardi."

"I thought they were both on leave," Donovan told his boss—although really, he knew better. He regretted the words as soon as they were out. He knew Eleri was on leave. He'd assumed Christina and Wade were, too. Wade had lost an immediate family member, tragically, and probably really *needed* the time off. He'd been thrown into the same last case as Donovan and Eleri, and it involved his own family. Donovan didn't know why Christina was on leave, but he was a firm believer that personal time should be respected. Westerfield did not appear to share that belief.

Even as he thought through the list, Westerfield disavowed him of any softer notions. "They can only be on leave for so long. There aren't enough of you guys to go around for the cases that we're getting."

It suddenly occurred to Donovan that he had known a handful of agents with NightShade, but he had no idea how big the division was. Only now, he was getting a taste that it might not be big enough.

"What about your two new recruits?" he asked, trying to be casual. Wondering if Walter and GJ might also turn up in Montana with him.

"No-go," Westerfield replied curtly. "One of those recruits brought her own case in tow, and they're cleaning up that can of worms."

Donovan understood that decision, but it meant that he would definitely not get to see his new girlfriend for a while. Hoping to keep the disappointment out of his voice and sound professional, he asked, "When does my flight leave?"

"Two hours."

His phone pinged with the information on his flight and Donovan headed out the door to catch a plane he was already late for.

6

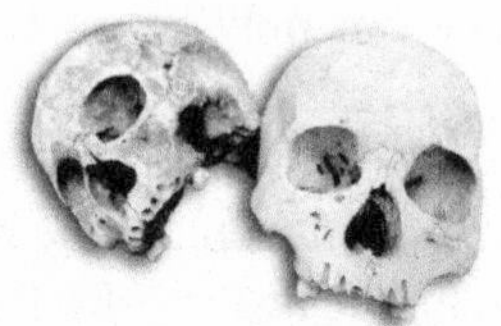

Afraid to take a day for herself, Eleri headed to the local FBI Branch Office the next morning. She was petrified that one day off would turn into five, and that if she started to relax, it would be easier to procrastinate than to solve her sister's murder. Though they all needed the closure, she was dreading the fallout.

Stomach churning, Eleri entered the building through the wide front doors, clearing security with her badge and ID. She wondered if anyone here recognized the bar with diamonds on it that signaled her division as NightShade. Even if they did, likely no one would say anything. So it wasn't entering the building as an agent off duty, or asking for family records, that made her stomach queasy. It was morbid curiosity about what she might find.

She knew Emmaline was dead. She knew this in a way that she couldn't explain to anyone—except maybe, she now realized, she could tell Grandmere. Maybe she *should* tell Grandmere. But she hadn't.

Deep in the back of her mind, she'd wondered if Grandmere had her own knowledge of Emmaline's disappearance. Eleri had waited, hoping Grandmere would say something. Perhaps she, too, had seen visions of Emmaline over the years. But Grandmere had not offered anything new this morning over oatmeal that she'd cooked in the crock pot during the night. Her great-grandmother had sprinkled brown sugar, pecans, and then strawberries without guilt and Eleri had eaten it but kept her mouth closed otherwise.

The Branch Office welcomed her. Despite her worries, they had no hesitation about helping her with the personal issue of her sister's case. She'd come with her copy of the file, but the office still had the set of bones they had found here in New Orleans that Eleri had reason to believe might be her sister's.

This area was correct for Emmaline's last live location. At least, in Eleri's gut it was—and her gut was so often right that she'd stopped doubting it. She was surprised when the man at the front desk walked her into a conference room and offered her a seat. She was still grasping her own file, which she'd pulled out of her bag as she waited.

Within a few minutes, an agent came in and sat down across from her. In contrast to her uptight nervousness, he managed to be relaxed and casual.

"Agent Eames, it's very nice to meet you. I've been working on this case since we reopened it." He was the official agent here, not her. She was merely the family in this situation and it was eye-opening to be on this side of the table. Even so, she understood she would never really truly be an outsider to the FBI. She had too much background to ever let that happen. The FBI would never treat her that way.

The look that appeared on his face as soon as she shook his hand told her news was coming that she might not want to hear—but the agent couldn't have known what news she wanted. Even Eleri wasn't sure what her best-case scenario would be.

Part of her desperately wanted this to be her sister. That would mean the search was finally over. Another deep part prayed that it would *not* be Emmaline—because if it was Emmaline, it would be the beginning of the end. If it wasn't, some distant piece of her heart—even though she didn't truly believe it—could hold on to a thread of hope that Emmaline was alive somewhere.

In her gut, Eleri knew that was not true. She'd known it for some time.

"Thank you so much, Agent Almasi."

He folded his hands and looked at her. "I'll get straight to it. We tested it against your DNA, as you requested. We drilled into a tooth and got a good sample. It does not match."

Eleri blinked. She'd been so certain this was Emmaline. That this case would lead her to all the discoveries she was missing about what had happened to her sister. But it wasn't going to happen.

Pausing, she sat back, staring at him blankly. In return, he looked at her with compassion and understanding that, on this case, she wasn't just an agent. She was processing the information as the deceased's sister—not as a scientist. Her reaction now was not going to be her final one.

When at last she sat forward again, he began speaking. "Something interesting did come up, though."

"What is it?" *If it wasn't Emmaline, what else could there be?*

"You were correct about the age of the bones and the general genetics. Everything that we can find on the alleles that we've matched appears to look very similar to everything we understand about your missing sister."

Eleri nodded. There wasn't much on Emmaline. Sure, there was a DNA profile matching to Nathalie and to Eleri, but Eleri was the best match. Her mother was half African American, and the other half possibly white, but it was unknown. Her own mother, the other Emmaline—Grandmere's daughter—had disappeared, become pregnant, had the child, and returned home with baby Nathalie. Nathalie's father remained, to this day, an unknown.

Eleri's own father was as white as white bread could be. Thomas Hale Eames was descended from Massachusetts colonists. That made Eleri one-quarter African American, and thus the closest match for Emmaline's peculiar mix of race and ancestry. Though they had collected hair with root balls at the time of Emmaline's disappearance, much of the DNA that they'd been able to keep as evidence had degraded over the years. Children didn't even leave lasting finger prints. All this left Eleri herself as the very best evidence for finding her sister.

"There was some level of match?" Eleri asked.

"Yes, a possible second cousin."

She blinked again and then began speaking. The two of them spoke the same language of genomics and alleles, of percent matches and statistics, and they talked back and forth rapidly. "A second cousin who looks like Emmaline and me? One quarter African American?"

"It appears that way," he replied, though with a small pause. "The heritage numbers all *match*. Given the tracing to certain locales within Africa, even that heritage seems to match."

"But," Eleri replied, "statistically, that may not mean much. She might be a second cousin but—well, what does a full-blooded Sub-Saharan African look like? Probably not 100 percent." She was busy calculating percentages.

"You're correct." He tipped his head as he conceded her point. "We don't have a full genetic panel yet to compare it against, so it's a 'best guess' at this point. But with her, all the percentages of the DNA match yours. And we thought this was even more odd: the time in the ground for this skeleton matches the guesstimate you originally provided. Can I ask how you came up with your sister's date of death?"

That stopped her. She'd put it into the file as though it was scientific and hoped nobody would ask. She'd been ready when she walked in for questions to be thrown at her. Eleri had planned how to have a few slick answers that rolled off her tongue and didn't include, "My sister visited me in my dreams for years." She did some quick math. "I calculated the approximate age of the skeleton, the time missing, and when she must have died to make her death occur at that age."

He nodded.

It all worked, but it wasn't how she had come to that date.

"Can I see the skeleton?" she asked.

"Absolutely," he replied, "but I think you might like to check out the genetic panel first."

The agent slid the pages across to her and Eleri studied the numbers. She'd practically memorized her own. She knew she had a handful of alleles that were uncommon in the general population. Even her hair—part African American—was mostly red from her father's side of the family. But Emmaline's hair had tended much more toward blond, and her sister's eyes had been blue rather than green.

When Emmaline was a child, the blond had been bright, shiny, pale gold. As she had entered her teenage years, it had turned a little darker—but again, Eleri was the only one who knew this. She also knew that their faces, despite the mild differences in coloring, could have been cast from the same mold. But that wouldn't show on a genetics panel. Science could conclude nothing from the genome about that—not yet. Eleri read through the panel, looking for something that might match her own odd genetics, but saw nothing.

Her phone rang just then. The picture of Grandmere's house popped up—because the house phone was the only phone Grandmere had, and the woman did not like photographs of herself on any digital device.

"Grandmere," Eleri said into the line. Grandmere would gladly talk on the phone, although she wouldn't allow her picture to appear on one. It was a connection Eleri still hadn't been able to make.

"Are you at the FBI Branch?" Grandmere asked, and Eleri flinched. She should've known better. She'd not told Grandmere the purpose of her visit to the city, only that she was visiting. She should've known her grandmother would figure out what she was up to. In fact, the next words solidified that.

"Is it your sister?" Grandmere didn't even wait for an answer before she asked again. "Are those bones your sister's?"

7

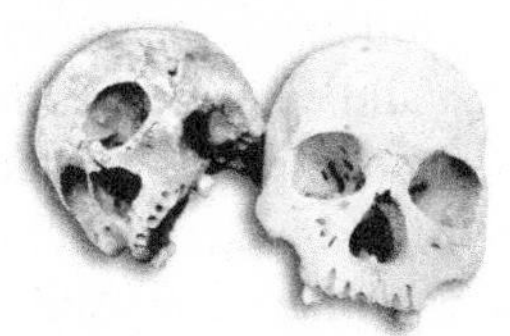

Darcelle Dauphine wondered about the woman who had come into her shop the day before. There had been a spark of recognition—first on her part, when the woman walked in the door, and then later on the woman's part. Darcelle never discounted her intuition.

To say she could follow her gut instinct was an understatement. She was fluent in hunches and psychic notions, as she'd been raised in every dark tradition the underworld of New Orleans would allow. She walked the worlds between the craft, voodoo, hoodoo, and more.

But recognizing customers wasn't uncommon, because Darcelle knew many people in town. Even the tourists were often repeat visitors. They stopped in one day to browse but came back the next day to purchase. Or they simply visited the city occasionally and came back to her shop, year after year. There were many reasons the woman might look familiar. Only a few were nefarious.

Her mother had owned this shop since Darcelle and her sisters were small. But her mother had not left it to all four of her children. She'd left it solely to Darcelle.

So when she had first caught that spark between herself and her new patron—when she had first looked at the woman's face—she thought maybe she was simply recognizing a repeat customer. Maybe she remembered her face from a visit the year before, or the year before that.

It only took a minute or two of watching the woman, as she gingerly handled the dolls on the shelf, for Darcelle to think perhaps something deeper was going on here. The woman had frowned at the wares. She'd picked up the poppets and narrowed her eyes. She read the spells on the cards as though she disapproved. And not in the way of the "good ladies" of town did—not in the way that said this was an affront to some other religion. No. Darcelle felt the rejection at a deeper level than just a surface judgment.

Surreptitiously, she'd followed the woman through the store, watching as she picked up and dismissed each item. It caused a small pang in her heart whenever someone did that. Even though Darcelle hated the shop, the idea that someone would dismiss the work that she'd been forced into was bothersome. And with the sharp pinch of that disdain, she'd felt a tight little knot form in her chest. So she'd followed along and whispered the word, wondering if she could throw the woman off her game.

She'd been satisfied when it had worked and the woman had startled. The endearment was not uncommon, but it wasn't well known either. It was not the kind of thing you would simply whisper to a woman on the street—and if you did, you wouldn't expect it to make them jump. Most people—in fact, even those who thought they were versed in the arts—might look at you as though you were strange. They might ask you if you were casting spells. This customer had done none of that.

Instead, she'd startled and gone pale, looking as though she'd seen a ghost. Darcelle had smiled softly to herself, stepping backward through the archway and disappearing into one of the other rooms. A few more patrons had come into the shop, and she'd been distracted, unable to spend her time following the strange woman—the one with the reddish hair, pale brown skin, and shockingly green eyes.

She'd ignored the feelings. The new customers might perhaps buy something. The shop was still her source of income, even though one day she was going to get out of it. She was constantly of two minds. One side of her was always plotting how to increase profits and make the store fare better, to make her income easier. Another was eternally devising ways to get out of owning and running the store altogether.

But then, she'd heard the clatter and watched the woman leave, unable to do anything other than raise an eyebrow to her two new customers. She'd shrugged at them as though to say, "Wow. That was strange."

Though it was surely odd, there was nothing more she could do.

In the end, she'd sold the newcomers a bag of trinkets and poppets worth several hundred dollars. They'd purchased candles that could cast spells from love to wealth, to the moon and back again, even though the two likely lacked the skill to conjure a single dollar. They were just playing. At least the sale had been satisfying, even if she didn't enjoy the work.

When she'd smiled and waved them out the front door and the shop was empty once again, she'd gone to the display in the back room where the strange woman had been. Darcelle was looking for something out of place, something she could see that the woman might have been holding when she so clearly startled. But there was nothing obvious.

Since no one was around to see, Darcelle waved her hand over the display, again looking for wisps of something left behind. Again, she found absolutely nothing. Strangely, the woman had left no trace.

8

Eleri followed Agent Almasi back to the lab in the New Orleans office. He spoke animatedly about his work with the skeleton that had come in, and about how—despite his last name and his obvious heritage—he was only now learning Farsi through the FBI. He was working this case but was also actively seeking out cases that might take him to the Middle East. This one that Eleri had requested they re-open had been unusual and interesting, but it had taken him in entirely American directions, he said.

He traced the genetics of the skeleton using statistical allele origin maps far superior to those the mail order gene companies could provide. And yet, he complained, the numbers were still lacking. There was not enough data to track anything with real certainty. Though he believed in his heart that soon they'd be able to do it, he could only shrug at some of the numbers now.

Eleri kept up with the conversation. It was an excellent distraction to help her keep her head in the game as she sat with the bones she had believed belonged to her sister. She could admit that she probably wasn't in any shape to talk with this agent, as she was still reeling from the news. She'd been so certain that this case was Emmaline that she'd not been ready for his answers. Her plan had been to use these bones to find out what had happened to her sister. It was a hunch she'd felt too deeply to imagine it was anything other than the truth. Now she wondered what had gone wrong.

When she first saw the skeleton in the lab, laid out on the large metal tray, it had hit her again—the feeling that this was *it.* Now she had clear and certain scientific knowledge that it was, in fact, not. She had no idea where that sensation or the confidence behind it came from.

Agent Almasi did a nice job at stepping back and letting her take a look first. Eleri then asked, "Do you know how she died?"

It was not obvious from the bones. At initial glance, there were no nicks from bullets or knives, and there were no breaks or obvious serious damage.

"No." He shook his head and shrugged. "We have some ideas, but no proof or even real evidence."

"She was fully skeletonized when you found her?"

"Yes."

Neither of them questioned that the skeleton was female nor that it had belonged to a girl in her mid to late teens. Those facts were clear from the developing pelvic girdle and the bone structure. Eleri could determine these things on sight these days, unlike when she was a student and had to count the flare of the hip girdle, the sharper arch in the sciatic notch. On the skull, she could see the rounder shape of the occipital orbits, the thinner depth of the edge of the bone, the size of the brow ridge. Now reading bones was as simple as Dick and Jane.

With a gloved hand, she reached up into the mouth, feeling behind the teeth for shoveling. Next, she held the skull and tipped it back to look inside, her eyes agreeing with her finger that there were no obvious marks on the back of the teeth.

Having checked what she initially could of the skull by sight and simple touch, Eleri turned back to the body. She examined the bones for size and placement. She looked at coloring, too, thinking that if the skeleton had been dug out of the ground in one spot—as the reports had stated—the color would tell her more about that location. If it was all one skeleton—all the bones belonging to one former person—the tint from being in the dirt should look relatively uniform across the pieces. Her initial assessment agreed with Almasi's.

Picking the skull back up, she looked now at the front and sides of the teeth, wanting to see if the growth was normal.

"Do you have an ID?" Eleri asked.

"Not yet, but I do have five dental records of possible matches. From young women like your sister, who disappeared at one point and may have been alive much longer afterwards."

"Are they from the area here?" That was common, Eleri knew. The first place to look was local. Only later, if that didn't pan out, would the feds begin searching through missing person cases farther away.

Again, Almasi surprised her. "Only one. Several are from other states, even the mid-to-northwest area. We did a full sweep."

She liked him and his science more and more. While she thought this, she kept her attention on the specimen in front of her. So Eleri only nodded and continued her assessment, slowly rotating the bones and checking for information that she hadn't caught the first time around. This time, she did catch something new.

"Look," she pointed.

Almasi nodded, indicating he'd found the same thing before but was waiting for her own assessment. It was common and not at all rude or calculating to do so. It was important that everyone get an unbiased initial assessment.

"I spotted that too," he said.

"Knife?" she asked.

"Also my guess."

Marks traced the length of the radius bone in the forearm on each side in similar places. When Eleri examined it more closely, she caught two more marks on the left radius. Heading back to the right radius, she found other, fainter marks as well.

"It looks like the damage was repetitive," she said.

Though she'd spoken almost to herself, Almasi nodded.

"And the timeframe looks long-term."

"Here." His own hands were already gloved and ready to go. A sharp metal pointer appeared in his hand, motioning to things smaller than a finger could delineate. "See this? This one looks very old, as though it originated when she was much younger. The scarring is faint, but that's because it's been there so long."

He then pointed to a scar that almost perfectly overlapped it. It would not have been obvious that there were two unless they had been looking as closely as they were.

"This one is very fresh."

That, Eleri understood, didn't mean recent. Recent would be long after the time of death and would look very different. Here, "fresh" meant very soon before she died. "Could it have killed her?"

"I don't think so. I put the bones together and rolled the radius along the ulna with the wrist rotation." He demonstrated, picking up the arm bones and fitting the notches together before moving them in a human-like way. "I don't see a point where this scar would have lined up with an artery."

It was an interesting phenomenon, the way the wrist end of the forearm could rotate back and forth and the radius rolled along the ulna to create this. But any scaring or marks on the radius were difficult to locate to their position on the outer arm, given that rotational ability.

Eleri, again like Almasi, held the bones together into proper position and rotated them for herself. She tried to visualize where the other internal structures—now long gone—might have been. It was ten or even fifteen minutes later when she finished rolling both arms back and forth, checking the cut marks that they had discovered. She finally looked up at the agent and said, "I agree. I mean, if the cut was deep enough that it hit the bone, she could have bled out from it. But it doesn't look like it was necessarily a fatal wound. And, because there are so many cuts in the same places that did heal, I have to assume that no individual cut was fatal."

At that point, without saying anything, he walked to the other side of the room, opened the desk drawer, and pulled out a file folder to hand to her.

"Lab results. Paper?" she asked with a small smile, the first one she'd found of the day. She had a bit of a soft spot in her heart for the old-school ways. Everyone else liked to pull results up on a screen somewhere. But with paper, she could move the pages all around, line them up side by side, and spread them out on the table with the bones to look at everything.

"Of course," he replied, as though anyone who thought otherwise was nuts.

Eleri liked Almasi a little bit better. She hadn't expected to like anyone on this trip. Then again, she'd expected to be examining her sister's skeleton, not analyzing an unrelated case.

He pointed to results on the page. "Tooth sampling for strontium gave us an initial position of where to look for missing children reports. She appears to have been in the Northern U.S., a little more Midwest, if you will."

Eleri nodded that she was following along, though she was looking at the strontium maps he'd printed out and drawn on in red-ink circles. Each circle marked a biome in the US where this girl's particular isotope ratio lined up to the local numbers.

Next, he pulled out another set of lab results.

"Bone sampling, too?" she asked.

"Of course. We know where she started. We need to know where she ended up."

That was important, Eleri understood. There was far too often an assumption that a body had died near where it was found. But that was just conjecture, and often a bad one. Had the person lived there for a long time? Traveled a great distance to get there? Had they been alive in this location for long—or at all?

This specimen was found in New Orleans and clearly—from the isotopes in her teeth—she had grown from a very young age—from birth to around age ten or so—in one particular biome. It stretched from Ohio to Nebraska and down into Oklahoma. It was a large biome. They'd not gotten lucky and hit one of the smaller ones. That happened, she knew.

"She was here for a while," he said. "Look, these are your isotopes for the New Orleans area and these are your isotopes in her bones."

"Wow!" Eleri hadn't meant to say it out loud. It wasn't common for her to be dumbfounded by evidence. But nothing about this was common for her—not the bones, not the location, and not the fact that her gut had been so wrong.

As a trained scientist, she was used to numerical surprises. But this one? This had been big.

She peeled her gloves, running her fingers down the numbers as each isotope was reported in. Then she looked at Almasi again. "What are we at now?"

"We don't have anything else definitive. Do you want to try doing a forensic odont match with the five dental records?"

So they sat with their heads together over a clean table surface on one side of the room. He had already taken X-rays of the teeth and the skull, angling the film in a variety of ways, attempting to match up as many of the X-rays taken from the five possible samples as he could.

Together they ruled out four and decided one was a match. The age between the dental records of children and the time of death made it difficult. Baby teeth had been lost; adult teeth had come in. But Eleri and Agent Almasi found more than fifteen points of corroboration and no rule-out options on one set of X-rays.

They declared the body a match to Mackenzie Burke from Nebraska. Her family had reported her missing just the year before Emmaline.

Eleri's heart had sunk. The location was so different, though other pieces of the two cases were the same. She couldn't reconcile the two abductions, nor could she tell herself that they definitely belonged together. The lack of conclusion was frustrating.

So she decided it was time to take herself out of the equation for the day, before she said or did something dumb. Standing, she thanked Almasi for his work and for letting her horn in on it. As she stood near the table with the bones laid out, she looked up at him. Not paying attention, her hand came to rest on the arm bones.

This time her fingers were ungloved. As she touched the ulna, the air spun around her. A rank odor crawled through her sinuses. Her vision sparkled at the edges, and Almasi disappeared in front of her as Emmaline appeared.

"Eleri," Emmaline whispered as she reached out for her older sister.

9

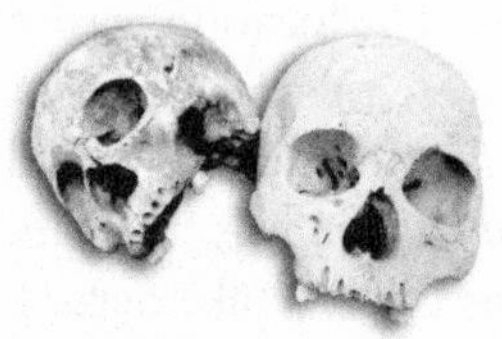

Eleri lay awake in her bed that night. She'd recovered from the shock of touching the bones with her bare hands.

She'd used gloves at first, as had Agent Almasi, simply so as not to contaminate anything should it be needed for evidence later. It had been a mistake to stand, talk, and wave her hands around, letting them eventually flutter down onto what she'd thought was the edge of the table. The metal lip at the borders of the body tray turned up, and she'd meant to lightly rest her hand there. But Eleri hadn't been looking. She'd let her fingertips land on the radius and ulna she'd been examining before.

Though she wanted to believe that she'd handled the shock well, she wasn't certain she'd achieved it. Agent Almasi had looked at her strangely.

"Agent Eames, are you okay?"

She'd said, "Yes." But it was a lie.

She wasn't okay at all. She was shocked both at the vision and at the return of her sister. Though she often saw things in odd ways, Eleri hadn't seen Emmaline in a while. Her sister usually came to her at night, in dreams, told her things she needed to know. She even helped her solve cases, sometimes.

As a ten-year-old child, when her sister had first appeared to her, she'd had no information. She'd not known what to do with the vision, or even that it *was* a vision. Ever logical, she'd thought it was just a dream. There was no reason to believe otherwise. She'd dismissed the whole thing as wishful thinking.

It was probably a good thing, looking back. Who would have believed her anyway? She'd later told her mother of her stark belief, saying directly to her, "Emmaline is alive."

Her mother had simply replied, "Of course she is, and we'll find her. We'll bring her home."

Those had been the days when her mother had run around frantically, worked with the FBI, handed over Emmaline's hairbrush and blanket and any beloved object that might contain fingerprints. She had worked tirelessly, doing everything she could to help her daughter return home. But slowly, their mother had faded into a shell of who she had been. She'd become the smiling, certainly-just-fine, brittle woman she was now.

Nathalie Beaumont had been raised here in Grandmere's house. The only clue to her parentage was the last name, Beaumont, although it was entirely possible Emmaline Remy had pulled the name out of thin air and written it on her daughter's birth certificate. No one was willing to put something like that past the first Emmaline. The Beaumonts had many wealthy branches of the family in New Orleans, but a handful of poor relations, too. It could have been a real clue—or it could have been a joke. They still didn't know.

When the first Emmaline had abandoned her daughter with Grandmere, she had not stayed long enough to let her mother in on any secrets of Nathalie's conception or heritage. There was only what was obvious—the baby looked part white. Emmaline had been dark as night, like Grandmere. Nathalie was paler, though whether that swayed her decisions, Eleri still didn't know. What she did know was that her mother had decided she was a blue blood.

"No idea where that notion came from," Grandmere always said. But Nathalie had done well for herself. She'd met and married Thomas Hale Eames, descendant of both Virginia first families and Massachusetts first families, owner of one massive trust fund, and the eldest son from a line of eldest sons.

Nathalie and Thomas had a beach house at FoxHaven. They had a farm in Virginia with a name—Bell Point Farm. And they had Patton Hall—their main residence—in Kentucky. It was from Patton Hall that Emmaline had disappeared.

The girls had been out riding and their instructor was watching them take turns cantering around the field and working over tiny jumps that he'd had installed for that purpose. It had been Emmaline's turn, since Eleri had just gotten her notes from her own trip around the training course.

"Heels down. Back straight. You're letting him pull to the right," Keith had told her. Eleri could still hear the words, as though they were saved on an audio file to this day. His vocal tone and inflection were forever seared into her mind.

After Eleri had nodded and accepted her corrections—what else could she do?—they had both turned toward the edge of the woods where Emmaline was supposed to be waiting.

But the younger sister and her horse were both gone. For a good thirty minutes to an hour, no one had panicked. It would be just like Emmaline to turn and ride off through the woods when no one was paying attention to her. She'd been eight that day. Eleri ten. Neither had been especially mature, but what did anyone expect? They were children.

They were children taking riding lessons. Both girls understood riding was something they should do, but neither girl had any particular love for the sport. They loved horses and they liked riding, but posting *just so* when trotting the horse and taking the jumps had not been anything either child had deemed necessary for her life.

Even today, Eleri was proud to say, "I can ride a horse. I can jump and I can do barrel turns," but that was all the skill seemed worth. Emmaline, at first, had hated the jumps but though she'd eventually gotten used to it and had even gotten better at it. But her dislike of jumping had seemed the obvious reason she wasn't waiting her turn. Keith, the trainer, only had her train over the smaller obstacles—but he and Eleri had initially believed that Emmaline simply hadn't wanted to jump her horse that day and had turned and cantered off through the woods.

Eleri and her teacher had entered the trail exactly where they presumed that Emmaline had gone. Thirty minutes later, when they'd found no trace of the younger Eames girl, Keith had turned Eleri around and sent her back to the house. The man was not willing to let Emmaline stay outside alone, and he seemed still convinced—despite Eleri's growing worry—that Emmaline would soon be found.

Even at ten years old, Eleri had known to trust her gut. And her gut had told her that her sister hadn't just run off to avoid a practice.

Unfortunately, it would take Eleri almost twenty more years, and a stint in a mental hospital, before she would find anyone else to believe her instincts as she did.

With Eleri not speaking her fears, the family tried to believe their younger daughter would turn up playing in a stream, hopefully having remembered to ground tie her horse or lop the reins around a branch. Her pale riding pants, black boots, tailored jacket, and matching helmet should have been easy to find in the woods. Hell, the *horse* should have been easy to find in the woods. But she and Keith had seen no trace of Emmaline or her mount.

Even now, Eleri remembered that frantic ride home. Her teacher had shown no outward signs, that she could recall, of panic or real fear—but Eleri had begun to feel them herself. She'd ridden not to the stables, but right up to the back door of the house, where she'd hopped off the horse, barely remembering to tie the reins to the railing, and had run frantically inside.

Her mother had scolded her for coming in the house in her riding boots and asked her why she was there when she should be at her lesson. Eleri, though she'd known she would get in trouble, had told Nathalie that Keith was still looking for Emmaline.

Her mother had frowned. It hadn't registered. A ten-year-old's panic didn't mean much in the adult world, and Eleri had wished she was tall enough to shake her mother by the shoulders. "Emmaline is missing, Mother!"

Still, her mother, ever the calm, cool, collected, mainline blue blood—even if she wasn't one—had looked at her older daughter and said, "I'm sure she's fine. Where is your instructor?""

"He's still looking for Emmaline. He didn't come back because he didn't want to stop looking."

Her mother had frowned again, and she'd asked, "Well, just how long has your sister been gone?"

As though Eleri would say, "Five or ten minutes," and everything would be okay.

"Almost an hour, mother." The lessons were two hours, too long by at least half for children of their age, but her mother hadn't thought of that. She'd told them, "Buck up, pay attention, and get your lessons in." Eleri had tried.

That day was the last time she'd ever seen her little sister, outside of her own dreams. She was twelve before Emmaline appeared again.

That night, she'd recognized her sister and had spoken with her, and woke up feeling better. She felt for the first time, that Emmaline must be alive.

It wasn't until the next night, as she was falling asleep thinking of her sister, that a realization startled her. In her dream, Emmaline had not looked quite like the picture she remembered.

That Emmaline had been eight. This Emmaline looked a little older.

Eleri had known by then that she was good with hunches, that she was a finder of lost items. Her mother had even asked her several times to help her locate lost objects. Nathalie said, "I don't know what it is, Eleri, but things always seem to turn up when you help me."

Eleri knew what it was. It was that somehow she would know where the missing thing was and she would ask her mother a handful of questions. The first time, she'd asked only one question, directing her mother exactly to the missing keys. Her mother had frowned and looked at her a little sideways, with a certain suspicion in her gaze.

After that, Eleri asked three questions about locations that she knew for certain would not turn up the missing item before asking about the spot where it would be found. Aside from being able to see her sister in her dreams sometimes, her intuition had seemed nothing more than a parlor trick. It was only in the past year or so that Eleri had begun to find out exactly what she possessed, what ran in her blood, what Grandmere had passed down to her two great-granddaughters, passed through the original Emmaline and then through Nathalie Beaumont Eames—whether Nathalie knew it or not.

Eleri felt the jury was out on her mother. Over the months after Emmaline had disappeared, Nathalie had slowly gone downhill. She'd faded away, from the fierce mama bear who was certain her daughter would be returned soon to the cold shell of a socialite who believed that somehow, sometime in the future, Emmaline would come home.

Though they'd eventually found her horse, they'd never found the girl. And now Eleri lay in bed at Grandmere's and slipped under into sleep, hoping to see her sister again.

10

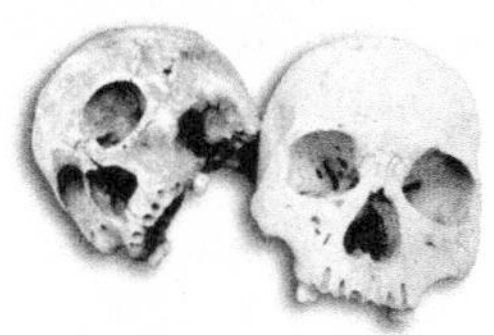

Despite the fact that she'd fallen asleep thinking of her sister and the day of her sister's disappearance, Emmaline did not show up in Eleri's dreams that night, nor did any clues to her personal "case" for finding her sister. She'd spent the next day with Grandmere, both in the kitchen, cooking, and also waiting around in the living room while Grandmere met with one client after another at the tiny table in the kitchen. The space afforded little in the way of privacy, but Eleri seemed to be the only one who cared.

"It's going to be a heavy day," Grandmere had warned her that morning.

Eleri had nodded in reply before realizing she didn't know if her great-grandmother referred to an influx of clients, the weather, or something else that Eleri hadn't counted on.

Times were harder here since the hurricane, Grandmere liked to point out. Eleri thought of that storm as something that had happened far in the past. Although the devastation still showed, Hurricane Katrina had come and gone long ago. Perhaps in Grandmere's long, long life, it was not so great a distance.

At first, Eleri had sat in the living room with her e-reader, waiting while clients came through. She curled up with her feet tucked under her, trying to read her book and not listen in on Grandmere's conversations with the people who came, but that had proved impossible.

One woman felt her husband was cheating and wanted a way to find out.

The woman offered to pay for whatever spells or help could be offered, but Grandmere was having none of that. She'd simply held the woman's hands and said, "I can already tell, you are correct. He is. If you follow him, you'll see."

No money had exchanged hands that time. Eleri discovered that was often the case. Grandmere had probably earned less actual cash in her lifetime than Eleri earned in a year. She paid for most of her life through barter, trade, and Lord knew what. In many cases, Eleri saw people appear and leave with no apparent method of compensating Grandmere in any way for the effort she put forth, and—as Eleri saw that day—it was effort. Though spry, her great-grandmother was old. Eleri didn't even know the woman's true age, only that she was at least in her nineties. She might have been over one-hundred.

When the parade of clients had gone for the day, Grandmere made her way around the house, walking boldly into the bedroom where Eleri stayed. From the hallway, she visually followed most of Grandmere's progress through the small house. She watched as the older woman went into the room and heard her in the closet. The rustling of plastic store bags told Eleri her great-grandmother was searching in the bag of fabric scraps, but she emerged with something that was definitely not fabric. Eleri wished now that she'd followed and looked.

Grandmere seemed unconcerned by her great-granddaughter's surprise. She pulled herbs from the other room, where they hung drying in the closets and along the walls. In the kitchen, she boiled pots of water, burned candles, and chanted prayers. Eleri heard her invoke the name of gods that Grandmere had prayed to for decades.

After a while of listening to Grandmere work in the kitchen, Eleri had gotten up from the couch and gone into her bedroom. She decided to search through the bag of fabric scraps herself.

It was shoved into the back of the closet, and this time when she pulled it out, it was much heavier than she had expected. She shouldn't have been surprised. As she pawed her way through it, she found hand-stitched, white cotton dolls. They didn't have faces painted on them, but some features were clear in the way they had been stitched.

Another bag, shoved down under the fabric scraps, held other bags with smooth sticks and crystals and even bones. Eleri frowned as she pulled out the crinkly plastic, and the pieces inside had rattled as she picked them up. She'd worried Grandmere might find her digging in here, but it was past time she knew about her own heritage, past time she knew what she really was.

Donovan had shaken her foundations when he pointed out pieces of her past that she'd never known. He'd simply paid attention to the ancestors in the paintings at Bell Point Farm. The canvases had hung there since before Eleri was born, looking down from the farm's white plaster, several-hundred-year-old walls.

Eleri—on her father's side—was both a Hale and an Eames. She was literally the great-great-granddaughter of the witches that could not be burned in Salem. That had been a shock. In turn, Donovan had been shocked at her surprise. These ancestors had stared down at her for her whole childhood. Engraved, brass plaques were bolted to the bottom of each one, stating their names, but Eleri had paid no attention. Donovan had put together the look and feel of the portraits along with the dates and names, and had gone online to look up information. Eleri had just known them as her ancestors. She'd thought nothing of it.

On the other side, her mother brought the Remy name into her blood. The Remys were a powerful New Orleans family with whispered rumors of spells and voodoo in the past. Eleri hadn't known that, either. She'd only known that Grandmere walked the French Quarter and the Lower Ninth Ward with equal ease. Two tiny girls had held onto her hands, and it had made no difference that the neighborhoods were considered "bad" or "unsafe." As a child, Eleri had known only her sister and the comfort of her Grandmere's hand in hers.

Now it seemed Eleri was a lightning bolt of strange sources of power. She was sure Grandmere knew a lot. Perhaps because her own daughter, Emmaline, had run way—disappearing into bad crowds, with booze and drugs—Grandmere had shied away from teaching Nathalie about the family, about the magic. It was also possible, knowing her mother as Eleri did now, that Nathalie had been raised in the craft and the family traditions, and had simply rejected them.

If asked, Nathalie would answer, without blinking an eye, that her family was Christian and always had been. Eleri now knew better.

On the floor of her tiny room, she pulled the bag of bones out, spreading its contents onto the floor to see it more clearly. She expected to find chicken bones. Instead, the bag held metacarpals, carpals, and the smooth end of a radius. She frowned.

These were clearly human bones. It was one of the first things a forensic scientist learned—what was and wasn't human. Human bones warranted investigations. The bones of raccoons and bears did not. She could only stare at the spread before her. Her grandmother had human bones in a bag in the back of her closet.

It was suddenly hard to breathe. Grandmere's house was not air conditioned. It was set up so that the central portion made a loop, helping the air to circulate, the way houses had been built before air conditioning existed. Wide ceiling fans blew the air around and gave the illusion that the heat was not as oppressive as it was, but there wasn't much that could be done about the humidity. While it hadn't bothered Eleri before she got that bag open, she now felt like she was dying to drag in air from underwater.

Should she confront Grandmere? Take these bags into the kitchen and shake them at her great-grandmother and demand answers? That probably wasn't the right way. Her only good thought was that Grandmere was as mellow as the day was long. Even if Eleri did run into the kitchen, shaking the bag, demanding answers, her Grandmere would merely smile at her. The problem was, the old woman was just as likely to suggest that Eleri had no idea what she was doing and that she had just cast a spell on thousands of local city folk merely by shaking the bag.

Eleri sat back on her heels and tried to get her thoughts together. She realized it was probably better if she confronted Grandmere after she thought about it for a while—not right now, when she felt angry.

An immediate thought grabbed her and clenched her heart even harder. Was this Emmaline? Could this possibly be her younger sister? But a quick look—her fingers scrambling frantically through the bag, pulling out bone after bone—made it clear to her that these were much, much too old to have come from her sister. These bones appeared to have been in the dirt for centuries. They also did not belong to a body of the correct age to be her younger sister. And, though these discoveries should have made her breathe easier, she gasped for the air she'd been missing while she searched.

With three, deep, harsh breaths—where she blew the air out forcefully between pursed lips—Eleri tried to get herself back together. She wanted to call Donovan. She wanted to call Avery and speak nothing of this, but she didn't really know how to do either. She and Avery had left things at a crossroads. They hadn't broken up, but she hadn't spoken to him in far too long. Had they ghosted on each other?

She didn't really know what else to do, so she pushed everything back down into the bag and back into the closet.

Eleri held no illusions that Grandmere would know, the next time she came in here, that the closet had been snooped on. But for now, her hatchet job would have to do. At least her searching wouldn't be obvious at first glance. Maybe.

Still trying to calm herself, she sat on the bed and texted the man who had been her boyfriend for some time. She apologized for her silence and then briefly explained about her missing younger sister and the bones and the lack of her expected genetic match. It was far too much for a text, but she sent it anyway, wondering if she'd get a response.

She stayed in the room reading—*hiding?*—until she heard Grandmere out on the couch, watching television. Eleri had joined her for several game shows that evening. She'd kept her fat mouth shut. At least, that's what she told herself.

Grandmere was clearly not paying attention to the TV shows, which weren't very interesting. The older woman was exhausted from the work she'd done in the kitchen that day. Eleri asked how she could help, but Grandmere had merely shaken her head.

Then, when the last show finished up, Eleri turned to her great-grandmother and said, "I found the human bones in the bag in the closet."

Grandmere tilted her head, as though she didn't know what the young woman was speaking of. Eleri knew better, and she realized that meant Grandmere might not know *which* bag of human bones she was speaking of. Popping up and heading into the bedroom, Eleri suddenly felt bad about her own lithe ability to jump up off the couch. Still, she came back in with the plastic bag and a few questions that weren't quite accusations.

"What are these?"

11

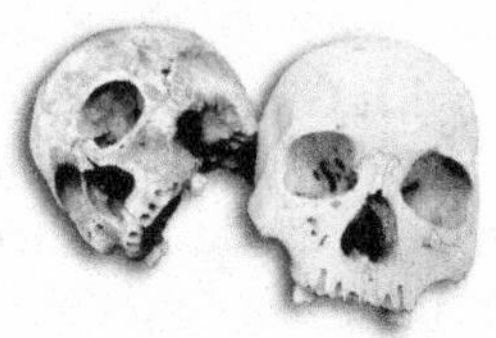

Donovan entered the shell of what had once been a large family home. The summer air around him heated his skin and stole his air.

He'd not been to Montana before—or not this section, anyway. Prior to joining the FBI, he'd traveled little. But then he'd become a NightShade agent, and now it felt like he was hardly ever home, hardly ever even within a hundred-mile radius of home. But his job here was clear: He had to glean whatever information he could from this, the home and the lands of the Little family when they had lived here in Montana.

The case was old. The local cops had investigated, found nothing of value, and closed the file more than a year ago. The buildings had been burned out and then rained on, snowed on, and baked through the summer. Donovan would have had trouble guessing why Westerfield was resurrecting this investigation now, except for the killings at the de Gottardi-Little compound in the Ozarks.

So Donovan knew the importance of this. He also knew the probability that the lack of evidence was going to be astounding. He had learned not to question his FBI orders, or at least not to do so out loud. But that didn't mean that he didn't question them silently.

He questioned Westerfield's urge to put him on a plane faster than was almost humanly possible. He'd barely made it here "on time," grabbing his go-bag without a chance to pack more. He'd rushed to the airport, racing against stop lights and nearly growling his way through the security check. Even though he was given a fast track, he still had a weapon that had to be examined every single time, in every single airport. They had been closing the plane doors as he arrived at the gate. Had he not been an FBI agent flashing his badge, he was certain they would have told him he was just too late.

And now, here he was, checked into his motel room in this small town in Montana, standing here by himself to examine the house. Agents Pines and de Gottardi had not arrived yet. Westerfield had specifically told him both Christina and Wade were coming—yet Donovan had spoken with each of them, and they weren't due until tomorrow.

Had they not been able to make it to the airport fast enough? It didn't seem right that neither of them would have. He'd almost asked out loud, "Was this the original plan?" Was he supposed to get here a full day before his colleagues? And what would Westerfield get from that? Donovan had no idea what he might find that Wade or Christina couldn't. Even then, keeping them back another day accomplished what, exactly?

He didn't know. Donovan had never proclaimed to understand how SAC Westerfield's mind worked. Some days, Donovan was pretty confident that it didn't work at all. But—supposedly—his boss was looking at some bigger picture that none of the individual agents could see. Donovan just had to trust that his boss was making those decisions well.

Instead of sitting in the motel room, he'd grabbed his kit for evidence collection and had come out to the house by himself. As soon as he turned onto the gravel road, he realized this was probably not his best idea.

Weeds grew up through what had once been carefully packed gravel. Since the family had abandoned the land, it had shifted again and again, with no tires traveling over the road to pack down the tiny imperfections. The cracks and dips had grown, creating a ride that wobbled the car back and forth as he hit ruts and potholes and made him glad he was in a rental car instead of his own. It also made him wonder what kind of damages the FBI might end up paying when he returned it.

Still, he'd kept pressing forward up the two-mile-long drive toward the house. Most of the foundations still stood, rows of cinder block with a basement carved out beneath. Only these portions had not burned in the fire. Floor joists, flooring, and even some cases of exposed sub-flooring greeted him as he climbed up the front steps, grateful for the cinder block. Whatever covering had been on the floors had burned, rotted, or broken away, but parts of the foundation felt stable enough for him to put his weight on.

As he stood in the doorway, he wondered if he dared to step inside. He stepped one foot forward, testing the charred, blackened wood planks and plywood that were now covered with a thick layer of brown, silty dust. This part of Montana was either wet or dry, and nothing in between—or so the local, older man who worked the motel desk had told him.

Donovan had now stayed in enough of these little places. He hadn't thought about it before, but in the past year, he'd learned to recognize which motels sold rooms by the hour and which were the nice, family-owned kind of places where the locals would talk your ear off. This was, luckily, one of the latter.

The man had told him about the Littles. He knew about the compound and the houses in the area. He knew the acreage of the farm they owned and what kind of vegetables they grew for themselves and what they sold at their roadside stands during the spring and summer.

He supplied a lot of information for a man who hadn't seen any of the family members in well over a year. Donovan already knew they had packed up what they could and fled, taking all their remaining belongings, and even a cache of secret documents. Then they had headed to the Ozarks to join family there, believing in safety in numbers. Well, they had believed until last month, though given the outcome, Donovan wasn't sure what direction their compass needle aimed on that one now.

Looking around what remained of the house, he cataloged random walls here and there from the studs, some still yellow but graying with age, with charred-out pieces. None of this property looked safe. He stepped gingerly across the floor. This wasn't the first time he'd been in the burnt-out shell of a home, and he shuddered when he thought back to the damage from Echo and Ember. But he brushed it off and pushed forward, one careful step at a time. With each move, he tested the floor and then leaned in, slowly putting weight on it, ready to jump, if necessary, and get off of any weak spot before he went crashing through.

His short time at the de Gottardi and Little home in the Ozarks had given him information about this property. He saw more now, because he knew what he was looking for. He'd found a trap door in the floor of what must have been a family room. The hinges had given it away.

Had there been carpet or better flooring still intact, it would have been smooth and nothing would have showed. But here, after the fire had come through, with dirt illuminating every crack and crevice, the trap door was outlined quite neatly. Donovan crouched down, trying to position himself directly over a floor joist and hoping it would hold while he pulled out the short, heavy crowbar from his kit. He wedged it under the edge of the wood and worked hard to pry it up. It took a few minutes, and several times he thought he would fall back on his butt and go crashing through the floor. Though that was probably the fastest way to find out what lay beneath, it wasn't the safest.

He looked around again for a moment. The walls provided no protection in three out of four directions. If anyone was out in the woods, they would see him in here, messing around and investigating.

He stopped and did something he'd been remiss to have skipped on the way in. Though it was second nature to sniff the air, he should have stopped and carefully checked what was around him, focusing on the scents that came to him. As he did it now, his hands wrapped a little tighter around the crowbar still tucked under the edge of the trap door. It was aimed and ready to crack and lift—or swing at an assailant who came too close. No one should be here.

Maybe not even me, he thought.

Donovan turned his head in all directions and carefully inhaled and tested the air, until he'd almost given himself a headache. He smelled nothing. No humans—none of the normal kind, none of his kind. He smelled no one like Eleri. No wild and crazy teenagers with a death wish. Nothing human was nearby.

Animals, however, came to his senses easily. Vegetation, too. Something, it seemed, was in bloom out here, despite the hot summer months. While he couldn't place the scent, he could smell that it was there. Deciding that was the best he could do and he'd already been foolish to come out here alone—and that the rutted road would hinder his tracks if he tried to escape quickly—he figured he should at least finish this part of the job.

The trap door at last pried open with a snap, almost sending him backwards as he feared. He barely managed to stay on the balls of his feet and he had to hold the door up with one hand, leaning into the dark space. He pulled the flashlight from the kit and shined it down.

In the Ozarks, a neat staircase had led into a well-lit cellar, which he later learned led to a pathway outside. Here, he saw only a ladder. The ladder had been wooden. It appeared to have been sturdy in its previous days, but now it had seen the ravages of fire and rot. He didn't trust the floor he stood on, and he sure as hell did not trust the ladder.

He continued looking around but left the cellar on his list as something he and Wade and Christina might examine more closely tomorrow. He would not be going down there alone today.

Just then, his phone pinged. He looked around once more for visitors and let the trap door slap shut. Pulling the phone from his pocket, he saw that Wade had forwarded him the map they'd been discussing earlier.

Donovan did not know much about his own kind, raised mostly by his father the way he was. As the map that Wade forwarded him lit up, it showed where all known people like him existed in the U.S.

Donovan smiled as the map talked him through the key. The size of each dot corresponded to the numbers of shape-shifters in each area. The key gave specifics so he could follow the dot sizes. But when it switched to the map, it was empty.

Then, Donovan grinned. Wade had found him an animated version. But his heart pounded harder as he watched red dots balloon across the map.

12

Still feeling adrift, but now knowing she had to get out of the house, Eleri left Grandmere's early the next morning.

She still didn't manage to get up before her great-grandmother, though, and when she finally rolled out of bed at half past six—so late!—breakfast was ready.

Biscuits that had been rolled by hand and tossed into the oven already sat hot and waiting on the table. A bowl of gravy waited nearby today. Oatmeal, apparently, was only good for some days.

Unable to sneak out of the house now, Eleri ate breakfast with Grandmere. She stayed quiet, thinking as she chewed. Her great-grandmother let her stay that way. She still hadn't fully accepted Grandmere's explanation of the bones: that they had been passed down from family member to family member until they arrived at her.

Eleri had almost shuddered at the thought. Would they become *her* bones some day? Much the same way she would inherit the family silver on her father's side ... She had tried to suppress the concern and the willies it gave her but, as usual, she had no doubt she'd gotten nothing past Grandmere.

Given that she couldn't say anything that might be a lie, Eleri mostly again ate her breakfast in silence. Then she got dressed and headed out, climbing into the rental car and driving into town. She coasted aimlessly around the Lower Ninth Ward for a while, going up and down streets but trying to stay far enough from Grandmere's that she wasn't spotted driving by.

That only lasted a little while before she realized the futility of her meandering. Turning onto Judge Perez Drive to take the bridge, she headed into the French Quarter. Parking was a bitch, but she paid it, then hopped out and headed down one of the side streets.

In no time, she found herself in front of the wooden sign for Mystic Vudu. The sign said "892 Rue Royal." Eleri stood across the street and gazed up at it, wondering why she had come back here. She had thought she was simply wandering. Now, as she looked up and down the street, she realized this had been her destination.

Should I go back inside? Should I touch the knife again?

She was here now, and something had pulled her, so she crossed the street, telling herself that this time, she would be quick. She pulled the heavy wooden door open and strode boldly back into the shop.

The same woman was there, her hands clasped in a nearly identical pose as the first time Eleri had seen her. Her eyes and nostrils flared just a touch as she spotted Eleri. *Did the woman see something special in her, or was she just ... memorable?*

In the FBI's Behavioral Analysis Unit, she'd been an analyst. She'd not been tapped to work as a field agent, though she'd been through agent training and had passed. There was never a consideration of sending her undercover.

Agents had to blend. That was a near impossibility with her unusual coloring and face shape. She looked partially African-American, but the red hair and green eyes were a startling mismatch. She'd never been able to decide if she was striking or freakish, and she'd ultimately decided she landed somewhere in the middle. Some men found her attractive. Some looked at her askance and walked away. She was an odd mix, she knew. Perhaps this woman just remembered the red-headed, mixed-race woman who had come into the store.

Did she also remember that Eleri had left so abruptly? Eleri smiled and hoped not. *Why would she?*

She once again wandered through the store, although this time, her feet moved much faster. She remembered the general layout and headed directly for the back room, toward the shelf with the knives. She paused only to look around and make sure she was not being watched.

The knife she had touched last time had not been sold. Slowly, she reached out and picked it up, prepared for the assault on her senses—but it didn't come.

Eleri blinked and set the blade back down. Was it the same? Once again, she touched it, picked it up, and turned it over. As she did it, she heard footsteps behind her.

"Does that knife interest you?"

Eleri smiled at the woman, deciding it was a great time to get some information. It was surely the same knife. She examined it in detail now. Although, to be fair, she couldn't say she had looked at it closely the first time. She'd merely found it interesting, picked it up, and immediately dropped it before running from the shop. Perhaps that knife had been sold and this one was on the shelf was its replacement.

Taking advantage, she turned to the woman, "Yes. Can you tell me about it?"

"Absolutely." The woman came over and gently lifted it from Eleri's palm. "The blade is hand-forged."

"Is it steel?" Eleri asked, thinking that was an appropriate question. She understood, from Grandmere, that steel was preferred for some tasks in the Hoodoo religion and disavowed for others.

The woman shook her head. "Not particularly."

Eleri tipped her head a little sideways, enjoying the expression on the woman's face as she waited patiently until the woman said, "It is a kind of steel, but it is not like the steel of the factories. It is a steel recipe that was made and handed down by my family. My uncle, in fact, owns the forge. He designs the blades and then gives them to us. We bind them and make the knives."

The woman did not discuss the spell work that the blade was obviously intended for. This one looked like a cross between an *athame's* straight blade and a *boline's* half-moon shape. Eleri noted the curve and the slight hook to the tip, that the sharp edge ran along the long outer side as well as the short, inner curve. This was not a knife for everyday use, nor even for specialty purposes other than ritual. She'd been reading up.

"This knife," the woman continued, "has been in my family for a while."

Eleri tipped her head again. "Yet you would sell it?"

That was hard to believe. Families did not sell their artifacts. Hell,

Grandmere had bones! She would not consider getting rid of the things she had, let alone selling them. Grandmere had scraps of fabric that her own mother had collected, perhaps during WWII or WWI or earlier. None of her family's odd heirlooms would have been sold. Grandmere wouldn't even take two chickens and a goat for some of the stuff she did. Yet, this woman claimed she was selling her family antiques in a storefront on Rue Royal?

"Yes," the woman said, nodding sagely. "Some days, I am not particularly fond of my family."

Eleri found she had to laugh. She also felt that things would work better if she played dumb. "What do the markings mean?"

She again picked the knife up out of the woman's hands, hoping she would see one of the pictures that had flashed in her mind. The first time she'd touched it, she had seen blood dripping down hands. She had seen white dresses and large bonfires and many, many people around them. She had seen animals—goats and chickens—though they were not being sacrificed, not as many people believed was the heart of voodoo.

In fact, most of what people believed was wrong. Eleri had believed it too, and she had learned from Grandmere's sharp words just how wrong she'd been. In the vision, when she saw the chickens and goats, she noted only that they were whole and live.

The flashes of hands and bare feet in the dirt and knives were of more interest to her now. Since it was all just random, rapid imagery, she'd taken it as an assault and fled. Now, however, touching the knife yielded nothing. She turned it over, looking at what she supposed were runes carved into the side of the pale gray handle.

"Those are powerful markings. For spellwork," the woman told her. Her wonderful accent lilted as she described what each mark was for and discussed how they created a shield to guard the user of the knife.

"Did it guard your family?" Eleri asked.

"Perhaps. My own mother lived long, long into her old age. She gave birth to me when she was well into her fifties."

"Fifties?" Eleri asked. She realized she was straddling two worlds: playing the agent, farming information out of this woman who owned the shop, and also playing the role of the new friend, standing in the store, asking honest questions about a knife that interested her. The woman tipped her head.

"What can I say? My family has a strong history of longevity."

Eleri's thoughts ran to Grandmere and she wondered about the lifespans in her own family. *Did Grandmere's brothers and sisters live a long time, too?* Grandmere was the only one left, as far as she knew. It was a thought she'd never pondered, like the paintings on the walls at Bell Point Farm. It was just something that had always been. There was Grandmere. And she was the only one.

Looking back at the knife lying across her hand, she turned it over and realized something that only a forensic scientist would know. "Is this real bone?" she asked.

Even without touching her tongue to it and feeling the telltale stick, she knew. In fact, she recognized that it was bone. And it was human.

13

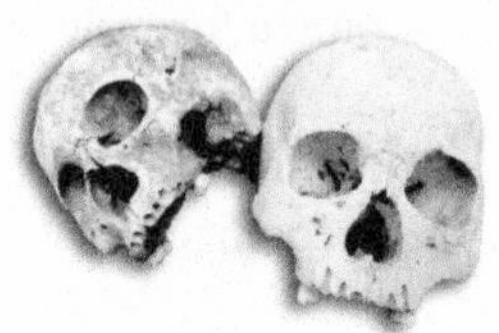

As her stomach turned, Eleri thanked the woman and left Mystic Vudu. This time, she didn't run. This time, she didn't have the cover of other patrons so she could sneak away without making a scene. Though she'd made some noise the last time, at least the shop owner hadn't seen.

Even so, her departure this time had also been abrupt. She'd managed enough decorum to say goodbye, and the woman had time to formally end the conversation. "If you are interested in purchasing or, if you have other questions, come back and visit anytime. My name is Darcelle."

"I'm Eleri," she'd replied and thanked her again, looking at her watch as though she had somewhere she suddenly remembered she needed to be. All of that was a lie. Eleri had looked briefly at the shelf, giving a quick visual exam to the other knives and wondering if they, too, were perhaps made of human bone or other forbidden substances.

They weren't, she saw—or at least, there was nothing so obvious to her own eyes. The bone handle she'd held wouldn't be obvious to an untrained observer. The piece of skeleton had been rubbed with oil, split with a thin saw, and shined with a patina. The tang of the knife was pushed down into the split and into the center gap, where the marrow had been. After that, leather strapping was wrapped around it to hold the blade tight to the handle. The cord was wrapped in a design as disturbingly beautiful as the cut of the blade was. It didn't obscure that something—some spellwork—had been carved into the bone. It was a stomach-churning piece of art.

Eleri felt it now, the surety that the knife she'd handled today was the same one she had touched the day before. In fact, she prayed it was. Sometimes she got visions on things—and sometimes she didn't. It was clear from her history that she was more susceptible when she wasn't paying attention. It was much harder to make a vision come to her than it was to be smacked upside the head by one she wasn't expecting. Although she hadn't seen the chickens, goats, bare feet in dirt, bloody hands, blood dripping into the ground, and the sharp curve of the knife this time when she touched it, that didn't mean it wasn't the same. She prayed to every God she had heard of that it was the same knife because—if it wasn't—that would mean the shop had a cache of human bone knives.

This time, she'd seen something else while she was in there. As she gingerly touched the handle, treating it as the delicate piece that it was—despite the morbid undertones surrounding it—she realized it was not very old.

It came from a human adult arm, though there was no more she could tell from sight. The whole bone was not present. Only a portion of the bone's length had been used. It was hard to tell, as it had been cut, sanded, and otherwise manipulated. It also sported the knob on the end of the bone, almost as a counter- weight to the blade. The fusing of the epiphyseal plates indicated the bone had once belonged to an adult—male or female, she couldn't tell from just the one sample. Sexing the bone required certain parts of the skeleton: a pelvic girdle, particular portions of the skull, or… there were lots of options, none of which were present on this knife handle. A DNA test would have yielded much more information. For just a moment, she thought she should go back and purchase the knife. It had been very expensive—a family heirloom, the woman had told her.

Darcelle. That had been her name.

Perhaps Darcelle understood what it was she was selling and that was why the price was so high.

At the end of the street, Eleri paused, standing at the light and waiting, thinking. *Should she go back?* Unable to decide, she walked straight across when the "walk" sign flashed and headed directly into an ice cream shop where she ordered a cone in a flavor she'd never tried before.

Though she didn't really like it, the ice cream cooled her down as the day warmed up. She found she wasn't the only one eating ice cream in the middle of the morning. Sitting at the small round metal table, she tried to make her decision. Should she tell Westerfield? Would it open an actual case? If it did, she was the only agent here in town—at least, the only one she knew of—from NightShade. Thus, she would be the one opening this brand new case when she had come for an entirely different purpose.

Then again, her true purpose seemed to have not panned out at all. The bones in the file folder did not belong to Emmaline. Eleri was crunching on the cone by the time she thought about the fact that the skeleton she'd fixated on did seem to resemble her and Emmaline, despite having come from the Northwest area.

The biome from the strontium isotopes in the teeth had placed the girl in a large area. The dental records had made her specific. As it turned out, she was from Nebraska—corn fields and all that. Then one day, she'd gone into the cornfields and had never come back. Somebody, somewhere, was now telling her family that, twenty years after their daughter had disappeared, her bones had been found. They were also relaying the disturbing news that she had made it to somewhere in the age of her late teens before she died. They'd had a decade to find her alive, and they'd failed. Eleri felt that same pain.

The girl had gone missing before her tenth birthday. Just like Emmaline. She'd grown to be a teenager, just like Emmaline. But exactly how old had she gotten? Had she made it to thirteen, but been a very mature thirteen? Or was she fully seventeen, but still developing the bone characteristics that identified her as an adult female? The problem of growth was that it was difficult to pinpoint anything more than an age range.

The ranges strictly determinable by bone development and markers got wider as the person got older. That was why so many forensic reports stated, "He was somewhere between thirty and sixty." At least the teen years offered slightly narrower ranges.

As she finished the ice cream, Eleri decided not to go back for the knife. She would return and check again tomorrow or the next day to see if it was still there, and only then would she make a decision. She wasn't here to pick up a case, other than the one she had first come for. She decided, as she chewed on the last corner of the sugar cone, that she was going to find Emmaline. They had all spent far too long waiting for something to break, for something to happen with her sister's case. Eleri was going to make it happen.

She left the ice cream shop in a bit of a daze, meandering along the streets and wandering the downtown area as she had originally expected to do today. She was out of Grandmere's house, away from the idea that the bones she'd found in the closet had been handed down generation over generation.

Sighing, Eleri thought about the numbers of bones she'd encountered. In her job, it was to be expected. But this was her normal, non-working life. She was on break. Why, then, was she still encountering human bones?

She was going to have to test Grandmere's little collection. Tomorrow or the next day, she told herself. It wasn't anything she could just let slide—but for today, she would.

She walked along the graveyards, enjoying the statuary and the raised tombstones. The white marble monuments were aged. Black mold had pushed into cracks, stood regal in full relief. Angels guarded the dead here: both hated and loved ones, both small and big.

It wasn't long before she'd passed two separate graveyards, one of which clearly belonged to wealthier families. In the poorer cemetery, bodies were stacked side to side—bones to bones, almost. Some of the graves sat on top of each other, as the poor families still needed to bury their dead but couldn't afford fresh land to do it. In New Orleans, the dead could no longer be interred underground, only stacked and pushed into the spaces. Land was too expensive for the old-school internments.

On her right, a salmon colored building with railings along the second- and third-floor balconies hosted flower boxes that trailed down pink and green vines. Flowers bloomed along them, despite the heat and humidity—or maybe because of it. Eleri didn't recognize the plant by name, but it was one she saw repeatedly when she came to town.

Music drifted to her from one of the alleys—either someone playing a horn or something from a radio or a record, she couldn't tell. Given the location and the number of people in the streets who appeared to not have a job to go to today, it was entirely possible someone was sitting down with a jazz horn, just out of her sight. The melody set her cadence as she headed down the street.

Lifting her fingers, she let them trail along the fence, slapping slightly and tapping each of the black, wrought-iron posts as she went by. Her thoughts disappeared. The day around her disappeared. Her fingers tapped and tapped and tapped along the spikes. When she looked up again, she saw her.

Emmaline was right in front of her, walking backward down the street, beckoning her to follow.

Eleri had no choice. This was what she had come for. What had Emmaline decided to show her?

She followed her sister for several blocks, despite the fact that she picked up the pace. Emmaline looked all of seventeen now, considerably grown up from the pictures at Grandmere's and on the walls at Patton Hall. While no one else seemed to see Emmaline as she wove in and out of other walkers, Eleri fought to keep up as the crowds got thicker on some of the streets and then thinner on others. She walked past tall buildings. Only the colors and quality changed, but not the style. Eleri occasionally glanced up at a street sign, trying to determine where she was. Once again, they passed black, wrought-iron fences, *fleur de lis* finials gracing the top of each of the spikes to deter anyone who might try to climb over.

The buildings were close to the sidewalks here, many of them without any yard to keep a space between the house and the passersby. The patios often brushed against the edge of the street, where Eleri could just reach over and touch them, but she didn't. She followed her sister, occasionally losing sight and frantically jumping to catch up.

Then Emmaline turned the corner, and Eleri did, too. Emmaline had made it there just a moment or two more, and then she was gone. Eleri was alone on the street. On her left was a graveyard, one she had not passed before—or was it? They all looked familiar. She studied it a little more closely and then felt a tap on her shoulder.

As she turned to face the building behind her, she saw a large, wrought-iron fence that opened into a courtyard. In the courtyard, a large tree grew in the corner, its roots pushing up between wide paver stones that held court underneath it.

The gates opened easily at her touch, and as she walked into the private space, she noticed bumps in the ground. Emmaline had come through here. She knew it. In fact, as she looked up, her sister stepped between the bushes and ducked out the back. For a moment, Eleri thought about following her, but it was the bumps under her feet that intrigued her the most.

Dropping to her hands and knees, she began to dig in the dirt. She had to get what was under there, though she couldn't have said why. Something important was in here and she knew it. Soon, she'd broken three of her fingernails and stuffed black loamy dirt up under the others, but she kept digging. Her purse was slung haphazardly across her back and her back was aimed toward the now-open fence, where anyone could walk in and find her. This was private property, she knew. She had no idea what she was doing here, other than the fact that she had to dig.

So dig she did, and as she did, she found what she was looking for. Slowly, she unearthed a human bone.

14

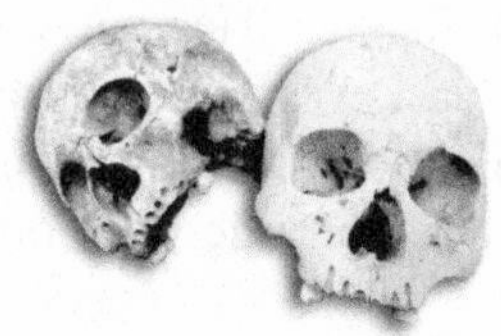

Eleri woke lazily, rolled over in her bed, and slowly blinked her eyes against the sun coming through the window. The slant of the rays told her it was much later than she normally arose.

She wasn't one of those morning people who woke themselves up with pep and the urge to go running. But neither was she someone who was irritable until she's had her coffee and preferred to sleep until noon. Today's late wake-up surprised her. Still, she stayed in bed, luxuriating in the feel of her own laziness for a while longer. Pulling the covers up from where they had slipped down, she rolled into a warm ball again—as though she needed anything more to make her warm. She'd probably kicked the covers off herself during the night in an attempt to regain a body temperature somewhat in the human range.

The city was sweltering and the interior of Grandmere's home was only mildly better than standing in the sun. Eleri considered going to see a movie just for the air conditioning. But the lull of the bed was pulling her back under. She was curled up, tucked into her covers, and falling lazily back asleep when her eyes snapped open.

How was she here? Yesterday, she'd gone to Rue Royal, to Mystic Vudu, and talked with the shop lady. Hadn't she? She'd wandered the streets and seen Emmaline, and then followed her down and around curves and corners, to a house she'd seen once before. In fact, the last time she'd seen it had been in a dream when she followed Emmaline through New Orleans—just like yesterday. Only this time, she'd opened the fence to the private courtyard and walked inside, and had begun digging in the dirt. That's how she remembered it.

Had she really done that? That was a massive violation of private property.

She was an FBI agent. Though she was on leave, the badge remained in her pocket and she could use it to identify herself. Like many officers of the law, her private life was not *completely* her own, even when she was off duty. She was still a representative of the Bureau. And, if taken to court, the idea that she had no concept of her own trespass and violation would be laughable. She'd clearly committed a crime.

She had wandered uninvited onto someone's private property, dug in their dirt, and taken—

She paused. She'd dug something out of the dirt. She'd taken it, she thought—slipped it into her pocket. Eleri pondered it further and then had a brief flash of memory. It was bone. She'd found human bone in the dirt. A worn knob from the end of a tibia, she believed.

The piece had been short, appearing to have suffered a serious break just under the epiphyseal plate. The bone had been old, and had been in the dirt long enough for the sharp edges to have worn smooth—not into a perfect knob, but smooth enough that it didn't cut or stab at her as she dug it up. She had only the vaguest, foggy memory of sliding the bone into her pocket. *Had she done that?*

She thought about it now. She remembered digging it up and how surprised she was to find it, and even more surprised to recognize it as human, inside this courtyard garden. She had taken it as evidence. But even that was something she couldn't claim under the guise of law. Though it was definitely bizarre, she supposed there might be any number of legal reasons for a family to have a human bone buried in their own courtyard.

In many places, bodies could be buried on family property at will. It depended on the laws of the state and local province. But although Eleri wasn't up to standard on exactly what New Orleans burial laws were—especially given the graveyards, the mausoleums, and the sarcophagi that made New Orleans so famous—she couldn't think of a good reason to have a human tibia buried in a private residence courtyard.

Still, maybe it hadn't been buried there at all. Bones could move.

Or maybe it had been buried there, but too long ago to associate with any current indictment. The problem in New Orleans was that buried bodies floated to the surface, because the ground was so very wet. Her find might make perfect sense. The area might have been an old graveyard. Urban growth, gentrification, reclamation—they all had a hard time here. It was entirely plausible that, at one point, any plot of land in and around the city might have been a graveyard. Who knew what tribe or ancient culture the bone might belong to? It might have just been someone's great-great-grandfather, floating upward.

Surely, it was human. She recognized it. But beyond that, she could say nothing other than that she'd trespassed and stolen from private property—and possibly, depending on the local ordinances, violated several other laws.

Eleri was sitting up in bed now with the covers thrown back, thinking she needed to get into her pocket and examine the bone more closely, before she could make a decision about what to do with it. But when she went to the closet and pulled out what she'd been wearing the day before, she found nothing in the pockets at all. *Had she put it down somewhere, or stashed it away when she came home?*

After searching her brain for whatever she might have done, Eleri was surprised to come up blank. She had no memory of coming home the previous day. Nothing, in fact, existed in her mind beyond putting the bone in her pocket.

Eleri scrambled to get dressed. The whole time, her mind raced. How had she even gotten home? Had she walked back to her car? Driven it here? That would make sense. It was exactly what she had planned to do. But she had zero memory of doing it. As she thought it through, she wondered how she'd even gotten back to the car. She'd been following a ghost through the streets. They'd taken twists and turns, and while Eleri had tried to pay attention, she'd lost the direction along the way. She'd simply been following the tunnel vision that showed her sister in front of her, beckoning her along.

Assuming that she must have driven home—and for whatever reason, her brain wasn't grasping the memory—Eleri searched her vicinity for where she might have put the bone. Though she was fully dressed in another pair of lightweight pants and a tank top—her best defense against the heat of the day—the familiar action of getting ready had not jogged her memory. Nor had it put her into contact with wherever she'd put that bone fragment.

It did not lie on the table next to her bed. It was not in the closet, nor in her purse, nor her travel bag. It should have been in a plastic baggie, the best method for carrying evidence. Though she was aware that, in Grandmere's house, she might not find anything that was petroleum based, she didn't know if she'd managed to protect the bone fragment at all. If she was smart, she would have stopped by a store and bought herself some paper lunch bags so she could preserve her finds and even label them somewhat properly—but it appeared that had not happened, either. She was combing through the room again when she realized it wasn't here, and her search radius needed to extend a little further.

Gingerly, she opened the door, wondering still—*How had she gotten home?* And now, *What might Grandmere think about her sleeping in so late?*

As she went through the house in small, ever-widening circles, she searched for the bone—and now also for Grandmere. The woman was shockingly absent. Though Eleri knew and understood in her heart that Grandmere must, at some point, leave her home, it was a rare occurrence that she'd not seen very often. Though Grandmere would walk the girls around the block when they were young, they would be with her—not left alone. Grandmere might send them out to places while she remained behind. Eleri and young Emmaline had walked to play at the water, some ten or so blocks away. But Eleri couldn't recall when her great-grandmother had ever left her alone in the house.

Now, Grandmere was markedly absent. Eleri continued searching for the bone. It could be assumed Grandmere was fine and would find her own way back, but the bone might be lost forever if she couldn't remember where she'd stashed it. So she scanned every surface she could find. Had she brought it home and shown Grandmere? Her memory was blank.

If she had shown it to Grandmere, Grandmere might have put it away somewhere safe or special. But where would that even be?

When Eleri craned her neck to see into the driveway, she found her car parked exactly where she had left it the day before. Shaking her head and wondering how she'd lost such a big chunk of the day, she aimed back toward the closet in her room. When she’d been dressing, something had tugged at the back of her brain.

She looked inside again, and her gaze snagged on the pants she'd worn yesterday. Her eyes widened. The knees had absolutely no dirt on them. She'd knelt while she was digging in the little garden. They should have been filthy. They could not have been washed and dried in such a short time.

Now the question arose: *Had she dreamed the whole thing?* But when she checked her phone, the date was one day forward.

15

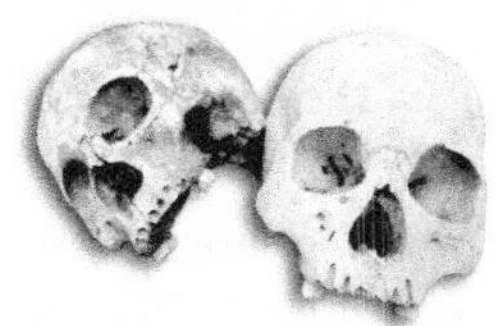

Donovan had waited almost a full twenty-four hours for Wade and Christina to show up at the compound in Montana. The area, just outside of Billings, reminded him of the de Gottardi compound in the Ozarks.

Though the areas were dramatically different, there were lots of similarities in the layouts. It seemed when the families had started these "family farms," they'd had a plan. Each place had lots of land outside of the city—far enough out not to be stumbled upon, but close enough that a run for milk could be made, if necessary. The gravel roads on the land deterred people from taking them on a whim and just driving up to see what was there. Blatant signs along the road warned "No Trespassing."

In the center of the property—much too far away to be seen from any passing roads—stood a handful of houses and buildings. Just like in the Ozarks, the largest homes dominated the center. Here, there had only been one other large home in the central position, though several smaller homes and other buildings held court.

Donovan had found what he thought looked like a schoolhouse. While it would hold about ten students and a teacher comfortably, it showed evidence of maybe five. He'd found another smaller, single-family home much further away from the large, multi-family home. It still remained close to the center of the property, simply because of the size of the acreage.

However, a second, even smaller family unit lay a little further beyond that, and a third one appeared to have been in the mid-stages of being built when it, too, had been burned. He found a small, burned storage building for furniture and perhaps cast-offs. He saw a storage area where he found that fruit and root vegetables had been kept. They weren't under the main house in the cellar, where one might have expected. On this property, that space had an entirely different purpose. So here, they'd been given their own building, with its own cellar.

Interestingly enough, in the school building—again built on a cinderblock foundation that was slightly raised—he'd found another trap door. He'd seen a third in the small family unit, the one closest to the home. And he was now confident that a series of tunnels had been dug underneath, connecting all the buildings.

He would have thought the ground was too rocky for tunneling, but since he was no geologist or soil scientist, he eventually fell back on the idea that it was farmland, and thus had pretty good quality soil. The land probably had a decent depth of dirt above bedrock, as well as a good water table. None of that mattered now. The family had been burned out, hunted, and driven from the state to the relative safety of another area. The good soil and secret tunnels had lost their value. Donovan figured the secrets here were reason enough not to sell the land, even though the family might never be able to come back.

However, it was the map Wade had sent that bothered him when he'd tried to sleep the night before. The red dots had started small and grown. They appeared in different places on the map at different times. Donovan wondered if that was simply animation or if the timing correlated to the arrival of his kind to the area.

He'd been as patient as he could, waiting for Wade to show up and explain it all to him. But once his fellow agent arrived, he'd wasted no time and followed the man into his motel room.

Practically in his friend's face and barely having given any greeting at all, Donovan assaulted Wade with rapid-fire questions. "You have to tell me what's with the map. Do the dots correspond to historical arrival times? How recent is the data? Is this current?"

He only managed to shut up when Wade looked at him with eyebrows up. "Good to see you, too. How are you doing?"

The words were sarcastic, but Donovan ignored the fact that

Wade looked at him as though he'd lost his mind. He pretty much probably had. He said a cursory "hello" and repeated the questions.

"What are you talking about?" Wade asked him now, almost deadpan, as he placed his go-bag onto the bed. It looked disturbingly similar to Donovan's own bag. It was made from black, ripstop nylon. It was duffel style, with wheels on one end so it could be dragged through an airport. The utilitarian quality allowed it to blend in at a military base, and Donovan wondered for a moment what Wade had given up to be here again, back in full mode with NightShade.

He and Eleri had visited Wade at his office once. He'd worked for a private company, solving physics problems to improve their designs and designing his own DOD materials. But Westerfield had called him back. Wade—like each of them—was unique, and his skills were needed.

But now, after the death of Wade's boyfriend Randall, he might have found an inner drive to be back in NightShade, back behind the badge. Maybe back here in Montana, where his extended family had been burned out and driven off. Maybe it wasn't just Westerfield's urging that had brought him back. He had no idea what the SAC might have held over Wade's head.

Donovan just stared at his friend, and then he said, "I'm sorry. I'll give you a minute. The whole red dots thing just kind of threw me for a loop."

"Oh, the map I sent you yesterday …" Wade seemed to catch on. "Sorry, I sent out a crap-ton of stuff yesterday. It took me a bit to catch on. The one with the family history and locations …" He trailed off again, seeming to think.

"Yeah, that one." Donovan let it roll out of his mouth, hoping Wade would pull himself back into the present.

"I'm hungry," Wade spit out, almost point blank. "There's a coffee shop about three blocks down. Give me a minute. I'll come knock on your door and we can walk down together. I'll tell you whatever I know."

Donovan wondered if Wade had checked out the coffee shop closely enough. He'd caught his own glimpse when he headed by the day before. It seemed to have only coffee, and Wade's hunger might not be taken care of there. But he suspected the town would have something to eat nearby. The place was not that large; they should be within walking distance of some restaurant. There was a McDonalds closer to the highway, but it was too far to walk. Donovan kept his fingers crossed. He'd wondered himself if he would spend this trip eating crackers and peanut butter he'd spread with a plastic spoon from the local mom-and-pop grocery.

He went back to his room and waited for what seemed an eternity before the knock came. Checking the time, he saw that it had been less than fifteen minutes. He threw the door wide and found Wade standing there, hands in pockets. "Come on, walk. I'll talk."

Wade continued as they headed down a relatively empty street. "That map was put together with information that I got in part from the compound and the documents we have there."

Donovan frowned. "I didn't know you made the map."

"Mm-hm." Wade only nodded. "It seemed an important piece of our history to have."

Donovan noted then that, of course, the map was entirely unlabeled. It could have been a map of small airports, or Listeria outbreaks, or clusters of cases of Parkinson's. As a former medical examiner, the latter two came easily to his mind. He often thought of populations in terms of disease and deaths. And the map could easily be for one of those issues. That was the point: It could have been anything.

"Does it correspond with times?" Donovan slowed down his brain and asked his questions now one at a time.

"Yes. These are records that we have of when our people came into the US and originally populated specific areas. Again, no labels, but it begins in the late fifteen hundreds."

"Wow." Donovan blinked and stopped walking, but Wade didn't.

"Actually, the records go back much further than that. You know that. But that was the point when our European ancestors came and we began populating the North American continent."

"We weren't here before then?" Donovan caught up and asked, suddenly fascinated by a history he'd never known he had. The problem was, it still wasn't his history. It was Wade's. It was a history of people who were like him—so like him it was a stunning match. But it wasn't *his*.

Wade couldn't hear his inner disavowal of the people on the maps. "Well, there were rumors of 'skin-walkers' here before us."

Donovan had long wondered about the stories of things that went bump in the night. Had his ancestors *been* those things? He skipped ahead a little, wanting to discuss this, but needing to get to a certain piece of information. "So, according to you, the largest populations aren't even in the Ozarks, where your family is."

Wade shook his head. "We may be a large cluster, and it's definitely our family. My family has all the histories, the documents etc., so we know that population well. I can verify that dot, but I can't do as well with the others. Still, according to my data, it's all pretty accurate."

"But the cities," Donovan said. He'd noticed that the major metropolitan areas on the map not only now seemed to sport red dots, but that the size of those dots was growing exponentially. He said so to Wade.

Wade nodded in return. "It's absolutely true. The ability to hide in plain sight has gotten better. And the ability to hide at all has gotten worse. Many have developed the attitude that we're going to be found out at some point soon. When we are, they expect to pass it off as a medical anomaly. But so be it. The idea is that—if we are going to be found anyway—there's no longer a need to make an effort to hide."

"Is it Lobomau?" Donovan asked, the word still not rolling off his tongue.

Wade shook his head. "No. Well, some, but a lot more are like you and me—just people out in the general population."

Donovan took a deep breath. The little red dots seared his memory with the shock of knowing he wasn't nearly as rare as he'd thought. Still, the one that had bothered him the most was the growing red dot over the city of New Orleans.

Should he warn Eleri?

16

Eleri left the house and started her car. This time, she drove directly to the parking lot where she knew she would be able to find a space, even if at this time of day. It would be a spot being abandoned by someone leaving, but it would happen. It had taken three passes around the lot playing parking shark to find the requisite spot, but it had opened up. She managed to snag it and headed down the street on foot, not quite certain where she was heading.

She realized that yesterday's path was still very uncertain. She believed she had come here. Then again, she also believed she had dug a portion of human tibia out of a central court garden in an area of the city that she now couldn't pinpoint.

Her first stop was confirmation. If the entire day was missing—if she really had slept it all away—this should tell her. And honestly, sleeping the day away made a level of sense. She was emotionally exhausted, deeply disappointed that the bones had not belonged to Emmaline, and traveling too much lately. When she added in that there was no dirt on her pants from the day before, sleeping more than twenty-four hours in one stretch began looking plausible.

She'd checked the gas gauge while she'd driven across the bridge, but she couldn't remember quite clearly how much gas she'd had the day before. Regardless, the drive from the Lower Ninth Ward into the French Quarter wasn't very far. If she'd only come in and parked and then driven back home, she wouldn't have disturbed the needle enough for her to know that she'd been anywhere.

She needed to find something else to confirm her story of the day before, so she headed toward Mystic Vudu with a purpose in her stride. She threw the door open, still not quite sure what she would say, and again found the shop owner standing there. Realizing her attitude was absolutely inappropriate—throwing open the door as she had, and then striding into a shop and barking questions—Eleri softened her stance and set a smile on her lips. Even though it felt forced, she tried to make it look natural.

"Hello," said the woman, the same wonderful lilt of mixed accents in her voice. "Can I help you?"

Ah. Eleri felt a vague sense of relief. She had *not* been here yesterday. The woman had not shown a flicker of recognition. But then, as the woman turned away and stepped behind the desk, she asked, "Did you come back for the knife?"

Eleri paused for a moment. At first pass, the phrase seemed damning. In her memory, she and the woman had looked at the knife together yesterday. The woman had described the symbols carved onto it. But then again, if the shop keeper had been watching on the first day, she might have seen Eleri pick up the knife and examine it, before she dropped it and ran from the store.

Eleri felt tongue-tied and only managed to shake her head. "I just had a few more questions."

The woman nodded and waited for them to come. Unfortunately, Eleri's statement was not a brilliant opener, designed to tease out information from the woman. She was underprepared. She'd thought this would be easier—that she would walk in and immediately understand what had happened, from the reaction she got. Now she needed to ask, "Was I here yesterday? And did you speak to me about the knife?" but without saying those words. Without coming across like an escaped mental patient.

She had a brief thought that maybe, for this past year or so, that was exactly what she had been—a parolee from the looney bin. She'd never finished her stay in the psychiatric institute and she'd practically loved it there. Despite the fact that people had been absolutely bonkers around her, she had stayed and worked her program, trying to find some semblance of mental balance, trying to reconcile what her bosses had accused her of and had never been able to prove.

Agent Westerfield had snatched her out of the hospital, demanding that she return to work—new work as a field agent, with a new partner—before her therapeutic stay was up. She was under the impression that Westerfield was still quite confident that her time in the institution had been unnecessary. Maybe he was right. She had not ever believed she was psychic, though they'd put her in for treatment of that delusion. On the other hand, she had solved a disturbingly high number of cases through the behavioral analysis unit.

Initially, she'd been a field agent, but then she wound up at a desk as an analyst because they'd needed her there, and because she'd been good at it. The very quality of her performance had ultimately done her in with her bosses. They wound up accusing her of knowing far too much about the crimes she investigated. The mental institution had been a welcome relief from the stress of accusation.

However, here she stood, in the open doorway of Mystic Vudu, wondering where her day before had gone. *Maybe my stay in the loony bin was appropriate and too short.* Closing the door behind her in an attempt to mimic a sane person, she walked inside, leading the way to the back room.

"You said a few things about the knife." She opened with that vague statement, realizing that if she hadn't been here the day before, any more details would sound absolutely bonkers. The woman merely tilted her head. Maybe she was used to customers coming in and thinking they'd been here before when they hadn't. Maybe they'd visited other, similar shops and confused them with this one.

Eleri understood. She had been in a few of these common voodoo shops in the tourist sections of the Quarter. Shops of all sorts lined the streets in this section of town. At least every tenth one had a voodoo theme—it was a museum, or a spell shop, or a bookstore specializing in craft and magic. Many looked remarkably similar, and Eleri could not say there was anything particular about Mystic Vudu that made it stand out from the others.

She asked a few boring questions, different from the one she had asked yesterday, things she wouldn't know even if their conversation had been real. And the conversation slowly went around in a circle. It seemed there was nothing Eleri could say to prompt the woman to give her a true clue as to whether she'd actually set foot in the shop the day before.

It was only as she was leaving that the woman said, "Come back anytime, Miss Eleri. I'm happy to answer your questions."

Eleri smiled and nodded in response, thanked her, and turned away. She headed out toward the left, down the block, aiming the direction she had aimed the day before—although she was still uncertain if she'd even been here.

Two blocks later, she stopped so suddenly that the man walking behind her had crashed into her. This being New Orleans, he managed to look at her as though she was insane even while apologizing profusely.

Only nodding at him and motioning him to go by, she stayed where she was in the middle of the narrow sidewalk. The woman in the shop had said goodbye *Eleri*. She'd known her name. That meant Eleri *had* been there the day before. It meant the woman's name was Darcelle, and that yesterday had happened—or at least the first part of it had.

Heading down the street with renewed purpose and trying to retrace her steps, Eleri remembered running her fingers along the black wrought-iron fence. She went back toward the graveyards and looked at them again. As best she could tell, she was looking at what she'd seen the day before: the weeping angels, the carved white marble headstones, the mausoleums blocking her view of the houses on the other side of the wide lot.

She walked on and became upset when, three blocks later, Emmaline still had not appeared, and Eleri was once again lost. She couldn't see or remember the turns she had taken. She saw wrought-iron fences that seemed familiar, but she was more than fuzzy on whether they were the same ones she had passed the previous day.

She took turn after turn. Because New Orleans has a certain culture and clear design style of its own, she saw things that she was confident were blazingly familiar. However, these home businesses sat next to buildings she was certain she'd never come across before. Her heart ached and she tried to stare into the middle space, hoping she could conjure an image of Emmaline, but she couldn't. Her sister did not come. Though she wandered the city for several hours—until she was hungry and tired, and her feet were sore—she never found the garden that held the human bone.

17

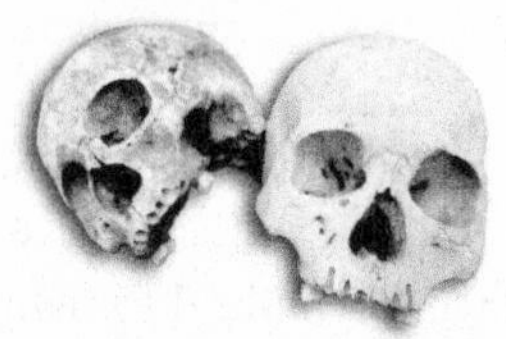

Darcelle flipped the door sign to Mystic Vudu, the golden script she'd hand-lettered to announce the store was now closed. Then she walked straight through the shop and headed out the back door, bolting it behind her. By habit, she added a little spell for safety and aimed straight for home.

She would have liked to walk the other way, into the city, but she wasn't able to. She would have liked to have stepped off her set trail and grabbed a meal at one of the places on Bourbon Street, or even one of the little hole-in-the-wall shops that no one really knew about—no one except the city dwellers. She could have driven the path, but she had long since given up on that.

The walk home was her only chance to look around and see the city, to have a little bit of the freedom that was mostly denied to her. Her world was only the shop and home—and home wasn't even truly her own home. It was her parents' house—or her mother's, to be sure. Her father had never had much hand in it, or truly, much hand in anything. He'd been cowed by one of the most powerful women Darcelle had ever met. So she and her sisters had been raised by their mother and her father had merely been an entity that existed in their lives.

It took a good thirty minutes to walk through the streets that led out to her house at the slow pace she kept. She did it for several reasons, mostly because the space between shop and home was the only freedom she had. She intended to make it last.

Also, she did not like breaking a sweat, and anything higher than a snail's pace would certainly do that in this weather. She wore a long-sleeved, button down white shirt, in lightweight cotton to reflect the heat. It was harsh, trapping her body heat close. Still, it seemed cooler and less humid than the outside air. Her long, flowy skirt swished at her ankles, and she wore sandals with little bells on them, as though it was important that everyone knew she was coming. That was laughable.

All she did was come and go. She had a mild amount of freedom on her days off. One night per week, once the shop was closed, she could go out. Alesse, who had never been nice to her about anything else—at least not that Darcelle could remember—had made momma concede to at least that.

"Momma, that'll kill her," her older sister had once protested on her behalf. Once.

Momma had snorted, "She'll kill herself."

Momma hadn't seemed to care that she'd just commented on her daughter's suicide due to a restrictive system she was setting up. Darcelle had watched in horror as Momma set out her rules. She'd attempted to scream and run, but she was held in place by forces she couldn't see or fight. Now, some nights, she tried to veer off the path, to test if this was her one night of freedom. On those nights, she was limited, but still freer than normal. She still couldn't leave the city limits at all. But it seemed tonight was not the night.

When she reached the front door of her home, it pleased her greatly to see that she had changed it. In fact, she had changed everything she possibly could. Momma had thought she'd be stuck living in her mother's plans and designs. Momma had not counted on the internet and fact that Darcelle could have just about anything shipped to her.

So now, the front door had been replaced. Instead of the old wooden version, she'd ordered something from the hardware store and had it delivered. Bright light came through the pane glass front. It was not a good, safe version, as the glass could be shattered and the lock inside reached. But Darcelle did not worry about safety the way most people did. She'd painted it a welcoming shade of bold blue. The house itself was now orangey-peach. In most parts of the United

States, it might have been too bright, but not here. Not in New Orleans, where color reigned supreme.

The blues she chose were not colors that normal people would put together, but Darcelle made them work, mostly because she had to. She had to scrub every inch of her mother from the house. She'd traded out the throw pillows immediately and then gone after the bigger pieces of furniture, spending down to her very last penny. For her own mental health, it was important that everything was different. She'd painted the walls, refinished the floor, and when she finished—when she'd changed every last piece of the house—she panicked.

What was there left to do? Soon, she'd taken on other projects. She had dolls to make, of course. But those could be done in the empty hours at the shop. She preferred not to bring the work home. A part of her hated it. A part of her knew it was in her blood, and the logical part knew it was all that there was. But she'd also taken up cross-stitch and embroidery, making beautiful things to relieve the stress of her imprisonment. Some kept for herself. Some she sold.

This evening, as she pushed the front door open—reveling in the cool air from air conditioning units she'd installed in windows around the house—she noticed something was amiss. The beautiful, bright throw pillows in pops of pinks and oranges had been taken from the couch and tossed about the room. One had a huge tear down the middle and oozed stuffing, as though a pet had clawed at it. But Darcelle had no pets.

The couch cushions, though not broken or permanently damaged in any way, were flipped up as though someone had been looking for loose change underneath and didn't have the sense to put them back. In the kitchen, cabinets stood open. One broken plate was scattered in pieces across the floor, though at first glance, the rest seemed to be intact. Darcelle strode boldly through the mess, not worried about her feet. She had shoes on, but more than that, she knew her magic would protect her.

Her bedroom was the only room that was untouched. She breathed a sigh of relief that her spells there had held. She had not thought of protecting the rest of the house she hated. In the bathroom, medicine bottles lay in the sink, directly below the cabinet where they'd likely been scooped out and let fall. Mostly, they were

Momma's. She'd turned to pharmacy to treat herself at the end, but had not finished any of her prescriptions.

Darcelle didn't bother with them now. She headed instead to her older sister's room. Though her sisters were free to come and go as they wished, this did not look like freedom. Alesse's room had taken the brunt of the damage. The mattress was flipped and lay partially off the bed. The closet stood open, clothing still on hangers tossed frantically about the room. Someone had obviously been searching for something. For all Darcelle knew, it might have been Alesse.

She looked around the room, and spotted a few key, empty spots. She could come only to one conclusion: Alesse was missing.

18

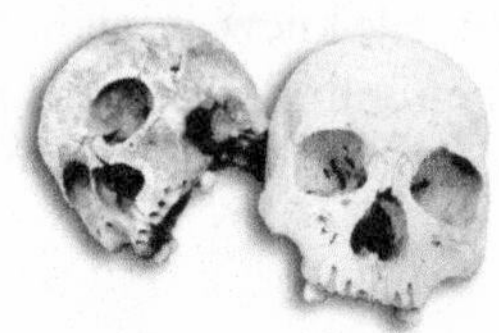

Eleri had come home to Grandmere's that afternoon after deciding she was completely unable to find the house with the fence and the garden in the center. She was certain now that she had visited Mystic Vudu the day before.

The woman knew her name, and Eleri had only said it the day before when she'd asked about the knife. So today had to have been at least her third time in the store. Eleri, as an investigator, knew not to discount the possibility that she had returned to the shop yet again in the stretch of time that she didn't remember.

Grandmere was still out when she got home. Again, she had the worrisome thought that perhaps Grandmere was missing. It probably wasn't true. Grandmere lived here on her own for months and months on end when Eleri didn't visit. Surely, Frederick came by. Eleri had a few other cousins that she didn't know well, but Grandmere was close with them. It wasn't as though no one was checking on her. Still, the house seemed unusually empty.

Heading into her own closet once more, she examined her pants from the day before again, searching for telltale signs she might have missed on the first pass. Had they possibly been washed? Had she simply not gotten them that dirty? Maybe the dirt was drier than she remembered and it was now gone, brushed off cleanly? There were no answers here.

She now knew she had been to the shop, but she might not have been in the garden. She had driven home somehow. She'd made it back to her car—or someone had—and her car had made it to Grand-mere's driveway. There was a comfort in being able to say at least those few things were facts after the screwed-up day before.

She sat on the couch, staring into space, wondering if she should make her own meal or simply continue thinking about the evening and the strange evidence before her. When her phone pinged, her heart leapt into her throat. Avery. Did she want to see what he had to say? She didn't know. It had been a while since she'd texted him—longer since they'd spoken. So much time had elapsed since she'd sent her apology that she wasn't certain he would return her message.

Then again, she'd also been doing too many other strange things to think too much about it, and maybe Avery deserved better than that from her. She should have been more worried about them than she'd had time to be. As she watched the message pop up on her small screen, she realized there was only one word in the message. *Good.*

Eleri frowned. Quickly, another bubble popped up. "I mean, good that you're still speaking to me. I'm sorry about your sister's case. I had hoped it was something distracting and not something I had done."

Eleri almost smiled. It was absolutely something he had done, and something she had done. They'd had a bit of a tiff over how her life went. Clearly, her life wasn't going any better now, and she didn't see it changing in the future. So they'd just faded away. But she found she missed him, despite the fact that neither had much room to give more. He was starting his pre-season practice. Then again, she'd nearly laughed at that idea that he was "starting." He'd barely finished the last one.

She'd known nothing about hockey before she met Avery. Most of what she'd learned had come from him telling her about his team and their games, about making it to the playoffs and so on. In addition, she'd looked up what she could. To call hockey time a "season" was a little on the ridiculous side. They played nearly eleven months a year, if you added in all their practices and playoff games.

She was smiling as she typed a message back. "It's not that. I miss you. I want us to be us." As vague as that was, she contemplated adding more to it, but couldn't think of any other way to explain her feelings in the text message.

Another return message popped up quickly. "I have to go practice, but we'll talk more later."

"Yes," she texted back, uncertain if he'd bolted immediately after hitting send and maybe never even seeing her reply. At least this was one thing going well, or better. This was a problem she was grateful to have the opportunity to fix.

She enjoyed solving things. She enjoyed closing cases and knowing that she and Avery were in the right place. Their relationship had a problem, and she wanted to fix it. It was that simple. Lord knew, despite how busy she had been since she had last spoken with Avery, she'd had plenty of chance to think about whether it was something she really wanted.

She hadn't had a boyfriend in a long time. The term "boyfriend" seemed silly and insignificant for their ages and what they were to each other. She hadn't been in a relationship for a while, was maybe the better way to put it, and for a short while—and she hadn't been sure she still wanted one. But now that she realized she missed him—even just his texts and chats—she would need to carve out time for him, get away to see him, and more. She'd have to put in the effort. She was beginning to think that was absolutely worth it. Even now, just looking at typed out words on her phone and knowing they were from him eased some of the tightness in her chest. *That is exactly what a relationship was supposed to do,* she thought.

The ease of pressure didn't last long. She was still struggling with things in front of her face, including her missing time, her missing bone, and her missing memory. Grandmere walked in the door just then, her hands laden with cloth bags, presumably full of groceries. Eleri knew the woman had to get food from somewhere, though as much as possible came from the small garden. Still, there was meat and flour, and Grandmere didn't have animals to slaughter and butcher, nor did she have a flour mill. Eleri knew she must've obtained it from somewhere.

The heavy cloth bags she held were not the grocery store brands that Eleri owned. In fact, these bags looked hand-stitched from old, faded pieces that resembled flour sack fabric from the Second World War. Eleri wondered if these were the bigger pieces the scraps in her closet had come from. It would be just like Grandmere to make her own grocery bags and make voodoo dolls out of the leftovers.

Eleri popped up. "Let me help you with those."

Grandmere had three bags hanging from each hand—a very heavy load for anyone, let alone a woman who must be in her nineties. Still, she balanced the bags on both sides and walked slowly, seeming determined to get everything into the house in one trip. They didn't speak as they stood in the kitchen, opening the bags and putting the groceries away.

At last, Eleri could hold her tongue no more and turned, unable to avoid the topic. "Grandmere, when did I come home yesterday?"

Her great-grandmother frowned at her.

It was an odd question, she conceded, but her grandmother answered, "Around five."

"Did we have dinner?"

"No. I offered and you shook your head and refused. I don't think you said a word." Grandmere stood now with one hand on her hip and one on the counter as she leaned against it. "You were acting weird, child. In fact, if I didn't know better, I'd say you'd been spelled."

It was a word Grandmere had not used with her before. Eleri tried to let the moment pass without her surprise showing on her face. She guessed she'd always known what Grandmere was, but only recently had Grandmere been telling more of the truth behind it.

"What kind of spell could it have been?" Eleri asked. It was time to start talking more.

"I don't know. What happened?"

Eleri, unsure if she should tell everything, edited together what she could. She said she'd gone back into the shop. She didn't tell Grandmere the knife was made of human bone, though she didn't know why she held back on that. Maybe it was because she considered opening an FBI investigation, and Grandmere might have other ideas, given that the woman had her own human bones in her home. Eleri told about leaving the shop and wandering the streets in a daze. She had not yet told Grandmere about seeing Emmaline in her dreams for years, and still saw her in visions now.

"I went down the street, Grandmere. I saw a house I'd seen in my dreams before."

"What did it look like?"

"It was beautiful," Eleri said. "It was in a U-shape with the U facing toward the street. Two small porches graced either side. There were French doors opening onto the patios," she said, thinking of the grand home and how to describe it, "and onto the wrought iron balconies over them. It had a ten- or twelve-foot-high wrought-iron fence across the courtyard.

“I opened the gate and went inside. I remember thinking that it was locked, but that it opened for me." She paused for a moment, wondering if that had any relevance to the story at all.

"What was in the courtyard?" Grandmere asked. Was it significant that Grandmere had asked about a courtyard, or merely just that she understood it was a common design of New Orleans homes?

"A tree, a garden, some paver stone s…" She motioned the size with her hands, but found her memory less certain than she'd previously thought. “I dug in the courtyard, Grandmere. I went in, and I dug. I brought home a human bone."

Grandmere looked at her and shook her head. "No, honey, you didn't bring anything human home except yourself. I would have known if anything like that had crossed my threshold."

19

Eleri struggled with the idea that she was standing in her great grandmother's kitchen discussing the fact that she'd had some kind of spell cast on her. However, her logical brain couldn't dismiss the possibility. She'd seen and done far too much to believe there wasn't "something else" out there. And Grandmere? Grandmere knew all about it.

While she and her great-grandmother had never had the conversation about the family legacy, Eleri knew more about it now than she had a year ago. Donovan had found information easily enough, and Eleri had begun to speaking to other people about what it meant to be a Remy.

She now asked point blank, "What kind of spell could it have been?"

"Well, there's lot of options," Grandmere said without qualifications. "But apparently, it got you to stop what you were doing and got you home without any memory to hold onto."

Eleri nodded. That much was clear—that she had actually done at least some of the things she remembered from yesterday. It was plausibly some kind of mild psychogenic fugue, but the idea was ludicrous. That kind of amnesia would have involved her having a full psychological break, but still finding her way home—to a home that really wasn't hers—and then forgetting exactly the portion of the day that seemed most useful. And all of this had to occur despite her never having had a psychological break before.

Even when she'd been working at the behavioral analysis unit, she'd stood psychologically strong. She didn't break when her bosses accused her of knowing far too many details about the crimes she was supposed to be investigating. She'd been clear. She'd done the research. Sure, she'd gotten hunches, flashes of visions sometimes when she touched the photographs or held the pieces of evidence. Those things gave her little clues about where to look, and she would head off in a different direction. Sometimes, her new directions seemed to come out of the blue and were disconnected, but her work had always panned out. She'd caught a number of serial killers and a child kidnapper. She had returned three children safely home in exchange for being able to provide more information than just that the perpetrator was a white male, aged twenty-five to forty-five, whose mother had emotionally abused him.

But then her bosses had accused her of being involved in the crimes. Their attacks had stressed her out to the point where she had checked into a mental institution. Still, at no time had Eleri lost any chunks of her memory. This was fully new ...

"So," she said to her great-grandmother, "the question is, did I just dream that I found the courtyard?"

"It's possible." Grandmere now leaned against the counter. Her hands on the edge, elbows crooked, feet crossed. It was the pose of a much younger woman, but it was also the position of a woman completely comfortable in her own home. "Here's what I'm thinking. Let's say someone just spelled you. You dream of the courtyard. That makes sense. You've dreamed of the courtyard before—right?"

She double-checked, and Eleri nodded.

"So," Eleri continued, "do you think it was the woman at the shop?"

"Could have been. I mean, it's a voodoo shop. Most of them are crap, but the Dauphine family owns a few, and they know what they're doing. Maybe other people do, too."

Eleri nodded, and said again to Grandmere, "Yes, I picked up a few of the pieces, and they seemed to have real ..." she hesitated to use the word *magic*. Though she fully understood it would make sense to Grandmere, it would not make sense to her. She didn't generally think in terms of "magic" and "spells." She kept the conversation on a track where she could have a logical talk about it. But she was beaten to the punch.

"So, option one," Grandmere said, and Eleri could see where her logical brain had been passed down through the generations. Suddenly, she saw it in her mother, Nathalie, and all the decisions she had made to move herself out of this tiny house and into Patton Hall with Thomas Hale Eames.

Eleri smiled as Grandmere continued. "So, you go to the shop. You ask about a piece in the shop, correct?"

Eleri nodded again.

"The shop owner spells you. You leave in a daze. In a while, you believe you find a courtyard you've seen before. Then you come home and sleep it off."

Eleri nodded. It was as logical a chain of events as one could put together when operating from the premise that there had been a spell involved.

Grandmere looked at her through narrowed eyes now. "But why?"

That was a most excellent point. Although this story made the most sense, step by step, why would anyone do that to her?

Eleri had gone to the store and asked about a knife. That was all. She wasn't threatening anyone. And if the knife hid some secret, why was it out on display? She spoke to Grandmere now. "The piece I looked at was very expensive. We discussed my buying it."

"Did you buy it?" Grandmere asked. "Did she spell you so that you would buy it?"

Eleri almost yanked her phone out of her pocket to check her bank account records. But in a moment's flash, she put the phone back in her pocket and looked at Grandmere and said, "No. I didn't. When I went there this morning, she asked if I had come back to buy it."

"So you didn't buy it yesterday," Grandmere confirmed.

"Maybe she put a spell on me that was intended to make me buy a knife, but it didn't work."

Grandmere looked into the distance for a moment. "Well, I suppose it's possible the person owning their shop doesn't know what they're doing, and they screwed it up."

Eleri thought on that one for a minute. "But the things in that shop do not speak of someone who's an amateur."

"So, then, option two," Grandmere proposed. "You go into the shop, you talk to the woman, and you leave. You find the courtyard you've seen in your dream, you go inside, you dig up a human bone ... and someone doesn't like it. *They* put a spell on you. They send you home in a daze."

Eleri thought the possibility through for a moment. "They take back the bone. They remove my evidence." She thought and thought, searching for holes she couldn't find. Sadly, that option made much more sense.

She'd found something she wasn't supposed to find. Someone in New Orleans had the power to either make her forget or make her believe it wasn't real. "There's no reason for the shop lady to spell me that I can think of," Eleri said, staring into space as she thought her possibilities through.

"Now the question is, can you find the house again, and can we figure out who owns it?" Grandmere then popped forward, basically interrupting herself as she hustled from the room. "Give me a minute, child."

Eleri stood at the kitchen counter, wondering what they would have for dinner tonight and what might have happened to her the day before. If someone had cast some sort of spell on her for going into the courtyard and finding a human bone, then that lent credence to her concern that there was *not* a plausible reason—or at least a legal or moral one—for the bone to be there. If there was, why would they worry?

Eleri also felt, deep in her own marrow, that it wasn't the only one. She'd found it so easily, it was unlikely there weren't others.

Right then, Grandmere returned. She held a small bundle of herbs wrapped tightly in white cotton ribbon. A lighter in her other hand almost made Eleri laugh. It seemed somewhat ridiculous that she would have these old school herbs, clearly dried upside down. The ribbon, Eleri was certain, contained no polyester or synthetic fibers. But Grandmere had no issues lighting it with a ten-cent Bic. Fire was fire, Eleri guessed.

By the time she had finished that thought, the buds on the herbs were burning and releasing a fine gray smoke into the air. Not knowing what her Grandmere was doing, Eleri stood still while Grandmere waved the pieces around her.

"Hmm," she said. And Eleri stayed quiet, the gray smoke dissipating into the air around her.

"Hmm," Grandmere offered again. A third time she did it again, before holding up the herbs, telling Eleri to turn around. Behind her, Eleri heard the puff as Grandmere blew out the tiny flames. The herbs had smoked like cigarettes, a red front line burning down into the stems.

The smoke they gave tripled after the flame was put out. Grandmere held it close to Eleri. Interestingly, she noticed no smell at all.

"What's this, Grandmere?" she asked.

"Checking you for spells," the older woman said.

"And?"

"There are zero spells on you, child."

20

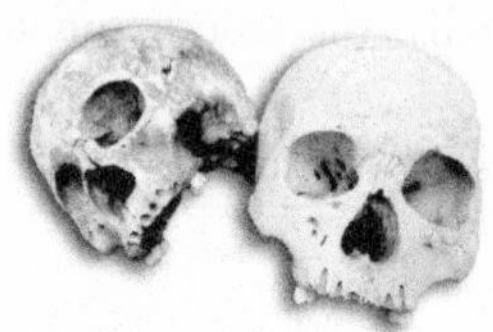

Donovan, Wade, and Christina sat on a picnic blanket on the grounds of the Little farmland. They sat on grass in an area they'd chosen, far out of sight from the family's homes. Though the buildings no longer smelled of burnt wood and charred hopes and dreams, they did still look like the aftermath of disaster. Donovan had preferred not to be staring at them as they talked about what they'd found.

Wade had found a sandwich shop he particularly enjoyed, though it was about thirty minutes away. So Donovan and Christina had the task of locating a tarp and a blanket, which they'd managed to scrounge up at a box store they'd found in the other direction. Then they'd met up here.

It seemed silly to be having a picnic when they were in the middle of a case, but the town didn't have conference rooms. The sheriff's station wasn't anywhere nearby, and there was no police station, since the population couldn't support one. There weren't enough people here to be a city.

The agents were staying in a motel that boasted seven units. The place was almost at fifty percent capacity, and the entire capacity was the three of them. Even if another room had been available, having a conference on beds in rooms that had slightly smoky smells—because the area still hadn't quite come around to completely embracing the no-smoking laws—didn't seem any better than where they were.

So they ate their lunches as they sat on the blanket and discussed what they'd seen—and for Christina, what she'd felt. Wade and Donovan had rehashed the physical investigation of the farm area. Wade looked at it with an eye of someone who knew the place. Though he hadn't specifically been here, his own family compound was similar. His relatives had lived here. The old families had shared designs and layouts. He looked for very specific things.

Donovan, on the other hand, had been unfamiliar with the compound. He hadn't even known they existed until the team had been in the Ozarks, just a few months ago. His was the untrained eye here, or at least the broad-view one.

Christina had spent her time in town talking to people. She got the stories of what had happened, or at least what the people in town knew. With a little bit of push from her mental abilities, she was able to persuade them to tell her all of it. She could easily get them to say if their information was rumor or fact. What evidence did they have? Where had they heard it? It made for an interesting story.

But then, as the three put the pieces together, the story got more and more disturbing. It had initially appeared that the hunting party raid in the Ozarks was a one-time attack on the compound. Though even then, those initial appearances were pretty easily swept aside, as it was clear no one could have done what was accomplished without being at least somewhat familiar with the place.

It was also believed that the group Dr. Murray Marks had run—or at least had been some high-ranking official in—had done the deed. And while that did still appear to be the case, it now looked like several more disturbing things were also true.

They'd found evidence of hunters on the land here—evidence of people outside the family hunting on this land. They had not been hunting for deer or big game other than the family members. Not only had the people who lived here been hunted on their own property, but a series of troubling incidents had occurred in town in at least the four years preceding the burning of the homestead.

"The locals told me about the time Jared Little was shot at the Seven-Eleven," Christina offered. "Then Bess Little was hit and killed in a car accident on Potter Street. Before that, four family members caught a very severe strain of the flu, and three of them wound up in the hospital. Two survived, but one didn't. Jefferson Little, who was once the family's patriarch, was murdered during a mugging. He was stabbed multiple times and his wallet was stolen."

It didn't sound too bizarre—just maybe a string of bad luck—until they added the numbers up. The family was big, but the area was small. The land was vast, but the population low. What Christina stitched together from each of the incidents was that they had been perpetrated by strangers. Small population or not, small town sentiment or not, there was still a criminal element. There always was. Someone would take advantage. Locals obviously knew who those people were. They had been in jail at times, or had CPS called on them, or more.

"Jefferson Little's murder still hasn't been solved," Christina added, "though people do recall the attack. One of the sheriff's deputies told me—though he shouldn't have—some detail about the case and the perpetrator. The witnesses also noted that the man who stabbed Jefferson fled the scene and was not anyone they recognized. The story in town is that some stranger had come through, gotten into trouble, and tried to steal a wallet. Jefferson Little fought back and got himself killed."

Another "violent drifter" story, Donovan thought.

On top of that, the woman driving the car that killed Bess Little had not only been a visitor in town who disappeared immediately following the accident, she'd been a small Asian woman. She'd managed to pass county lines before sheriff's deputies could stop her and question her. The deputy told Christina the case was still open for lack of being able to interview the woman.

Donovan and Wade both looked at Christina as she relayed this information to them. "Do you think it's the same woman we picked up in the Ozarks?"

"I wouldn't put it past them," Christina said. "This set of random attacks and accidents started four years ago, and with nothing prior to that. In fact, the townspeople say that, except for one or two hospital cases of severe illness—walking pneumonia, or the like—nothing had hurt the Littles in the past twenty years. Then suddenly, four years ago, they start turning up dead. There's a rash of crimes where the Littles are the victims—and all perpetrated by strangers. In fact, even the flu case seems to be the same."

Donovan must have frowned at her, because Christina nodded and continued. "The sick ones had all met in town with someone the week before they turned up in the hospital. They met in the back room of the one restaurant with the door closed. And none of the locals can give me any identification of the person they met with. He was average—height, coloring, way he carried himself. So on. No one knew his name, including Bob over at the motel."

Donovan blinked. Bob kept track of everyone. Donovan would bet his MD license that—barring floods or hurricanes—Bob still had records of families that had come through in the seventies. The information Christina had gathered was far too much of a coincidence.

The hunters had systematically come after the Littles, attacking them not just with silver bullets, but by any means possible. They'd winnowed the population down as much as they could.

Wade looked back and forth between the two of them. "It gets worse."

"What?" Donovan looked now to his friend, shocked. He couldn't imagine what "worse" might entail.

Wade had not gone into town and interviewed people. He'd been out at the homestead with Donovan. So Donovan thought he'd seen, or heard, what Wade was going to report already. But it seemed now that Wade had more to tell.

"Bess was one of the elders. She was medically trained, delivered the babies, treated most of the diseases. When our people get cancer, they generally don't go to the hospital. It means they can't change. They can't run. X-rays will show some differences. Sometimes doctors want to study us, and we can't let that curiosity grow."

Donovan understood that. He'd been asked to become the subject of a paper for a physician in Los Angeles when Eleri had taken him in to the hospital. He, too, had begged off.

"We don't always know if medications will affect us the same as the general population." Wade continued. "Things like morphine might make someone talk or reveal things. They might make us change right there in the hospital, deluded into thinking that it was safe."

Donovan hadn't really thought about that. He and his father had not been to the hospital when they were ill, but he'd thought it was more because they were poor than anything else. As a teenager, he'd learned otherwise. Wade kept going.

"Jefferson Little, as Christina said, was the patriarch of this family. The three names you said, those people wound up in the hospital with the flu, but there was another who stayed home. He died. I didn't put it together before this. But those four, they were out and they were meeting with that man because he'd told them he had information. He'd somehow convinced them he was one of us."

"You know this story?" Donovan asked.

"Somewhat. The Littles contacted my family about what this man said he could provide. They vetted him, contacted all the elders, and more. There was a vote. I was called in for that vote. It was big. But they met with him and nothing really came of it. It turned out his information only corresponded to things we already had. Ultimately, I guess he wasn't trying to share information. He was trying to make the elders here as sick as possible, and hopefully kill some of them."

Wade looked back and forth.

Christina nodded in support of his statements. "It was Flu A."

Donovan blinked. You did not want to tangle with Flu A. "It could have easily killed all four of them. It's actually more shocking that it didn't, given their ages. So these people were systematically taking out the elders."

Donovan turned the subject a bit. "Wade and I found evidence that they were hunting on this land long before the Littles were burned out. There are shells from pistols and shotguns Wade swears his people don't use. There are old sites littered with shells that don't belong to the Littles.

"I would have done better with Eleri or GJ here, but on my own, I'm passable. I found places where there were soil samples worth checking. We ran a few field tests, picking a spot just from the smell that Wade and I sensed. Those revealed there was human blood in the soil."

Christina looked back and forth at them. "But that could be from anything."

Now Donovan and Wade shook their heads together.

It was Wade who answered her. "It's been a year. We still smelled it. It means that there was enough blood soaked into the dirt that someone lost all of it, right there. That kind of blood loss means death. So the things you got were the things that the townspeople knew about, the things that they saw evidence of or things that had been reported. But Donovan and I found even more evidence of murders here on the property, long before the family was burned out."

21

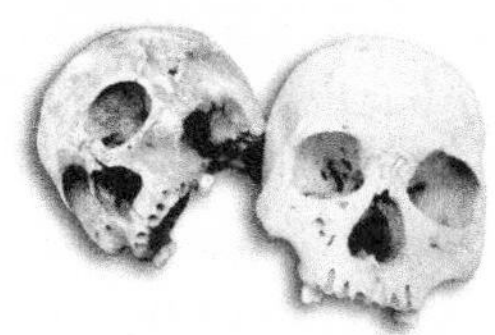

Eleri headed out the next morning. Grandmere had declared her "spell-free" the night before. At first, Eleri thought that meant the theory that she'd been cast on was wrong. But Grandmere had set her straight.

"No, it only means that if it was a spell, it was by someone strong enough to dissipate that spell before we thought to look for it." She'd paused for a thoughtful moment. "I'm not sure I like what you're getting into."

Eleri wasn't sure either, but it was too late. She was already into it.

Driving around the French Quarter again, she started in the area she expected the house to be in–a neighborhood that was as far as she thought she might have gotten on foot. She drove a grid pattern, checking every possible spot she could for the beautiful courtyard home. She slowed down and took long-winded turns as she carefully inspected her surroundings for clues. Using her turn signals as best she could, she still managed to piss off a handful of tourists and locals alike.

She'd asked Grandmère if she wanted to ride along with her, but her great-grandmother had refused, as Eleri had expected she would. She couldn't recall ever having seen Grandmère in a car. Certainly not driving one—and, as she thought back further and further, not riding in one, either.

Grandmère had not come to visit them in Kentucky or Virginia when Eleri was a child, nor even when she'd been an adult. In all cases, whoever was going to see Grandmère had traveled to her, to the same small house in the Lower Ninth Ward. Grandmère, it seemed, relied on public transportation—and public transportation wouldn't make a grid. It wouldn't do a systematic sweep and find the specific house Eleri was looking for. Now she drove her car back and forth, the bright sun in her eyes until a series of sharp turns brought the sun behind her.

She had to backtrack to fill in her chance to see the side streets. After three hours of cruising back and forth in the French Quarter, she was tired out. Occasionally, she would get excited about finding streets and buildings that looked familiar or gave her a vague sense that she had been here before. Again, she thought to herself, the architecture in New Orleans was so clear. The city had a style and a voice. It was wonderful when she was playing tourist, but incredibly hindering when she was looking for a specific building and had no idea where it was.

She was three hours in when she got hungry and realized she needed a sandwich and a break. And a soda, too—something to keep her going. Wearing herself out would do no one any good. She needed to find the house, and though she knew the bone she had dug up was merely a distraction—albeit a seemingly pertinent one—she still had to find Emmaline.

Deep in her heart, she knew Emmaline's body was here. So, while the lead she'd followed had not panned out, she still believed that this was where it would end, where she would be able to find the closure she needed. The evidence to tie up the knots of Emmaline's case lay in New Orleans, and so did the pieces that might begin whatever massive undertaking would be required to fix the emotional gaps in her parents. She knew it would be far easier to close Emmaline's case with the missing children division of the FBI than to deal with her family. Still—for herself—Eleri found the task necessary. So, she would look for the courtyard home and also continue to look for her sister.

She was sitting in a small café, enjoying a fried shrimp po' boy—a place that she decided she needed to make note of, so she could come back and have this sandwich again—when her phone pinged. *Donovan.*

She'd been checking in with him, and she'd spoken a little bit to

Avery the night before. Not that anything was solved, but at least she now knew that things between her and Avery had reached a level she could call "okay." She appreciated Donovan keeping tabs on her, telling her where he was, and making sure that she was safe, now that the FBI no longer had a stake in her whereabouts.

Though Donovan and Grandmère got on like a house on fire, Grandmère wasn't exactly the kind of source you could trust if you were trying to follow someone's whereabouts. Her lack of cell phone and transportation were just part of the hindrance.

This time, all Donovan texted was, "Call me."

She knew he was on a case in Montana. It was his first case without her, and she felt a bit of a pang in her heart. Would he enjoy working with other agents more than her? She almost sounded like a jealous girlfriend, but a partnership as FBI agents was at least as attached as any other relationship or a marriage might be, if not more. Married people rarely entrusted their lives to each other. Eleri and Donovan, in the short time they'd known each other, had depended on each other for survival more times than she could count.

Since she was sitting and staring into space and almost finished with her sandwich, she took advantage and rang him back.

"How's the Montana case?" she asked, already relatively up-to-speed with the idea that they were investigating the property the Littles had owned and lived at prior to moving to the Ozarks and combining the Little and de Gottardi families there.

"Beyond disturbing," was his two-word reply.

She hadn't really expected that. Eleri had thought he and Wade and Christina would find a few pieces of information that were useful to the case. In fact, she'd gotten the distinct impression from Westerfield that was all their SAC had expected as well. He'd merely wanted to know that he'd sent agents and that they'd closed the case.

From Donovan's tone, the situation was much more complex than they'd predicted. Donovan's next words confirmed that. "It appears someone was here—or, perhaps, several people. Possibly the same organization we saw in the Ozarks. And they've been hunting the Littles for at least the past four years."

"Hunting them? Like we saw outside of Bull Shoals?"

"Well, yes, there's evidence of that. But there's more. The attacks on this family include car accidents, a mugging that turned into a murder, and even an incidence of bio-warfare."

"What?" Eleri asked, stunned. Her mind was racing to Ebola or poisoned water supplies.

But that wasn't what Donovan responded with. "They met with someone who said he had information. He was checked out through the family council and vetted. Then, this man came in and gave everyone who attended the meeting a case of flu A."

"That could be a coincidence," Eleri said. Flus were often highly contagious, and the people who were exposed to them were susceptible at different rates, depending on their exposure to other things. The Little family lived on an isolated farm, schooled their children there, grew their own vegetables, and left only when necessary. Thus, their level of inoculation to airborne and fluid-borne diseases was likely low. Eleri couldn't even begin to account for the altered physiology that people like Donovan and Wade had. While she wouldn't have suggested that being a changeling had an impact on the immune system, it was entirely possible that it did.

She mentioned these things to Donovan, and even as she said it, she realized she was being ridiculous. The man was a former medical examiner. He held an MD. He understood infectious diseases, probably far better than she did. If he believed that this was an incidence of bio-warfare, then probably he was right. She apologized and said so.

"No," he said, "The points you make are all valid, and if it was not for the other pieces of evidence, I would have agreed with you. But the other deaths have come in shockingly high numbers starting four years ago, and all targeted at the elders and at specific people in the family who are possibly the most useful. It appears that someone outside was undermining the family and trying to collapse it."

"Wow," Eleri replied. "Do we need to warn the de Gottardis in the Ozarks?" Even as she asked, she realized Wade was right there with Donovan. "Oh, Wade's on it, isn't he?" she asked, chagrinned. They didn't need her help with this case. She was off duty. She needed to remember that.

"Yes," Donovan replied, and she wondered for a moment if this week away, as short as it had been, meant her investigative skills were going completely out the window. So far in this conversation, she'd merely suggested things to people who were experts and given out ideas for actions that were already under way.

"Eleri," he said, "there's also evidence of Lobomau here."

"The Littles weren't involved with Lobomau at all, were they?"

"No. They were emphatically not involved. They disowned family members systematically if there was any hint of involvement with Lobomau."

"Wow," she breathed, thinking that was a harsh punishment for what might have amounted to a teenage mistake.

"Yeah. And I have to tell you something else, too. Wade gave me a map of ..." He paused for a moment, and Eleri knew what was coming. "... our kind of people all over the US, but I asked him specifically for one with Lobomau, and we put it together last night."

They are in New Orleans, she thought. Though, before she could put thoughts together about what that meant—if anything—Donovan shocked her again.

"It's not that they're in New Orleans. Of course, they are. It's that, in the past decade, their numbers there have exploded.

Eleri, you have to watch out."

22

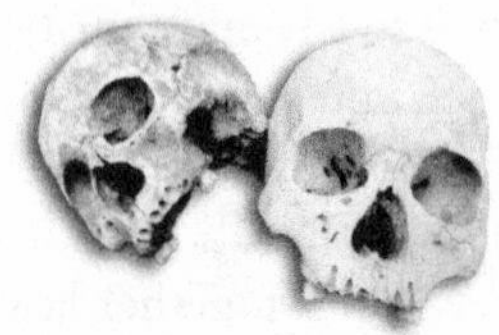

When Eleri hung up after talking with Donovan, she stayed in her seat in the tiny café for a few more moments. Her food was eaten, the wax wrapper for the sandwich spread out on the table in front of her. Only crumbs of bread crust and small dabs of mayonnaise remained from her sandwich.

She was disturbed by more things than she'd like to admit—including her inability to find the dark peach courtyard house. Donovan's revelations about what had happened at the Little farm had shocked her. GJ's grandfather— and whatever group Dr. Murray Marks was involved in—seemed to be doing far more damage than just showing up on a whim and trying to take people out.

Apparently, before it was over in the Ozarks, they'd learned Dr. Marks was quite the zealot. He and his people believed that Donovan's kind were remnants of an ancient and dark evil—magic, even. Eleri almost laughed. She sat in New Orleans, searching for a building that she believed was hidden from her by exactly that same kind of magic—although if this was dark or light, she couldn't tell.

She was even more unnerved by Donovan's revelations about the Lobomau. According to him, the Lobomau had begun exploding in population in New Orleans in the last decade.

She'd asked him to clarify that. "Is that a phrase of speech, 'a decade'? Is it a general timeframe, or is it more literal?"

He'd replied that he meant it literally. Wolves like him had been there for a long time. Their population in the city had grown steadily in the last seventy years—well within the averages of wolves moving into other big cities—although he'd been disturbed by that, too. But recently, in New Orleans, the growth of wolves like him had been far greater. They'd been turning up at a higher rate than in other cities, like New York or Los Angeles. So it was clear that New Orleans was a place for "his kind."

Yet when he and Wade used only the data that they knew were from Lobomau and made a map just of those populations, the numbers in NOLA exploded. It was exponential, and had begun to increase almost exactly ten years ago. In fact, they'd even seen reduction in Lobomau population in several other cities, or stagnation.

But New Orleans? New Orleans was now full of them. Eleri was left wondering who passing her on the street right now might be a wolf—or Lobomau. Why were they coming here? She was bothered by his description of the ongoing and systematic attack on the Littles, though there was nothing she could do about any of it sitting here in this small café. Her stomach was now full and her mind back on track. The call from Donovan had jolted her again.

So she left the cafe, headed back to the car, and resumed her gridding of the city. It was another hour of slow driving before she saw it. There, on her right—nestled amid other stately homes in white, gray, and pale blue—stood the peachy-orange courtyard home.

Eleri drove past, trying not to look like she was rubbernecking the place, but she was. Her heart rate kicked up as she made a very large loop around the block and drove the street again, this time in the other direction, passing slowly in front of the house.

She breathed in deeply, not realizing how much she had doubted that it even existed until she felt the relief, seeing it there. But now, she knew that just looking at it as she drove past was not going to be enough.

She felt couldn't afford a third pass in the car. There was every possibility that this was where she had been spelled. If the house existed, then it stood to reason there *were* actually human bones in the courtyard.

This time, she made a point to memorize the address. But now that she knew where it was, how could she get back in? She needed to see the courtyard. Could she see where she'd dug? Were there more bones?

A block and a half away, she found a spot and parked the car. This time, she approached the house cautiously on foot, coming around the corner, walking up casually. She stepped slowly near the patio that bordered the sidewalk, trying to figure out what she could do. *Can I just peer into the courtyard? Do I look like a tourist?* She wasn't sure if she even looked like one now.

Something about her spoke of purpose and need. She knew that much. So surely, she wouldn't pass as a random tourist. If someone was in the house, they'd get an odd vibe from her.

But as she approached the courtyard fence, she saw a young woman standing just on the other side. Her hands interlaced the wrought iron spikes and she looked out. "Hello," she offered in greeting, almost as though she'd been expecting a visitor. She'd not been standing there when Eleri had last driven past.

Unable to do anything else, Eleri replied, "Hello," and quickly added, "I love your house!" It seemed like a nice thing to say—touristy, maybe not too creepy. "It's just beautiful. The courtyard is stunning. And the garden is amazing."

"Yes," said the girl. Something in the way she dragged out the letter S, something in her tone, told Eleri that she didn't quite buy what Eleri was selling. Whether that was because she was not keen on tourists in general or Eleri in particular, Eleri couldn't have said. Still, she was unprepared for the young woman's next words.

"My name is Lafae. Welcome to my home."

Eleri smiled and held out her hand. They clasped hands through the gate. No shock or tremor hit her, although Eleri had been braced for something when she touched this young woman's hand. Something about her face looked familiar. Still, despite all the thoughts racing through her head, she forced her standard etiquette. "My name is Eleri."

"I know," said the young woman. "You were here before. You came into our courtyard."

Well, shit, Eleri thought. So much for thinking the young girl just didn't like tourists.

She wasn't that young, actually. Something about the way she had stood with her hands on the fence, almost hanging on it, one hip shot out to the side, had made her seem almost like a petulant teenager. But Lafae must be at least partly into her twenties.

She threw the bolt on the gate, and Eleri realized it was an easy thing to do—simply a flip bolt. Had she reached through the bars the other day, she could have flipped it herself, easily letting herself into the courtyard. In fact, anyone could walk in.

Lafae turned as Eleri followed her into the open but shaded space and looked over her shoulder. "No, ma'am," she replied. "Not just anyone can come in."

She didn't illuminate the idea any further, but left it to stand *had she said her thoughts out loud, or did Lafae have some kind of special skills?* Maybe she just read people well. Maybe she just realized she'd opened the bolt and wanted to be sure she wasn't advertising to the street how unsecure her home was. Somehow, Eleri doubted a reasonable explanation was at work here.

As she stepped onto the grounds, it felt like something seeped up through the soles of her feet. Despite the grass, and despite the shoes she wore, she felt something leaching up and into her—something separate from this strange woman. Eleri walked carefully. The feelings coursing with her blood told her this ground was hallowed.

Even as Eleri was registering the sensation, a door from the home opened onto the courtyard. Practically hidden by vines, the door swung forward and suddenly became visible. Another young woman, who looked much like Lafae—and again, seemed very familiar to Eleri—emerged into the space.

Lafae beckoned to the newcomer with brightly colored fingernails that tipped graceful hands, but something underneath the show lurked a feeling Eleri couldn't quite place—or maybe didn't want to.

"This is my sister, Gisele," she said. Her accent lilted. It rode the words instead of forming them.

Eleri put out her hand again in yet another attempt at etiquette, but once again, the new woman beat her to it.

"You are Eleri," she said, and Eleri only smiled. The day was getting stranger and stranger. And then Gisele added, without mirth, "You tried to steal something from us the other day."

23

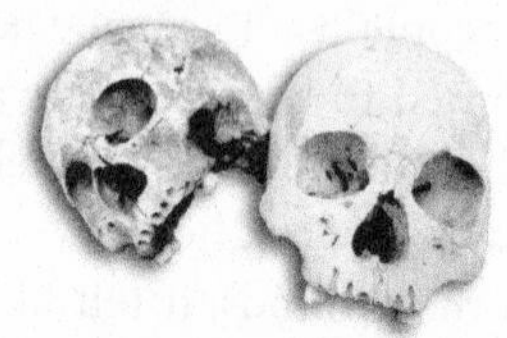

"Would you like to come in?"

Gisele swept a graceful hand to her side, motioning Eleri into the home. She had no long nails and wore no bright colors, unlike her sister. Something flowed from her that was more natural, something that told of magic in her touch.

Eleri smiled as best she could and offered up her nicest, "No, thank you."

She was not stepping foot into this house. There was something under the ground, and she could feel it. These two sisters were toying with her. She wasn't about to let them.

"So," Gisele said in little more than a whisper, "we shall speak here, but you can't raise your voice."

Eleri shrugged. Why would she? Unless she needed to attract attention? Did they know she was a federal agent? They knew many other things about her. How had they figured out her name? Unless—well, factoring in her lapse in memory, anything was possible.

Perhaps she'd even been inside the house before, but nothing swam to the surface in her in recollection. What she remembered and what was real were certainly at odds.

It was Lafae who spoke next. "You found our house and you entered. That speaks of something."

That was a vague sentence, Eleri thought, and she merely raised an eyebrow at the other woman. This was an old trick from interrogation training: Keep the other person speaking and let them give themselves away.

Lafae either fell for it or played along; ultimately, Eleri couldn't tell.

"Those gates are protected. What are you, that they let you in here?"

Eleri shrugged again. It wouldn't be fair to answer when she really didn't know what she was—but she wasn't going to reveal that to these two.

They stood in front of her, the two sisters as close to each other as they were to her, the three of them forming a triangle. Eleri had her back to the street. She didn't feel completely safe, but anything else would be a far more vulnerable position. In any other configuration, they would block her exit. Right now, the two women had their own home at their back—and she had no idea what else might be in that house.

"You tried to steal from us?" Gisele nudged the topic again, the Ss lingering just a little bit. The Rs were swallowed ever-so-slightly, almost as though she were British, though nothing else in her accent spoke of a UK origin. Though the tones were distinctly New Orleans and definitely local, they lacked any of the drawl of the south.

"I found something," Eleri conceded. "Stealing" was a harsh word for confiscating evidence—though Eleri couldn't yet prove that was the case.

Gisele *tsked* twice with her tongue and played the return game on Eleri. Waiting in silence and hoping Eleri would speak. Eleri obliged. "It was a human bone."

She wondered if she could shock them enough to return what she'd found, or at least acknowledge the enormity of the problem. Instead, neither reacted at all.

She tried again, playing another card. "So, you are aware that you have human bones buried in your courtyard?"

Lafae laughed. "This is New Orleans, honey."

Eleri found it humorous to be called "honey" by a woman who appeared to be her junior, but she didn't let it stop the forward momentum of the conversation and she didn't let it change her expression.

"Human bones can be found all over New Orleans," Lafae protested. "Finding one in our courtyard doesn't mean much of anything."

"Doesn't it?" Eleri pressed, again tossing the ball back to them. This time though, they both stayed silent. Eleri waited a beat and, when they didn't speak, she said, "I found the human bone, and you're correct. They exist in abundance all through a city as old as this one. Old Graves and bodies float to the surface all the time. Any yard might contain who-knows-what ..."

She acted as though their excuse was perfectly normal, but then turned her expression on a dime. "However, when I found this one, you stole my memories and sent me home. You took the bone back. You cleaned the evidence."

She waited again. The two women shrugged their acquiescence to what they had done. That was shocking in itself. Eleri only barely believed that magic like that was possible. A quick admission that it had been perpetrated against her was not what she'd expected.

Who were these two and what in God's name were they up to? She was considering drawing her badge from her back pocket when Lafae and Gisele suddenly went on alert. Both women, though it was subtle, quickly tensed, their eyes darting toward the left. Their noses lifted slightly into the air.

"Cabot," one whispered to the other. Eleri wondered if it was an incantation, or another spell on her, or a name. She had no idea. Then they resumed the interrogation on her.

"How did you get through the gate?" Gisele asked a second time. "No one can get through that gate without an invitation. Yet you walked in when no one was home. What did you do?" She almost hissed as she repeated the last question. "What did you do?"

The second time she said it, her tone demanded an answer—and for the first time, Eleri felt threatened. These were two women who had successfully erased a portion of her memory. She had gone home with no idea where she'd been. It had taken hours to find this place again, and now they were hissing at her like snakes, asking what she had done. She decided to turn the tables.

"I opened the gate. It pushed open quite easily." That much she remembered, and she would use it against them—even though she was unsure if her memory was accurate. Their eyes widened, but she didn't give them a chance. "What did *you* do?" she demanded in return. "You stole my memory. So I stumbled onto something you very much want to keep secret. Tell me. What did you do?"

Both women slightly shook their heads, refusing to answer. Eleri aimed another direction. Whereas she wanted to tell them she'd found the anterior end of a broken piece of adult tibia, she felt that pulling out her professional vocabulary—though it accurately described what she'd seen—would out her as the scientist she was. She wasn't ready to do that. She wasn't ready to tell them she was a federal agent, either. She wanted more information before they possibly clammed up and turned away.

This time, it was Lafae who smiled at her, and the smile was neither welcoming nor warm. One edge of her lip curled up, revealing white, even teeth. Eleri thought they must be orthodontic—but then again, with these two, who knew how they accomplished anything? Lafae's grin opened a little wider and she spoke. "Doll, if you can open our gate, then you should know very well what we did. Tell me—" She leaned in closer. "What *are* you?"

"A visitor," Eleri replied. She saw Gisele's eyes narrowing as she scanned Eleri from head to toe. Her nostrils flared as though she was sniffing at her, and Eleri wondered, *What in God's name is she looking for?* Lafae's twisted grin did not leave her face.

Gisele motioned to her sister and Lafae glanced at Eleri questioningly before running through the same motions. Eleri stood still, taking it. Let them look. Let them sniff. Let them examine her. What would they possibly come up with?

Lafae's focus turned away for a moment as a man approached from the street. He pushed the gate open easily, and Eleri couldn't remember if Lafae had locked it behind them. Regardless, he was in with them now and somewhat behind her, where she couldn't get a good look.

Eleri didn't like it. Her agent training had only been short on how to get out of these situations, and most of it had emphasized how to not get stuck like this in the first place. *Too late*. If the three were in league and if they wished, they could box her in. So she turned to look at the newcomer. She wanted a good look it his face.

This must be Cabot. He wasn't a spell, but a person—and as she took in the long face, the lean nose, the thick but narrow jaw, she realized what he was. He was like Donovan. And here were these two women with human bones in their yard and a wolf amongst them.

Cabot also looked Eleri up and down, and he came to a conclusion the two women had not. He looked at them and said, "Remy."

24

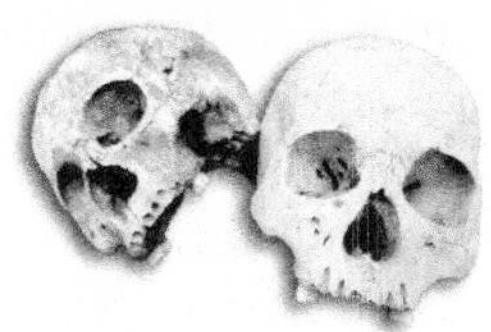

Eleri stood still, trying not to let her expression show that she already knew what Cabot was. The average person on the street wouldn't have been able to understand his skills and ability just by looking at him, but GJ Janson's research and the skeletons in her grandfather's lab had made a number of skeletal anomalies in Donovan's kind quite clear. Still, Eleri never would have guessed it the first time she met Donovan—and she knew the human skeleton like the back of her hand. So there was no reason at all for Cabot to be alerted to her knowledge.

She was happily surprised to find that she could simply look at Cabot and know right away. The shape of his face, the hair along his forearms, the way he carried his shoulders—because his scapulae were longer and thinner than normal, his rib cage slightly rounder and less flat front to back—gave him away.

She almost smiled, but fought the urge. She didn't want any of these three to know that she knew. She also had to figure out how Cabot had immediately known she was a Remy. Though it was her family name, she hadn't shared it with them. The way he'd said it, "Remy" didn't mean anything good. He hadn't introduced himself, either, and hadn't spoken directly to her. He'd simply looked her over, smelled more than whatever the two sisters had, and declared her a Remy.

She looked back and forth now between the three of them, taking a short step backward so that Cabot was no longer behind her. She was calculating a clear path out. She noted from the corner of her eye —without glancing over or turning her head—that the fence remained slightly open. Unfortunately, only one of the two halves was open. The other appeared to still be locked in place. The open one was on her side, meaning it swung toward her, and she couldn't simply push through it as she fled. She'd have to duck around it.

Still paying attention to the conversation as well as her escape route, Eleri neither confirmed nor denied what Cabot had said. However, it didn't appear that anyone doubted him. Lafae and Gisele glanced to each other for a moment, side-eye, never taking their attention off of Eleri. Apparently, being a Remy meant they trusted her less now, and they hadn't trusted her when she showed up.

She almost said "Eleri Eames," but clearly, the name Remy meant something to them. Maybe that was because it was New Orleans. Maybe it was because they were involved in something. The problem was, if they *were* involved in something, the name Eames might mean just as much. She didn't know, so she decided silence was the best strategy.

Slowly rocking her weight to one side, then the other—as though she might just be nervous—she managed to get another half step backward. This time, though, Cabot turned and stared at her, narrowing his eyes once more. "What are you doing here, Remy?"

She raised her eyebrows, trying to look innocent, and said, "My Grandmere lives in town." The French term for grandmother didn't faze any of the three, though with names like Gisele and Lafae, Eleri was not surprised by that.

"It's more than that," Cabot declared, an obvious demand for more information from Eleri. When she didn't volunteer it, he volleyed more specific questions at her. "Why are you here? Why are you at this house? How did you find it?"

Eleri shrugged and answered only his last question. "Stumbled upon it two days ago, and—well, let's just say, these lovely sisters took something from me." She wanted to say she was going to head out, but that didn't feel right. If she announced she was leaving, they might try to stop her. She did not want to have to make a break for it. She wasn't certain they wouldn't try to physically detain her. There were three of them. Two had some kind of powerful voodoo and one was a wolf. Though he likely wouldn't change fully, right here in view of the street, he still could bare fangs and grow claws in a heartbeat.

She'd seen it before. What she didn't know about him was whether he was Lobomau—but given the numbers Donovan had spouted to her recently and his warning, the safer bet was that Cabot was.

Eleri decided taking the offensive was a better option. She looked between the two sisters. "Any chance you still have that bone that I dug up the other day?"

Again, without moving her eyes, she tried to change her focus to the ground near her feet. It wasn't difficult to spot the wound in the earth where she'd removed the piece in question. The sisters had not tried to cover it up, and the damage further cemented the facts, though her memory was still a little spotty.

"You need to leave right now, witch," Gisele hissed.

While the two sisters had been toying with her cat-and-mouse style before, now the atmosphere had turned an ionic cold. Cabot's pronouncement had changed everything, although Eleri had to admit she was grateful for the invitation to go.

She shrugged at them and said, "Thank you so much for your time and hospitality. I do love the courtyard. It's just lovely."

Then she turned and forced herself to walk sedately through the gate. She turned left, winding her way back to the car and wondering if she was being followed, either on foot or by some mysterious power that she still didn't understand. Only when she was in the car did she let herself suck in a deep breath and feel the weight drop from her shoulders with relief. Still, she couldn't let any of those feelings show. Were the sisters watching her, even now? She knew they would be if they could. Eleri just didn't know if they could.

Carefully, she turned on the engine and shimmied her car out of the parallel spot before turning around and taking her first left. She did not drive past the house again, not wanting them to see her or catalog her car if they hadn't already. Though she had no doubt that Lafae had been watching her go by earlier, she wasn't going to give them a chance to catch anything they might have missed.

She headed quickly back across the bridge and home to Grandmere's. Her Grandmere threw open the door when Eleri came up the back walk.

"What have you been doing, child?" Grandmere confronted her.

The distress was very unlike her, although Eleri had to admit her recent forays into the city had been very unlike anything she'd done before.

"What do you mean?" Eleri asked cautiously, as the answer could refer to any number of bad, stupid, or careless things she might have inadvertently done.

"I've been worried! And you've got spells again."

"What?" Eleri stood up straight, confused. No, she didn't.

"You've got spells," Grandmere told her again, waving her hand up and down Eleri's form, as though Eleri might see them. She didn't. Before she could ask again, Grandmere was pulling her into the kitchen and closing the back door behind her.

It appeared she'd been sitting here at the ready to check her great-granddaughter this time. Picking up the partially burned bundle of herbs and flicking the tiny Bic lighter at it again, she held the herbs near Eleri.

This time, the smoke clung to Eleri, and she frowned.

"Told you," Grandmere announced with a defiance that was unexpected. Then she stared her great-granddaughter in the eyes and demanded an answer. "Where did you go?"

"I went to the ... with the ...." Eleri stumbled over the words, because her brain had nothing to tie them to. She'd gone to see the house in her dreams, she knew—but what did it look like? It was tall. She forced herself to remember specific facts. Did it have colors? What street was it on?

"You can't remember," Grandmere accused.

"No, I made a point to remember it this time," Eleri rebutted the old woman. "I memorized the address." That much, she knew was true.

"Okay," Grandmere said, almost taking a stance with her hands on her hips but clearly fighting the urge, wanting to be kinder. "What is the address?"

"It's ..." Eleri began the sentence with confidence, but after two words, "It's at ..." she was done. She didn't have it. "Damn it!" she shouted into the kitchen air, despite knowing how Grandmere felt about curse words. But this time, her great-grandmother did nothing to stop her. Instead, she sighed and moved closer, offering kindness and maybe pity. Eleri took it. She probably deserved it.

"Let me remove these, to see if it helps. Close your eyes."

Eleri smelled strange smells and heard clinks along the counter that perhaps were crystals or bones hitting the surface as Grandmere picked them up and used them and then set them aside again. A soft hum came from her grandmother's throat, but Eleri couldn't distinguish the words. When at last she opened her eyes, she asked her Grandmere, "What did you do?"

"I called upon every God I know," Grandmere told her.

25

Darcelle sat inside her grand home. Something was going on outside with her sisters, and she didn't like it. Then again, her sisters were always involved in something she didn't like, so she wasn't about to join in now.

She hadn't cleaned up Alesse's room, but she had tried to put the rest of the house back together. Why had someone tossed the place? And why was Alesse gone?

She should have been more worried about her sister, except—well, all of the Dauphine girls could take care of themselves. Momma had made sure of that. She was worried less about Alesse and more about what Alesse might have brought into their home.

Lafae and Gisele came in through the side door, Cabot following close behind. A scowl rode across Cabot's features, but when did it not? Darcelle didn't like him and she didn't like what he was. But he was always here, unfortunately, almost like family.

"What crawled up your ass and died?" she asked him. She was bitter right now. No one else ever cleaned the house. That was up to her. It was her house. It didn't matter that it was hers, though. Everyone lived there.

But everyone else could leave. She was stuck. She could have gone out into the courtyard with them, but she didn't really like playing her sister's games. They came and went freely. Often enough, their freedoms served to stop her from trying to break free. She wasn't going to join their games, and her captivity was her only valid excuse. She wasn't going to do them any favors if she could help it. Cleaning the house was the extent of her service, and she did it for herself, not them.

"Some witch walked into our courtyard two days ago," he announced, and Darcelle raised her eyebrows.

She almost asked him, "*Our* courtyard?" Although Cabot was in and out often, this wasn't his, though he seemed to speak of it like it was. She really didn't care that some woman had come into the courtyard. It was actually a major coup. Maybe it meant the forces on the house were weakening, but she worked to hide her excitement.

Her lack of response bothered Cabot, and he glared at her. "Did you let her in? Is she the one who did this to the house?"

Darcelle sighed. "If she came two days ago, then she didn't do it to the house. This happened to the house late last night." She didn't like his tone, his topic, or his complete lack of math. Clearly, the timing was wrong, but in typical Cabot fashion, he didn't care. He just wanted to lay blame. Truly, Darcelle didn't give two shits about who specifically walked into the courtyard—only that someone could.

Instead of dealing with Cabot, she turned to her sisters. "Do either of you know where Alesse is?" They shook their heads in unison. Either they both knew and were lying, or neither did and they cared even less than she did.

Lafae offered, "Probably ran off."

Honestly, that would be more like Lafae than like Alesse. Alesse was the oldest of the four, and yet somehow still the least dependable. The award for "most dependable" fell to Darcelle, the second sister, though that wasn't by choice. Lafae's scowl remained on her face, almost matching Cabot's.

Darcelle was not fond of the way the others let the wolves into the house. She wasn't fond of wolves in general, but she became more concerned when they were in the house. Momma had been the first to let them in, to start alliances between them. Her sisters had merely followed suit. But these days, the house seemed an open pass-through for all sorts. Darcelle would have kept it for herself. But like many things, it wasn't her choice.

She looked Cabot up and down almost disdainfully and asked him, "Where's Caspian?"

His younger brother was usually a constant attachment at Cabot's hip, except when Cabot was out causing trouble. Caspian must have gotten the recessive genes, for he didn't change, as Cabot did. He also seemed to be recessive in many other things, Darcelle thought snarkily. He was nothing more than a lackey. At least she had been able to make him into her lackey, as well.

Unfortunately, Caspian owed her something—and Cabot didn't seem to care. In fact, Cabot didn't know about the deal she'd struck with his younger brother. It might have been the only reason she tolerated either of them in the house.

"Well." Darcelle looked at her sisters and felt her mouth pull down. "Have fun playing with your little witch. And let me know if Alesse returns."

She walked away as they spoke animatedly behind her. She caught only the words that came out the loudest: "witch," "Remy," "open gate," and "bone."

Apparently, whoever had come in had found something human in the courtyard. Darcelle shook her head. Her sisters would have taken care of that. It was truly no threat to them and wouldn't make her lose any sleep. In fact, as she listened, even walking down the hall, it sounded like her sisters had cast a nasty spell on the woman. So the witch had left, hopefully never to return.

Darcelle walked away, heading into her room and thinking about Caspian. Caspian owed her blood.

26

Eleri was grateful to Grandmere for removing the spell, which had brought back at least some of her memory. Though she still couldn't recall the address of the house with the courtyard, she now remembered that it was the house with a courtyard.

She remembered the beautiful, orangey-peach color of the exterior and the distressed paint that made the house appear old and stately. The black wrought-iron that ringed the patios butted up against the sidewalk and the upper floor's balconies. She remembered the gate across the courtyard. She did not, however, remember the address—though she knew she'd made a concerted effort to memorize it.

"Do you remember who was there?" Grandmere asked her.

Eleri nodded. Now, she did. The faint scent of thin gray smoke lingered in the kitchen and, once again, the bundle of herbs sat on the counter, smoking ever so slightly after the flames had been doused. "There were two women initially. One was named Lafae and the second was Gisele."

"How do you know their names?" Grandmere asked.

Eleri shrugged at her. "They introduced themselves." She wondered why Grandmere might ask, as though it were unusual for anyone in the South to say hello or offer their name and the shake of a hand. She was surprised she hadn't been invited inside for lemonade—although, then again, maybe she had.

Grandmere turned away sharply, shaking her head and pacing a short circle in the kitchen. "Lafae and Gisele," she said. "How old were they?"

"I don't know," Eleri said. "We didn't trade ages."

"But were they close to your age? Closer to mine? Middle-aged? Teens?" Grandmere wouldn't let up, agitated in a way Eleri couldn't recall having seen her before.

"Close to my age, maybe just a little bit younger."

She could have sworn she heard her great-grandmother swear slightly under her breath. That, too, was new. "What is it, Grandmere?"

"Dauphines!" she said. That meant nothing to Eleri, so she looked at her grandmother, raised her shoulders and shook her head, indicating she had no clue what was going on.

"The Dauphines. Remember the family I told you about, the one that runs some of the voodoo shops? The ones who know what they're doing."

"Oh." Eleri began to catch on. "That might be why Cabot, the wolf —" she mentioned, watching her grandmother's scowl deepen even as she progressed with the sentence, "—looked at me and said *Remy,* as though it was some kind of curse."

"To them, it is," Grandmere said, enunciating each word.

Eleri could feel the blood in her veins starting to chill and run cold. "What was it, Grandmere? I don't understand."

"The Dauphines and the Remys have been ..." She didn't finish and Eleri looked up sharply.

"What, is it a blood feud?" She said it as a joke. Only as the words came out did she realize that this was exactly where Grandmere was headed. "A *blood feud?*" she asked again, this time incredulous.

"No, not like that. We've been on opposite sides of disagreements over the past ..." Her great-grandmother let the sentence trail off. That made Eleri more nervous.

"For how long?" Eleri demanded. She couldn't imagine Grandmere having gotten into an argument with anyone. Frederick, maybe. When he was younger, he'd run a little hot-headed. He'd had to cool before Grandmere agreed to make him the new head of the family.

But even if Frederick had gone to the Dauphines and started some kind of witch fight, Eleri thought—almost laughing at the term herself, though she couldn't because of the fierce expression that remained on her Grandmere's face—*she could not imagine her Grandmere getting involved.* No way would Grandmere have picked up Frederick's mantle and followed him. If Frederick had a tiff with someone, the old woman would have told him to stuff it.

So Eleri wondered and repeated, "How long, Grandmere?"

"Since the seventeen hundreds," Grandmere said slowly, almost as though she understood Eleri would have a tough time swallowing it, and she did.

"Literally, the seventeen hundreds?"

"Well, the late seventeen hundreds. The Dauphines and the Remys were some of the first families in this city. We have ancient roots."

Eleri knew that about the Remys already. Donovan had looked up as much and shared it with her. She knew the family had been in town for a long time, but it hadn't occurred to her that they had a "Hatfield and McCoy" relationship with some other local family.

"Are they Haitian?" she asked, thinking of their dark skin color and voodoo roots. Of course, it seemed everyone in New Orleans was a mix of something—French surnames, skin tones, religious backgrounds. She and Grandmere were the same as the Dauphines in that sense.

Grandmere shook her head as though shaking off a thought she didn't like. "I don't know if any of us even remembers truly where we came from. Sure, there are stories about our roots, and we believed them for a long time. But I must admit, the new advances in science disprove a lot of it."

Eleri found it interesting that her Grandmere might be invested a little bit in science to go along with her voodoo—though, again, she was forced to admit she'd seen the two hand-in-hand.

She stuck with her original line of questioning. "So these Dauphines ... what are they? And if this feud goes back to the seventeen hundreds, why is anyone still carrying it on?"

"It's old. One does not simply drop something like that. And it's difficult." Grandmere looked to the side, a shadow of something like shame passing across her face.

Jesus, Eleri thought. This evening was full of revelations, and none of them were good news.

"When I was younger, they lashed out at us," Grandmere told her, though she avoided Eleri's eyes. "I, well ... I helped lash back. It didn't make any friends of the Dauphines, you could say."

Eleri didn't ask, not even sure what "lashing out" and "lashing back" might have looked like in Grandmere's youth, which had been close to a hundred years ago. She wasn't sure what kind of voodoo might be involved, what might have been real slights, and what might have just been perceived or blamed, that might have prompted retaliation in an ongoing feud.

Whatever this long-standing feud was about, though, it might explain why she was so unwelcome in the Dauphines' home—even though she had seen that vision of Emmaline and followed it to the building, and even though she had dug up the human bone. She put those pieces together now for Grandmere.

"The tibia I found, Grandmere—it was in their courtyard." Grandmere merely nodded.

That was not a revelation to her. "I'm not surprised they have human bones there."

Eleri remembered that Grandmere had human bones in her closet. *So I guess it doesn't seem that strange that the Dauphines have them in their courtyard.* She changed the subject. "There is also a guy there named Cabot."

"Cabot," Grandmere frowned. "Not a Dauphine? Did he look like them?"

"Well," Eleri said, "he was lily white, so no." The Dauphine sisters had been dark as night, beautiful in the way that their skin glowed. But now, Eleri wondered, maybe a little scary.

"Was there anything special about this Cabot?" Grandmere pressed.

Eleri started to answer before thinking twice, and then she said, "He's like Donovan."

"So the Dauphines are hanging out with a wolf?" Grandmere leaned forward, her curiosity piqued.

Eleri nodded, her brain struggling to process the ease with which this conversation occurred.

"Oh, I've heard rumors about them developing some kind of alliance."

Grandmere gathered her supplies from the counter in a rush. But as she did, she looked back over her shoulder at Eleri. "Do not go back there, child. It is not safe. I was worried when you were spelled, but I thought some random practitioner had spelled you. If it's a

Dauphine— well, that worries me more. You must promise not to go back."

Eleri nodded at her Grandmere, but did not consider it a promise. She wasn't sure it was something she could promise. She'd have to look into it more. It depended on whether Emmaline turned up again. She couldn't promise to not follow her sister.

Just then, her phone beeped and she saw a text from Donovan. The case in Montana was getting wrapped up. The report would be written once they got home, where they had desks and computers at hand, though they were sharing all of their notes and sending copies to each other.

She smiled and texted back, telling him just a little about the courtyard, including the Dauphine sisters and Cabot.

Donovan texted back immediately. "Eleri, be careful! Stay put. I'm on my way."

It surprised her, the two warnings coming so closely together, but she sat at the counter and scrolled through her phone absently for something to do. That was when she caught the email from Agent Almasi.

27

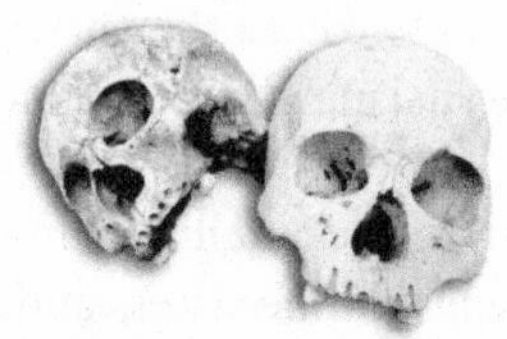

Donovan changed his flight leaving from Montana, and instead of heading home to South Carolina, he bought a ticket directly to Louis Armstrong airport in New Orleans.

He booked the change in his flight before contacting SAC Westerfield. If Westerfield said no, it would already be too late. He was prepared to push back with "yes." He would leave the FBI before he would leave Eleri in a lurch, and she didn't seem to know yet exactly what kind of lurch she was in. He'd told her what he dared over text, but it wasn't everything.

Though he and Wade had looked at the numbers, they had not created a second map with cute red dots growing as populations did. However, the numbers in New Orleans were alarming—no, beyond alarming. Not only was something going on there that had been attracting the Lobomau for the past ten years, but something was also happening with specific groups of Lobomau.

Wade's family kept tabs on wolves all over the US, allowing them to trace specific members. He had the names of children born into his own family and related families. The families that had come to the New World back in the day, seeking freedom for their kind. They'd tracked themselves, looking for safety in numbers, even when they were in distant locations. Families like the Littles and the de Gottardis had grown up, spread out, and even spawned members that had gone off to join the Lobomau.

There was nothing really strange about that. The Lobomau groups weren't limited to specific families, per se. Many times, they recruited members as they went. Sometimes, younger members of one family would be recruited in by older members who'd already passed whatever tests were necessary.

Wade's family, and perhaps some of Donovan's relatives, had been seduced into a lifestyle that let these Lobomau run roughshod over cities. They acted like gang members. They had leaders like gangs. They stole, fought, and killed like gangs. Donovan couldn't deny the appeal of it. As someone who'd been taught that he had to live in hiding—by seeing the reactions to his father when his father changed —he understood the allure of a life that allowed him to believe his own genetics and nature were superior to mere mortals.

It was human nature to want to come out on top. Donovan had never felt the need for violence, only acceptance. Then, just when he'd accepted that he was good as a loner, the FBI had come knocking and tipped all his beliefs on their heads. He didn't have it in him, but he could understand why some joined up with the Lobomau.

Wade had told him—since Donovan didn't have the same family history and didn't know as much as Wade did—that the Lobomau were somewhat scattered. The ancient term "Lobomau" had been used for all of them, though originally they only used it to refer to an individual considered "a bad seed."

It now was the name of the group, and the group had adopted the term, calling themselves "Lobomau." The group had branches, but they followed one leader—and as went the leader, so went the gang. Some caused only mischief, especially those living in small towns and rural areas. Others in cities ran in packs that were as bad as the Bloods or the Crips. That's what worried Donovan.

The greater numbers gathering in New Orleans were highly problematic. The more that were there, the more likely they were organized and dangerous. On top of that, it looked like several groups of Lobomau had immigrated to New Orleans in just the past several years. An entire gang seemed to have picked up from New York City and headed to New Orleans. Another had come from south central Los Angeles. More had come in clusters of three or four, perhaps brothers and sisters, perhaps friends from an area.

As Donovan and Wade traced the movements of individuals known as Lobomau as best they could from records, flights, residences, utility bills, and other records, they saw the pattern growing. The more they saw, the more worried Donovan became—because Eleri was sitting in the heart of it and didn't even know.

Donovan raced to the airport, and while he waited for his flight, he called Agent Westerfield.

"Sir, I just wanted to let you know that I've changed my flight from arriving in South Carolina to arriving in New Orleans later tonight."

Westerfield let the silence hang in a long pause, and Donovan was afraid his boss wasn't going to say anything. It was pretty clear what Donovan was doing.

But then Westerfield asked, "Why, pray tell, did you do this?" He sounded exasperated.

That was an odd question Donovan thought. Wasn't it obvious? But Westerfield was going to make him say it. "Eleri is there, sir. You know that. There's a large contingent of Lobomau in the area—the exact area where she's staying and investigating."

He could almost hear Westerfield nodding on the other end of the line. "Yes, that's absolutely true. But Agent Eames is on personal leave, and she chose this. She's seeing family. The fact that Lobomau are there has nothing to do with her."

"Do you truly believe that to be the case?" Donovan asked. "I'm sure she's not the reason that they have been converging there for the last decade. However, she is in the middle of it. She knows what they are, and if she sees them or they encounter her, what will happen?"

Westerfield had no answer for that. Only as he replied, "You don't know either, Heath. You're welcome to go and stay in New Orleans between cases. You have reports to file. I don't have anything on my desk yet."

"Yes, sir," Donovan replied. Then he added, "There is nowhere in Montana that was suitable for the writing of reports, so we scattered again, heading home. You should have all of those filed within the next twenty-four hours. You'll get my report, as well as those from de Gottardi and Pines."

"Excellent," Westerfield replied. "I'll reach you on this number when I'm ready to put you onto a new case."

Donovan paused. It was acceptable, but not really good enough. Westerfield could have a new case for him the next day or the day after that, and Donovan did not think Eleri would be done. "Sir, I might need a few days in New Orleans. What if I'm not ready to leave?"

"Well then," Westerfield said. "Are you actually going to defy an order from your boss, from the FBI?"

"If I must," Donovan replied, surprising himself, even as the words came out of his mouth. His brain scrambled for a solution should it come to that. He knew he could find another job as a medical examiner. True, he was odd, quiet, and kept to himself. He would have no one to write a personal letter of recommendation for him. But his work spoke for itself. Prospective employers wouldn't know it, but it was his nose that solved a lot of the cases. He always knew to test for particular toxins because he *smelled* them in the liver first. His keen senses made his work exemplary, and he was certain he could find another position. He wouldn't wind up homeless.

However, his position in South Carolina had been filled soon after he joined the NightShade division and Westerfield's team. A new job might mean moving—but even facing that reality, he wasn't going to back pedal on his stance. He wasn't going to tell Westerfield that he would cave because he knew Eleri wouldn't cave in to their boss if it were about him.

Westerfield paused, and Donovan filled in the space. "Is it better that I request leave, should that come up?"

"It's better that you request leave *now*." Westerfield put emphasis on the last word, and Donovan understood his boss wasn't happy about it. However, it was the only consent he could give that didn't involve him completely caving to what Donovan was demanding. And Donovan had no doubt now: He was demanding the option to go and stay with Eleri.

"I'll do that," Donovan replied, making it clear he wasn't budging on his position. However, the thought occurred to him suddenly, and he posed it to Westerfield before he had time to think about it. "What if there's an actual case to open when we're there?"

Westerfield sighed. "You know we don't go looking for cases to open," he said, as though he was weary of this conversation, as short as it had been.

"No," Donovan said. "However, Eleri has already commented on a few things that concerned me during our phone calls." He'd called her Eleri instead of Agent Eames, and he wondered if Westerfield noticed the slip. He didn't know if Westerfield wanted his agents to be tight partners or if he wanted them to maintain a more professional relationship. Donovan had no clue how to go about forming either kind of relationship. The only thing he knew how to do was avoid them completely. The bond between him and his partner had simply happened. "We know there's a large contingent of Lobomau in the area, and that they've been congregating there for the last decade. Their numbers are exploding."

"How do you know that?" Westerfield asked, suddenly sounding more invested in the discussion.

"Agent de Gottardi and I pulled the data over the past couple days." He almost heard Westerfield cussing on the other end of the line, as if he was irritated that his agents were pulling data not directly related to the case they were working on. Donovan added, "The Lobomau were at the home in Montana. You'll see that in our reports."

Donovan wanted to clarify that he hadn't simply been looking for reasons to go to New Orleans—and truth be told, he hadn't. He and Wade had just been looking at the data about wolves across the US, and the Lobomau had come up. He didn't say any of that to Westerfield. Didn't want to defend his position any further, to create places where Westerfield could poke holes.

"Also, Eames's sister is a known missing child case. That's standard Bureau jurisdiction," Donovan pointed out. And as he said it, he realized his idiocy. Of course, Westerfield knew that. Of course, Westerfield knew that's why Eleri was in New Orleans. And of course, Westerfield understood, as did all three of them, that her search was intensely personal—not an FBI case.

Unable to stop his runaway mouth, Donovan pointed out, "As soon as she finds evidence, it reopens Emmaline Eames' case."

"Yes it would," Westerfield said. "But it's not our division."

"Isn't it?" Donovan asked. "I know Eleri's family history." Dammit. He'd said *Eleri* again, but he didn't pause. "Which means Emmaline Eames' family history is the same. She's a Remy, a Hale, a Llewellyn, and an Eames. That's NightShade business."

28

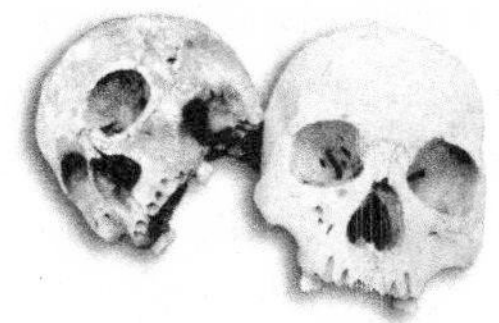

Eleri watched as Donovan pulled into Grandmere's driveway, parking his rental car next to hers. His car doubled the number of vehicles here, and since Grandmere didn't own one, they massively upped the use of her driveway this week.

It was well into the middle of the night when he finally pulled in, but Eleri had stayed up waiting. He wouldn't let her pick him up at the airport, insisting that two cars might be necessary at some point and he would drive out to her with his own rental. The FBI wasn't footing the bill on this one, though. Not hers and not his. She wanted to pick up the tab on his car. She had a trust fund. It would do no damage to her account but he didn't let her. She was happy she could make the offer.

Just over a year ago, when Agent Westerfield had called her in and introduced her and Donovan for the first time, she'd not foreseen this.

Even Avery wasn't here in New Orleans to support her—but then again, how could he be? Avery had no idea what she was, no idea what Donovan was, and no idea what threats existed in New Orleans. He did know Eleri's little sister had been kidnapped at age eight and that Eleri, as an FBI agent, had put herself on the case. She had no way to explain wanting a hockey player with a slate of pre-season practices clogging his schedule—hours and hours every day—to leave his team. Even if he came and offered help, she wasn't sure how useful he might be. He had no science, no Bureau training, and no missing children's background at all.

Eleri was inordinately glad that Donovan had showed up, and Grandmere was overly grateful as well. Not only had she fussed about setting up his room, but she'd cast spells and smoked herbs into it. Eleri almost laughed imagining Donovan walking in and getting smacked back by smells he could surely perceive more acutely than either of the women.

Without asking, Grandmere had barged into Eleri's room, rummaged through the bags, and pulled out the bones. She'd walked through the house tossing them on the floor, mumbling spells and citing gods' names. Then she would pick up the bones, move five paces further, and repeat the whole sequence.

Once she had finished doing this around the perimeter of every room in the house—wearing an alarmingly worried expression on her face—Eleri had expected her to stop. But no, Grandmere had merely gone outside and paced the entire rectangular yard this way. Then she'd climbed into the passenger seat of Eleri's unlocked rental car and proceeded to do what Eleri could only presume was more of the same.

Maybe she should start locking her car, Eleri thought. *But on the other hand perhaps the Dauphines would detect the spells cast on her and her car the next time she pulled up.*

Though Grandmere had eventually cast on everything she could find before she went to bed, she'd awakened and come into the living room just moments before Eleri saw Donovan's car lights turning onto the street at the corner. Cars passed through here with reasonable regularity—not often, but often enough that car lights alone hadn't meant it was Donovan.

However, Eleri had just seemed to sense it. Grandmere's presence in the archway to the living room only confirmed it. She couldn't tell if her great grandmother had slept at all in the last several hours, but Grandmere once again held the bones in her hand. Eleri figured she'd have to warn Donovan that Grandmere might need to slip into his car and mumble some curses, prayers, chants, invocations or something.

She watched as he unfolded his tall frame from the small rental, and by the time he made it to the back door, Eleri was standing in it. She engulfed him in a hug, thanking him for coming. It felt natural enough that she realized she had no idea if this was the first time she'd ever hugged him or not. If she had, it hadn't stuck in her memory. But this ... this was personal. This was not a case they were working on together. This was her realizing she might be in some kind of danger—although at this point it seemed she might be imagining it. Donovan had showed up to help her.

As soon as Eleri stepped back, Grandmere stepped forward, engulfing him in an even bigger hug than Eleri had managed. Grandmere, however, also gripped the bones tightly in her hands, and she knocked them ever so lightly against his spine as she murmured something.

Over Grandmere's shoulder, Donovan raised his brows at Eleri, asking if she knew what was going on. She shook her head and motioned her hand in a forward circle, indicating that he should just roll with it.

"Do you have your bags?" Grandmere asked him when she finally stepped back and released him, apparently satisfied that her work was done.

"I have only the one," he said, and Eleri recognized the black ripstop "go bag" in his hand.

"Excellent," Grandmere said. "Put it in your room. I'm going out to your car." She was gone before Donovan could ask what she was doing, and Eleri explained about the spell Grandmere had cast on her own car several hours earlier.

Her partner disappeared down the hall only long enough to drop his bag and use the restroom and then he was back on the couch before Grandmere had returned. Eleri would have worried about her great grandmother outside in the Lower Ninth Ward, sitting in a car, chanting spells at almost two in the morning—but she didn't. Surely, Grandmere could take care of herself, and surely Grandmere's home was protected against all things evil.

"So, what have you found?" Donovan asked.

Eleri proceeded to tell him. The bones she'd originally followed did not belong to Emmaline. She'd told him this before, but Agent Almasi had given her new genetic information, sending her the entire profile they'd worked up on comparing her DNA to the skeleton.

He'd explained that, at the time they'd spoken at the branch, he hadn't wanted to contradict her because he hadn't realized and hadn't counted the numbers for sure. Many times, people believed something about their family history and didn't want to hear otherwise. But, having examined it again since they'd spoken, he'd developed a new set of numbers for her and wanted to share them.

"It turns out," she told Donovan, "I'm not one-quarter African American. I'm something closer to seven sixteenths."

Donovan took in that information with little surprise. "Almost half. What does that mean about your mother? It means she's almost full-blooded, right?"

They both assumed that had to be the case, given Eleri's new information. Thomas Hale Eames appeared to have crawled from a bag of Wonder Bread, so the extra genetics that indicated genes of African origin likely would not have come from her paternal lineage.

Eleri agreed. "I mean, I suppose there could be some on my father's side. We'd have to test other family members to see. But it appears my mother's father was more African- American than not."

"Seven sixteenths," Donovan said. "Seven out of sixteen great-grandparents. No, great-*great*-grandparents," he corrected his math, thinking through the numbers and implications.

Eleri had already figured on that. "But as Agent Almasi had pointed out, it's not as though my great-great-grandparents were pure-blooded in any way, either. Grandmere says the Remys have been here in New Orleans since the 1700s, when the city was founded. Many came from Haiti after a Haitian revolution, and so that's in the family mix as well. Basically, at this point I'm a full-blooded mutt." She smiled, thinking how her ancestors on her father's blue-blooded side of her family might roll in their graves. Well, likely none of them were as pure as they thought, either. She loved the genetics but didn't place much stock in the idea of bloodlines.

Donovan only nodded in response, and Eleri wondered if he was thinking of his own genetic history. It might be something they would look into one of these days. But right now, she had more information to reveal. "So, the kicker is, if I'm not one-quarter African-American, and I'm more like seven-sixteenths and my historical pieces are a mix of genes from Northern Africa and sub-Saharan Africa and Haiti, which showed up as well—and if all that is a match to another person—that makes the match all the more significant."

"Not Emmaline?" Donovan asked.

"No. The bones we found that I originally thought were Emmaline, that matched her case so closely—well, they also matched me, genetically. They might have belonged to second cousin or something. I thought we were both one-quarter African-American, which isn't that uncommon. But now, even with this new, unusual mix of genetic history—we test as having a very, very similar mix."

Though Agent Almasi's initial suggestion that the missing girl was a second cousin had been surprising, this was even more concerning. "The similarities of the case to Emmaline's, the mix of bloodlines—that has to make the case related, doesn't it?" she asked Donovan.

"Sounds like it," he said. He asked when the missing girl had disappeared and when she had died, and Eleri told him. Again, the details were disturbingly similar to Emmaline's.

"Shit," Donovan said, running his fingers through his hair. "I didn't realize before, but it's something we need to consider. Two young girls with very similar genetics , living on different places on the continent disappear within a year of each other. One of them turns up here. We have a passable reason to believe the other will, also. They both die within a year of each other. One here, one likely here—and all within a year after that the Lobomau population explodes in this city."

29

Eleri did not sleep well. Donovan's revelations tied things together in ways she'd not expected. He'd mentioned the Lobomau in his texts before, but she merely thought it was some issue of the city.

Grandmere had stayed up into the late hours talking with them as well—another surprise. She, too, seemed to think that the Dauphine family being tied to the Lobomau was another concerning bit of evidence.

Something was clearly happening between the two. Also, the details concerning the missing girls didn't add up well. Eleri listened with her heart on her sleeve. It was the first time her great-grandmother had talked much about losing Emmaline.

Almost a decade ago, Emmaline had died. This young woman from Nebraska had also died, around the same time. Then, within the year, the Lobomau began appearing in the city in record numbers.

None of it made sense. None of it was anything that Eleri could tie together for any reason she understood, but the numbers must mean *something*. The facts lined up in a way that she and Donovan were certain they could not discount.

Donovan had suggested calling SAC Westerfield. He'd thought there might be a real NightShade case here. Maybe this was that case, but Eleri wanted to wait. Making this into a Bureau case would mean turning control over to Agent Westerfield. It would mean he could invite other agents in and take them out at his will. Eleri wasn't willing to let it go. The situation wasn't bad enough to bring in the cavalry. Not yet.

It was the wee hours of the morning before they had finally gone to bed. Eleri had awakened late, nearly screaming from a dream where she was once again in the courtyard in the garden of the peachy-orange house. In the dream, she dug in the dirt, checking under roots and pavers, lifting them up and finding skulls. She found the skulls of children. She found skulls of adults ... or they found her. She found long bones, fully intact, and fingers that pushed their own way up out of the ground, reaching for her.

Once she was fully awake, she knew it was completely impossible. The connective tissue of a hand would have rotted away, and the finger bones would not have stayed in position. In fact, forensically, hand and foot bones were notorious for scattering as rains penetrated the soil, as predators carried them off and ate them and scattered them out in a wide radius, sometimes of miles. So the idea that a stack of finger bones would come out of the ground almost the same as an intact or wired skeleton was utterly laughable, in the light of the late morning.

However, as she'd been digging and the bones had pushed their way upward in her dream, it had been terrifying. In her dream, she'd ripped her fingernails and bloodied her hands trying to get through the dirt. She'd held the skulls in her hands, staring at what had once been faces of children, and she'd watched as the teeth had wiggled and fallen out onto the ground around her.

But even in the dream, she had not found Emmaline.

The thought of digging and finding bones in the courtyard at the Dauphines' home had horrified her, even without her sister being part of it. She got out of bed, awake now. Donovan and Grandmere were still asleep, despite the late hour. Donovan sleeping late, she understood. But Grandmere sleeping in was surprising.

Despite their late hours the night before, she had still expected her great grandmother to be up with the crack of dawn, as usual. It seemed almost nothing deterred Grandmere's schedule.

Eleri wandered the house for about fifteen minutes and, when no one rose, she decided to begin making breakfast. She put together pancakes from flour, milk, eggs, and a shot of the rich brandy she found in Grandmere's cabinet. She cooked bacon in the oven, not in

Grandmere's cast iron skillet. Though she was Grandmere's descendant, she was definitely several generations younger.

Donovan must have smelled it. He rolled out of bed just as it was ready—and yet Grandmere still did not appear. Asking him to man the pancakes and flip the last few and slide them onto a plate, Eleri went down the hall to check on her great-grandmother.

By the time she made it to the last bedroom, her heart was racing. She'd not thought of it—not often, at least—but Grandmere was quite elderly. Though her health appeared perfect, there was no telling what might happen or when. She found she was suddenly afraid that last night might have been the last of Grandmere.

Petrified, she screwed up her courage and swung the door open, her heart pounding out the rhythm of her fear. It was a thought that she had not really let enter her mind while Grandmere had slept away the long morning. Now, it was suddenly very real.

There were people in the house now, though Grandmere was used to living alone. That should have woken her up. There was someone in her kitchen using her food and her supplies—and that alone should have stirred Grandmere, as should the late hour. Eleri saw her on the bed, facing the wall.

For a moment she stopped and watched with a focused gaze, hoping to see the rise and fall of Grandmere's chest. When she didn't, she held her own breath. Stepping forward, and knowing she had to check, she placed a hand on Grandmere's shoulder. Luckily, at that moment, the body jolted. The heavy arm swung back and the old woman sat suddenly upright in bed, once again as spry as Eleri had always thought of her.

"What are you doing in here, child?" Her words were clearly enunciated.

Nothing about her spoke of Eleri's fear that she might be gone. "You didn't wake up, Grandmere. It's late. I made breakfast. Pancakes and bacon." She said it with a cheery tone, as if she'd just come to rouse the woman for breakfast, with no morbid thoughts of death lingering on her tongue.

"You made me breakfast?" Grandmere asked her. It wasn't *that* unusual. Eleri had, of course, cooked here a few times before, but it certainly wasn't the norm.

"Donovan flipped some pancakes for you, too, Grandmere. In fact, he's setting up the plates right now."

"All right then, child. Leave me alone," Grandmere told her and Eleri happily obliged. She headed back down the hall. Donovan must have noticed the expression of her face was very different from the one she'd left with, because he seemed to understand that all was well.

They ate the big, heavy breakfast happily and, as she emptied her plate, Eleri turned to Donovan. "Look, there's a knife in a shop that I found down in the French Quarter," she started. Then she turned to Grandmere. She hadn't told her great-grandmother this before but with Donovan here, and possibly an actual case on her hands, she mentioned it this time. "Grandmere, the handle is human bone. They're selling it in the shop."

"I don't like that," Grandmere said, her tone conveying far more than the simple words did.

"I know, neither do I." Eleri pushed on, knowing the older woman would like the next part even less. "And that's why I have to follow up."

Grandmere shocked her by asking, "Are you armed?"

Of course, Grandmere knew she was an agent. She knew of Eleri's training, but this was the first time she had seemed to demand that Eleri use it.

"I wasn't the last few times I went, but today, we will be." She turned back to her partner. "Donovan, I'd like if you can come into the shop with me. Perhaps there's something you can smell or sense, something I didn't see. The first time I stumbled on it, I just went in as a tourist. There seems to be something about the shop owner, too —and, well, anything you can sniff out would help." She used the common phrase but meant it literally.

"Of course," he replied. They finished the last of the breakfast, cleaned up the kitchen, and left Grandmere in her home.

Someone was walking up the walkway as they left, and Eleri was relieved that Grandmere recognized a client of hers. At least the woman wouldn't be home alone today. Everything here had gotten much, much messier in the last twenty-four hours. Or actually, Eleri thought, it was exactly as messy as it always had been—but only in the last twenty-four hours had she realized what it was.

Driving Donovan into the French Quarter, Eleri pointed out things that she saw and knew. They agreed to try to find the Dauphine house later, but first headed to the shop.

She parked on Royal Street and they walked a half block to the shop doors. As they entered the small store, she was grateful to see Darcelle again. She wondered if the woman ever took a day off.

"Eleri," Darcelle welcomed her back, her hands once again folded in front of her.

"Darcelle," Eleri greeted her with a return smile, almost as though this woman was a friend. She had no idea if the shop keeper knew she had a human bone-handle knife in her shop, though she suspected Darcelle did, given her willingness to speak of it and of the spell carved into it. "I brought my friend Donovan to see your shop today."

Darcelle's nostrils flared and her pupils widened just a touch at the sight of Eleri's friend.

"Have you come to look at the knife again?" Darcelle asked. Her tone was overwhelmingly pleasant, though suddenly, it held a slight edge underneath.

"Yes," Eleri replied, thinking this was now a surface game the two of them were playing. "I wanted to show it to Donovan. I thought he might be interested in it." She took his hand and led him into the back room. This time, Darcelle followed closely.

As Eleri picked up the knife though, the woman had a surprise.

"Eleri Eames," she said, suddenly knowing Eleri's full name. "You are the witch who visited my family yesterday."

30

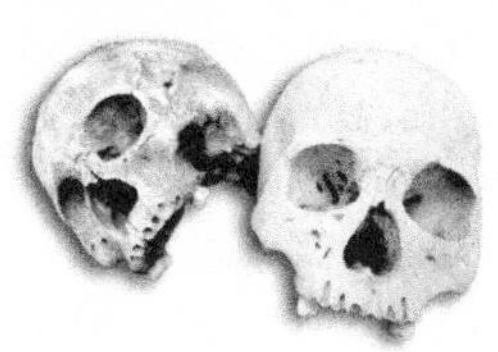

Eleri stopped dead at Darcelle's words. She stood still and silent, stunned for a moment, until something she had thought yesterday became clearer in her mind.

This was perhaps why the two women at the courtyard house had looked vaguely familiar to her. Now that she thought about it, they looked stunningly similar to Darcelle—and the three were clearly sisters.

Beside her, she felt Donovan stiffen and a short motion he made gave her the impression he was reaching for his gun. Everything was happening too fast. When Grandmere had asked if they were armed, that had stunned Eleri. The fifteen minutes it had taken to drive over and park here had not been enough to process everything, and Eleri was still reeling from Grandmere's suggestions. Then, to walk in here and have Darcelle suggest that she knew more than Eleri did was another slap in the face. She was grateful that—while Donovan had positioned himself to get to his gun quickly—he hadn't actually pulled it.

The three of them stood facing each other. They were in the back room of the shop, just feet away from the bone-handled knife, but Darcelle was standing in the archway. Eleri was glad now for the way the little house was constructed. There was always another arch and another wall leading to another space. Darcelle did not have them completely blocked in, though they didn't have a truly open path, either.

The shopkeeper's eyes narrowed slightly. "Did you come to my home two days ago? Did you come inside looking for something, *witch?*" She asked the question with an emphasis on that last word.

Strange, Eleri had never been called that before these past few months, yet now enough people in enough different places had referred to her as "witch" that she was beginning to think there was something to it. Perhaps it was a fact about her that they had all known long before she did. She could feel her own eyes narrow in response to Darcelle's question.

"Darcelle Dauphine?" she asked. Eleri was waiting for it to settle on her own tongue before she went any further. She knew better than to answer before she was prepared.

"You met my sisters, Gisele and Lafae."

Eleri only nodded this time and Darcelle asked again if Eleri had gone inside the home and moved things around.

"No," Eleri replied with as much confidence as she could convey. "I've never been inside your home." Then she paused. "At least, *not that I remember.*" She emphasized every word, indicating her irritation and anger that she'd been spelled and her memory had been stolen. She paused, curious about how Darcelle might respond to that, but the woman merely stared at her, as if she didn't comprehend.

Eleri decided it was time to explain. "A spell stole my memory after I was in the courtyard, that first day."

Darcelle shook her head and looked almost confused. "I have cast nothing on you."

"And how do I believe you?" Eleri asked. "Your sisters don't seem trustworthy. Apparently, it's your home."

That was another mystery, Eleri thought. She'd come to this street and come into this shop. She'd visited no other voodoo shops, and—besides getting an ice cream or a sandwich—set foot in no other shops in the French Quarter at all.

But why this one? She thought she'd just come in because it looked nice to her. Something about it had made her want to check out the wares and explore. Was that merely good advertising in the shop windows, or was there some kind of voodoo involved? Was it a generic spell, to pull the public in and get them to buy Darcelle Dauphine's wares? Or was it something that was more attractive to Eleri in particular? Did she recognize something in these sisters that not only brought her into this shop, but then led straight to their home?

And was it Emmaline?

While Emmaline had played no part in getting her to the shop—that she knew of—it had been her sister's image walking backwards, beckoning with fingertips, that led her directly to the Dauphine home.

Darcelle repeated the sentence. "I have cast nothing on you, sister," she said. And Eleri found her use of the word interesting. The Dauphine women were not *her* sisters.

"So who did?" Eleri asked. "The first day I was here."

Darcelle nodded. "You touched the knife. You dropped it and ran. You say that was when you went to the house?" she pressed in return, not answering Eleri's question. The two were playing back and forth, neither willing to give up information first.

Eleri nodded, conceding to that little bit in hopes of a better return and finding it strange that this woman who lived in the house seemed to know less about the incident than she did. These were her sisters—but Darcelle seemed to not know anything about what they'd done. The question was, was that legitimate, or was she merely digging for information?

Eleri paused again and tried to look into Darcelle. She wanted to see if she could feel or sense anything, but she smacked up against a hard wall, and Darcelle narrowed her eyes as though she knew what Eleri had tried.

Darcelle then shot her gaze back and forth between the two of them, almost as though it was first she had noticed Donovan, despite the fact that they had introduced themselves when they walked in the store. This time, her eyes snapped to him and lingered, leaving Eleri to wonder, *What did Darcelle think?*

However, that curiosity did not last long. "Are you a friend of Cabot's?" Darcelle barked out the words at Donovan. The tone made Eleri think Darcelle was no friend of Cabot's, despite her sisters' clear relationship with the man.

Donovan shook his head, likely only recognizing the name from the information Eleri had given him earlier. This, too, was a distraction from the topic at hand—from the idea that Eleri had been spelled. She stepped forward, wanting to direct the conversation a little more on her own.

"Who spelled me?" she asked again, this time with force behind the words.

Darcelle shrugged, dropping the forward momentum of her earlier anger. "Probably one of my sisters. No one is allowed in our courtyard without an invitation."

Eleri tilted her head. "Funny, I just walked in. Does that mean I have an invitation?"

Something flickered in Darcelle's eyes, but she didn't answer. Eleri wanted to push, and push hard, but she couldn't think of what to say or how to make it happen. Even the mild search she'd tried met up with a brick wall. Whatever Darcelle Dauphine was, it was powerful.

This time, though, she didn't relax, and Darcelle took a short step backward. "What was the spell?" she asked, as though she truly didn't know.

The tone of her voice and the set of her shoulders were all that Eleri had to go on. Her hunches, her new talents were no good here. Darcelle didn't let them be, and so Eleri was relying heavily on the training she'd received at Quantico. All she could do was read the body signals Darcelle sent out.

The tension in her hands, the relaxation of her brow, and the fact that her eyes did not flick to the side said she either truly did not know what had happened to Eleri or she was an excellent actress. Eleri hedged her bets. She told Darcelle about walking into the courtyard the first time, about digging up the human bone, and about the spell. The shopkeeper raised her eyebrows higher and higher through the few sentences Eleri spoke.

"You dug a bone out of our courtyard? With what?" she asked incredulously.

"My fingers." Eleri held up her hands as though to demonstrate her nails were broken and short—but they weren't. It had been several days, and they were clean. There was no evidence, despite the way Eleri held them up. Still, she pressed forward. "That bone was in my pocket. But now it's missing."

"Of course it is," Darcelle told her. "You tried to take it from our courtyard. I don't even know if it *can* leave."

Again, something flickered in the woman's eyes and Eleri wondered, did she *truly have some unique power to walk into the court-*

yard, or was this something the sisters were selling her, trying to make her think she was special? Did they just mess with everyone? Because truly, who would push open a private gate and walk into the courtyard of a residence?

Yet Eleri had done it. And whatever they thought she was, they had spelled her.

"Most likely Lafae," Darcelle eventually volunteered after seeming to think about it for a moment. "Possibly Alesse."

"Alesse?" Eleri asked. She'd not met Alesse.

"My older sister."

"But two evenings ago?"

Darcelle's chin went up in a subtle stance of defiance. Eleri recognized it well. Her next sentence indicated why. "My house was tossed. And my sister is missing."

31

Darcelle's heart twisted as she watched the two of them standing in her shop, staring at her as though she was weak.

Outside the window, people moving around caught her attention. Despite the fact that she could barely see through the archway and onto the street, they worried her. Moving quickly and startling the two who stood staring at her—though she did not care—Darcelle darted to the front door and flipped the sign to Closed. This conversation did not need to be interrupted.

Her smaller guest, Eleri, frowned at her—but it was the larger one, Donovan, who bothered her more. Not only was this Eleri Eames a witch, and not only did the name sound slightly familiar, but it had rolled off her tongue when she introduced herself fully this time. Somewhere in the deep recesses of her history, Darcelle had recognized her from the first moment she stepped foot in the shop, though she could not have told you where or how.

To have the woman show up now with a wolf in tow—and one not related to Cabot in any way—was so strange. The entire week had been strange, and Darcelle did not like it. It seemed the whole mess had started the first moment this Eleri had set foot into her shop. Was Eleri Eames to blame for *everything* that was going wrong?

Turning now, seeing that Eleri and Donovan had followed her and that they still looked at her strangely, Darcelle put her back to the front door and crossed her arms and stared at the two of them. Then, she turned her focus to the smaller one.

"Why did you come into my shop?" she asked, anger simmering at the back of her words. They had messed up all of her plans.

The woman started to shrug, a far too casual gesture for the conversation at hand. Then she replied, "I truly don't know. I was walking down the street. I saw your sign. So I came in to see what you had."

"You crossed the street to come into my shop. You jay-walked to come in here," Darcelle pointed out.

She remembered seeing the woman beeline for her front door. Her first thought had been, *Excellent. A dedicated customer!* But as soon as the door had swung open, she'd seen something else in Eleri's face, something she couldn't define. She'd politely said, "Hello," and waited, knowing that this one was different. She still said none of this to the two standing in front of her, but once again merely waited for the winds of this conversation to shift without her. When neither of her visitors spoke, she had to turn the sails herself.

"What you are suggesting," she said, jabbing a finger to make her point, "is that you came into my shop on a whim and then turned around and went down the street to my home, also on a whim. Once there, you passed a secured gate with ease, walked into my protected space in the courtyard, and dug a human bone out. And then got yourself spelled."

Eleri looked at her and blinked. "That's pretty much the order of it," she agreed, still far too casually for Darcelle's boiling anger.

"Did you walk straight to my home when you left here?" she asked.

"Pretty much," Eleri said.

Darcelle wondered if the woman had walked the same path as she. Had she connected with Darcelle in the shop and then followed directly along that line? It was plausible, if the two had connected, that Eleri would feel the thing that pulled Darcelle home every day. Plausible, she thought—but that didn't mean she liked it. She felt her eyes narrow again and could not stop the sweep of emotion that she felt cross her face.

"What led you there?" she demanded again, fighting the urge to pace or yell or even breathe too heavily. Though the woman did not respond openly, this time, Darcelle caught the slightest flare. Interestingly enough, the same flare caught light in the wolf's eyes, too.

Donovan reacted to that question—though, apparently, he had not been with Eleri Eames that day. Darcelle had not seen him. Though the Eleri woman shook her head back and forth, she lied. She would not tell Darcelle what had taken her to the home, but something had. She'd followed the path or someone had led her there.

Had Lafae or Gisele come near the shop and picked this Eleri out for some purpose? They likely would not have told her if they had. Darcelle didn't like that idea either, but she also didn't like throwing her lot in with her sisters. Perhaps they had recognized the Eames woman the same way that Darcelle did on some deep, inner level. Darcelle still had no idea what that was about.

Another option that came to mind was that this whole mess had something to do with Alesse. Alesse had still been home that day. Maybe she'd stalked the Eames woman and sparked something, something that got the house tossed and made Alesse disappear. Darcelle changed her direction. "What do you know of Alesse?"

Eleri shook her head. The Donovan man was not speaking at all. The wolf stood still, sniffing at her, holding court, and offering backup for his small friend.

"I don't know anything of Alesse," Eleri said. "I didn't know she existed until you mentioned her. Who is she?"

"My older sister," Darcelle said.

Once again, Eleri shook her head and shrugged. She was clearly trying not to offer up anything she didn't have to.

"Why did you react?" Darcelle pushed, for the Eleri woman and Donovan man had both reacted to her statement. This time, it appeared Eleri thought for just a moment—but when she answered, it was not what Darcelle expected.

"Darcelle, you have to understand. You, and now your sisters, are tied to some very strange things."

She pointed back over her shoulder into the other room.

"The knife on the counter back there is made from human bone. Did you know that?"

Darcelle did know that. She didn't blink, though, and as she stood her ground, she realized perhaps she should have. Perhaps she should have played dumb, but she wasn't fast enough on her feet to make that happen.

Eleri used that lack of reaction to move forward into Darcelle's space. But Darcelle didn't give ground. Eleri Eames did not want to go up against her. She might be in this shop and she might be stuck under her Momma's thumb still, but she was not one to be trifled with.

Eleri spoke evenly. "Your sisters put spells on me. I don't know why I went from your shop to your home," though, again, something in Eleri's eyes told of the lie behind the words. Whether it was true or not, her explanation wasn't complete.

Eleri spoke one more time. "You say your sister is missing. Well, so is mine."

That grabbed Darcelle. Had Eleri's sister gone missing the same time as Alesse? Did the two know each other? Was that perhaps what had brought Eleri into the shop, and then all the way down the street through the several turns that would lead her to the courthouse home? She started to ask the question, but Eleri interrupted.

"My sister has been missing for twenty-one years."

Darcelle felt the impact of those words. She felt it hit her, pass right through her skin, and shock her to her very bones. She wanted to ask more questions. Why had Eleri come with a wolf this time? She had no idea, but she did know one thing. She turned to the two, putting the force of all nature behind her voice.

"You need to leave my shop right now."

32

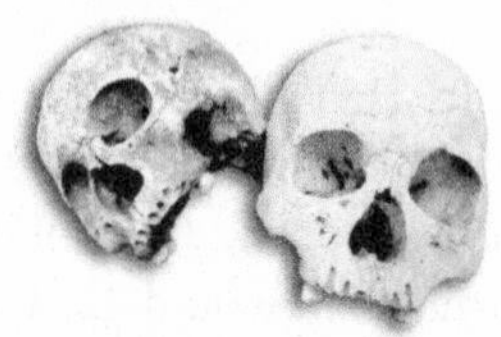

Though outwardly he was calm, inside his chest, Donovan's heart pounded. What appeared to be a casual conversation was scaring the shit out of him.

The shop with the human bone had seemed an anomaly, the house was weird—but the connection between the two was stunning.

When Eleri had commented about her missing sister, Darcelle had turned pale and ordered the two of them to leave immediately. They'd complied, Eleri holding her head high. Donovan hadn't aimed for decorum, but to keep his hand close to his gun and be ready for any sudden change in the air.

He'd seen Eleri in action before and he had no doubt that Darcelle could do as much as—if not much, much more than—his partner could. Darcelle Dauphine worked in a shop called Mystic Vudu. Though he couldn't feel whatever vibes the dolls and spells gave off like Eleri could, he could feel that they were creepy. He could also tell that the shop didn't cater to idiots. Tourists, maybe, but the woman didn't sell crap on her shelves. That scared him maybe a little more than the rest of it. If Darcelle wanted to try anything, she was sitting on a powder keg.

He and Eleri sat in the car for a moment before Eleri turned the key. She was the one to drive, being more familiar with the city than he. She turned down the street and, without addressing his major concern, she said, "I'm going to head to the Dauphine home now."

He put his hand on hers, effectively stopping her from turning the steering wheel before they started down a path they weren't ready for. "No. Not right now."

Eleri blinked.

He said what he could to sway her from her plans. "One, there's every possibility that Darcelle is on the phone to her sisters right now, warning them that you are on the way. Two, she also now knows that you are bringing someone like me. Apparently, her family is involved with others of my kind here. Three, given the percentage of wolves in New Orleans, versus the percentage of Lobomau, it's more likely than not that the wolves they're with are Lobomau. I am not prepared to deal with any of that. Are you?"

He waited just a heartbeat, and then dove in again. "What if there's more than one? You already said there are two sisters, and now with Darcelle, there are three. With Alesse, there are four. Are there more? Darcelle is strong. I cannot imagine ticking off four of her."

Eleri shook her head, not to answer his questions, but because she didn't know the answers. He removed his hand from hers, now allowing her to make turns and to drive where she wished. He still hoped that, with his input, she would make a different decision.

"We don't know enough to go there. Not yet." He said it softly this time. If he went to the Dauphine home, he wanted to be as ready as he could be, though he doubted that would even be possible.

"So, where do we go?" she asked.

"Somewhere new. Somewhere neither of us has been before. We talk and we regroup."

Eleri nodded. She drove the car out of the French Quarter, away from the Lower Ninth Ward and into more residential areas. She drove through the neighborhoods and out the other side. It was a bit of a challenge, with the roads bumped and buckled from the damage of Hurricane Katrina. In other places, they were smoothed as though brand new. It felt almost as if there was nothing in between the extremes.

They drove past stately homes that showed almost no damage and poorer ones that still showed some, though few houses stood as obvious testaments to the hurricane, the way some did in her Grand-mere's neighborhood.

Eventually, Eleri came to an area with a small bodega next to a tiny hole-in-the-wall shop and she parked the car.

"I don't know about you," she said, "but I could go for a soda."

"Me, too. It's hotter than blazes," Donovan agreed. Perhaps they could walk the street and make a decision. They were far away from everything associated with the Dauphines, and he hoped they could speak freely here.

The streets appeared relatively empty; no one should be picking up on their conversation. Still, they stayed quiet as they stepped inside, ordered large drinks, and took them out where they inhaled them quickly as the outsides of the plastic cups sweated down their hands.

Donovan spoke first. "There are thousands of Lobomau in this city, Eleri. It's insane, but there are literally thousands of them." He thought about the overall population and wondered if that number was really a cause for concern.

Eleri, having met Cabot, made him think it probably was.

Eleri started them off with a long-suffering sigh and the two launched into their usual co-brainstorming, where they each just threw facts onto the table.

Eleri threw the first one. "Darcelle clearly knows that the knife has a human bone handle. She knows what's in her shop. She's not a random curator getting these things from other people. There's a reasonable possibility she and her sisters make her wares themselves."

Donovan agreed. "They're also Dauphines, and that's one of the names your grandmother used."

"Actually," Eleri said "it's the only name my grandmother used, aside from our own. And the sisters recognized me as a Remy yesterday."

Seeming to think more like the agent he now was, Donovan offered up, "Well, we can arrest Darcelle Dauphine for trafficking in human artifacts."

Eleri smiled. "I suspect there's more than just that knife, though that was the only human artifact I found in the shop."

Donovan switched the subject and threw out another fact. "You are closely related to the other young woman who was missing."

"Second cousins," Eleri said.

"Close enough," he replied. They walked further down the street, having moved several blocks away from the car.

"We need to learn everything we can about the Dauphine family," Eleri said.

"Yes." Donovan nodded. "We need two major sources. One, we need Grandmere. She knows a lot, and two, we need the FBI database just in case Grandmere is misinformed."

Eleri nodded slowly but her eyebrows rose, indicating that she had not really considered that. Clearly, she was glad Donovan had. Grandmere knew the Remy family history. Apparently, she knew it from being a Hatfield to the Dauphines' McCoys.

According to Eleri, it was entirely plausible—as Grandmere had once pointed out—that the family stories were wrong. Still, the stories, whatever they were—whatever myths or legends the two sides were operating from—were just as important.

"I'm curious as to where this Alesse has disappeared to as well," Eleri said. "Apparently, she just didn't come home the other night. From what little I gathered, the house was ransacked or something."

She asked if Donovan had gotten the same impression, and he nodded that he had. So perhaps looking into Alesse Dauphine's history might yield a little something more. He added it to the mental list he was tallying.

"I want to go back to the courtyard," she said. "I'm curious about what the two of us can dig up, literally."

"Not today," he said, this time not suggesting any more. He still didn't like the thought, but the more ideas the two of them tossed around, the more he realized visiting the home was an inevitable necessity. "They're expecting us today. In fact, they're expecting us at any moment. We need to wait, at least until tomorrow, or maybe even a few days. And we need to plan on going when none of them are home—if we can figure out when that might be."

Eleri seemed to think on that for a moment, Donovan could tell she was considering everything from spells to tear gas to drive them out. Perhaps even a warrant, but that seemed a little extreme. So far, he hadn't seen the need to pull his badge. According to Eleri, she'd not let that little tidbit about her occupation slip, either. So, unless Darcelle Dauphine had some other method of looking into online databases that he wasn't aware of, she did not yet know the two people in her shop were federal agents. Official capacity or not, Donovan was quite certain it was something Darcelle would find interesting.

As they turned and headed back to the car, Donovan suggested putting a wireless hot spot in Grandmere's house. Eleri merely raised one eyebrow. "Grandmere is not a fan of wireless."

"Well," he shrugged, not liking the alternatives. "I suggest we ask, because our other option is to go somewhere like the library, or a café, and you know how easily those connections can be hacked by proximity."

Eleri was starting to agree that they should at least ask Grandmere—obviously, they wouldn't do it without her permission—when someone bumped her shoulder on the sidewalk. Something in her eyes changed, and as Donavan watched the exchange almost in slow motion, his brain caught up. His nostrils had flared. He'd not gotten a good glimpse at the guy, but he suddenly felt things fall into place. The man had been following the two of them.

Why hadn't he noticed it before? How had he let it slide so badly? He could smell the man! He had been behind them. Donovan had known that, but he'd brushed it off. Obviously, so had Eleri.

Whatever hunches they had—whatever sense of scent he possessed or intuition Eleri might have had—it had all been disregarded, and so had their standard Quantico training. Now, with the shoulder bump, it all came into play, suddenly blooming in his mind as an obvious conclusion.

Donovan turned and whispered down at her as he sniffed the air one last time. "Lobomau."

33

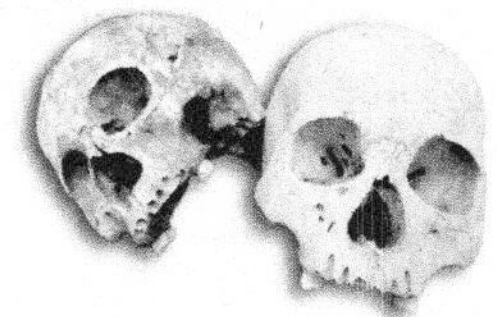

Eleri and Donovan returned to Grandmere's to find Eleri's great-grandmother flinging the door open wide to meet them, a worried expression on her face.

Eleri wondered if maybe this visit hadn't put that fold in Grandmere's brows permanently. She had not planned on involving her great-grandmother in this hunt. In fact, she'd barely even mentioned it, saying only that she wanted to visit and stay at her house. She'd known she'd be welcome. Now she almost wished Grandmere hadn't been so ready to open her doors. Look what Eleri had brought to her doorstep.

Grandmere had even looked left and right before closing the door behind them, as though she were checking for some kind of threat coming down the street.

This case had gotten away from her, Eleri thought. It was so much bigger than she had intended it to be. She sat back on the couch as a loud sigh escaped her. A second later, Donovan plopped down next to her. They looked like wayward teenagers who'd been out too late, even though it was only four in the afternoon.

Grandmere came and sat in front of her, nearly staring her great-grandchild down and then looking the two over as if for cuts and bruises.

"Grandmere, I'm sorry," Eleri started, but she got no further.

Grandmere interrupted her. "Were you followed?" Grandmere was paying no attention to Eleri's apology.

"No," Donovan spoke up confidently. "You have no idea the circles we drove in to make sure that didn't happen, but we were not followed."

Eleri noticed, even if Donovan didn't, that while he was confident they had not been followed, he was also conveying the information that he was confident someone was trying.

Grandmere nodded, looking back and forth between the two of them, and Eleri tried for her apology again, "Grandmere, perhaps Donovan and I should leave."

"No." Again, the woman wouldn't even listen to the suggestion, but Eleri held her hand up.

"Hear me out. I did not intend to bring this to your doorstep. I thought when I came—" She was surprised that her throat clogged up a little bit. The words were harder to get out than she'd imagined. "I thought when I came that I would go to the branch office, and that the DNA testing would tell me the bones that I had followed to New Orleans belonged to Emmaline. I thought I would go to where they'd been found and dig up whatever information I could."

Grandmere nodded slowly, this time seeming to absorb the words.

"Did you know that's why I came, Grandmere?"

Grandmere nodded again, though her words were slightly different than her acquiescence. "Yes, though I know you've come several times over the years. And that you've gone around the city looking for clues. But as I understand it, in the past, you never truly found anything."

Eleri shook her head. "How much do you know, Grandmere, about Emmaline—about how long she lived?"

To her side, in the corner of her vision, Eleri could see Donovan looking between the two of them. She felt his urge to jump up and leave the conversation, to let it be a private family matter, but she reached out and placed the palm of her hand over the back of his for just a moment. It was nothing that would force him to stay in his seat, but it urged him to do so. Though the case was hers and hers alone, he'd put himself in the center of it. He'd sensed she was in danger and had come immediately. He deserved to know the background.

Grandmere was sitting on the coffee table in front of them.

With a slight bit of effort, she heaved her large frame up and moved over to the side chair. She often sat there. In fact, Eleri wasn't sure she'd ever seen the woman sitting on the small couch that she and Donovan now occupied. Grandmere looked comfortable, which was good, because the conversation to come was going to be difficult.

"When Emmaline disappeared," Grandmere began, not looking at either of them, "I was frantic. I looked everywhere I could."

"What does that mean?" Eleri asked, having no idea how Grandmere would "look" from three states away. Surely her great-grandmother had not been out in her boots with a search party, cutting grids through swampland. Had she put up signs? Had she phone-banked? All those things were normal in that situation to Eleri, but not to Grandmere.

This time, her great-grandmother turned and looked her in the eye. "I scryed. I went to all my friends. I had them scry, too. But wherever Emmaline had gone, it was dark."

Eleri frowned. "I never got that impression. I sensed that she was actually okay. It may be why I didn't look for her harder."

Donovan turned and looked at Eleri then, and this time his hand moved to the top of hers, a gesture, not of keeping her in place, but of comfort.

"By dark," Grandmere continued, "I don't mean that Emmaline was in the dark or that things were bad for her. I mean, there was a wall. Whoever took her knew how to stop us from looking."

That hit Eleri hard. For all these years, merely that her sister had been kidnapped. Then she had died before Eleri had gone to Quantico, before Eleri had learned too much. Until that time, Eleri had seen Emmaline in her dreams. She'd seen Emmaline growing and changing. She'd spoken with her sister. They'd run through the woods and played together, in the dreams. Emmaline had shown her a few things, and only occasionally did Eleri get glimpses of anything sinister or evil. In many ways, it seemed Emmaline was growing up as a happy child.

Those dreams were the only reason Eleri survived what she found when she studied human trafficking during her Quantico training—and when she'd learned what the protocol was for a missing child of eight. She did not share it with Grandmere now, though she didn't doubt Grandmere understood what happened to pretty eight-year-old girls who were kidnapped, particularly when they were blond-haired, blue-eyed, and from wealthy families.

"I told myself, as I saw her getting older—" Eleri paused, realizing that to Grandmere, it was not a revelation that Emmaline had gotten older after she'd been taken, that she had not died right away. It was also no revelation to Grandmere that Eleri knew this.

Sensing that and understanding there was no need to speak of it, Eleri continued. "I saw her getting older, and I saw her happy. I saw her playing. She wore clean clothes. She ran around barefoot. I got occasional glimpses of scary things, but overall, nothing major. Emmaline herself told me not to worry. For whatever reason, I was never quite able to ask where she was or how I could come and get her."

Grandmere nodded again, still staring into the distance. "That's because you weren't allowed to ask, child."

Eleri had only now just begun understanding. "Is that like when I tried to look inside Darcelle? I wanted to see where she was going, where she'd been, but I couldn't learn anything about her?"

Grandmere nodded. "You smacked a wall, didn't you?"

It was interesting, Eleri thought, that Grandmere not only described it, but used the same terms she had used when she experienced it.

"There was always a wall around Emmaline," Grandmere said. "And the wall only began to come down after Emmaline died."

Eleri leaned forward. "What about Mama? What did Mama do? Did she not feel any of this? It seems like it runs through our blood, Grandmere, and Mama's blood is between yours and mine." Eleri heard her voice almost cracking. She was no longer an FBI agent relaying facts, no longer just a granddaughter asking questions. Now, she was worried, frightened, and unsure. Her own mother was at stake, and she'd already lost her sister.

"Nathalie was—" Grandmere started once then tried again, this time with a sigh. "Nathalie was something else. Nathalie's powers lay mostly in denial. You're absolutely correct. She has everything you have. No," Grandmere said, "I take that back. You and your sister also have a lot from your father's side of the family."

Eleri and Donovan both nodded at that. That made sense, she thought.

"Nathalie did not have Hale and Eames blood. Nathalie did not have Llewellyn running through her veins—but somehow, she had managed to pick the man who would make her daughters even stronger than she was," Grandmere said. "She wanted nothing to do with this life, and she managed to find a man who, on the surface, looked as far away from it as she wanted to be. Yet underneath it all, he was dug in even deeper than maybe she was."

Eleri had not thought of it that way before. She'd heard of her parents' history as a love story. They'd met, taken one look at each other, and had been together ever since. Blue blood colonial Thomas Hale Eames had taken one look at Nathalie Beaumont and decided he had to have her. He had seen an African-American beauty who faked being mainline very well and he'd understood that she would fit into his life the way he wanted a wife to fit. More than that, Eleri thought, the two did truly seem a love match—not just a societal one.

When Emmaline disappeared, her parents had come together in a way she'd not seen in other families. It didn't seem to change the fact, though, that over the years her mother had grown distant and cold—which didn't seem to change the fact that Thomas Hale Eames loved Nathalie Beaumont Eames with all his heart.

A thought occurred to Eleri. "Speaking of bloodlines, my bloodlines are strong and strange," she said to Grandmere. Grandmere only nodded. "But they're the same as Emmaline's."

Donovan's head snapped toward hers, and she understood he was thinking what she was.

"Grandmere," she asked, "do you think that had anything to do with why Emmaline disappeared?"

Grandmere looked at her sagely. "I'm confident of it."

34

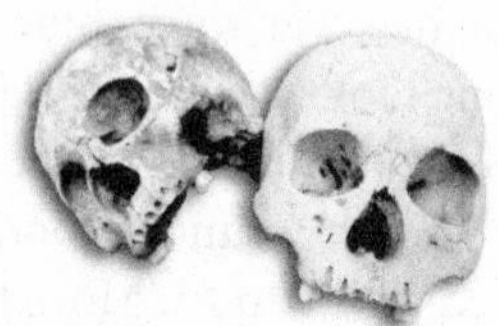

Eleri sat back. The words had come as a shock to her heart, strong and sharp.

"But Grandmere'" she began cautiously, "if someone took Emmaline for her bloodline ... what about me?"

Grandmere shook her head. "Do you really want to hear this?"

"No," Eleri replied suddenly. "But I have to know, if I'm going to find her. If I'm going to bring her home, then I need to know everything."

Grandmere leaned forward, elbows on her knees. It was a position Eleri wasn't used to seeing her great-grandmother in. She clasped her hands and looked at her great-granddaughter intensely. "Eleri, child, there is nothing to bring home."

"I can bring home her bones," Eleri said. "I know that they're out there."

"Yes. I, too, am confident they are," Grandmere replied. "But Emmaline has been gone for more than a decade."

"I know," Eleri said. "And my mother needs to know that. My father needs to know that. They're still waiting for her to come home. They haven't healed. And to be frank, neither have I."

Grandmere started to open her mouth.

"And neither have you!" Eleri cried. "Whatever happened to her, it wasn't okay—and, well, I need to know."

Grandmere nodded and sat back. "I think you're right about the bloodlines. I've always been confident that's why they took her."

Donovan leaned forward then, too. The conversation and the tension in the tiny room was getting tight as all three of them ratcheted in.

"Anyone who took that girl for her bloodlines took her because they knew what those bloodlines were worth. It means they used her for something," Grandmere continued, her gaze in the middle distance.

Eleri nodded. "That's probably why I had visions of her with blood on her hands."

Grandmere nodded. "I never saw that, but it makes sense. Emmaline was powerful. Like I said, I'd expected her to inherit the family line. However, there's something else that you should know."

Grandmere paused, but when she started again, her words still rambled with the difficulty of speaking them. "Well, the good news is that you're an adult now, and it wouldn't be easy to take you. But the fact is, the two of you are the same. Emmaline was the one I thought would lead the family—not because of her blood, but because of her temperament. It was never for you. But if it came down to blood and power, I don't know that there was a distinction between the two of you. The day that Emmaline disappeared, I got the clear impression it could have been either of you."

Eleri inhaled sharply. It had not occurred to her that was a real possibility. Though looking at it as an FBI agent over the years, she'd wondered why anyone would take an eight-year-old girl, and the answers to that question could not be good. However, no matter what those reasons were, they would have made Eleri just as vulnerable.

Emmaline had always been more serene than Eleri. She'd always been more pliant, friendly, and willing to please. But it had not come from stupidity or lack of caring. Emmaline had not been malleable. Even at eight, she'd been sharp.

There were family members Emmaline would not go near. Eleri had never understood why. Perhaps Emmaline was a little more in touch with the feelings she had earlier in her life. But despite those differences, the two little girls were—for all intents and purposes—the same.

It struck Eleri then that it could have been she who was

kidnapped, raised by another family, and murdered at the age of seventeen. That was a harsh pill to swallow, because while it frightened the crap out of her, she desperately wished it had been the case.

Grandmere shook her head. "No, you can't go there," she said, clearly understanding the direction Eleri's thoughts had wandered.

Donovan took over the conversation then, realizing they'd hit a point where they probably shouldn't go any further. At least, he knew, Eleri needed time to digest what she learned.

Maybe Grandmere and Donovan needed time to digest this new information, Eleri thought.

This time Donovan went for the basics and talked logistics. "Grandmere, we need to do research. We need to interview you about what you know, and we need to do it less like a conversation at the couch. We need to have recordings and make notes. We need to treat it like a case."

Grandmere shook her head. "This is no FBI case. This is my family."

"I understand," Donovan said. "But what I need you to understand is that Eleri and I are very good at working cases. So while there won't be FBI involvement, we're going to work it that way."

Grandmere's lips pressed together. "The Feds couldn't find Emmaline before," she announced, clearly disappointed in the agents who had searched for her great-granddaughter.

Donovan managed to keep his expression neutral. "Well, the science is a lot better these days, and they didn't have a team like ours."

Eleri smiled at the thought. It was good to know Donovan understood what a great team they were. Though neither of them mentioned that much, they worked especially well together, and she was aware that Westerfield knew this, too. However, it felt good to hear her partner understand what they were. Then again, he'd risked his own career to come here.

When Grandmere nodded her concession to Donovan's request to record their interviews, he lobbed another request at her. "We need internet connection. Eleri and I need to get into FBI databases, and we need to research what we can from right here. I have information from Wade, and Eleri needs to be able to get in touch with him. Right now, I have my phone, but it's not secure. Right now, the only internet access I can get is at the library or at the bakery or Starbucks down the street." He motioned out the window, but his expression made it clear he didn't think conducting his research in public was suitable.

"Grandmere," he said—Eleri loved the fact that he used that term as though it was the woman's given name—"If we need to use internet anywhere other than this location, we will not be secure. And if we work from the FBI branch office, we run the risk of anything we find becoming a federal case."

Grandmere nodded. "You want to set up one of your internet routers in my house." The tone of her voice told Eleri exactly how much she disliked the idea. So Eleri was shocked when Grandmere added, "Okay."

Eleri blinked and looked at her grandmother. The easy acquiescence began to pull her out of her shock at what she'd just learned about her little sister's kidnapping. "Okay?" she asked. "I mean, we need it. But I know you don't like Wi-Fi in your house."

"I don't." Grandmere's tone was matter-of-fact. "I don't like digital technology. I don't like what it lets in. However, I can't protect you at the FBI branch. This house is the safest place you guys can be, and I want you here as often as possible. Protecting you while you're out is so much harder."

Eleri had not thought of it that way. She did realize that Grandmere had been casting spells around the house, of course, and that she'd been casting them on Eleri and Donovan. She looked to Grandmere. "How much work is this costing you?"

"That does not matter, child," Grandmere said. "None of that matters. How is it you think you got home after going to the Dauphine's house and digging up bones in their graveyard? Their spells are powerful, but so are mine. Had you only suffered from theirs, you might not have made it home for several days."

Eleri accepted that. She understood the surprise that the Dauphine sisters had felt when she'd walked through their gates. As it turned out, she didn't have the magical powers to counteract a spell. Grandmere did.

Donovan stood up abruptly, headed into the back room, and brought out his go bag. He laid it on the table and started pulling things out. Apparently, he'd removed his clothing earlier and put it into the drawers. Now the pieces inside rattled, and Eleri saw that he was already getting started.

Donovan turned to Grandmere. "Look, I want you to understand I haven't turned any of this on, but I had it with me because we needed to set up mobile hotspots in Montana. Now I need to do it here as well."

"This technology," Eleri told Grandmere, "is as secure as it can be."

Grandmere nodded, and Eleri understood that Grandmere's understanding of "secure technology" was that the words were an oxymoron. But Eleri was ready to welcome any security she could get her hands on, whether it was the FBI's or Grandmere's.

Donovan continued setting up on the table. Eleri knew that most people set up routers in the corner of the room or tucked under them the furniture. Donovan was setting this up smack in the middle, where Grandmere could see it and know that technology was not invading her home from the corners. *If he did it on purpose, it was a kind gesture,* Eleri thought.

In moments, his laptop was open and he had begun his research. Grandmere stood. "Best I start fixing dinner, now," she said. And slowly, things began to turn toward normal.

Eleri stayed on the couch for just a few more minutes trying to absorb the blows that had come her way. But she knew they weren't done coming.

Donovan motioned to her. "El, you've got to come see this." He pointed to his computer screen.

35

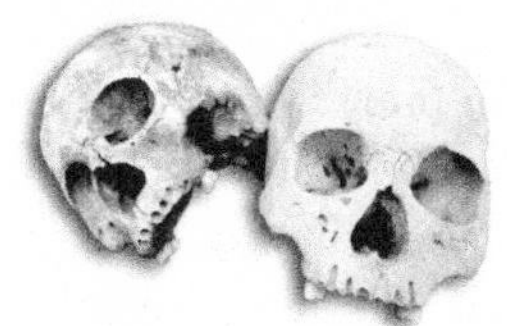

Not sure what she would see, Eleri forced herself to walk over to where Donovan pointed to his computer screen.

He'd wasted no time. Grandmere had said yes, and within minutes, Donovan was researching. What he showed Eleri on his screen was land tracts, which she had not expected. She frowned at him.

"Well, I wanted to find the Dauphine home," said, looking up at her. "This building says it's a courtyard home. That matches what you've talked about. It's also inside a radius of walking distance from where Royal Street and Mystic Vudu are." He mentioned that the property was deeded to a "Tempeste Dauphine" and a few other bits of information that had gotten him this lead.

Eleri nodded along, following his reasoning. He'd even pulled up a street view and given her the street name. It all suddenly sparked her memory.

"Yes! That's it."

"So take a look, Eleri. This is an interesting block. Most of the other blocks have a street that cuts through, with houses facing each direction." He tapped the laptop screen. "But here, the street stops and picks up at the next block, almost as if two blocks were fused for this one, creating much larger-than-normal tracts of land—slightly over twice as large as the others in the neighborhood. And look at this house," he added, pointing to a different spot on his screen.

Eleri followed where he led, but she was thinking that the courtyard home's size was deceptive because of its shape. The houses next to it had not had the courtyard center. Looking down from the top, in a birds-eye view, it was easy to see that the Dauphine home sat on a tract at least twice as wide as the others. The depth also pushed into the yards of the homes that butted up against the back of it. She sucked in a breath before saying anything out loud. "Donovan, the amount of land that they have in the middle of the city is incredible."

Grandmere walked in then. "The Dauphines are wealthy," she said, "but I would not count on where that wealth comes from."

Eleri took that as a solemn warning and nodded. Then she decided she should get out her own research.

So the Dauphines had a lot of land. She wasn't quite sure what Donovan was getting at. But as he soon pointed out, "Look El, there's space back here. There's space for whatever they want to be doing. The courtyard—the way the house is designed, the way the entry doors are—it would be easy for several families to live there and go relatively unnoticed."

Eleri headed back into her bedroom, retrieved her own laptop, and plugged it in next to Donovan rather than using the batteries. The first thing she did was log into FBI databases, wanting to get as much information as possible on Mackenzie Burke, the girl missing from Nebraska. Eleri dug up what she could of Burke's case as well as her parents and lineage. Her ancestry was the most fascinating to Eleri—not the mix of her heritage, per se, but that this girl had shared the same mix as Eleri and Emmaline. And how had the Burke family wound up in Nebraska? Eleri wondered. They had Haitian bloodlines and early colonist bloodlines, yet they lived in the middle of the country.

After only thirty minutes of searching, sure enough, the name Hale appeared in the girl's paternal lineage. Eleri almost smiled. That was certainly the second-cousin link. The girl looked like Eleri and Emmaline had, and she had the same genetic heritage—because it had come from the same family.

Eleri looked further but found she had to request records to get some of the maternal names going back over the generations. In a short while, she had looked up everything she could about Mackenzie Burke's disappearance and family lineage. She'd filed requests to find the missing pieces—putting her fingers in many different pots—and she would simply have to wait until someone stirred one of them.

Donovan turned to her, having sat idle at his keyboard for several minutes watching her. He sniffed the air. Only then, Eleri noticed that good smells were coming from the kitchen as dinner simmered on the other side of the wall. She was grateful for something as normal as dinner. She desperately needed some normal.

"I emailed Wade," he said. "He just got back to me. Do you want to look?"

No, not really, Eleri thought, but nodded her agreement and scooted the chair closer. "What about?"

"The Lobomau in New Orleans, of course." Didn't Donovan already know about that? Hadn't Wade already given him that information? She must have let that question show on her face, because he answered it immediately.

"Well, before we were looking at numbers. Numbers of wolves, numbers of Lobomau, numbers moving over certain years. This time, I want to know what parts of the city are involved. I want to know who Cabot is and who he's related to, for example. I want to know who came with him. So I asked Wade for as much of that as he could gather."

"And he has it?" Eleri asked. It seemed quite specific, the kind of information people always worry about the government getting its hands on.

"Almost," Donovan said. "Remember, the family kept records. They kept records of births and deaths and who shifted and who didn't."

The family records were more extensive than Eleri had realized. That detail might have been the reason for the raid on the Ozarks and the one several years ago outside Billings, Montana. If they could hunt down and locate individual wolves with the kind of data the family held—well, it was incredibly useful to her and Donovan, and incredibly dangerous to those being tracked. She was surprised more of the family members hadn't voted *against* keeping all that documentation.

So it turned out Wade had not sent Donovan everything he'd asked about. But he sent the bits and pieces he had, so the two of them could begin work. She got Cabot's full name. Cabot Lucerne Salzani had moved to New Orleans almost a decade ago.

The Salzani name indicated he was Italian, though like Wade, he didn't really look it. The family must have married into other families and mixed ethnicities in the U.S. Once again, Eleri dove back into the databases and pulled everything she could on the Salzani lineage. Although much of it Wade had already supplied, there was more to find. In fact, the Salzani name went back and connected with de Gottardi a couple of times, making Cabot some distant cousin.

Along with Cabot, three brothers had come to New Orleans in short order. One was Caspian. Younger by a good seven years, he was listed as not shifting. The other two were both wolves, one older and one younger than Cabot, but both within a year-and-a-half of Cabot's age. Eleri wondered if that meant anything as they had reached adulthood. Surely, Caspian had been the odd man out when they were children. Eleri wondered if that meant anything as they had reached adulthood. She almost smiled, but pushed the thought aside, thinking it had little to do with how they would function now.

Carson was slightly older than Cabot, and Cameron slightly younger. Eleri noticed the cute use of consistent "C" names for the boys, which seemed funny given that Cabot was such an asshole. She checked Wade's records on Cabot as well and was disturbed to find a long list of infractions against the families in the Ozarks before he'd even come to New Orleans. Cabot Salzani wasn't that old. It meant he'd been perpetrating crimes as a teenager and the de Gottardi group had kicked him out. Perhaps the Lobomau had not found him so much as he had found the Lobomau.

Typing his name into the FBI database shocked her further as even more information came up. Not only was he a bad wolf, he was a bad citizen in general. He had an arrest record long enough to scroll well off the page, and this particular list was limited to more major crimes, like felonies. It didn't begin to cover petty infractions like speeding tickets and parking violations. Eleri frowned at the screen and clicked that link.

Cabot had a number of parking violations, but interestingly enough, they weren't from all over the city. The majority clustered in just one district. She pulled the individual locations of the tickets. Next, she pulled up a map and scanned the positions of his immediate violations. Sure, he'd parked illegally in a few random places, she discovered as she checked closely—including a few times in front of the Dauphine home. But the vast majority appeared within a three-block radius in a different section of town. The parking times didn't reveal any standard pattern. Eleri began to wonder what might be there that was so important.

"Look, Donovan." She motioned to the map and explained about the parking tickets she'd tracked.

Donovan frowned and noted the address on one of the Post-it notes he'd stacked next to him, ready to jot things down as he went. She was still looking at the location, trying to figure out from the map where it might be, when her email pinged. Flipping over screens, she popped the message up and found that somebody had gotten back to her with more genealogy information about Mackenzie Burke.

Three generations back was the name Dauphine.

36

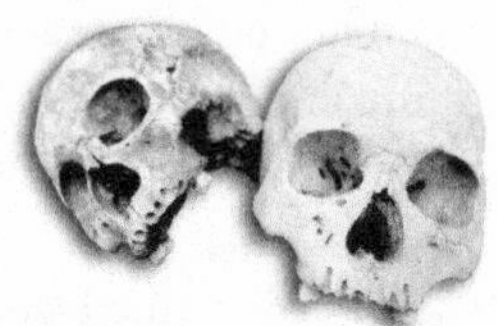

Darcelle closed the shop and followed the path home. It was the first time she had truly tried to close early without something as disheartening as an illness driving her. As she'd locked the door behind her, she was shocked to discover it worked. Testing her luck, she stepped off the path, but was pushed harshly back by unseen hands. Once again, today was not her day.

She cursed her Momma fluently under her breath as she headed down the street. She made it one more block before she turned around and headed back to the Mystic Vudu.

Again, this was something new. In all this time, she'd never tried to turn around and retrace her steps. She wondered—had she ever tried to avoid going into the shop in the morning? She didn't think she'd ever tested that water. And she thought again, what would happen to her if the shop failed? She'd mused on it often, but truly didn't know. Despite the fact that her Momma had tied her neatly to the store, Momma had been gone for more than a year. Yet Darcelle remained stuck under the spells the old woman had cast on her—and she'd had damn near enough. She'd had enough of all the bullshit *years* ago, which was the reason Momma had tied her to the store in the first place. Darcelle wanted to leave. So her mother made sure she could not.

But today, she headed back to the store, unlocked the back door, and stomped her way through the place. She should have been meticulous, but she wasn't. Grabbing a cloth bag from under the front desk where she rang out customers, she slid through the store like a snake, swiping things off the shelves, dumping them into her bag, collecting everything she might possibly need to finally break free.

Fuck this shit, she thought adding both tansy and belladonna to her bag.

Fuck this shit, she thought again, bypassing the displays of white ribbon and heading straight for black. She wanted—needed—black ribbon that had been soaked in an alcohol mix and infused with tiny crystal pieces and wolf's bane. She was done with all this crap.

Slinging the heavy bag over her shoulder, she repeated the process of letting herself out the back door and locking it. When she turned and faced the alley, she saw Carson standing on the other side.

Fucking wolf, she thought. Clearly, her attitude had gone to hell.

"I came to walk you home," he said with a crude smile. His expression fell short, but he seemed to want her to think of this almost as though he were a boyfriend or a family member coming to protect his one of his womenfolk.

Darcelle knew the difference. He was not protecting her. He was corralling her, making sure she came home and stayed on the path. Still, the very thought that she had rattled her sisters delighted her. They had sent Carson to make sure she stayed on her path. He sisters knew well and good what Momma had tied her to. Momma had told them she was doing it. They all knew what the spell entailed, and that had made Darcelle hate her sisters a little bit more.

They wanted the money from the shop. They wanted the shop to run—it was an excellent front—but they didn't want to make the effort to actually run it. So they'd all stood back and let Momma "bequeath" the shop to Darcelle. And many times, as Darcelle had just done, they'd walked into the store and plucked from her goods to supply their own spells.

Even then, the magic wasn't always for the family. It wasn't always for anything reasonable. She'd watched repeatedly as Alesse had come in, pulled things from the shelves, dismantled her stock and more, all for whatever personal gain or revenge she wanted that day. Her sisters had been using her for a long time.

Why was she the one who'd been tied down? It was because she had bucked all restrictions when Momma had been alive. Her sisters —hideous creatures, just like Momma was—had always been allowed to run wild and free. Not Darcelle. They had behaved far worse than she ever had, but perhaps that had been the issue. Momma had approved of what her sisters were.

Interestingly enough, when Momma had bucked her own parents, the family had nearly disowned her. Tempeste Dauphine had wanted nothing to do with the Dauphine name. She'd felt the family was amiss in their decision. And being as strong as she was, and as stubborn as she was, she spent five years honing her skills. Darcelle still remembered being small and her older sister Alesse remembered it, too—though Gisele and Lafae had been so tiny that they probably didn't understand exactly what her mother had done. Tempeste brought her four daughters to live in the Dauphine family home, and Darcelle had never asked exactly what had happened to her grandparents.

"Thank you, Carson." She turned to him, confident that he would know that her thanks were sincere only in the way that they benefited her. If everyone else was going to be terrible and be awarded freedom for it, then Darcelle could be terrible, too.

Carson dropped her at the gate. She could tell he hadn't been on the way to the house, or on any mission of his own. That meant only one thing: her sisters had sent him to fetch her. Darcelle wondered now if she would have to fight not just Momma's spell, but theirs, too.

There was only one way to find out.

She passed through the living room, finding Lafae lying on the couch and watching some afternoon crap on TV.

"You're home early," Lafae commented in her droll tone, not taking her eyes off the screen.

"You're home always," Darcelle replied, even though that wasn't exactly true. Lafae wandered about plenty, causing her own mischief. She just didn't have a job.

Not waiting for a response, Darcelle headed up to her own room, briefly opening the door to Alesse's room to see if anything had changed. It had not. The room was still in disarray, the mattress still off the side of the bed. That told her that Alesse had not slept here, but didn't necessarily mean that her sister hadn't been back. It would be just like Alesse to come into the room, see it was tossed, grab a few things, and leave, never letting her sisters know she was safe. Darcelle decided that, at this point, she didn't care.

Darcelle's own bed was made, though whether that was something Momma had instilled in her, or spelled on her, or just something innate to her own characteristic, she didn't know.

She looked around, wondering what changes might be wrought with her spells. The house was beautiful. The courtyard was full of magic—both dark and light—that she tapped into. Her sisters were here. While she hated them sometimes, they were the only family she had ever known. Still, it was time to find out what she was like on her own.

Darcelle dumped the bag from the shop out on her bed and went to work.

37

Eleri and Donovan worked through the next day, not leaving Grandmere's house. With all the secure logins they had, they had access to multiple FBI and government databases from where they sat at the dining area table.

Grandmere tended to eat at the small, Formica-top folding table in her kitchen. The formal dining table in this section of the great room seemed to be used mostly for casting spells and meeting guests. This meant that Eleri and Donovan's Wi-Fi hotspot—their laptops, tablets, and other assorted technological devices—sat between bundles of herbs, blocks of minerals, crystal spheres, and various earth substances Eleri wasn't quite sure she could identify. There were also many more scraps of old fabric. Twine and twigs sat in tiny piles, waiting for Grandmere's deft fingers to pick them up and create something.

In the meantime, Eleri and Donovan tapped away at their keyboards. No guests showed up that day. Eleri wondered if that was coincidental or if Grandmere had managed to keep everyone away so the two of them could work. She didn't ask, just kept her head in her computer and took copious notes.

She let Donovan interview Grandmere in between making meals. Though Eleri didn't try to eavesdrop on the interviews, the house was so small that she could hear what Grandmere said. At times, she stopped and sat back, wondering if Donovan or Grandmere would notice that her keys had stopped clicking for a while. She listened to the stories.

It was shocking what she learned. She learned things about the first Emmaline, her grandmother, and what she'd been like growing up. She heard about Nathalie had been like. That was interesting. Her mother had been a tomboy, nearly kicked out of the public school system for casting spells on other children. It wasn't unusual for little girls in New Orleans to be referred to as witches, especially if their last name was Remy.

Young Nathalie had embraced the craft. So who knew if she'd actually cast anything on any of the other children? Lord knew, Grandmere claimed, she'd not taught the child any of it yet—because she knew Nathalie was so hot-headed, she couldn't be trusted with even a small amount. But Nathalie acted as though she had some kind of magic, and that was enough to worry her teachers and some of the other parents.

Grandmere laughed about it now, but Eleri easily imagined a younger Grandmere not thinking that was so funny.

Turning back to the task she was supposed to be working on, Eleri gathered emails, many from Wade, and when she found a name that sounded familiar, she would email back to him and ask how that person was listed with the database—whether the person was listed as a wolf or upgraded to the status to Lobomau. Too many of the names she found in New Orleans had the L next to them when Wade returned the email.

Shit, she thought. She was putting together a mental picture, much as Wade and Donovan had—but the more she learned, the more she thought their original number had drastically undersold the situation. The Lobomau were being drawn here like magnets. The problem was—given what she now knew—she had no idea if they were being openly recruited or if they had simply decided to come to New Orleans on what they believed was a whim.

More than once, she tossed her pen down onto her notepad in frustration. Everything added up, and nothing did. Mackenzie Burke, the kidnapped girl, was both a Hale and a Dauphine. No wonder her lineage looked so much like Eleri's and Emmaline's. The exact mix of New England colonizer and African-American, with Haitian influence, was stunning—but perhaps it wasn't as odd as Eleri had originally thought.

But why had the Burkes been in Nebraska? She'd been looking for answers during a good portion of the morning, but nothing had given her anything to work with yet. While she waited for return emails with database searches and birth and death records, she watched satellite images of the Dauphine house. She hoped she could use them to puzzle together when the women came and left. Was someone always there guarding it? It was difficult to tell just from an aerial shot. Even the courtyard was shaded by the one grand tree and several smaller ones, so it was often difficult to ascertain, from the angle she had, whether someone was home—and if so, who it might be.

It appeared none of the Dauphine women owned any cars, or at least none they parked at the house. Perhaps they went on foot everywhere. The satellite passed by and took intermittent shots, so it wasn't as though she had cameras watching every move like some kind of reality television. Eleri was not able to see anything inside the house, and she only occasionally caught glimpses of the occupants, usually a still image of someone coming and going. As it was a residential street, there was nothing like a bank nearby or a business that would have a security camera watching the street. If that existed, she might subpoena the footage—not that she had any power to do that while she was off the job.

Right now, she had zero official power, and she intended to keep it that way. Having no power meant no one had power over her. It meant she was her own authority, no longer a cog in the FBI system. She'd been waiting all day for Westerfield to call to ask why she and Donovan were using FBI information and databases so freely. Surely, he was aware of all of their logins, but no call had come. For that, Eleri was grateful.

Donovan came back to the big table and joined her. He was mostly silent, but he kept his laptop pushed up against hers so they could look side to side and see what the other was doing. Grandmere came out with lunch and—where the spell-making tools that she had out had initially been shoved aside to make room for laptops and towers—now everything was shoved aside one more time to make room for bowls of rice, steaming chunks of meat, and some kind of red sauce that Eleri could not name, but could smell the magic of.

Grandmere served it with brown bottles that she pulled the lids off of using a crank opener.

Eleri had frowned at the obvious alcohol. It was so unlike her great-grandmother.

"Trade," Grandmere said in answer to the unasked question. "Payment from a client."

Beer? Eleri wondered. She didn't think she'd ever seen Grandmere drink beer, but she put nothing past the old woman.

"Pear cider," Grandmere said, and Eleri caught a hint of the smell coming from the open neck of the bottle. Donovan surely had known what it was as soon as the lids had come off. Sometimes, she envied him that ability.

She was halfway through the bowl, watching cars go by on the street for something to distract her. She was working to not pay attention to the pings on her computer as emails and information and records came in.

Her hand shot out suddenly, grasping onto Donovan's upper arm. "That's the third time I think I've seen that car go by."

Her spoon clacked down into the bowl as she strained to see where the car went without standing up and giving herself away. On the other side of her, Grandmere went very still as she looked out the window at the white sedan. Having spent some of her morning in the kitchen at the back of the house, Grandmere had not been sitting in this position, looking out onto the street.

"Third time, you say?" Grandmere asked and Eleri only nodded in response. "He should not be able to do that."

Pushing her bowl aside, Eleri scooted over, lining herself up once again with her laptop. A few key strokes and she pulled up state IDs. Those pictures were easy to differentiate. Looking into the car through the slightly tinted windows made it harder to distinguish individual features. Still, he'd turned and looked at the house, and she suspected she could identify him.

"Well," she concluded, "it looks like either Cabot or Cameron." One of the Salzani brothers was casing the house. Donovan peeked over at her computer, his own bowl still warming his hands, his spoon still moving back and forth to his mouth despite this new development.

"Looks like," he said between bites.

Grandmere, too, spooned the last several bites of her smaller serving and stood to walk away from the table. "You two stay here. I have more work to do on this house. He shouldn't have been able to pass that many times."

When Donovan had finished the last of his food, he turned to Eleri. "I think we need to go sniff out some Lobomau."

38

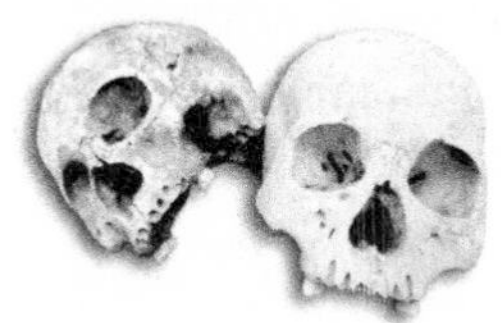

Donovan drove his rental car this time. One, he wanted to turn the engine over and let it run a little bit. Two, he didn't want to let it sit in the heat and the sun for too long—although he had to admit he regretted his decision to drive the moment he sat in the driver's seat.

The steering wheel burned his hands and, despite the fact that he was wearing pants, his legs tried to fry like eggs on the seat. The car didn't even have leather, just rental car fabric, but it was black. In New Orleans, the combination left him with what he suspected might be burn marks.

He had adopted Eleri's aim at casual clothing. Lord knew, they'd tried on a variety of different looks over the last handful of months. He'd sported every outfit from obvious federal agent, wearing his suit and earpiece, to decked out like a SWAT member, to trying to blend in with small town Texas. Now, they weren't trying to blend in or protect themselves from anything but the humidity, the heat, and the sun.

Now Donovan, too, was wearing lightweight pants he'd picked up and a tee shirt he hoped would reflect the heat as much as possible. None of this was anything he could expense to the FBI, but that was okay. As he'd reminded himself earlier, he'd be able to get another job as a medical examiner if this one didn't pan out. He could make do;

he'd saved and saved for years. It hadn't yielded much, but it had been his only security when he started.

Now he had friends. He truly didn't doubt that, if his money ran out, Eleri would offer him FoxHaven for however long he wanted to run out on the beach, or Bell Point Farm, where he could run in the forest. He'd be okay, he told himself. He had friends. The thought almost made him smile, even as the backs of his legs sizzled while he waited for the air conditioning to kick in.

He watched as Eleri scooted her own car out of the way and parked on the grass before climbing in with him. She held a paper map in front of her on which she'd drawn out the area where she wanted to go.

They'd both taken to turning their phones off and having them on only if they needed them. It wasn't as if Grandmere was going to reach out. And if Westerfield did, Donovan wasn't sure he wanted to hear it. He was on leave, after all. Having his phone turned off was an excellent excuse. Walter, maybe Wade, maybe GJ—those were the only ones he wanted to hear from, and he would turn his cell on and check periodically. This way, if the phones were ever stolen, they wouldn't let anyone know where he and Eleri had been. With them off, any hackerware added would not be able to track them as they headed around the city. Like today, when they were heading out to see the area Cabot had kept visiting.

Eleri held up the map toward Donovan. "Do you see where you need to go?"

He'd paid enough attention the last time she was driving to not worry about it too much, and he backed out of the driveway only using his fingertips on the steering wheel. Gingerly, he made turns for the first few blocks until the entire car cooled down.

"It isn't just that he goes here," Eleri commented. "It's that he goes here and stays for long enough to get parking tickets."

"Or he parked illegally in the first place," Donovan pointed out.

Eleri nodded. Both were possibilities, he'd thought. They hadn't been able to tell without driving and looking for themselves what the parking meters looked like or how they were run. She'd brought coins and a disposable credit card, as they wanted to be able to pay the meters when they got there and not incur any of the charges that Cabot was known for.

Had the meters been changed over to credit card readers? Or were they old enough to still take coins, where you could hear them clinking into the box inside? As they drove closer, Eleri rattled the change in her pockets, a sound Donovan could hear, though probably she couldn't. He recognized the kind of area they were heading into before she did.

This was an older area, full of graveyards and houses made from marble and granite. The houses were bigger, but also older and rundown. Black had creeped into the cracks and run with rain, identifying each original seam and any new ones that were unintended. All the places the water had seeped were now highlighted in stark relief against the old, cold buildings.

Yet another cemetery created an anchor amid the houses. They turned right to curve around it. Every neighborhood had a graveyard, it seemed, in New Orleans. It was the age and care that interested him. This one had a look similar to the houses. The old money had left the area a good while ago, leaving the current residents to fall on harder times. Maybe it had happened when Katrina had come through.

They parked several blocks away and walked in. The only area they could find for reasonable parking was a lot in front of a strip mall. Once again, they headed inside a convenience store for drinks. Donovan thought it was nearly impossible to stay hydrated enough in Louisiana. He felt his only hope of doing so was to absorb the humidity like a frog. He poured himself a fountain coke, trying to stay light on the ice, thinking it would melt and water down his drink far too quickly. Unfortunately, given the heat and the pressure of the air, he would still drink it.

He looked at Eleri with her Gatorade bottle. "You know you don't need that right? Water is just as good."

She raised an eyebrow at him. It was always fun to know something Eleri didn't.

He added, "You don't need that many electrolytes unless you're an athlete playing a game or participating in an actual competition."

"Hm," she said, but she didn't put the bottle down. "Water doesn't taste like winning." She said it with a grin, and he laughed at her.

They were walking down the street already guzzling their drinks when they made it to the corner and the first point where Cabot had gotten a ticket. Looking around, they checked the paper, almost like they were tourists with maps—which, in a way, they were.

Eleri had marked each of the points to be checked. Cabot had only gotten a ticket here once, and Donovan guessed this was slightly farther away from wherever the man had been visiting. When nothing in the neighborhood popped as someplace Cabot might frequent, they continued along.

They hit a second of the spots, and then a third, before finally coming to a very close cluster of tickets over a number of nearby parking spaces. Eleri pointed to the meters, and Donovan saw that they were the old kind that took coins, just as they predicted.

"Perhaps that was why Cabot got tickets," he told Eleri. "So that makes sense."

"But he comes here all the time. How many times does he have to come here and get a forty- or seventy-dollar ticket before he remembers to bring coins?"

Donovan shrugged. He didn't know the answer to that. He wanted to say Cabot was smarter than that, but that wasn't anything he knew, either. Eleri seemed to think so, but he shrugged again.

They headed to the next spot and the next, chucking their empty cups in a street-side trashcan, the two drinks having disappeared just as quickly as he predicted.

"This is probably the easiest one to get to next." Eleri pointed to a spot on the map. In fact, it wasn't very easy at all. In order to catch all of them, and to catch this anomaly that still managed to statistically make the cluster, it was fastest to cut through a side neighborhood than to head directly toward the location of the bulk of the tickets.

They quickly found themselves in an area that had more little strip malls and shops than homes. A graveyard was behind them once again. The walls around it were high, and as the edges of the houses and apartments crept in, the streets got narrower. The spot where Cabot had his ticket was best reached by heading down an alley, and Donovan and Eleri turned right as Donovan smelled it.

Shit.

Without stopping the momentum of his stride, he thought on his feet. It was probably more dangerous to go back. He reached out and tapped Eleri on the hand several times. It wasn't a prearranged signal, but it was one she immediately understood.

Turning, she looked up at him, concern in her eyes, and he only mouthed the word "Lobomau."

He could tell that she changed the pattern of her steps and made her footfalls slightly softer so that she could listen to what was behind them. But he could hear it well. He wished he could change his skull just enough to flick his ears back and better capture the sounds behind them.

He heard at least three of them. They stayed at their current pace, and Donovan worked his hand toward his hip, closer to the gun he'd slid into the large pocket of his pants. It was a dumb place to carry a weapon—but with the heat, it was the only place the gun could go to be ready if he needed it.

Eleri had kept hers in her purse, and she now slowly slid the zipper back so her hand could reach in. He knew she would have no problem aiming and squeezing the trigger without pulling the gun out. That, at least, might surprise someone. But Donovan's gun would be obvious if he pulled it.

The footsteps were getting closer, and Donovan heard the sounds behind them change rhythm. The followers were gaining on purpose, stepping a little bit heavier. There was no mistaking that the three behind them were not moving randomly, but were trying to catch up.

"Hey, witch!" one of them called, and he knew it was time.

39

Eleri felt her muscles tighten even as she fought to relax them. The best way to go into a fight was to go in loose. The best way to go into a fight was actually not to go into one at all. And she wondered if she and Donovan could talk her way out of this, though the words "Hey, witch" made her think that wouldn't be possible.

She didn't wait for a second invitation. She didn't want to look cowardly or like she was fleeing. Donovan seemed to have the same idea. So she spun around and looked at the first of the men who'd been following them.

It was not Cabot. None of the others was anyone she was supposed to know, either, though she recognized him from the driver's licenses they'd pulled up earlier. So she asked, "Do I know you?"

"You should, *witch*," he growled, the emphasis on the last word as though it were some kind of slur.

"Nah," she said, as relaxed as she could possibly make it sound. "I don't know you at all. You must not be anybody important."

She was goading him, she knew. Beside her, she watched as Donovan tensed. Apparently, he didn't quite approve of her methods. Honestly, neither did she, but the jab had just come out of her mouth. She wanted to ask this man what he called his witch friends if it was such a horrible thing to say, but she held her tongue on that one.

"My name is Carson Salzani." He spoke clearly and cleanly,

although there was definitely an implied threat in the tone. Eleri stared at him, blank-eyed. She did know that name, but he was going to have to follow some of her micro expressions to get it out of her.

She looked up into the corner of space over his shoulder and then shrugged her shoulders again. "No," she said, "It doesn't ring a bell."

"It will."

"Why?" she asked. "Are you going to do something dumb?"

Again, she pulled the corners of her lips up a little, making just the tiniest of smiles. And again, she thought, *Don't poke the wolves.* But it was too late. She had already poked.

"Not dumb," he said, "but you need to stay out of what you've been sticking your hands into—or you might wind up with no hands at all."

"Interesting," she said. "Are you threatening to cut off my hands? You might not want to threaten me."

"You think you're that powerful of a witch?" he asked. "You think your friend here, the wolf, is going to protect you? Maybe you don't know what I am."

This time, she threw her head back and laughed, exposing her throat and doing her very best to demonstrate absolutely no fear. "I don't think I'm that powerful a witch," she said, "but I do think you might be that much of an idiot."

She wanted to tell him that he'd just threatened bodily harm to a federal agent and expand on what classification of crime that was. But she bit her tongue; she was still holding that card for later. "And yes, I do know what you are. My friend here can smell you. Unfortunately, he said you guys smelled even before you came down the block." She wrinkled her nose in distaste. It was impossible to abandon this tactic now, not once she'd started it.

Donovan stayed silent beside her. He knew what she was doing, and he was deciding to stand back, though he was perfectly ready, should things turn south.

Carson came closer, one slow step, then another, and another ... until his face was inches from hers. Behind him, another wolf—one she didn't recognize—curled his lip, revealing a long canine tooth and offered up a growl, as though after all this, that might stop her. Donovan stepped in closer. None of it stopped Carson.

Eleri stood her ground. "What is it that you want, little boy?"

He didn't flinch at the insult, which was a shame. He only told her his list of demands. "You need to stay away from Mystic Vudu. You need to stay away from Darcelle Dauphine."

"Ooh," she asked, "because she and I are such good friends? Does that mean I need to stay away from the other Dauphine sisters too?" She prattled on purpose, her hands sneaking into her purse, and she wondered if he noticed. "Did she ever find her other sister? What was her name? I think she was missing…"

Carson was having none of it. He growled, too, this time. "*Stay away.*"

"Sorry, dude," she said. "You can't tell me where to go in a U.S. city."

"It's *my* city," he said.

She laughed again, despite his closeness, despite the lightning speed at which she knew his claws could emerge and the fact that he could slash her throat if he so decided. He was close enough. There was nothing she could do, and probably nothing Donovan could do, either. But still, she laughed. "Oh, honey, it's not your city. If anything, it's the Dauphine sisters' city."

His open hand came out with lightning speed and smacked against her shoulder, shoving her back a couple of steps. Eleri stumbled. Her right shoulder blade struck Donovan in the side. She hadn't realized he was quite so close. Carson's hit had almost made her spin, but she managed to stay on her feet.

Still, it wasn't graceful, and it was an affront. Carson had made the first move. Eleri was going for the second. Lifting up both of her hands, even as she stumbled back, it looked like she might be trying to protect herself. But she was angry. Carson was going to learn that she might be a witch, but she had no control over this shit yet.

She shoved her hands forward. Even though she made no connection with his skin, he too went stumbling back, colliding into his friends. They jostled into each other, almost like bowling pins. Unfortunately, that was enough. It was now a real fight.

The three of them rushed toward her, coming in one unit, seeming to forget that Donovan was there. Before she could react, Carson's hands were on her throat. But she had her fingers wrapped around the butt of her gun, aiming it up toward his chest and smacking her purse into him.

"There's a Glock in here," she managed to gasp through his grip, "and it's loaded. It's right on your chest. You can squeeze my throat, but it takes approximately three-and-a-half minutes for a human to die that way." That was actually a little long, but she was going for it. "Guess how long it takes a man to die from a bullet directly to his heart?" She pushed forward with the gun hoping he would get the message, but he didn't move.

Instead, the two behind him leaned forward, growling. They had finally noticed Donovan, who was balanced on the balls of his feet, ready to spring. The other two were starting to change, but Eleri was watching Carson. Despite the hands around her throat, she stared the lead wolf in the eyes. "You might want to tell your little lackeys to change back. This is public, you know. I don't think you want to learn what the general good folk of New Orleans will do with your kind."

Carson laughed this time. "Honey, a lot of them already know about us."

Still, he slowly stepped backwards away from the gun, away from her perfect aim. With her throat now free, she took deeper breaths, though she was careful not to show any damage. Eleri pulled the gun from the purse now, but Carson didn't seem to care.

"Are you really going to shoot me on the street?" he asked. "Do you know what kind of a crime that is? My people will make my body disappear and more will come after me in waves." He seemed to have the threatening down pretty well. But when he leapt, that was when Eleri went into action.

Sadly, he was right, and she didn't want to pull the trigger. She was, however, more than willing to pistol whip him. She brought her free arm up as though aiming for a blunt hit toward his nose with the heel of her palm, a typical female self-defense move. He caught it handily, moving her hand out of the way and coming in close to her space, which was perfect. Her reach wasn't as long as his, but now that he was close, she brought the pistol up against the side of his skull. What she hadn't counted on, and what she should have remembered, was that his skull was a little bit thicker than normal. So while the heavy hit dazed him, it did not knock him out.

Meanwhile, the other two had lurched at Donovan, and that worried Eleri more. Though he also had a gun, they were federal agents. And if they shot people on the street, there would have to be some accounting. Westerfield probably could get them out of it, but he could only do so much.

While she might not be on duty, a federal agent was never fully off duty. She tried again with the gun. Instead of hitting him with the side of it, she brought the butt directly into the cords of his neck. That at least made him gurgle and step back. His hands let go of her, but he came at her with a roundhouse kick this time.

Eleri ducked. She thought it was quite graceful, and it put her in the perfect position without warning him. As she came up, she rammed a fist into his groin. Carson toppled backwards. But the problem was, while she was winning her little section of this skirmish, Donovan was handling two of them. And though Donovan was plenty big, so were they. It wasn't a fair fight.

He was holding his own relatively well, though. Eleri was coming toward him, trying to help out, when something caught her arm. She was spun around, and Carson surprised her. She'd not expected him to recover that soon. A fleeting thought went through her brain: *Perhaps he doesn't have any balls and that's why it didn't hurt so bad.* But the wry thought dissipated with the connection of his fist to the side of her jaw. Dazed, she felt herself going down. And dazed, she was no good.

But over his shoulder, she saw a new person enter the fight—a woman with dark hair in braids tucked up along her head and some weapon that flashed silver.

40

Eleri watched as one of the Lobomau crumpled. His legs simply went out from under him with an expertly delivered hit to the side of his head. He was falling from the first contact.

She was impressed by the level of coordination it took to take him down, to get his knees out and be ready to knock the exact right point at his thick-skulled temple as he twisted. She saw the device in the woman's hand was a sai, a pronged, stabbing weapon. It was not the kind of weapon you usually encountered in the streets. She didn't have time to frown, though, as she was spun around by another hand grabbing hold of her arm.

Carson, again. He was on his feet, and Eleri didn't like that. He just kept getting back up. She went for his legs, but he neatly sidestepped and avoided the hit. When his arm swung toward her, trying for a punch, she pushed both of hers upward, her fists clenched, blocking his. As soon as she made a jarring contact with his hit, she swept her arms together, down and around, trapping his with her own. Using the motion as momentum and holding him closely, she swung her back toward him and brought an elbow up in a neat jab to his throat. She was no longer aiming for his head, having realized it might easily hurt her more than it hurt him.

He gurgled again just a second after she heard the sound of her elbow connecting with the side of his windpipe, but it wasn't quite enough. He was strong. She found herself again considering the gun. This time, though, he was angry.

She jabbed a second time in rapid succession, and the gurgle turned into a growl. The growl turned into a roll of his shoulders, and he leaned forward, his face extending, his teeth bared. His fingers changed as his wrists rolled, and though his carpal and wrist bones shifted spots to make his hands shorter, his nails extended a little bit —enough to be dangerous.

The growl he let out altered to a scream of fury as he lunged for her. There was no mistaking his gaping jaws going for her throat. Eleri was trying to duck, but she wasn't quite able to. Carson hit her full force. She saw Donovan looking sideways at her, but he had his own Lobomau to deal with. Whatever his name was, he had changed, too. And the one on the ground was beginning to stir.

The dark-haired woman spun over Carson and tapped him on the head again. This time, she hit his other temple with another sai that almost magically appeared in her hands. Eleri hadn't seen the weapons when she'd first spotted the woman, so she had no idea where they had come from. The woman had been walking casually down the street before the fight had begun. How she'd wound up in the alley with sais was not clear.

Before Eleri could think about it, though, and before she could strategize, her back hit the pavement with a jarring thud. Gravel and loose pieces of glass, most likely, dug into her shoulder blades. She tried to get her knees up for protection, but Carson was on top of her, his gaping maw aiming for her throat. She tucked her chin, knowing that it put her face in jeopardy. But better her face than her throat. Right?

She aimed up, a sharp fist punching him in the solar plexus. It was good, but not good enough. One could punch a dog repeatedly and it didn't faze the animal much. Carson was more dog than man now. And Eleri had to think again about what the best strikes would be. His neck was bad. Dog necks were invariably strong from carrying the head forward for so long. Canines were almost impossible to strangle. Curled knuckles punching at his throat wouldn't do much good. That was probably why they hadn't done a good enough job when she'd delivered them the first time, and they certainly wouldn't work on him in this form.

She brought her elbows up again, more in an effort to protect her face and think about where her gun might have gone. As she'd fallen, her purse had slid from her shoulder and slung far enough away that if she reached out for it, she could grab the strap and pull it back. But reaching out would mean exposing herself.

Her mind was searching for what weapons she might have nearby. Feeling along the pavement beside her with her right hand, she kept her left elbow up over her face for protection. She was feeling nothing much of value: tiny pieces of gravel everywhere that might be flung in his face, but likely wouldn't do much. There was nothing big enough to stab or bash with.

As she was thinking she was going to have to make due with her bare hands, something stabbed him. He squealed and reared up, one of his feet digging into her thigh. The long nails would surely leave marks, but it was far better than him still attacking her. She watched as he lifted up and off of her. She thought perhaps Donovan had gotten a better handle on him.

But, as she looked around, she saw Donovan was still fighting with the other one. Relatively evenly matched, they'd both landed blows. Blood came off of Donovan's left eyebrow, and the other one had cuts along his collar bone. But neither man was down.

Eleri looked again, up where the wolf was lifting off of her. Once again, she saw the woman with her dark braids, dark cargo pants, and a loose jacket. One of her hands grasped the scruff of Carson's neck, lifting him off. *She must be remarkably strong,* Eleri thought in wonder. She was small, like Eleri, but she lifted this wolf.

Eleri understood conservation of mass. Despite what people saw on TV, these wolves didn't leap and become forty- or sixty-pound woodland creatures. They were still full men, often a hundred and eighty to two hundred pounds, if not more. Carson was lean enough to not top two bills. For a young woman to lift him by the scruff of his neck, leaving him balanced on only the one leg, claws digging further into Eleri's thigh, was quite an impressive feat of strength.

As Eleri twisted and tried to get out from under him, she rolled her leg, suddenly leaving his foot hanging, and he dropped to the pavement, though the woman did not let him get purchase. It was then Eleri saw the sai had been stabbed into his side, upward through his ribcage. She sat up, scrambling, and listened to the menacing words of the woman.

"I don't know what you are, *dog*. But this is close to your kidney.

Up a little further, I'll puncture a lung. You can suffocate in clear air. Down a little further, you'll bleed out before any ambulance can get here. Do you hear me?"

Carson, tongue still lolling out of his mouth, fangs bared and wolf face showing, nodded as well as he possibly could, given her grip on the scruff. A good several inches of the tip of the sai was dug into his side. That was gonna require stitches, if not surgery.

"Call off your friends," the woman demanded, her voice low and brooking no disagreement.

"Call them off, Carson," Eleri reiterated. "You don't want to dick with us."

Carson could not call them off, but he managed a bark that ended on a whine. Eleri was grateful for the pain he was in. The woman slowly pulled the sai out, letting the wound drip blood as she set him on his feet and cautiously let go. Eleri was amazed she hadn't hit something more vital—and given the way she'd spoken to him, she seemed to know it. Eleri tried not to let her eyes go round.

Carson and his friends drew back, the fight with Donovan ending almost as abruptly as it had begun. Carson turned and ran. The other man transformed back quickly, although Carson did not, staying in wolf form as he headed down the street. The one who'd been fighting Donovan roused the man lying on the ground, grabbed him by the shoulders, and lifted him up until he gained his own feet and ran with them. He seemed to have taken the knock to the head, gone down for the count, and missed the majority of it.

Eleri stood then, watching as the woman carefully wiped her blade on her pants. *Interesting,* Eleri thought. *The blood doesn't show.* She had to wonder how many other times the woman had done that. But now was not the time for that question. She was starting to ask what she was, but the woman looked at her and said virtually the same words.

"What was that?" For the first time, emotion laced the sound.

She seemed stunned by what she'd seen, and Eleri could not think of how to explain it. She opted not to. "Thank you for your help. You probably saved us both."

The woman merely nodded. She was obviously a professional—but Eleri wondered, a professional *what?*

. . .

"My name is Eleri Eames," she said. "Nice to meet you." She noticed the other woman shook her hand but did not offer her own name.

Instead, she repeated her question. "What is it that I just saw?"

Again, Eleri thought about how to best answer. And so she replied with, "Nothing you can repeat."

"No worries," the woman said. "I don't talk to much of anyone. It's not like I'm going to feed the gossip mill."

"Still," Eleri said, "it's nothing you can repeat." She dug her card out of her purse and handed it over. "I'm Special Agent Eleri Eames. I'm with the FBI."

The woman merely looked at the card, and Eleri saw a small smirk turn up at the side of her lips. "Federal agent," she said. "I should have known. Well, I've got to get going. Good luck to you two." And she let the card drift to the ground as she walked away.

41

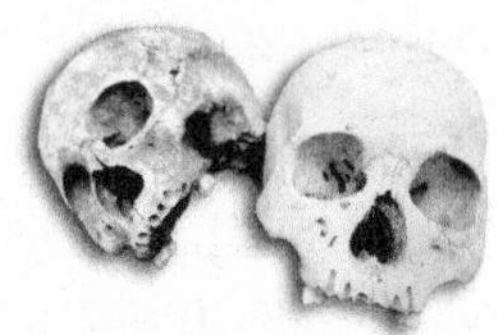

Eleri and Donovan practically limped back to the car. Neither of them had escaped the fight unscathed. As she walked away, Eleri, of course, discovered new bruises and small cuts.

Donovan's face was still bleeding, and he'd pulled up the hem of his T-shirt to stem the flow. She almost smirked. It wasn't every day you got to see your partner's bellybutton. And that answered a question: yes, he had a bellybutton. Unfortunately, it answered a question she hadn't asked.

"Donovan," she sighed, turning toward him. "Hold still."

"What?" He sounded surly, probably from pain or from the encounter or, honestly, any number of things.

"You have gravel in your back." She could see it where he'd lifted the shirt. She grimaced and slowly brushed it off his skin, grateful that none of it was embedded enough that she had to pick it out.

Shit, she thought. She turned around, lifting the back of her shirt. "Me?"

"Not much gravel, ugh," he said, making the odd noise. "But you have glass. You must have fallen into a broken bottle or something."

Lovely.

"Okay, I don't have anything like Band-Aids or alcohol wipes on me. You?" He was a doctor. She had hoped he was better prepared for medical emergencies than she.

"Not in this rental. Crap."

She jerked slightly at the sharp stings as he plucked the glass from her back.

"Well, now you're bleeding," he said, almost cheerfully. Though she couldn't see what he was doing, she felt it as he wadded up her T-shirt and held it against the spot. Taking her right hand, he pushed it over the worst of the wounds.

"Here, hold this in place," he told her. He had to tend to his own cuts, apparently. The gash on his face was starting to bleed a little more profusely, now that he was no longer holding pressure against it with his T-shirt. Lifting the hem, he went back to his own task.

They decided to avoid alleyways, thinking they were now the better part of crime occurring in this area. So they wound up taking the long way back to the car.

As she walked, Eleri noticed her calf muscles wanted to cramp up. That was odd. Then, again, she'd been very tense during the fight. Her shoulder started to throb, presumably from where she'd been slammed into the ground, and a slow headache had begun forming on the lower right side of her skull. She wanted to reach up and touch it, check to see if a goose egg was forming, as she suspected it was. Instead, her right hand was occupied, holding her T-shirt, so she wrapped her arm up, around, and behind her head, using the fingers on her left hand to gingerly probe the back of her skull and find a good bit of what she'd expected.

Her fingers came away slightly sticky. She must have been slammed harder than it felt at the time. Adrenaline was a good painkiller, at least.

When they finally made it back to the car, Donovan began patting his pockets for his keys. For a moment, she had a brief fear. They hadn't checked. What had they lost in the alleyway?

"Gun?" she asked.

He patted it in his pocket. At least the weight of that would have been hard to miss. She, too, reached into her purse and felt it, the Glock was safe there, but she had only her own keys. They were both driving rentals, which meant there weren't spares.

"Ah!" he said finally, pulling the key fob out of a random pocket. His happy expression must have pulled the wound above his eyebrow in just the wrong way, and a slow trickle of blood started again.

"Lord, tell me there's a Kleenex in the car," she said.

"Nope," he replied, with a forced optimism as he handed her the key. They were both banged up, but she didn't have blood running down her face.

They climbed in on their respective sides, Eleri sliding into the driver's seat and leaning back, her head resting against the padded headrest. When at last she was breathing again, at least somewhat normally, she turned to Donovan and said, "What was that?"

"Lobomau, is my best guess," he said, almost immediately. The word rolled off his tongue with little impediment. "Lobomau telling us that we were exactly where we need to be," he added.

That much was true, Eleri thought. The wolves were following Donovan and Eleri. Despite not turning their phones on, they'd still been tracked.

Shit, she thought. Then, out loud, she said, "We have to check the cars."

It hadn't occurred to him either, apparently, from the look on his face, that trackers might have been put on the cars.

"Do we need to check it now?" he asked.

"Shouldn't we? Before we go back to Grandmere's, house? Before we let whoever this is follow us back there?"

He'd offered a quick agreement, but she was already seeing another problem.

"We've got cuts we need to take care of. I was figuring it was faster to go back to Grandmere's and let her dose us up with alcohol and Band-Aids than to head into a store and buy ourselves a kit."

Donovan shook his head. "I think we need the store and the kit. I think we need new T-shirts, and then I think we need to hit someplace where we can find something to sweep for tracking devices. And you're right. We need to do it *before* we go back."

Eleri was forced to agree. Somehow, they were being followed. They thought they'd gotten ahead of the game, but they were still behind. She was grateful that she knew at least some parts of the city well enough to know a store where she could find a reasonable first aid kit and T-shirts. She probably didn't know the closest one, and she probably didn't know the nicest one, but maybe that was for the best. Maybe it was better if whoever was tracking them had no idea where they were going, or why. She could've found something much easier, much faster, if she'd been willing to turn on any of the devices in the car—but now, more than ever, she refused to do that.

In the parking lot, even before they went inside, they walked the exterior of the car and checked the wheel wells and other obvious places to hide a tracker. Physically, they'd found nothing. It would be easier with a radio-sweeping device.

Ten minutes later, they emerged from a quick round through the store and sat in the parking lot, on the back of the car, probably drawing attention to themselves, but rubbing alcohol wipes over individual spots, waiting for it to dry, and then slapping Band-Aids on. She'd looked to Donovan for advice on that, unable to see her own back, of course, and with him being a physician and all.

"Do we need any stitches?" she asked.

He shook his head. "Nothing too severe."

"Not even that one over your eyebrow?"

"Well, just to be safe, I think I'm going to ask you to put butterfly bandages on it. If we went into the ER, that's probably all they would do."

She laughed at the thought. If they went into the ER, the staff would definitely ask what they'd been doing. They'd either have to show their badges and admit they'd gotten in a fight or make up a story. Of course, the best one Eleri could come up with was that they'd been fighting with each other. She mentioned that to him, and Donovan shook his head, not finding it as funny as she did.

"Great. Get me arrested for domestic abuse," he commented.

She hadn't thought of it that way. Then again, she wasn't the physician, and she hadn't done a rotation in the ER, like he had.

"This is better," he said. "Honestly, they probably wouldn't have stitched me up. They'd just butterfly me anyway. Instead, you get to do it."

Now, at least, their T-shirts no longer had blood on them, and that was helpful. Eleri wasn't one for changing in the parking lot, like Donovan was already doing. Even though they'd parked near a small stand of trees that mostly covered things, she'd climbed into the backseat of the car, taking advantage of the tinted windows. As she headed forward into the front seat, she said, "Now, we have to find someplace that can sell us the kinds of devices we need to build a tracker tracer."

"We can go to the FBI branch and just ask," he said.

"I know." She'd already thought of that—but going to the branch and borrowing a sweeping device would mean admitting that they thought they were being tracked. "It would get cataloged, and Westerfield would know," she told him. "I'm really not in favor of pinging Westerfield on any of this."

"Well," he thought. "This area is well enough off, there's probably a store like that. Do we just drive circles until we find something?"

"No," Eleri thought. "We ask."

She headed back into the store, going through the other doors and hoping no one recognized her as the woman who'd walked in with the bloody T-shirt thirty minutes earlier. She simply asked one of the cashiers, who pointed her down the street, said "three lefts," then gave her some wonderfully New Orleans-based directions.

Eleri smiled, "Thank you," and popped back out to the car.

Donovan was sitting inside with the air conditioning running, and she was grateful to climb into the cold, enclosed space.

"I need food," she said. "But first, a sweeper."

They found burgers and silently ate them, along with fresh-cut fries, out of Styrofoam containers. As soon as they were fed and Eleri was starting to feel better, they assembled their device from the parts they'd bought and swept the car. After they'd done so three times, Eleri announced, "There's nothing on here."

"Nothing we can find, anyway."

They climbed back in the car and headed to Grandmere's. Halfway back, Eleri turned and looked at him again. She repeated her earlier question, but this time she clarified that she didn't mean the Lobomau.

"What *was* that?" she asked. "I mean, the woman with the sais?"

42

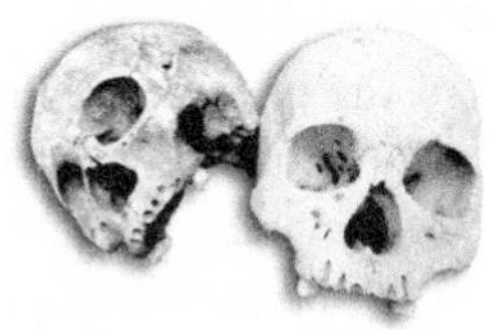

Darcelle left the store at noon. Closing up early was the one piece of freedom she had found. She wasn't sure if she'd created it or merely discovered it. She also wasn't sure how much freedom it was, given that she was only able to walk along the trail back home.

She had been angry when she woke up on time that morning, her body rising and unable to fall back to sleep. She'd wanted to stay in bed. She'd gotten up and gotten dressed, and she'd gone out the front door, aiming to walk down the street, away from her house—and away from Mystic Vudu. But as she'd gone farther toward the end of the block, the tightness had come in on her again. It happened every time she tried to stray. It squeezed. It pushed on her rib cage, her heart. If she walked any farther, it felt like a vice on her brain. Even on the evenings that she was allowed some kind of freedom, it squeezed her if she tried to leave the city limits.

Once, she'd been in the car with friends, not telling them what she could and couldn't do. They'd known of a bar with wonderful, home-style food. They'd driven her toward it, but apparently they'd crossed the city limits—or at least her mother's limits.

They hadn't known, but Darcelle had. She started to have trouble breathing. She started to feel her heart rate slowing and slowing and eventually her blood pressure dropping. When the headache had started, and her friends had turned and said, "You look pale." She'd barely managed to reply, "I think I need to go home."

It was a shame, she thought, that she couldn't tell anyone what was really going on. It was a shame to waste a free evening. She knew she'd feel better as soon as she was back in the city, and that's the way this worked. She was Darcelle. She had a job. She was not allowed to deviate. She was given exactly as many freedoms as her mother had seen fit to dole out, and no more. What good were freedoms when they were parsed out that way?

It appeared her spell of the previous night had not worked. She'd thought she would at least be able to get farther away. She'd known she was fighting against an inevitable force. Her mother had been all that her grandparents hadn't—all that the legends had told of, all that their ancestors had been. Tempeste Dauphine had been that and more.

Had her grandmother known what she was doing when she named her only daughter? Darcelle's uncles had left town long ago, not caring much about the family and thinking that her grandparents were a little bit crazy for the legends they told and the rituals they practiced. Tempeste had embraced it all—but not the way the family had wanted. As a child, Darcelle thought her grandparents had been reasonable, but now, as an adult, she wondered.

She'd grown up in a culture where the Dauphines circled their wagons and took care of their own, whether there was an outside threat or not. It didn't matter what was happening to anyone beyond that circle, either.

The Dauphine family had always stayed in that tight ring, but now … now that the ring was closed around her, and she had no chance to get out. Once she'd started thinking about it philosophically, she had realized she didn't like the way the wagons closed, the way the family sheltered each other, even when they hated one another. Even when they disagreed. Even when one of them was wrong.

Darcelle wasn't sure she had morals, per se. She understood the universe went round and that things changed. She believed death was release and not something to be feared. She'd watched many of the white folk shake in their shoes. She'd even seen a few dying on the streets, pleading for help, petrified of the other side. But Darcelle was beginning to think death might be the only way out of this prison.

Her worst fear was that, even in death, she might walk this same path. So rather than die, she had to break the curse.

Unfortunately, today was not the day she'd break free. She'd spilled her own blood last night working the spell—but her own blood was apparently not as strong as the ghost of her mother.

She thought about heading into the back yard, to the stones at the far corner where they had buried Momma. She could rail at her grandmother's ghost in person, though she was well aware that the ghost did not reside there. The spirit did not linger with the bones, although the bones themselves had power.

She wondered if maybe she should dig them up. She started thinking perhaps she ought to. The bone-handled knife that she'd taken with her and used for her spell had not been as powerful as she wished—but perhaps one made of her mother's bone would suffice to break her mother's spell. In fact, her mother might be the only one who could do it. She thought about that a little further.

What would she need to crack this? She already had the spell work and the anger to drive it, but even together, it had not been enough. She thought about when her mother had cast that spell, how she'd offered the cut on the meat of her thumb. In movies and TV shows, people always slit across the palm of their hands, but that was stupid and dangerous and likely to leave you unable to hold anything with that hand for the rest of your life. The backs of arms, long ways, were a great place to get blood. But for simplicity, the meat of the thumb was optimal. Sliced with the striation of the muscle, a nick there would bleed heavily and avoid damaging tissues, Darcelle knew.

That's what she had done last night. Even so, it had not been enough, and the bandage across the lower part of her palm was a reminder of that.

Not knowing what else to do and not having many options, she'd walked to the store and opened it up. But again, this time, she'd taken her lunch break not for lunch, but to raid the shelves. This time she took poppets and tiny crystal balls. She rummaged through the knives they had on sale, each one unique. And, as she had told the Eleri woman, many of them were pieces of her family's history. She hadn't been lying when she said she wasn't that fond of her family. The spell that had been cast on her had been cast with her mother's blood.

Maybe, she thought, it would take her mother's blood to break it.

43

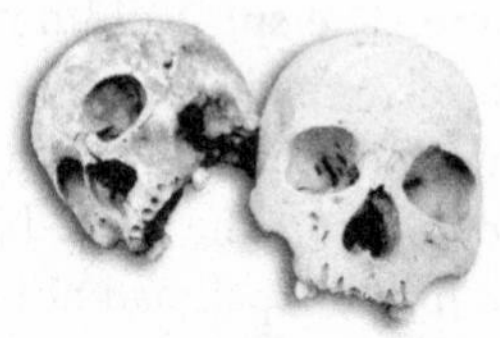

"Grandmere," Eleri said, trying to get the older woman to understand. "We've swept both cars. We can't find any tracking devices. It means that they're watching us carefully. I'm afraid they're watching you, too." She tried to emphasize the danger that all three of them were in. "I think it's better if Donovan and I leave."

Grandmere shook her head, much the same way she'd done when Eleri had been a child and had come home covered in mud or with a crawdad pinched on her finger. This idea appeared equally as stupid and possibly as inane. Eleri was working to convince her otherwise. Luckily, she had Donovan at her back.

The two tag-teamed Grandmere, trying to let the woman understand that something far more serious was going on than they originally anticipated. Now Grandmere turned that look to Donovan, and Eleri almost raised an eyebrow.

"Children," Grandmere began, with the same word she'd used when Eleri and Emmaline had run amok. "You can't find a tracker, because there isn't one—at least not physically. Think about who you've been up against. Do you think the Dauphine family is using toys from Radio Shack?"

Eleri felt the words like a smack. Grandmere was probably right, and if she was ...

"Grandmere," she said, "Donovan and I don't know enough to deal with this."

Grandmere had nodded at them sagely. "True, but I do."

Did she? Eleri wondered. If Grandmere had truly known enough, would they have been followed? Would they have gotten into a fight with wolves?

Grandmere tilted her head, as though she were able to hear Eleri's thoughts. For a moment, Eleri wondered if she might actually be able to. Her words didn't quell that idea.

"I can't save you from everything. I certainly can't save you when you go looking for trouble," Grandmere chided. "You came out of your fight, at least relatively unscathed. Am I correct?"

Eleri nodded.

"You're better off than the other guys, aren't you?" Grandmere asked. Her tone was smug, something Eleri wasn't used to hearing. Again, Eleri had to nod and she noticed Donovan doing the same thing.

Donovan was quick to add, "That was because a woman came along with some sais and saved us."

"Hmm," Grandmere said. "The universe works in mysterious ways."

Eleri decided she could go crazy or be grateful, and so she opted for the second. Though sadly, she didn't think she'd see the woman again. The stranger had not kept her card and would not be getting back in touch.

"If we don't leave, what do we do then?" Eleri asked. She wanted to sit at the table, but she remembered the beautifully carved chairs were also hard, and they pressed on the constellation of cuts on her back. She'd seen them when she'd looked in the bathroom mirror, pulling her shirt up. Donovan had done a good job at patching her, but tomorrow, she'd be black and blue. A few precocious bruises were already starting to bloom. Donovan looked much the same.

"Well, for starters," Grandmere said, "we need to do something stronger. They're still following us. We need to become invisible." Eleri wasn't sure about Grandmere's use of the word "us," but she wasn't going to argue.

"What do we do that's stronger? Haven't you already cast spells on everything?"

Grandmere nodded. Her eyes turned solemn. "I haven't done everything I could do."

"Why not?" Eleri asked.

"I don't move easily into that level anymore, child. I haven't for years, or actually decades. I think we need to call Frederick."

"Is he stronger than you?" Eleri asked, considering for the first time that perhaps her Grandmere was maybe not the most powerful woman in the universe. It was a belief that had lingered since childhood—Grandmere could rule the world if she wanted. Eleri had never seriously considered that it could be otherwise. Now that Grandmere wanted to call Frederick, it made her think the consequences through.

"No. He is not stronger than me. He has not practiced long enough to know what I can do, or to do what I can do. However, two is stronger than one. You can be our third, Eleri." Grandmere said it as an offer.

Eleri felt a lightning bolt go through her at the idea of finally becoming part of one of Grandmere's rituals. It was not something she had ever intended to do, but it was an invitation she could not deny. Eleri had no idea what she'd be walking into, or what would be expected of her. It was the great unknown, as far as she was concerned, but it was also clearly part of her history.

She nodded. *If Grandmere asked, she would do it.*

What Grandmere asked was for her to call Frederick, and to tell him to arrive at dusk. Eleri loved that her Grandmere did not use clock time to describe what she needed. In the meantime, she set them to work—though Donovan was of little help—as they dug specific herbs out of the garden. Donovan kept offering to do more, but Grandmere turned him away.

"We're the ones doing this," she said. "We have to be the ones to dig. It builds the power."

Donovan seemed to graciously accept the strange things that her great-grandmother was telling them to do. Then again, he knew he'd been followed in a car that had no known tracking devices on it, no GPS turned on, and cell phones turned off. Unless they'd swallowed trackers inadvertently, there was nothing that should be tracing them.

That idea had stilled Eleri's hand when she'd first thought it. She'd told Donovan to sweep his own body, which he'd done. But that, too, yielded nothing.

When she stood in front of him for a few minutes and found no tracking devices were on her—or seemingly *in* her—it further solidified the idea that the way they were being followed was not something they could find with a tech sweeper.

Unable to help with the spells, Donovan got on the ground and crawled under the cars, though Eleri didn't like the makeshift lifts he had designed. He stayed underneath each car for only a few moments—for which Eleri was grateful, as it looked horribly unsafe—hoping to find something that was perhaps radio-invisible.

That kind of device most likely existed. The sweeper that the two had constructed should have swept for all kinds of frequencies. Still, he was looking for something newer and hoping only that he'd know it when he saw it. In the end, he shook his head. He hadn't found anything.

As the day wore on, Eleri thought about the things she'd been reading up on since Donovan had discovered her family history. Pure American Witchcraft on her father's side. Her Grandmere's side brought Haitian rituals, Voodoo, and Hoodoo into her bloodline.

She'd begun to wonder if she, Frederick, and Grandmere were going to wind up in the backyard, around a completely wooden altar, with water, salt, wine, chickens, poppets, and no clothing. Eleri wasn't really sure she was ready to participate in that. She was grateful when the sun started to set. Frederick had sent her to change—not into her bare skin, but into "cotton and natural fiber clothing only," he said.

She'd wound up checking tags and looking for stray pieces of metal, like zippers and buttons and snaps. When at last she'd found two pieces that worked, she was dressed in red and brown. She looked reasonably ready for an afternoon strolling through New Orleans, but not for a powerful spell. Also, she was grateful that Grandmere did not plan to hold this ritual in the yard. She had cleared off the coffee table, pulling it to the center of the living room.

"Does it have no metal?" Eleri asked, thinking of the witchcraft reading she'd done.

"No metal." Grandmere smiled at her. "I see you've been reading up, little girl."

Eleri grinned. Then, things turned serious. Frederick had barely said two words to her, other than, "Hello cousin," offering her a hug and commenting how far she'd come. Eleri hadn't been sure how to interpret that, so she'd simply ignored it.

Pieces for the spellwork were laid out on the table—poppets, bowls of water and salt, and knives. Donovan had been banished to the back room. Eleri found herself grateful he wasn't there to witness. Embarrassment was not the right emotion for a spell.

"Not to be rude," Grandmere started. Eleri almost laughed. When had Grandmere ever been concerned with such things? "But Eleri, my dear, you are our weakest link."

Eleri only nodded. It was the truth, no rudeness required.

Grandmere looked at her. "What prayers or spells do you know?"

Eleri shrugged. "I only know the one you taught us as kids, the one to Aida Weddo."

"Then you lead us in that," Grandmere said.

Looking to both of them to see what to do, Eleri watched as Grandmere took her hand and then Frederick's, and Eleri reached out to Frederick. Then she started speaking the one chant she knew.

"*Bon Dieu,* keep me safe. Bind me from trouble." The other voices joined in with hers at the first syllable. "Aida Weddo, protect me from this forest I walk."

At Grandmere's urging, they repeated it twice more. And then, Grandmere pulled out the knife. She looked to Frederick and then to Eleri, and ran the knife down the back of her arm, releasing blood in its wake. She did the same to Frederick, and then turned to her great-granddaughter.

44

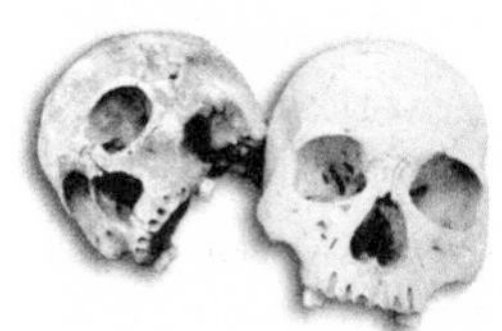

Donovan had been dead asleep. Whatever spell Eleri, Frederick, and Grandmere had been casting, it had gone on into the wee hours of the morning. Banished to his room, Donovan had been bored and began reading a novel. Eventually, he'd fallen asleep almost sideways on his bed with his phone face down on his chest. The soft knock on his door, around two-thirty, had awakened him.

Eleri stood there, one hand across the other arm, holding something onto it. "Hey, Donovan," she whispered. "Can you help me?"

Of course, he could. He hadn't even changed out of his clothes, so he sat up and motioned her to come inside. The light was still on, so it was easy to see now that she was holding a scrap of fabric and something that smelled odd against her arm. It tickled his nose, and he pointed to it, raising his eyebrows in question.

"Yeah, that's what it's about. So ..." she drew the word out, "apparently, this spell involved human blood."

Donovan's eyebrows climbed higher. "Yours?"

"All three of us." She said it as though it was not a big concern, but Donovan was beginning to think it was. At least they hadn't just sliced Eleri open.

"Anyway," she said, "Grandmere offered up this poultice ... and a piece of fabric ... to hold it." She paused periodically through the words, as though it was difficult to describe to Donovan what she was doing.

"I can smell it," he said. "Let me guess. You want me to take a look?"

She nodded with a smirk. "You're kind of an MD. The poultice is something we made from the herbs in the garden. I think it has some dirt in it, too."

Donovan tried not to laugh. He didn't want to offend Grandmere, and from the noises he was hearing, she was settling into the room on the other side of the wall. She didn't make much sound, so he had no idea how loud his and Eleri's voices were. He wasn't confident that the old woman couldn't hear their conversation.

"Let me take a look," he whispered, motioning Eleri forward.

She was holding the poultice to the back of her right forearm. Lifting the fabric and carefully peeling it back, Eleri looked down at the makeshift bandage as it took with it a soggy chunk of mashed herbs and grasses and something that looked like a red clay mud. He had no idea where one would find exactly that color here. He hadn't seen dirt like that anywhere in the city.

"What is it?" he asked.

"I don't even begin to know," Eleri sighed as she held her arm steady out toward him.

"You want me to clean it up?"

She nodded, and Donovan got to work. "This isn't going to feel good," he cautioned, "but I want to check."

He probed the wound, looking at it and into it. Seeing a flash of color, he probed again. Eleri winced. "Holy shit, El. This is deep."

She nodded. "There was some blood."

"And Grandmere did this to Frederick and herself as well?"

"Yes," Eleri said. "I watched my great-grandmother take a knife to her own arm, and she didn't even flinch. I was also very brave when it was my turn," she added, almost as though she were a child. Donovan regretted not having a lollipop to hand her.

"Honestly, part of me wants to put in stitches, but I'm shocked. It's a very clean cut, and it's not still bleeding, not really."

Eleri looked at her arm then. She didn't seem to be bothered much by blood or gore, but that kind of reaction often changed when a person was looking at their own blood and gore, Donovan knew.

She still didn't seem to flinch as she pushed and tugged at it with her other hand. "Is that bone?"

He nodded at her. "She managed to miss anything major. This is surgical precision, Eleri, really an amazing cut. And honestly, it's so clean, I think we can just bandage it."

"Clean?" Eleri said, flicking her eyes to the side and looking at tiny pieces of what appeared to be grass cuttings still clinging to her arm.

"Well, the poultice is for crap." He sniffed again, actually picking up the scent of several kinds of wild grasses that he recognized from the back yard. He didn't tell Eleri that, though. He also got lavender and a strange mineral scent, maybe the thing that looked like red clay.

"All right, we've got to clean it. It's probably going to hurt like a bitch."

Accepting that, she nodded and held her arm out to him while he began rummaging through the materials they'd put together that afternoon. It seemed like a million years since they'd walked into the store.

Eleri had suggested a prepackaged first aid kit, but Donovan knew better. He had specific things he wanted, and he was grateful now that he wasn't limited to the alcohol wipes that the basic kit had offered. Instead, they'd purchased a big bottle and full pads of gauze.

The way the week had been going, they might very well again. If he was a betting man, that's where he would put his money. He had not, however, thought he would be cleaning Eleri up after her grandmother cut her open.

Eleri seemed entirely undisturbed by it. In fact, she held the arm out, and he squeezed her hand to let her know this was it. The gauze was ready, soaked in alcohol, and he rubbed it down her arm. She didn't wince.

"Something's been bothering me," she said.

He raised his eyebrows. "Not the alcohol I'm using on the gaping wound on your arm?"

"No," she said.

"Did that not hurt?" he asked, surprised.

"Not really. It felt like a little sting."

"All right," he said, "but I've got to warn you, I have to pour it this time. Should we go into the bathroom over the sink?"

Eleri thought for a moment, and he could tell she wanted to. It seemed like the wise decision, but she still didn't want to offend Grandmere, who had made such a lovely poultice for her, and probably cast spells on it. To be fair, so far she said it hadn't hurt, and it did seem to have stopped bleeding.

"Can we just use a towel?" Eleri asked.

"Sure," Donovan said, pulling aside the one that Grandmere had set on the end of the bed for him. He had a towel, a hand towel, and a washcloth. He would make do.

Carefully tipping the bottle and having learned long ago how to clean a wound without splashing everywhere, he poured a small stream of alcohol into the cut on her arm. As he poured, the wound seemed to pull itself together. Nothing came out of it, either. Though the strange little cut grass pieces had clung to her skin, none appeared to have gotten *inside* the wound.

He wouldn't have put it past Grandmere to have sterilized the knife she'd used, and for that, he was grateful. He wanted to put Eleri on antibiotics, but he didn't have any. Tomorrow, he thought, when the pharmacies opened, he'd run her by and get her some penicillin. Grandmere might have special skills, but so did he.

Eleri barely even flinched as the alcohol ran down the gutter that existed in her arm now. "That doesn't hurt?"

"Not really."

"Do you normally not react to rubbing alcohol?"

"Always. Burns like a motherfucker," she said. "But I've got to tell you, this cut didn't hurt that bad going in."

"Eleri, you saw bone."

"I know." She said it as though understanding just how weird it all was.

Maybe, Donovan thought, they should get out of Grandmere's house. It was one thing when the woman was making them jambalaya, or when she was serving them andouille sausage and rice and keeping her spells private. It was another thing when she was slicing her own great-granddaughter's arm to collect blood.

"It's bothering me," Eleri said.

"The alcohol?" *Finally,* he thought. It should burn. She should flinch, at the least.

"No." She said it as though he was being nuts. Apparently, the alcohol didn't sting.

"What, then?" he asked.

"I don't know," she said. "No, part of it ..."

"Go on ..." Slowly, he patted her skin dry, pushed the wound together, and laid tiny butterfly bandages across it. He had managed to pick up some Steri-Strips—a more professional-grade version of standard sticky butterflies—and he'd also managed to get himself several little breakable capsules of first aid glue.

"It's Grandmere," Eleri said, paying almost no attention to the medical work on her arm, which really should be hurting. "She has these scars down her arm. She's always had them," Eleri said, "and tonight, I think I learned what they're from."

"They look like this one?" Donovan said.

"Yes. Very thin, white lines run the length of both of her arms. She must have been gathering her own blood for ... I don't know."

"That's weird," Donovan said.

"And I don't know what it is," Eleri continued, looking mystified, "but there's more. It's important. I just can't place it right now."

45

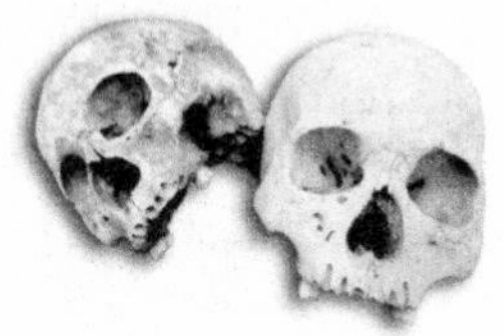

Eleri slept in late the next day and woke to find Donovan and Grandmere cooking breakfast—or perhaps brunch—by the time she had risen.

Grandmere smiled and acted as though nothing out of the ordinary had happened the night before. Frederick was long gone, too, his presence having disappeared from the house. Grandmere must have cleaned up the coffee table, as it was back to normal. A few scraps of fabric, a few out-of-date magazines on making pies, and a handful of coasters as mismatched as everything else in the house were the things that now adorned the top of it. Gone were the makings of her altar.

Eleri ate breakfast, noticing that Donovan was as quiet as she was. She didn't mention the spell from the night before, but did ask Grandmere if it was safe for her and Donovan to take the car out again today. Grandmere shrugged. "We won't know until we try it," she said. And she went back to eating her pancakes.

Eleri and Donovan decided to drive out. They still hadn't managed to figure out where Cabot was going all the times he'd gotten the parking tickets. Eleri had tried a little harder, before leaving, to figure out what he might be looking at. Using the maps, she'd checked out local landmarks and found a small number of buildings that involved the city works in some way. There were also several homes owned by older families, where the records seemed to trail off forty to fifty years ago. And a singular graveyard.

She told Donovan about all of these things, but he didn't seem to be paying attention. She tipped her head. She was the one who'd had her arm sliced open and had participated in a spell. "Are you okay?"

"Yeah." He nodded, but it was just as absentminded as everything else. When she pressed him he said, "I smelled something yesterday." But he wouldn't tell her more.

Turning back to the work, he finally helped, but they were unable to narrow down which locations were most likely the important ones. They still had no idea what Cabot might be doing or why. In fact, they were working backwards now, hoping that if they got there, they would see a place and understand, from the location, what it was that was bringing Cabot there so often.

Eleri decided to check one other thing while she was at it. Again, using the hotspot Donovan had setup, she logged into the local database.

"Donovan, look," she pointed out. "None of the tickets has been paid."

Donovan blinked at her. "With that many tickets and that much money, there should be a warrant out for his arrest."

"But there's not," Eleri replied, still staring at the information on the screen. "In fact, it appears all the automated triggers are turned off on these tickets. All the overdue notices that should automatically happen—it's all gone. The tickets are there if you look for them. But no one is actually trying to collect the money. And when they see the car, they seem to just ticket it rather than notice that it should be booted. His car should have been towed months ago," she said.

Donovan agreed. It was unusual, but they couldn't figure out what it might mean.

As they drove, Eleri mulled it over. Hand over hand, she turned the wheel. And word over word, she spoke to Donovan, trying to figure out what was happening. "Do you think they did something, or do they have somebody on the inside making it so he doesn't have to pay his tickets? Do you think they cast a spell?"

Donovan seemed to think about it for a moment. "It seems silly," he said. "If you were going to cast a spell to not have to pay your tickets, wouldn't it be better to cast a spell so that no one noticed your car was in the parking spot? So you wouldn't get the ticket in the first place."

Eleri had to agree, that made more sense. "But that requires the person casting the spell to think of it," she pointed out. "I would have thought—given the length of time that Cabot has been accruing the charges—that someone would have thought of that."

There was a moment of silence in the car as the two of them tried to figure out what was happening. They couldn't. She added, "We need to assume that he has someone on the inside in the city finance department."

"That makes sense," Donovan said.

Neither of them spoke after that for a bit, because Eleri knew Donovan understood as well as she did that city employee corruption made the whole case just a little bit bigger. It put them in more danger if someone in the city could give them tickets—or maybe even issue warrants.

Worse than that, she still hadn't found Emmaline. In fact, she had nothing aside from the fact that the bones of McKenzie Burke seemed to resemble her sister so much. Perhaps she should go back and figure out exactly where they'd come from. That might lead her to Emmaline.

Something told her that if she stayed on this path, she would solve her sister's case. She'd started to believe that, though the bones she'd seen had actually not belonged to Emmaline, that they were, in fact, the pathway to what she was looking for. She hadn't said this to Donovan. In fact, it seemed they'd just been following the trail laid before them by the mystery that was Darcelle Dauphine, and the courtyard with the bone.

"We should go back and talk to Darcelle tomorrow, I think," Eleri threw out into the space of the car.

Donovan agreed. "What specifically should we ask her?"

"I think we should ask her about McKenzie Burke."

"And also Emmaline?" Donovan asked, pushing the words slowly through the air, understanding it was a touchy subject. But Eleri didn't flinch.

"Yes."

They arrived in the area where Cabot had gotten his parking tickets—but this time, instead of going on foot and possibly encountering someone, they drove around. Both paid special attention to any car they saw multiple times and to anyone they saw on the street. While doing this, they also tried to assess if they were being followed.

Nothing they'd been trained to watch for at Quantico popped up. There was nothing that seemed suspicious in the people on the street —they walked by and disappeared around a corner and weren't seen again. Even Eleri's "Spidey-sense," if she could call it that, said that they hadn't been followed this time. She could only hope Grand-mere's spell worked. If it had, that further confirmed nothing physical had been tracing them in the first place. It was a disturbingly creepy thought, even to Eleri.

The first building on their list was an ancient mansion. It was marble-fronted and black with mold or dirt, Eleri couldn't tell. Though columns stood in the front from an era seemingly unrelated to New Orleans, a black, wrought-iron gate enclosed the porch, helping to make it look as though it belonged. The home sat directly against the sidewalk. The columns were close enough to reach out and touch, if a person stood there. The double front door was painted black, and so were the shutters.

The colors, at least, were very New Orleans, Eleri thought. Though planter boxes lined the railings of the second floor, any plants in them had long since withered. It was difficult to tell if anyone even currently resided there.

She and Donovan drove past and looked at the next place, which was a startling contrast. It was a small, ramshackle house on a piece of property as large as the one belonging to the mansion. It squatted quietly amongst the more elegant homes.

Donovan thumbed through the notes they'd brought. "It's not owned by the Dauphine family, but the owner does have a family history that involves a Dauphine grandparent. And the land was at one point owned by a Dauphine."

Eleri frowned. "You'd think they'd keep it in better shape." But again, there was nothing they could tell from driving by, and they weren't going to get out on foot until they had checked everything.

The last place they checked—after seeing several more homes and even a small business—was the graveyard. Like most in the city, it was bordered by a low, stone wall and a high, wrought-iron fence. But as it was the last place, Eleri and Donovan finally got out of the car.

A tremor ran up Eleri's spine, thinking about the last time they'd come through here on foot. They'd have to be more alert this time.

She turned to Donovan and asked, "Do you smell anything? Do you hear anything?"

He paused for a moment, and Eleri let him. After she waited, he shook his head. But the look on her face made her ask, "What?"

"Last time," he said, "when we were fighting those Lobomau ... I thought one of them smelled like family."

46

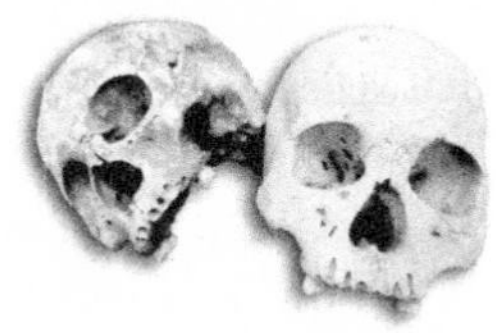

"What do you mean?" Eleri asked.

"One of the men who attacked us smelled like family." Donovan shrugged. "I don't know. I never smelled it before. Wade said something about it—that you could smell when somebody was your family member."

Eleri glanced at him and then turned her gaze back to the headstones she was passing as they walked through the graveyard. They were still just looking, hoping they might stumble onto something that would tell them if this was where Cabot had been coming. Now she was also trying to get her mind around this interesting comment Donovan had made.

"It makes sense," he said. "Family members share a large portion of genetics. The genetics goes into things like your immune system. And you already know you can smell when someone has a complementary immune system from their sweat. That's with a standard human nose. So, it makes sense that I can smell a familial relationship. I just ..." he paused. "I've never smelled it before .. .and it was so strong."

"Which one was it?" Eleri asked.

"Not Carson." Donovan shook his head.

Eleri breathed out a sigh of relief. "One of the other two?"

Donovan nodded. "The taller one."

She thought back. "I guess he somewhat looked like you."

Donovan didn't add to that comment, and Eleri kept going.

"You're right. Your sense of smell is probably far more reliable than anything else. But what does it mean?"

"I have no idea. I asked Wade, but he didn't get back to me yet. I would assume brothers and sisters could definitely be scent-detected. Parents and children, too."

"Makes sense." Eleri turned and walked another row of headstones, not seeing anything that caught her eye. Not yet. She remained hopeful. "Cousins?"

"Probably."

"Couldn't you smell that relationship with your dad?"

Donovan smirked. "My dad was drunk so often that if I could smell anything other than alcohol, it was a miracle. He was just my father. I never thought about how he smelled and whether or not that signified our relationship."

"Biologically speaking," Eleri offered up, "it would make sense if you could smell any relationship that would make it inappropriate to mate."

"Well, that's a lovely thought," he replied, following down the next row of headstones and reading the inscriptions, seemingly as a distraction for the weird conversation they were having.

"Well, isn't that the whole reason for the evolutionary development of being able to sense family relationships?"

"So, what you're saying," Donovan asked, "is that I *shouldn't* mate with this guy."

She laughed. "Well, I'm saying your genetic relationship must be close enough that if you were going to, you should reconsider."

"I'll take that under advisement." He then turned and pointed. "Look, Eleri."

"What am I looking at?"

His fingers motioned again to the headstone. "Not new, but not horribly old either."

The large name at the top read *Burke*. In fact, the whole name was *Nelly Mackenzie Burke*.

"Huh," Eleri said. "Do you think it's any relation?"

Donovan shrugged. "I think it's highly probable. They named their daughter Mackenzie. Maybe it was a family name."

"That's not uncommon." Eleri nodded, thinking she bore a family name of her own. "We know that Mackenzie Burke has lineage ties back to this area, to the Dauphines. It makes sense she might have an ancestor buried here." Eleri thought for a bit. "We still don't know why they wound up in Nebraska. It seems strange to me."

"I don't know," he said with a shrug. "Your mother managed to get her family into Kentucky, of all places."

Eleri had to smile at that. Nathalie Beaumont had certainly achieved a lot, and Donovan was right. It could be something as simple as a job that had taken the family to Nebraska.

"Okay," Eleri said. "So, let's play this out. Let's assume this is a relative of our missing Mackenzie Burke. What does it mean?"

"Well," Donovan said, "I didn't come to this grave site because of the name on the headstone. I came because of the smell."

She raised her eyebrow at him, wondering if he was telling her he was smelling family relationships in dead bodies. He didn't take the bait, though.

He dropped an entirely different bomb. "The earth here has been freshly turned."

"What?" *No. There was grass growing, much the same as the others.*

"This graveyard is only passably well-tended," he said, "and I think that's an advantage."

"What do you mean?" Her heart was beating faster at all the possibilities freshly turned earth brought to mind.

"Well, if it was beautiful, even, green lawn, then it would be obvious someone had been digging. However, I think, you could smooth out the top layer, maybe dig it up like sod?" He said it with a question mark, as though he was thinking his way through it while he was speaking. "Set it aside. Dig up the earth. Do whatever you wanted, and put it back, and because ..." He looked left and right, and Eleri did, too, now taking stock of the way the grass grew in patches. "Because of the patchiness of the grass all around here, I don't think anybody would really notice."

Eleri was forced to agree. "But why would the earth have been recently turned here? It doesn't make sense." She looked at the headstone. "This body has been in the grave for a half a century. There's no reason to dig here—unless it was to dig up the body."

She wanted to get on her phone and at least look for a little bit of information, but once again, they weren't turning their phones on. They weren't going to undo the power of Grandmere's spell with the flick of a button on some tech. She wasn't willing to waste the cut she'd taken down her arm, which was still bandaged, just to turn on the phone.

Besides, she couldn't log into the databases from her phone anyway—and that was where she really wanted to look. She needed to find out if Nelly Mackenzie Burke truly was an ancestor of the first missing girl.

"What we really need," Donovan said, "is to get somebody in here with GPR."

They'd used ground penetrating radar before, but Eleri thought it would be difficult now. "It's like the sweeper for bugs on the car, though," she said with a touch of irritation. "We can do it, but as soon as we requisition it from the FBI and make them pay for somebody to come out and operate it ..."

Donovan nodded. "Right. Then it's not our case anymore. It's theirs."

"Exactly." Then Eleri had another thought. "You know, we don't have to requisition a T-bar to check the soil."

Donovan nodded. Checking the density of the soil was something they'd done often before, something most forensic scientists did when looking for bodies. It was easy enough to find the edges of a grave by looking for differences in the pack of the ground. A piece of metal spike, maybe half an inch to three quarters of an inch around with a slight point at the end and a T across the top, was just right for pushing into the earth to see if you encountered rocks, caskets, or loose enough earth to sink in easily.

In many cases, they could use a T-bar to define a grave close to six feet by eight feet, where a body had been buried. It was even possible to tell exactly how deep the grave was. The stick test was done the vast majority of the time before scientists began digging.

Donovan wanted them to have two sticks, as they were in a cemetery and needed to be fast and non-obvious while they did it.

"I didn't bring mine," Eleri said. "It's a rental car." She sighed out the words as though "rental car" had become her new, go-to issue for every piece of equipment she didn't have on her. She'd really thought she'd packed well for this trip. Apparently not.

She thought about coming back with the sticks as she looked around from where they were standing. The good news about New Orleans cemeteries was that they were above ground, which meant that, as they walked through the lanes, they were relatively hidden from people walking by. Mausoleums stood a full story tall, the marble gray and rough from age. She could only see the street in a couple of places, and there were only a few straight lines of sight through the headstones, the standing angels, and the buildings where someone on the street could see her.

If they could get the stick into the graveyard, they could certainly come back to this grave and poke around without anyone much the wiser.

"It's probably better that we come back tomorrow and do this right," she offered.

Donovan agreed, but they didn't head out immediately to purchase the tools. Instead, they continued their walk through the graveyard aisles. They checked headstone names, now specifically looking for more Burkes and more Mackenzies.

They found a handful of each, but there was nothing unusual about that. Families tended to want to be buried next to loved ones, and the majority of them ended up buried in clusters in the same cemetery. There were even a small number of Dauphines buried here. The dates on the headstones went back well over a hundred years.

Even so, that wasn't what surprised Eleri. It was Donovan, who told her where the earth had been turned. Before they left the cemetery, they had more than ten sites to check.

47

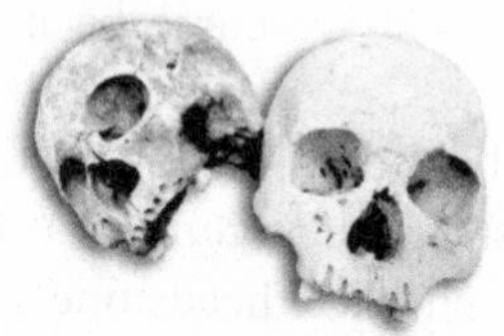

Donovan stood inside the open door of the car, looking at the edge of the cemetery the next morning. It was early enough that he could still smell the sunrise on the grass. They'd stopped by a home improvement store on the way back to Eleri's great-grandmother's and had been lucky enough to find two of the soil probe sticks they needed still in stock.

The checkout lady had looked at them oddly, though Donovan couldn't imagine this was the worst she'd seen—even just in the past twenty-four hours—so he'd merely offered his credit card and taken the two out the door. Eleri had pushed him, suggesting she pay for it.

"No," he'd said. "You're going to buy me dinner."

She joked about the quantity of dinner he ate, but readily agreed. He thought again how this was coming out of both their pockets, and how her pockets were much, much deeper than his. He was on leave, and that meant not getting a paycheck. But when he had looked at his tiny partner next to him, he thought about what a rock she was and how very different this was for him—radically different from just a few years ago.

Eleri was neck deep in her own troubles here. He kept himself from telling her that Wade had texted him back. Donovan worked under the weight of that message—if the smell was strong enough to notice without Donovan trying to finding it, then it was immediate family.

He'd lain in bed last night, staring at the walls and thinking about that. *Immediate family.*

It wasn't his father or his mother, obviously. He had no children, and even if he did, this guy had been too old for that. An uncle? But that didn't make any sense. While he didn't put it past his father to lie, his grandparents had never mentioned having another child. It would have to be an uncle, but younger than Donovan.

Given the man's looks and *that scent* … all Donovan could think was *brother*. But how?

He pushed the nagging thought aside and tried to pay attention to Eleri's problems.

Before going back to the cemetery, they'd found yet another hole-in-the-wall restaurant and taken a table at the back. They'd eaten deli sandwiches, piled high with turkey and roast beef. To Donovan, those sandwiches tasted a lot more like home than Grandmere's cooking did. He loved what Grandmere made—and he was a fan of food in general—but it was nice to have a simple sandwich. It also was nice to have Eleri pull out the scrap of paper from her purse and look at the list they'd made while walking through the graveyard the day before.

When they'd entered the tiny eatery, they had headed for the back and he'd cautiously sniffed at everything as they went by. It was easy, because Eleri understood what he was doing and walked slowly, as though she was having trouble picking out a table. She made it seem normal for him to meander through the diner.

There weren't any wolves in there at all, and he was grateful. It didn't mean they weren't followed—only that if someone was tracing them, they'd learned not to send a spy he could smell.

It was the best the two of them could do. Since they hadn't been harassed or even seemingly followed at all at the cemetery today, they'd taken a chance and had their conversation at the little restaurant the night before. He preferred keeping it out of the house. He didn't like the feeling that they dragged something into Grandmere's with them each time they came home.

So here they were, in the cemetery again, just after dawn. They were well-fed again and walking among the graves. The humidity almost made dew on the grass, but not quite. It didn't get cold enough for the water to condense here. Instead, it hung in the air and settled on everything that brushed it, including his skin.

This was such a strange feeling for a boy who'd grown up all over the North and West. He thought he'd experienced change in climate while heading to South Carolina, but nothing had prepared him for New Orleans in the summer.

"Okay," Eleri said. "Let's do this."

He looked at her cargo pants, which were bulky enough today to make her look several sizes larger. She'd insisted not only on the soil probe sticks, but on stockpiling anything else they might need. He'd bought the sticks, but she'd bought every other tool known to mankind.

She was irritated about it, too, saying she hated buying things twice. But it didn't stop her from gathering paint brushes, a three-pointed hand rake, and several trowels. Then she'd added a tiny dust pan with a stiff-bristled hand broom. Clearly, she was planning on digging up some bodies, or at least finding something in the dirt.

Donovan hadn't asked. He'd only been prepared to poke at the ground with his pointy stick. Eleri was loaded for bear. Instead of carrying her purse, which she left locked in the car, she carried only her ID and credit cards with her, tucked into a back pocket. She'd slung everything into each possible pocket on her pants and followed by handing him the last few pieces that didn't fit on her person. Now he felt that his pants were overloaded, too.

The Glock in the side pocket along his right thigh added to his bulk. He could see that Eleri's left side sagged a little bit under the weight of her own gun. She'd not been willing to leave it in her purse this time.

As they closed the car doors and walked up the steps into the cemetery, he'd once again taken a cautious inhale. Grandmere had been up as early as them, and despite their speed getting out the door, she'd managed to get a reasonable meal into them before they left. He was going to miss that when he headed home.

He could still smell the remnants of gravy and biscuits on his own breath, but it didn't change the scent of earth here in the cemetery. He could smell the hard-packed, old soil from most of the graves. He could smell the spores that clung to the marble, eking out a living in the rough spaces as the rock weathered. Some of the stones were still buffed to a reasonable shine, the letters carved with precision. But the older stones, though the letters were very neat, were now rough to the touch. All manner of things had embedded in the pores over the decades.

He could smell flowers that had been brought and left, and he knew some of them were placed here just a few days ago. He didn't smell that anyone had passed through since he and Eleri had been here yesterday evening, and that made him a little more comfortable with what they were doing. Still, though the trowels and the guns were in their pockets, it had been harder sneaking in the T-bars. Eleri had joked about sliding it down her pants leg, and Donovan thought for a moment she was serious, pointing out that she wouldn't be able to bend her left knee if she did it.

"I know," she said. "I'm better off pretending it's a crutch and that I have a twisted ankle."

He'd laughed, and then he'd taken both of the T-bars in his hand as they'd walked up the street. Better it looked like one person carrying something than two. But now they stood over the grave of Nelly McKenzie Burke and began poking at the dirt. Eleri's bar slid in almost all the way up to the T handle.

"It's very loose," she said. "You were absolutely right."

Donovan tried his own spot in the space between two graves and found that the bar barely went in at all.

"It doesn't go out this far," he said, and he rapidly jabbed the stick at the earth from a series of points about six inches apart. One, two, three, four. It suddenly sunk in several feet. Eleri motioned to him, and the two of them began marking out a space. Once they'd found it, it seemed to cover the same size—width and height—that the original grave had.

"Do you think they dug this woman up?" Eleri asked. Donovan shrugged. Given what he'd already seen from these people, anything was possible.

He had to admit that he wasn't looking forward to possibly digging up a body, whether partially decomposed or still in the casket. His best hope was to run into a skeleton, and that was saying something.

He looked at his partner now. Case or no case, they were partners. She would lead the way here.

Once the space was all mapped out, he glanced at her as though to ask *were they really going to do this?*

Eleri tipped her head. She glanced back over her shoulders, an action as guilty as it could possibly be, and Donovan only laughed.

"So, do we do this *now?* Or come back at night?"

She just stared at him, the tools in her pants clearly saying "now."

"Okay, let's do a test dig now. You keep alert. Hopefully, if someone comes up, we can cover what we're doing."

It didn't sound like much of a plan beyond *"Hope it doesn't happen but scramble if it does"*—but Eleri was going for it. She managed to dig a test space several feet deep without hitting anything, and then said, "All right, next one."

Still, no one had come to the cemetery, though several people had walked by on the sidewalks surrounding the edges. The space was large, perhaps even a few acres, and Donovan tried to appreciate the land value of that. They saw people passing on the street, but when they stayed low, the people didn't seem to see them or notice that they were digging.

Before they left the cemetery, they had performed test digs on three of the graves. It was Eleri who decided they needed to head home. The sun was directly overhead, and both of them had sweat dripping down their temples. Donovan felt it tracing his spine. He didn't dislike it, but Eleri squirmed.

He put his hand out over her wrist, trying to avoid the bandage there, and stopped her hand. "Is your arm bothering you?" he asked, suddenly thinking about her injury, though he'd been looking at the bandage off and on all day.

"No," she nodded. "It's just getting hot and it's daylight. I think it might be best to come back and actually do a full excavation on one of these at night. I don't know why, but I know we need to keep digging."

48

Eleri once again parked at the edge of the block and walked with Donovan through the gates and up the steps into the cemetery. She was a little surprised when the gates opened so easily. She'd fully expected someone to lock the place up at night—but in this neighborhood, that apparently wasn't the case.

There were things she'd made sure she wasn't carrying—her purse, all the extras she usually walked around with, full wallet, credit cards—and still several things she made sure she had on her. Her Glock was primary, and her state-issued ID. She'd reminded Donovan to bring his FBI badge, and she had hers. God forbid they get caught actually grave-robbing in the middle of the night without some kind of federal identification. They would definitely be arrested.

According to Grandmère, no one was going to see them. Or they might, but their brains wouldn't process the sight. This had something to do with the spell they'd cast the other night. Eleri thought back to the number of times people had walked by on the street that morning but had not noticed the two of them poking at the dirt and digging. She would have expected someone to call out to them, or at least report them to the police, but it never happened. While their seeming invisibility wasn't definitive proof, it was possible Grandmère was right.

She and Donovan had gone back to the home store and bought those nerdy-looking headlamp lights that came on an elastic strap. They'd found some with a low-level red light that would be less noticeable at night while providing them with enough light to work by.

Eleri was concerned the red light would mask the natural colors she'd want to see, should she find any bones. Her other concern was that she and Donovan were becoming regulars at the home supply stores. She did not want to be recognized anywhere in this city. They'd run out of hardware shops and would have to become repeat customers in at least one of them, should they need anything else. With food, it was easy to eat each meal at a different location. But for the supplies she needed? Not so much.

They walked between the graves now, using the tall ones as concealment. They noted the names they had marked on their last visit, each of which was an older, in-ground grave. It was only in the newer century that the residents had figured out to bury the dead above the ground. A cemetery like this involved a mix of above and below-ground graves. Some of the older graves had floated up and were replaced with waist-height tombs. Others had—for whatever reason—managed to stay in the dirt.

Nelly McKenzie Burke's grave was one of those, and it was there that Eleri and Donovan started digging.

On her hands and knees, Eleri paused a moment. She did not have her full kit with her, and she wondered why she hadn't brought it to town. What had she thought would happen? Honestly, she'd been hopeful she would simply come and identify the original bones as Emmaline's. Then, she would do research, maybe walk around town. She'd thought she might interview people who had known her sister when she lived here. It occurred to Eleri that Emmaline had lived here, away from her home, for longer than she'd been with her own family. It was a sobering thought.

Still, it hadn't occurred to her that she might need to dig her sister's remains out of the soil with her own hands.

They started now at the small hole she'd begun at their last visit. Using the trowel tilted on its side, she lightly scraped back layers of grass, widening her test hole to the full grave size. Donovan helped by grabbing the tufts of green and tugging on them, and letting her remove the soil underneath, almost as though they were lifting sod.

They carefully set several chunks aside, thinking they might do the same as the original grave-robbers had and put the grass back so that in the morning, no one would notice. Given that no one was even locking the cemetery at night, Eleri thought it was highly possible the excavations might be missed.

Slowly, they worked their way down through the earth. It was a good foot before they hit anything, but as Eleri pointed out, someone had already re-dug this hole. Though it had been some time since that person had been here, the dirt was still noticeably looser. This was much easier than digging one of the other old graves, where the dirt had settled for decades or centuries.

She continued using the trowel sideways, scraping off one fine layer of dirt at a time, slim enough that even something like a small finger bone would show up, rather than getting scooped and tossed to the side. Normally, she would have a sifter to push all the dirt through, so that anything big enough to get caught would remain behind. The problem wasn't just the bones. It was that bones aged. The soil leeched nutrients, and they got brittle as they sat in the dirt for a decade or more. If a finger bone had been there, she might find only a chip of it. The tip of the pinky toe was one of the smallest bones, and it was often lost in these situations. When she added in that the pieces she found would be covered with the same dirt they were hiding in, it might be extremely difficult to locate a bone—even in a gravesite.

Eleri was hoping to find what she could. She troweled up layers of dirt and handed them off to Donovan to mash against his own fingertips. Without a sifting pan, that would have to do.

Almost an hour later, she found the first bone, much to her surprise. She'd truly thought she would end up robbing a grave. She would get to the top of the casket or burial tomb and have to pry it open. But that was apparently not the case—not if this one bone could lead them to others. She frowned and held it up.

"Rock?" Donovan asked, and then he looked more closely.

He should have known better, she thought. The ME should absolutely be able to identify wrist bones on sight. Then again, she thought, maybe he didn't. Maybe he was so used to working with bodies that were still intact that her holding up a single, small, oddly shaped bone wasn't quite enough—certainly not in the red light. She shook her head and named it for him.

"It's a scaphoid. Left side, I think," she said, and set it aside.

Another inch or two down, she came to the next bone—except it wasn't a bone. It was three bones, located toward the foot of the grave site.

"Tarsals and a metatarsal," Eleri said as she handed the oddly shaped pieces over to Donovan to bag and label.

The bones were intact. She thought that was rather odd. For starters, this body was not inside a tomb or a casket of any kind. It wasn't even wrapped in a tarp or cloth, or encased in anything that might slow down the decomposition. The red light made it difficult to inspect the soil thoroughly, but she thought, *Maybe the whole body was buried directly here*. But the dirt wasn't sunken enough for that.

"Donovan." She waved a hand to get his attention. "Whoever did this either returned later to fill in the dirt as the grave sank, or they'd mounded it up enough to begin with, which would indicate they knew what they were doing. It's difficult to get a grave flat after a body decays."

"It was only relatively flat," he commented. "The ones we marked are a little more sunken than the others."

She nodded, thinking he was right and thinking that the graves seemed to shift and flatten at different rates. She sat back on her knees and looked around. This cemetery was old enough that most of the burial sites had flattened out through weather and time.

Donovan pointed to the one next to them, where marble, brick-shaped markers that had been used to delineate the edges of the gravesite. It was something she saw here in Louisiana in much greater proportions than she did at cemeteries in other parts of the world. "It's harder to tell if it's sunken or mounded with the markers around it. If it isn't a lot, it's difficult to measure."

She nodded, agreeing, and aimed her view back into the grave she was digging. The red light made it hard for Eleri to get a good estimate of how long the body had been here, but given the weather, it could have fully skeletonized in as little as a year.

"When we get to the next grave," she said to Donovan, "we need to see if dirt layers were added to the top." She explained her concern about the soil sinking. "We'll need it as evidence."

He only nodded and looked over their little stash of four bones. Neither of them asked the question. Neither of them had to. The bones they had discovered were clearly human. Eleri kept digging.

"Aha," she said, noting she had found something that wasn't budging. Slowly, and using the brush from her dustpan set, she moved the dirt away.

"Water bottle," she said, holding her hand out, and Donovan handed it over. She drank a swig, and then poured about a third of it onto the knob of the bone, using the brush to create mud, which more easily moved away from the piece she was trying to look at. She tried using the trowel around it ever so slightly but wound up going back with the three-pronged rake. She only needed to loosen the dirt. If she dug in with the trowel, she was likely to nick a bone.

It was still possible this was just a pile of bones thrown in the dirt. But the few parts she'd found indicated the body was originally laid into the grave site, head on one end and feet on the other, and that meant she was very likely to jam her trowel into another bone and possibly damage her evidence.

Her heart stopped for a moment, and she sat back on her heels again, wondering if she was doing the right thing. *Best to ask Donovan,* she thought.

"Hey," she said. "We have human bones. This is evidence. Did we just walk outside the jurisdiction of my own case?"

He looked at her, his brows pulling together and his face concerned. "Probably, but what happens if we quit?"

Shit, Eleri thought. It was the middle of the night. The graveyard wasn't locked. They'd come in through one gate, but she'd seen at least two others. There was probably one more on the fourth side of the rectangle that enclosed the space. If they quit now, anyone else could come in and finish the job. Anyone who was visiting would see what they had done. Even if they filled the dirt back in—probably the safest option, but still not smart, evidence-wise—then someone was bound to notice. They had dug so much that they were going to leave an obvious depression behind, even though the original gravediggers had not.

She was no longer thinking of herself and Donovan as robbers. In fact, she was beginning to believe that Nelly McKenzie Burke had stayed in her original resting place, undisturbed—and that perhaps a new body had been buried on top of her. It was a simple and ingenious trick, she thought. If something smelled, no one would think much of it. They were in a cemetery after all. Between the humidity and the heat down here, as well as the fact that they were standing in a graveyard, no one would question a mound of freshly turned earth. They might, if they knew the graveyard well—but the unkempt state of the place made it seem like nobody did.

Eleri looked at Donovan and then went back to the grave, her decision made. She kept digging.

49

Donovan watched as Eleri leaned over the third grave. They'd been digging all night. No one had bothered them—despite the stupid red headlamps they wore and despite the fact that they'd been in a graveyard well after normal hours, when it should have been locked. No one had even looked through the spikes of the wrought iron fence to see what they were doing. But, as Eleri had said earlier, it seemed nobody was in charge of watching over this cemetery, and that's why none of the gates had been locked in the first place.

After they'd found what they were looking for in the first grave—human bones that Eleri had painstakingly extracted from the soil—Donovan had gone around to each of the gates and fashioned a makeshift lock. It wouldn't really keep anyone out, but it would make enough noise that they would get a warning before anyone came in. It would give them a chance to cover their work, or at least disappear.

Still, if they were found, it wouldn't look good. They'd now dug up three whole sections of earth directly on top of existing graves. On the last one, Eleri had commented the grave had been so old, it had been sunk into the earth the way many had been before the people of the area learned not to bury their dead underground.

"Look, Donovan," she'd said, thunking her trowel on the top of the concrete box that housed the casket. "It's floating."

"What? Floating? Like, currently rising to the surface?"

She'd nodded. "It takes decades, but it happens. It's why all the new graves are above ground."

"How do you know it's floating? How do you know that wasn't where it was buried?"

"The hole is far too shallow," Eleri said. "Given the date on the headstone, it should have been buried about two or three feet deeper. They knew better by then."

Interesting, Donovan thought. Though her degree wasn't in anthropology, she knew many historical facts about graves. *Maybe because she'd spent so much of her time digging them up.*

Still, he'd watched as she bent over the task again, slowly dragging her brush and her three-fingered rake across the ground. She delicately disturbed more and more dirt, gradually bringing up more and more bones. After they'd dug the first test spots over the three graves, Eleri had decided to do it right.

It was part of why they'd left and come back tonight. She'd brought a camera. She'd brought string and stakes, this time. If he'd thought her pockets had been full the first time, he'd been mistaken. His pockets were now a full backup system for everything Eleri needed. Small air bubble levels hung along the string. Compasses sat next to them, to help them make sure the staked lines oriented North-South, so that anyone looking at the pictures would know where the bones had originally been placed.

Eleri also had begun hanging measuring tapes—although she didn't have access to her usual, professional ones. She'd spent a while at Grandmere's earlier showing Donovan how to mark the inches, half inches, quarter inches, and eighths in different colored dots on the brightly colored twine that she was now hanging from the crosshairs she'd made.

Everything had to be photographed and labeled. She knew what she was doing, and the pictures confirmed that. Because of the meticulous labeling, anyone else who looked at this would know how the bones had come up. They would have evidence in case this was ever prosecuted as a crime.

But the fact that she knew to do all this—along with the FBI badge in her pocket—indicated that she also knew she shouldn't *be* doing it.

The night had been long, and she spent most of it on her hands and knees, hunched over gaping holes she was carving into the earth. She reached down in repeatedly, in what must have been an uncomfortable position. Donovan did some of the digging, too, but mostly he was the assistant and the work was hers. He could only begin to imagine how her back felt, and he could only wonder if—before she'd come to Nightshade, before she'd been in the FBI in this capacity—she'd done this for hours on end as a student. She looked disturbingly comfortable pulling human bones out of the dirt.

Or so he'd thought for the first two graves. On the third, he noticed she was silently dripping tears into the hole as she dug. It had prompted him, after an hour of such silent work, and four more bones pulled up, to ask her, "Do you think that this is Emmaline?"

She shook her head, "It's not."

She sounded so confident, despite the tears.

"This is a boy," Eleri said. "He was somewhere between ten and fifteen years old." She was unable to offer a better age range than that, and Donovan understood. Bones didn't grow the same in everyone. They didn't grow at the same time, the same rate, or even always have the same changes. So from the bones alone, chronological age was hard to tell.

Eleri checked the teeth when she could, and that helped narrow down the age estimate, but not by much. She didn't have a skull for this boy yet. But the changes she saw in the clavicles and scapula, while laying out the pieces from his upper thorax, told her that this skeleton was male, and not merely a tall, immature female.

Donovan hadn't asked it before, but now that he'd broached the topic, he thought it was time. "Was one of the others Emmaline, do you think?"

Eleri shook her head again. "The first was too young—not even old enough for me to determine the gender. Emmaline was eight when she left. But I'm confident that she lived for a full decade after that."

So that couldn't have been Emmaline, Donovan thought. "What about the other?"

"A female of the right age." Eleri spoke in short non-sentences, indicating she was more tired, or at least weary, than she appeared. With the back of her hand, she wiped at the tears on her face, and Donovan didn't comment when she left a streak of dirt. It only joined others she'd already put there. Her work was more important.

The way she looked wouldn't matter until they got back in the car and were driving down the street, he thought. *If an officer stopped them, they would have mud on their faces and knees, and human bones in the trunk. None of that would look good.*

They already had six different cloth bags that Grandmere had provided. Inside were various-sized paper bags, stapled shut and labeled carefully with Sharpies. Eleri had insisted, and Donovan had thought it a solid, make-due idea. Of course, he'd seen excavations in action before, but it wasn't his job. So he'd merely done as she told him.

It was his handwriting on all the bags. His job tonight was to do everything he could to keep her aimed in the right direction.

Sitting up, he looked around, as he did approximately every five minutes. He scoured their surroundings not only with his eyes, but also with his ears and nose. What he wouldn't have given to be able to change and run along the borders of the cemetery, checking for interlopers. But he knew that was impossible. And, to be fair, Eleri was using the heck out of him. Despite the fact that he wasn't hunched over the grave site, he was not sitting idle.

"The teeth on the second one were wrong for Emmaline. She was the right age," Eleri added, "but the shape of the skull and the indentation on the back of the teeth indicated someone of Asian, perhaps, or Native American ancestry."

Donovan figured, given the case they were on, Native American made more sense. But what did he know?

When the first rays of sun broke through at the horizon, Eleri decided it was time to quit. She hadn't retrieved a single whole skeleton, and that bothered her. It bothered Donovan as well. But it seemed unlikely that their perpetrators had buried only body parts here, and he said so.

She shook her head. "I couldn't find them. I mean, we could have stayed at the first site, and dug out all the corners, and looked for every last piece of the skeleton. But things here drift. The water tables shift. It's why the graves are rising. So it's conceivable—more than conceivable, actually—that the bones also moved away as the body decomposed ... but ... wait."

She stopped and Donovan watched as she sat up ramrod straight, a thought brewing. *The missing bones are from hands and feet. So carpals, tarsals, metacarpals, and metatarsals—and long bones!*

Donovan looked at her, wondering where she was going. Whatever she'd just put together made sense to her, but not to him. Not yet. The hand and foot bones, he knew, tended to disappear easily. Those bones were tiny and hard to find, even if they hadn't drifted away. It was more than possible that many of them sat in the piles of dirt that they had shoved aside, and then pushed back into the grave sites when they were finished, just as he was doing with this one, now.

"No," Eleri said. "It's not the metatarsals and carpels that I'm thinking about, that's a normal issue. It's the long bones. There are a few missing long bones. In fact, there's at least one missing from each of these skeletons. Maybe we did find everything, Donovan! But maybe whoever buried these bodies kept a few bones *on purpose*."

50

Darcelle's head snapped back as Lafae yelled at her.

"What did you do?" her youngest sister demanded.

Gisele had joined in, ganging up on Darcelle. "Alesse is missing, and now we can't find the witch and her wolf."

Darcelle shook her head at the two of them. This wasn't what she thought they'd be yelling at her about. When they had asked what she had done, her mind had immediately snapped to the spells she had had been casting in her clearly inadequate attempts to break free.

"It didn't do anything," she said staunchly. It was a bit of a lie. She'd done a great deal—so much—but not that.

"Alesse is missing," Lafae said, her tone demanding nothing less than total compliance. It was what they were used to from Darcelle. It was the power her mother had given to them when she'd tied Darcelle to the shop. Darcelle had to be dutiful, and she was sick of it, all the way into her soul.

None of this fazed Lafae, who kept bitching. "And now, so are the two who came into our shop. We had spells on them. We knew where they were. We had our people show up, but they fought off our wolves, and now they're gone!"

Darcelle shrugged.

"Has the woman come back to the store?" Gisele demanded, the two of them talking in tandem. Either they had practiced this verbal assault, or they could read each other's minds.

Darcelle wondered now, *Did they do that? Did they cast spells on themselves so they could read each other's thoughts? Are they even capable of that level of magic?* It was possible, especially if they'd gotten their heads out of their asses and worked together.

She'd always been the odd sister out—smack in the middle, age-wise, and yet lingering at the outskirts in every other way. She was the one who'd worked with Momma and developed her power carefully, rather than only when it suited her. Alesse had been forced into more, but by the time Momma got to Gisele and Lafae, she'd been more indulgent, letting them learn what they needed only when their little hearts had desired something.

Darcelle shrugged again in answer to the latest demand. "I haven't seen her at the store. Not in a little while, anyway. You knew about it the last time she was in. You followed her." She paused dramatically and then offered her sisters a smirk and sarcastic comment, "Maybe you can't find her because she actually left town."

Gisele's head tipped in response to that, as if no one could possibly believe that would truly happen.

Honestly, Darcelle didn't believe it either. The woman had chosen to come into her shop, out of all the shops on the street. Then she'd honed in on the bone-handled knife and walked out, leaving a trace of something Darcelle recognized in her wake. She'd known from the moment that Eleri Eames had stepped into the store that something was up.

"Did you do something to Alesse?" Gisele asked, her arms crossed, suspicion in her tone. It wasn't the sharp demand of earlier. It wasn't intended to make her head snap back, and it didn't. However, the very idea that Darcelle might harm her sister was astonishing. In fact, the idea that she *could* harm her sister—with her hands tied, as they had been for years—was startling to her.

Her sisters must believe her more powerful than she was, and she was beginning to wonder if she was the only one who didn't believe. Was that part of her mother's spell? Had she been mentally pushed back, too? The thought churned something inside her. She might have been tied to the path by more than just the pain of breaking her boundaries. What had she missed in all this time? Now her resolve to break free grew stronger. But her sisters were still demanding an accounting that wasn't hers to say.

"Alesse is missing of her own accord," Darcelle told them. That was something she had decided when Gisele and Lafae didn't seem to have any better idea than she did where their older sister had gone.

"Has she come back?" Of course, they asked her. She was stuck at the house, in the shop, and on the path in between—nowhere else. If Alesse had come back, she was the one who would know. She hated it. If her sister had come back, she would have lied. But she told the truth.

"No." She shook her head. "I haven't seen her."

"Well, we have to find her. We need to know what happened. We need to know where she is."

None of them imagined that maybe Alesse was dead. It wasn't an option. The way the four were linked—the same way they'd been linked to their mother—made it an seem impossible that something heinous could happen to one without the others knowing. Darcelle thought again that perhaps her sisters had given themselves the ability to read each other's minds, but it appeared now that, if they had, they hadn't included Alesse in that. Or perhaps, for some reason, the oldest had blocked them.

"Well, we have to find her," Lafae repeated. "You have to help us, Darcelle."

Darcelle shrugged, almost laughing at the thought. "What can I do to help? I can't even leave this damned house."

"You can get her things, and you can cast from here," Lafae offered sulkily, as though it were obvious—and as though she, the youngest, was in charge of everyone above her. She was nothing close.

In this family, age mattered. Their great-grandparents had been revered. Their grandparents had done everything and been the top of their hierarchy, which was exactly why their mother had cast whatever magic she needed to remove them. Darcelle preferred not to know what Tempeste Dauphine had done.

"You'll help us," Gisele snarled, repeating the demand. Darcelle merely shrugged again. She would, but it was because she, too, needed Alesse back for her own purposes. She needed her mother's blood to break the spell her mother's blood had cast, and she knew four places where her mother's blood existed. Three wouldn't cut it—so she needed her sister back as desperately, if not more so, than her sisters did.

She had to admit, she was worried about what might happen to the Eleri Eames woman, once her sisters were all together again.

She knew Eleri was looking for something.

Darcelle was beginning to think this whole mess was tied together.

51

Eleri looked up from the bones she had spread out on the table at Grandmere's.

Donovan had just returned with another plastic sack of goodies in his hand. The costs were racking up, and though she'd insisted he take her card and spend her money instead of his own, she was pretty certain that he'd not done it. He'd insisted on helping, in every way that he could. For that, she would be forever grateful.

This time, he'd brought her a variety of toothbrushes and flat Tupperware bins—all the things that she would need to clean the bones. She'd been downloading the thousands of photos she'd taken at the cemetery.

Managing the photos was an epic job. She'd taken countless pictures, and she'd had Donovan snapping a shot each time a new piece of bone emerged or didn't. In school, she'd been trained that there could never be too many pictures of a scene. But she hated photos. They never fully captured what you wanted to look at. Having a shot from every possible angle and lighting was the best that you could do. They'd had red headlamps on all night, and she'd cringed every time the flash had gone off.

She knew she should be exhausted beyond the ability to stay upright. She should have come home and gone directly to sleep. Donovan had been tired, but she had been the opposite, strung tight and wired, ready to keep going. Still, he'd volunteered to go to the store so she could get started. She needed to do things he couldn't help her with. In this, she was the professional and he was the assistant.

Had the body been recently dead, she would have stepped aside and let him take over. But as these were fully skeletonized corpses, there wasn't much information he could get. So instead, he fetched toothbrushes and bottles of hydrogen peroxide, although she needed only a drop or two. He'd gotten rolls of paper towels, because she could not use Grandmere's linen closet for this. They now had straight, clear plastic rulers and swatches of black cloth to lay the bone out on so they could take additional photos.

She began to go through the stash he brought, turning away from the downloaded pictures she'd been sorting. Some were just the grass within the confines of the marble bricks marking the rectangular shape of the grave. In other shots, she'd just oriented to the headstone, and a few were taken of places so deep in a hole that all that showed was the pink crossed lines of her brightly colored nylon twine, marking the orientation of the compass.

She'd added her full set of bagged bones to the computers and everything else she'd set out on Grandmere's table before. Without any extra room, Grandmere was now forced to remove whatever she'd had out. Eleri could not afford for Grandmere's human bones—the ones from the closet, or any others she might have that Eleri didn't yet know about—to be mistakenly mixed in with these fresher ones.

Grandmere didn't balk at being moved aside in her own space. Instead, she made piles of her fabric scraps, her sticks and twigs and herbs. She moved some of them into growing stacks of her displaced crafts in the corners. Others, she carried back into her bedroom for safer storage.

Eleri next laid out three towels that Grandmere had given her—the only ones she was willing to use. They were dark colors, as she'd requested. She fervently hoped that later the dirt might wash out easily, should her Grandmere ever wish to use them again. Also, the dark color would make the lighter shade of the bones stand out for yet more photos.

Though many of the specimens were still quite muddy, she hoped to have them cleaned up and more photos taken soon. She lined up each part, pulling out bag after bag. She grouped the tiny carpel bones that formed the wrist and the base of the hand, sorting left and right, mezza lunate and trapezoid.

She sorted them easily now, but she still remembered being a grad student and trying to figure out which dent aimed which direction meant the bone belonged to the left or right hand.

She had them mostly aligned and three skeletons mostly reconstructed by the time Donovan returned, the bags in his hand a godsend to the task before her. But she still wasn't tired.

"Were you followed?" she asked.

He shook his head. "Not that I could tell."

Good. It went through her brain like a balm, loosening just a bit of the tension she now constantly carried. Perhaps the tracker that had been on them had not been physical in origin. Perhaps it had been, as Grandmere suggested—and perhaps it had been thwarted. She could only hope.

"You should go to bed," she told her partner. Glancing over her shoulder, she caught the gesture as he shook his head.

"I need to eat something."

That phrase sent Grandmere into action. Popping up as though she were thirty years younger than she actually was, she headed into the kitchen.

"I didn't mean—" he called out only the first part of the sentence before she interrupted him, putting a small grin on Eleri's face.

"No worries, child. This is how I can help, so help I will." Grandmere disappeared beyond the doorway, and soon the sounds of her clanking pots and the clicking of the gas stove echoed into the dining area.

Eleri smiled at Donovan. "Let her."

He nodded. "So what do we do next?"

"Well," she said, pulling lids off the Tupperware bins that he'd brought so she could inspect them. The largest was almost two feet long and seven to eight inches deep. They were intended for storage, but as a scientist, Eleri had learned that anything could be repurposed for her needs. "Fill this one with warm water and a little tiny bit of dish soap, and then this one—" she held up another bin, "with water and just a little, tiny bit of hydrogen peroxide."

She paused and held her hand up to stop him. "Actually, let me add the peroxide."

If he added a drop too much, it would bleach the bones, and she did not want·to affect them in any way. She just wanted to clean them.

Donovan nodded, either too tired to brook an argument or truly not offended by her need to control every last thing here. He quickly brought her back a sloshing bin with tiny bubbles forming each time the water rocked.

She picked up a femur, slid it into the water at an angle, and began using one of the toothbrushes to gently remove the last of the New Orleans cemetery dirt . As she cleaned, the color became brighter and brighter.

She would never get it to fully white, even with the very mild peroxide solution, but she patted it dry with a paper towel before setting it back on the dark bath towel. A few clumps of dirt still sat where they'd first shaken off, something she decided she could no longer worry about. Eleri picked up the next bone and worked this way, piece by piece, bone by bone.

But as she cleaned, a few things began to disturb her. Shockingly, Donovan stayed awake and at her side, picking up bones, scrubbing them with toothbrushes, working from those with firmer bristles all the way through medium and down to soft.

"I see now," he said, "why you wanted me to get multiple toothbrushes in each density." He'd almost laughed. "I really thought you'd lost your mind."

She grinned. "Different kinds of dirt require different levels of toothbrush bristles. Artists need a full array of paint brushes—and I need these."

She held up a radius and an ulna from the forearm of one of the victims. "Hey," she pointed to thin lines running the length of the bone. "Look at *that*."

Donovan frowned, and it occurred to her then that he didn't know—*he didn't know* what she knew from her visit with Agent Almasi. Right then, she sat up straight, suddenly snapping her spine into place.

"What is it, El?" he asked, noticing her change.

"*Shit, shit, shit!*" she said. Everything had started coming together in her mind.

"Eleri?" His hand reached out and touched her forearm, absently covering the white bandage that still wrapped it from the cut her Grandmere had made.

That cut pulled everything together. Without any clear idea of how to best explain, she began at the beginning.

"Donovan, sometimes when I see my sister, she's in the woods, she's in a white dress, and she's running barefoot, sometimes in the grass, sometimes on the dirt, sometimes down a sidewalk. But always wearing a dress, usually white, sometimes like a ..." she looked for the word, "a chambray."

He shook his head. Though he was following, she still hadn't given him enough to catch on.

"It's always cotton, *only cotton.* I didn't know that before, and I didn't put it together until Frederic had asked me the other night to only wear natural fibers."

"Like for spell work?"

She nodded. "The dresses are pretty—and I've been thinking back, *trying* to remember—but never, in any point in my memory, can I recall a single button, zipper, anything."

He nodded slowly.

"And several times when I've seen her, in my mind, she's had blood running down her hands. It's dripping into the dirt. I didn't see it then. I didn't know where it was coming from. But it would run down her hands. When I met with Agent Almasi—before you came down here—" she was rambling, but she couldn't get her thoughts any more organized than this. She could only hope Donovan followed. "When I saw the bones of the girl that I first thought was Emmaline, we found marks on the forearms, just like this."

She tapped on the radius and ulna in front of her. Then she quickly stood up and reached for the other two skeletons, ignoring the larger bones, the femur the tibia, and went straight for the forearms.

Quickly she scrubbed at them, easily finding more white lines down the front while her partner patiently waited through her madness.

"Donovan, they were bloodletting these kids. I'll bet they all have ties back in some way to some important family. It's about their blood. They were using them for spells."

Donovan nodded as he pointed at the laid out skeletons. "McKenzie Burke was one. And here we have two, three, and four."

"Yes," Eleri said. "We have to take these to Agent Almasi. This will blow his case wide open."

52

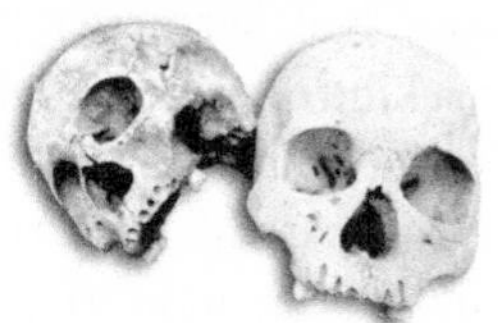

It had taken Eleri three hours to get the bones cleaned to the point that she was willing to let them go. It would have to be enough that she had examined them for herself, made her notes, and kept copies of all the photos.

She *wanted* to keep the actual bones. Eleri knew that having them in her hands was the best evidence and would give her the most information about what was going on. But she also knew she couldn't keep them. These bones belonged, most likely, to missing children. The families would want them back. The families had been through enough and *deserved* to have them back. She understood that better than most.

When she said she needed them for several more hours to finish her photos and her own assessment first, Donovan had easily agreed with her. Maybe he simply understood that she had to make the decision herself— she wasn't sure. She didn't ask. She just went about her work.

The day was moving on and leaving her behind, and she had to get to Agent Almasi before the sun disappeared. Not that an FBI agent actually *had* an end to their day. She knew that, when she called him and told him what she knew—what she had lain out on Grandmere's table—he would come immediately, regardless of the hour. But that wasn't how she wanted to do this.

She'd found the marks on the forearms of all three victims. And that's how she thought of them now, as *victims*. It was also a chain, indicating a serial killing, though not like what most people would think of as a serial killer. And—her own suspicions were, though she had no proof yet—these murders likely were not the work of a single person.

One of the sets of bones had a severe notch on the cervical vertebrae. Eleri strongly suspected that victim's throat had been slashed or the bone had been damaged in an attempt to cut the head off. She could not accept that a child had died that way. Not that there was any acceptable death for someone so young, but that kind of ending would not have been kind.

Whoever was taking these children was bloodletting them over timespans of at least several years. The scarring on the bones showed that time passage, with older scars indicating healing of the first time the bone had been breached. Fresher scars showed that the cutting continued for these kids.

Eleri had ignored some of the femurs and tarsals, leaving them dirty, with little pieces of Louisiana grave dirt clinging to them. Perhaps there was something there, but they no longer interested her the way the cut bones did. She wouldn't have had time to clean and inspect everything. She had to choose what she worked on.

She also realized that holding these bones in her possession any longer than necessary would constitute further crimes than she'd already committed. She was only willing to go so far. Right now, she thought, Agent Almasi might find a way to forgive her her trespasses —but if she waited any longer, he wouldn't be able to protect her identity or her illegal activity here.

She laid out the arm bones, the radii and the ulnas, of each of the three victims. Lining them up, she shot photo after photo. Two showed evidence of repeated cutting over long periods of time. The third skeleton, however, the youngest at time of death, had only a few cuts on each arm. Just as her Grandmere had done, whoever had done this had flayed the forearm down to the bone.

If it was anything like what her Grandmere had done, the perpetrators likely also had the skills to heal the wound as quickly as they could cut it. And if they could do that, they could use one of these children as a blood source for an extended period of time.

But the third, the smallest victim, the one who had the notch in the cervical vertebrae, indicating something had happened to him—

something severe and almost definitely fatal—at his neck. He had the fewest scars on his arms.

Eleri began to form a theory.

She suspected all these children had gone missing right around the same age. Given what she knew of Mackenzie Burke's and her own sister Emmaline's disappearance, she suspected that age was somewhere between seven and ten. Still young enough to be lured away, still young enough to grow and be manipulated by the family's needs or machinations.

Eleri suspected it was a family that was doing this. It might be a cult. That was still a possibility. She wouldn't reveal all of her suspicions to Agent Almasi. She had a few more.

After a full night without rest, she had become so tired, she was unable to shake the feeling "in her bones" that something was wrong. She looked up at Donovan.

"Are you ready?" he asked.

She nodded, unable to voice the words, still a little trapped in the stories the children's skeletons told her.

He'd made yet another trip out, this time fetching file boxes packaged as flat pieces of cardboard. He'd neatly folded them up into their proper shapes.

She'd labeled them, Subject One, Subject Two, Subject Three. She'd had Donovan write up a sheet of paper to put in each, indicating her findings and the suspected age range for the victim. She included the locations of each of the major bones, the skull, and the name on the grave from which they had been collected. It was obvious that the tombstone inscriptions did not name the victims she'd found. She hadn't breached a single closed casket, but maybe the inscriptions held clues. At the least, they were necessary evidence, something Almasi would have collected had he done the dig himself. So she provided it.

In the second two boxes, she'd included small Tupperware containers, just regular plastic ware that could be bought at a big box store, with soil samples from various layers they had scraped. Each plastic storage box had a corresponding photograph and a notation of the depth where they'd retrieved the sample.

She couldn't tell just by looking if someone had been coming and filling in the dirt over the graves. Donovan had not been able to sniff out a difference in the dirt layers, either. So that would be up to the labs to determine.

They'd added a USB drive with copies of every single picture she'd taken at the graves, but not the ones she'd taken of the bones laid out on Grandmere's table. She didn't want to implicate her great-grandmother in this. The USB would have to do. She taped it to the inside of one of the boxes. She couldn't sort all the photos with their proper victims, because of course, Grandmere did not have a computer printer available, and this wasn't the kind of thing they could run through the local copy shop.

Donovan looked at her again. "You're not ready, Eleri."

He motioned with his hand up and down her form as she stood and she realized he wasn't referring to the fact that she was loathe to give away her evidence. He was instead pointing out that she was still in the same pants she'd been digging in all night. The dirt stains on her knees revealed less dirty rectangular patches from the knee pads she'd eventually put on, which had only done a little to protect her knees and nothing to protect her back. She was wondering now if her spine would ever straighten out again. But if she found Emmaline, it would be worth it.

She showered, as Donovan had done when they'd first come home, and tried to make herself presentable. They stacked the boxes in the back of the car and asked Grandmere if they were safe to leave.

Grandmere looked back and forth between them. "You're as safe as I can make you," she said again. Eleri thought that would be pretty good until her Grandmere shook her head. "I've done what I can. But I am one person, and I don't know how strong the other side is."

Eleri listened carefully to the phrasing her grandmother chose. The *others,* Grandmere said when referring to them now, as though they were in some kind of epic battle. She'd thought once again of the Hatfields and McCoys. But how simple those gun battles seemed compared to this.

Before they walked out of the house, she picked up her own phone and turned it on. She saw several messages and texts from Avery. *I should return those,* she thought. But she needed to call Agent Almasi and turn off her phone again before she left the house. She'd have to reply to Avery later tonight, perhaps after she got some sleep. She didn't want to say anything that didn't make sense or, God forbid, anything she might regret.

She bypassed those messages and dialed up Almasi. He answered right away.

"Eleri Eames!" he said, surprised. "I didn't expect to hear from you again, or maybe not so soon. What's going on? Did you find your sister?"

"No," Eleri replied, not liking the sound of the single syllable falling off her tongue. She wanted to say *yes.* Deep in her spine, she felt that she was much, much closer. Instead, she offered, "I have something for you."

"Do you want to bring it by the office?" he asked.

"No," she said. This time, the same syllable sounded stronger, determined. "I can't." She left it at that. She could almost hear the frown pulling his features together.

"Can you tell me what it is?"

"No," she replied, "but it's bigger than a breadbox."

"Ohhhkayyyy?" He drew out the word, but the question at the end was one she would not yet answer.

She needed him to be away from the office. She needed to not get caught on video meeting with him. And she knew the branch offices were thoroughly monitored. "Is this some clandestine meeting in a park?" he asked almost jokingly.

Eleri replied, "Yes. My partner, Donovan Heath, will be with me. But please don't record any of that. I'm going to give you something, and I'd like you to take it into the office as your own find."

Through the silence she heard his curiosity building—and then the dawning recognition. "I'm not going to like this, am I?"

"Well," she replied, "I think it's going to crack some things wide open for you. You might love that part. But the rest of it—no, you're not going to like it at all."

53

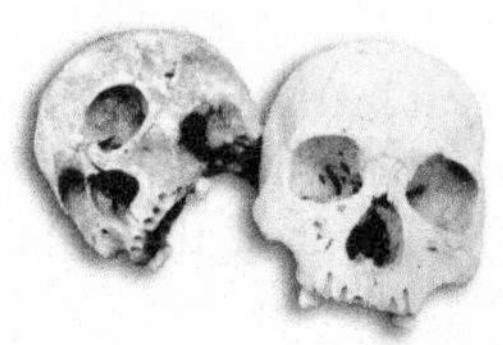

"Walter called," Donovan told her, and Eleri's ears perked, glad he'd heard from his girlfriend. He continued, "I called her back last night."

"Oh, that's wonderful." Eleri was relieved to hear that he was managing to maintain that relationship. It had been hard in the beginning, with Walter in Los Angeles running a private investigations business. She figured Westerfield snatching Walter up for the FBI division probably put exponential pressure on the two of them. She was grateful every time she heard that things were going well.

But Donovan's expression turned darker, and Eleri had only a moment to wonder before he dropped a bombshell.

"She gave me some news that she and GJ are dealing with." He paused dramatically, in a very un-Donovan-like way. "Dr. Murray Marks has gone AWOL."

"I'm sorry, *what?*" Eleri's head snapped up. She'd been expecting "Walter says hi," or something equally inane. Though his statement was totally unrelated to this case, it was a shock she'd not been prepared for.

She felt the thought pass her mind at warp speed: at least, she *hoped* this news was totally unrelated. But who knew? She filed the thought so she could work it over later and turned her attention to him, surprise still coloring her features.

"Are you serious? Wasn't he in prison?" she asked. Even as her brain wrapped around the thought, she still didn't fully believe it.

"That's what we were told, but he wasn't being held in any prison Walter could find. Not in gen pop and he wasn't in solitary. They had him in some specific, unnamed holding area."

"What happened? Did his people come and break him out?" It was the only thing Eleri could think of that might have worked. If he was at a safe house, if they found out where he was … if someone had leaked information …

She was trying to put the pieces together when Donovan said, "I asked Walter the same thing, and that's what she and GJ guess, but no one is saying anything. So as of right now, they don't know where he was being held or specifically how it was that he got out. The only thing Westerfield will confirm is that he was alive when they last saw him—"

"Oh my God," Eleri interrupted, actually putting her hand to her heart. "The case has been hard enough for GJ. She had to arrest her own grandfather and investigate the sordid activities he'd been into. But now?"

"Exactly," Donovan said. "So he was alive the last time they saw him, and then he escaped. They didn't say that he was on his own, if they expected to catch up with him, or anything else. Only that he's gone."

"Shit," Eleri muttered. "He was probably gone for several days by the time Walter and GJ heard about it."

If they'd been able to recapture him, Westerfield might never have mentioned it. She was pretty sure she knew how her boss worked after several years in his employ. She had to let all these thoughts turn over for a few moments. Although Donovan had known this since last night, he gave her the time to think about it. Then, as the thought struck, she looked up at him.

"This means we're even more likely to be pulled back into this case," she said. "We're going to have to look for him."

He nodded. "It's either us or else Westerfield's going to hand it to GJ again. She's probably the best one to track him."

"Or the worst," Eleri said with a shrug.

If Westerfield gave them the assignment, it was going to be a hard call. She did not want to be yanked off of this—not when she felt so close to finding her sister and her sister's killer. She knew now, from the scars on the bones and from what she had dreamed of Emmaline, that her sister had been used as a source. Spells had been cast using Emmaline's blood. Eleri shuddered again at the thought that it just as easily could have been her.

They'd both been out riding that day. Whoever had taken Emmaline could just as easily have arrived fifteen minutes earlier and taken Eleri instead. They shared the same blood, and that's what the kidnappers had been after, it seemed. It was a crap shoot which girl they got. Either would have sufficed. Once again, she wished it had been her. Still, there was nothing she could change about the past.

With her heart heavy, she looked at Donovan. "I don't know if I'll go if Westerfield calls me."

In the few seconds since she'd first thought of the possibility of getting yanked off her own investigation, Eleri had made up her mind. She needed to finish this search—even if it cost her her job.

Donovan nodded, but she couldn't tell what that meant. Did it mean he understood her dedication? Would *he* go back if their boss demanded it?

She understood that. Donovan needed to keep his job. Most people did. She was the oddball here, both in her trust fund and her missing sister. *Still, she wanted to keep working for the NightShade division,* she thought. It would just need to be after Emmaline's remains were found. She wasn't sure that refusing an assignment would put her job in jeopardy, or worse, put Donovan's job in jeopardy, but she knew it might.

He didn't deserve that kind of friendship from her, but her sister didn't deserve to be let go either. Not after all these years.

For now, she would wait. She would decide whether to cross that bridge when they came to it.

Eleri truly hoped that they wouldn't come to it—because she didn't know what it would look like or if she would have to burn it down.

54

Donovan had tried to sleep the night before, but found he just couldn't slide over the edge into rest.

He was tired enough. The day had been well over thirty-six hours long, and the work had been back-breaking. He'd dealt with the constant addition of tasks. Every time he thought that his work was done, something else came up. He'd turned around and driven back to the store more than twice. He'd fetched multiple rounds of goodies for Eleri to clean her bones or set them up nicely for delivery to the FBI branch office.

Donovan had not met with Agent Almasi, though he'd gone along. Eleri was trying desperately to shield him from the effects of their little grave-robbing expedition, and Donovan appreciated the effort, although this was the only time he took her up on her efforts to minimize his role. This time, they'd actually borderline committed a crime. So he laid low, knowing that she had a relationship with the agent she was meeting with and it would likely go well.

It had gone as well as it could. When they returned home, he had once again believed he would crash and finally sleep. But he hadn't.

Eleri stayed up and helped her Grandmere make dinner before she wandered off to her room. He, on the other hand, had helped Grandmere eat the dinner.

Apparently, being what he was burned a mega shit ton of calories. He'd long assumed he was just one of those big-eater kind of guys.

But the more he hung around Wade and saw the others, the more he realized it wasn't a personal trait so much as a species one. Still, he should've rolled into bed and been well asleep before he was fully horizontal.

It hadn't happened. Instead, he lay still with his eyes aimed at the ceiling, counting the swirls from whatever kind of paintbrush had been used to cover Grandmere's ceiling with a thick, puffy paint. He wasn't even sure what era the paint job was from, only that it wasn't from this one.

He couldn't shake the memory of the smell of the man in the alley. The word *brother* kept running through his head. But he was an only child. He tried to think it through, tried to remember. What did he know? That his mother had died when he was young. But how? Had he seen her body? He had no idea. He was torn between wanting to tell Eleri more and not burdening her with his imaginary sibling, when her real sister was in the ground somewhere. He continued staring at the ceiling, unable to sleep.

Eventually, he turned his phone on and collected several texts from Walter. He'd texted back, not expecting anything in return. He was happy when he'd gotten a quick response.

In short bursts, Walter relayed to him GJ's anger about her grandfather escaping. Apparently, it had been hard enough that she'd had to tell her mother that her grandfather was a criminal. Telling her family that Dr. Marks had escaped opened a whole new can of worms. Unfortunately, GJ had been left to relay that information to her family—because no one really knew where he'd been held. The FBI wasn't giving out information. GJ might not have either, but there was a very real possibility the man might turn up at his daughter's home. Thus, the task had fallen to GJ's irritated shoulders.

Walter had no updates on anything beyond that. At least, she said, she and GJ had not yet been sent out to find the man. For that, she was grateful. However, the assignment that she thought would last three days to a week to clean out Dr. Marks' lab had now become exponentially longer.

They'd started with an assignment of a few days. But the time frame had grown from the moment they'd begun cataloging the information and realized it was a bigger task than planned. It got longer again when they found the body in the kettle and tried to identify it. Now, it stretched out even further, because Dr. Marks had escaped.

She and GJ were officially on guard duty at a large home with a large staff and an even larger basement laboratory. They were asked to guard the secret entrance to this lab—despite the fact that they still had not found it.

Walter was not pleased.

Donovan thought about helping her out. He could call Westerfield and even Wade and ask what they thought of the likelihood that Marks would head to the burned-out family compound outside Billings—or maybe the family compound in the Ozarks. But he didn't call. Walter didn't need him stepping in. Besides, she'd gotten her information from Westerfield, and Westerfield had surely considered all these options. If he'd told Walter, then he would have also told Wade. So, in the end, there was nothing for Donovan to worry about. It wasn't his responsibility to let anyone else know.

When Walter's texts had slowed to a trickle and finally stopped, she'd said, "Goodnight," and signed off. He hadn't told her about the man in the alley, either. He didn't want to do it over texts, or even the phone. So instead of saying anything, he had said he was going to sleep.

But it still didn't happen.

His mind roiled with ideas as pieces of Eleri's case churned through his thoughts. He realized it was time he started to treat this as a real case. He was no longer just helping out a friend. He was investigating. So, he did what they did best when they got a new case, and he laid everything out in order. Then he began clicking it together.

One—they had met Darcelle Dauphine, who had a knife made from human bone. There were missing human bones from the children he and Eleri had dug up in the cemetery.

He had no idea—and he made a mental note to ask Eleri—if the bone-handled knife in the shop had been made from a child's bone. His best guess was that it hadn't. Eleri most likely would have told him, because if would have been even more shocking if the knife handle was part of a child. So he would ask her, but he thought he knew the answer.

He moved to the second piece of evidence they had—a cemetery with at least ten patches of turned earth. Three of those sites—the only three they had dug—had contained human bones. Children's bones, or at least those of minors.

They had not yet had a chance to dig the other seven patches that they found. Still, right now, at one-hundred percent of the sites where the earth was unsettled, there had been the decomposed body of a child. That was unsettling. He could only assume the other seven sites also had bones. Statistically, it made sense.

He was glad Eleri had turned in the locations of the un-dug sites to the agent at the FBI, along with the file boxes full of human bones they'd collected. Donovan suspected the cemetery might even now be crawling with agents. It might already have yellow tape wrapped around the corners and crossing the gates, cautioning anyone who dared to enter.

He almost thought it was funny. It was likely he and Eleri were the only ones who had dared.

He tugged his thoughts to the next piece of evidence and clicked it into place with an almost audible snap from his mind. They had found the cemetery by tracing Cabot's movements. Cabot had gone to the cemetery so often that he was willing to incur parking tickets for those visits. Not a big bit of willingness, Donovan amended. As apparently, Cabot wasn't paying the fines, so it wasn't too great a risk.

Click. Another piece snapped into place. Cabot led them back to Darcelle Dauphine and the younger sisters, Gisele and Lafae. Were all the Dauphine sisters in league with Cabot and his brother Carson? Donovan made another mental note that they thought Cameron was involved—but what about the fourth brother? Where was he?

At least according to Eleri, it wasn't clear if Darcelle, the second oldest Dauphine sister, was in cahoots with the younger two. Still, just because they hadn't seen it, didn't mean he could set the idea aside, either. There was no evidence either for or against it, so he couldn't count it out.

Next piece. *Click*. Grandmere had said the other big family in town was the Dauphine family. She'd said this before Eleri even knew that the woman she was speaking to in the shop was a Dauphine, before she knew the Dauphines had knives with human bone handles.

The facts made a big circle when he looked at them that way. It also meant the likelihood was that the Dauphine family—or someone close to them—had been kidnapping children over the years and using them for bloodletting.

That sounded bizarre as shit, he thought, his eyes still trained on the weird swirls in the ceiling. If someone had mentioned this to him even two short years ago, he would've laughed them off the planet. He, a man who'd known for several decades, that he could snap his bones in a series of double-jointed moves, roll his shoulders, stretch his feet a certain way, watch the hair on his arms stand up and thicken, and become what looked like, basically, a wolf—*he* would have laughed these people off of the street.

Westerfield and his FBI unit had certainly made Donovan think differently. He wasn't sure he appreciated it, but the scientist in him did appreciate knowing everything possible.

Since there was nothing more he could do about his situation now but accept it, he left it at that. Finally starting to get tired, he felt his eyelids closing and the ceiling growing dimmer. As he drifted off, he decided they needed to meet with Darcelle one more time.

55

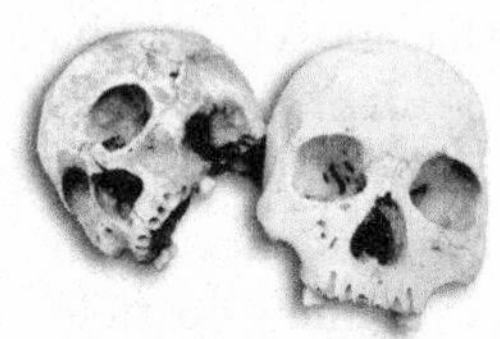

Once again, Eleri had slept like the dead. It was a phrase she was beginning to think was not inappropriate, in this situation. She'd risen, the hour late, the night long, and met up with Donovan and Grandmere as they polished off breakfast. Of course, there was a plate waiting for her.

Eleri wondered how Donovan was doing. He'd gotten up before her, despite the fact that she'd heard him rolling around on his bed until the moment she'd fallen asleep. But she'd passed out so quickly, she had no idea how much longer he's stayed awake.

She'd desperately needed every hour of sleep she'd stolen from the night. It had been a physically taxing day and an emotionally trying one, too. She knew she might have just handed away her ability to find her own sister. Agent Almasi had agreed to keep her out of it and claim that he'd been given the bones and the tip from an anonymous source. Still, she was pretty certain there was no way anyone of reasonable intelligence would not connect her to the bones that had turned up. Who else in this town could—or would—dig bodies out of shallow graves with such professional precision?

She wondered if the cemetery was now crawling with FBI agents. When she asked Donovan what he thought, he laughed, saying he'd figured that out last night probably around one a.m.

"Why wait for morning light?" he'd asked her.

Then she'd eaten her breakfast as she listened to him talk all the little pieces together, the same pieces she'd clicked. Good. They lined up in their thinking. She was comforted that they had independently arrived at the same conclusions. Though, that might be a mistake. Maybe they thought the same because they'd been in each other's pockets for so long. In the end, she agreed they needed to go back to Mystic Vudu.

It was time to confront Darcelle Dauphine.

Her stomach turned, the heavy breakfast sitting like a rock as they parked the car down the street and walked in. It felt odd to her—almost at odds with their purpose—to be coming back here.

This was the one piece of work that Agent Almasi could not finish up. He might look at the Dauphine sisters and see a cult and a weird belief in the paranormal, but Eleri saw action. Eleri saw things that had actually happened, not just based on her belief. And not just murder. Still, after they'd worked so hard using Grandmere's spells, trying to stay off the radar, it seemed wrong to walk right into the store.

If she'd had her way, she would have arrived as the store opened. But now, doing that would mean waiting until tomorrow, and she didn't want to wait. So they were here now, in the late morning, with tourists roaming up and down the streets as she and Donovan pulled open the door and let the air conditioning wash over them.

With the cool air came a breath of awareness. Darcelle Dauphine must have known the moment they entered the store. It took only as many seconds as it took heartbeats for her to appear in the doorway and ask, "Eleri, Donovan, what brings you back?"

Eleri almost shouted at her, "*Where is my sister? What did you do with her?*" But Donovan's hand, lightly clasping around the small bones of her wrist, stayed her.

Luckily, he was doing the right thing. Perhaps he'd smelled others in the shop or heard them. Regardless, Eleri hadn't noticed if they were alone. Perhaps that was why Darcelle Dauphine's opening conversation had perhaps been so generic.

Two men and a woman were rattling about in the back room. At least, that was what Eleri could see through the archway. Darcelle raised an eyebrow at her and turned away from them to wait on her customers.

Frustrated, Eleri roamed the shop. It took two rooms before she realized she already knew what was in here and nothing had changed. But what she wanted to know about was the knives. She wandered through to the last room to see that several of the knives she'd seen on her first visit had gone missing. Perhaps sold, perhaps taken home for personal use. New ones filled the gaps they left behind.

Donovan pointed to one of the replacements, which looked like the end of a femur. Eleri examined it more closely. It took only a moment to lift it and assess that it was a resin cast model, not an actual bone. In low tones, she said to so Donovan.

"Shit," he whispered. "It looks good."

"It does," Eleri agreed. She pointed to small spots where the bone had pock marks, rubbed dark with some kind of stain. The piece had been aged to look like it had been in the ground for some time. Even the way the edges were chipped and splintered made it look more real.

Eleri picked it up again then and gave another look. It was just resin. She did not doubt that initial assessment, but as she twisted it in the light checking all the angles, she became more and more convinced that it was a resin cast of an actual bone.

She pointed out features to Donovan. "I can't imagine an artist would carve this," she said, pointing to the kinds of pock marks and defects that one might find on a real bone.

Donovan had tilted his head, trying to get a better angle himself. "Do you think it's here to throw us off? Maybe to make us think you didn't actually see a human bone the first time—or to discredit us?"

"What do you mean?" she asked, her brows pulling together.

"Well," he whispered, his head still occasionally tilting to listen to Darcelle chatting up the customers in the other room. Certainly, he heard it better than she did, so Eleri merely continued the conversation, trusting his judgment not to lead her off track. "I mean," he said, "that if we come back later and claim that there were human bone knives here ..."

Eleri caught on. "Then they pull this out and say, 'No, it's just resin, it's a big seller' or something ..."

He nodded. It would make them look like fools. But the fact was, Eleri knew the other knife had truly been bone. She also knew that, if it came down to it, it would merely be her word versus theirs on the witness stand—and she didn't like that.

They waited almost thirty minutes, browsing the shop and acting like patrons while her nerves ratcheted up. Another set of customers had wandered in off the street just as Darcelle had rung up the previous ones. Eleri held her patience on a taut wire while the woman sold these next two—two very young women—books on witchcraft and Haitian voodoo.

As she thanked them and watched them leave, it was Eleri who ushered them out the door. She had decided, if anyone else tried to come in, she would pretend she worked here and push them out. Instead, she merely walked to the door and flipped the sign to "closed" while Darcelle once again raised an eyebrow.

"What is it that you want, little witch?" the woman asked, her dark skin gleaming, her teeth white in what wasn't quite a smile.

Eleri started with a softball question. "Where is the bone-handle knife?"

Darcelle shrugged at her. "I don't know what you are talking about."

"You know exactly what I'm talking about," Eleri replied, her tone calm, not even having reached mother-to-toddler level yet.

"Perhaps I sold it," Darcelle said, and Eleri was grateful for all her FBI training.

It did not take any witchcraft to see the micro-expression in the woman's face—the twitch of her cheekbone near her eye, the slight tick in her jaw. Darcelle Dauphine had not sold the bone-handled knife and her face revealed the truth. Eleri only smiled.

"All right then, enjoy your little lie," she offered, and watched the tick appear again as Darcelle found she was caught, but still didn't say anything. Eleri lobbed something a little harder next. "It's my understanding that your friend Cabot keeps ..." She almost said "racking up parking tickets," but as of yet—and she didn't know what Darcelle knew—she'd not revealed that she was a federal agent. There was no clear way for her to know about Cabot's nasty little habit without some kind of legal access. She wasn't quite ready to play that card yet.

So she rephrased, wondering if Darcelle also might read her micro expressions or even the hitch in her phrase. "... that Cabot has been visiting a cemetery over on Villere street quite frequently."

Darcelle tipped her head, the same eyebrow going up, and Eleri watched as she continued talking.

"Interesting little thing there." Perhaps she shouldn't be giving this information away, she thought, but she had. She'd already given it away once to the FBI and she was ready to give it away again. While it might hinder the FBI's case, she did it because she thought it would help her own, and she was dedicated to finding Emmaline now.

"The interesting thing is that we found a grave for Nellie McKenzie Burke."

Darcelle crossed her arms as though the story bored her, and no micro expressions gave anything away.

"We found several other graves"—Eleri didn't list the number—"that had freshly turned earth. And when we dug them up, we found human skeletons, Darcelle. Children. We found *children* buried on top of existing graves."

Darcelle was trying to play it cool, but slowly, while Eleri had spoken, she'd lost her natural stance, her movements becoming stiff and finally still as Eleri talked.

"I don't know what your family has been doing, Darcelle, but I do know that you'll go down with them. I have only one question for you. Where is my sister?"

She said it as a demand. Darcelle was stock still, seemingly unaware of what had hit her. Eleri was not prepared for the return question.

"What, witch? You want your sister?" Darcelle snarled. "First, you tell me—where is *mine*?"

56

Eleri felt the air crackle between them.

She hadn't thought of her own power in this situation until it was obviously spreading out around her and sparking off an equal or greater power from Darcelle.

It took her a moment to gather her voice and her thoughts. "What do you mean, your sister? I came to find mine."

Darcelle's eyes narrowed. "I don't care what you came to find, little witch. I have my own problems."

Eleri almost laughed out loud. She believed not only that Darcelle *had* her own problems but that she *caused* them. She was not sure that her negative opinion wasn't showing across her face, even as she did try her best to hide it.

There was another pause as the air cracked and sparked. Donovan's gaze volleyed back and forth between the two women. He looked as if he was about to step between them to create a physical barrier, to stop whatever was going on. He tried instead to become the voice of reason.

"Let's wait a moment," he said to Eleri, and then turned to the other woman. "Tell us about your sister, Darcelle."

As Eleri heard his voice break the tension, she thought what a good idea it was. She had been so stunned and so angry, she wouldn't have been able to think of it herself. Perhaps they could get Darcelle to give up some of the information without playing their own hands in return.

"Is it still Alesse who is missing?" Donovan pushed.

Eleri realized then that he had let Darcelle know, by his very words, that they knew about her sisters. Had he meant to do that? She wouldn't have given up their knowledge so fast, but she hoped he had some ulterior motive.

It probably wasn't a shock to Darcelle that Donovan knew at least what Eleri knew. For a moment, the woman paused and looked as though she wasn't going to say anything. Eleri wondered about that. Had the original question about her sister just slipped out of her mouth? Was it even true? Had she simply bantered back to Eleri?

Slowly, a pout formed on Darcelle's features. Her eyes narrowed, her lips pursed. And at last, she said in low tones, "Yes, Alesse."

The oldest, Eleri thought but didn't say out loud. Then, gathering her wits and thinking before she spoke this time, she asked, "Is this what you were talking about before? How long has she been gone?"

So, she hadn't disappeared at the age of eight, like Eleri's own sister. Alesse had been accounted for even recently by the reports she and Donovan had pulled from the FBI and local police force databases. Still, she did not mention all that she knew to Darcelle.

"Yes." Darcelle nodded and added, "One week."

"Are you concerned about her?"

Darcelle shrugged slightly. Eleri found it hard to tell if Darcelle wasn't concerned because she believed nothing bad had happened to her sister or if she wasn't concerned because she simply didn't care what might have befallen Alesse. Eleri stared, waiting, still hoping to drag the silence out and force the other woman's hand. It only worked so well.

"Tell me about your sister," Darcelle demanded softly. *Quid pro quo.*

Eleri realized the woman wasn't going to be quite so easy to play. She looked to Donovan, wondering if he had any ideas on how to proceed. His return expression was subtle, but it told her to do as she thought best.

Eleri opened up and cut her own wound a little bit deeper. "My sister disappeared when she was eight years old. I'm confident she lived to be seventeen before she died. And I'm confident that she wound up *here*."

Darcelle nodded, as though none of this was surprising—not that

Eleri's sister had gone missing at such a young age, had stayed alive so long after, or even that she herself was looking like one of the prime suspects. None of it seemed to faze her, which almost fazed Eleri.

Eleri pushed back. "Tell me about Alesse. What happened when she went missing last week?"

Darcelle nodded, knowing it was her turn. "Her room looked like it had been tossed," she said, the accent coming through again, the words both crisp and lilting, almost as though the language itself was magical.

Eleri worked to pay attention to the words as Darcelle continued speaking.

"She often does this," Darcelle said. "She leaves for several days at a time. Usually, she's back before the week is out, though. This time, her return is overdue."

"It didn't bother you that her room had been ransacked?"

Darcelle threw her head back released a deep and throaty laugh. The dry amusement almost made it difficult for her words to get through. "My sister's room often looks like a nuclear bomb has exploded in it. It was difficult to tell that it was more messy than normal. I was only able to do so because I had gotten tired of looking at it and had gone in and straightened it up the day before. Otherwise, I still wouldn't know when she'd last been home—or even maybe that she was missing."

Interesting. "Do you think she left because she was angry that you went into her room?"

Again, Darcelle laughed. Only this time, it was harsher. "She expects me to clean up after her. So, no, she was not angry that I did what she expected."

"Did she say anything before she left?" Eleri knew she was going through the standard questions. Though she was trying not to sound like law enforcement, she couldn't help being what she was.

Darcelle stopped and mulled it over for a moment, as though she were actually accepting help from Eleri and Donovan on this topic. Even though no one had yet agreed to anything, they were exchanging information. "I don't believe she did," Darcelle said. "My sister says strange things all the time. I think she may be a little bit ... "There was a slight pause, a moment, and then the words, "... mentally ill. Either that or perhaps she is just a full-grown brat. But she does not warn me where she is leaving or for how long—unless she is just trying to taunt me."

Eleri went for the next standard question, grateful to be on the asking side of things for a while. "And you've received no text messages, phone messages, no indication that she was home while you were out?"

Darcelle looked at her as though Eleri must think she was stupid and that Eleri was equally dull-witted for underestimating her. And Eleri, had she been sitting on one side of the interrogation table, would have informed her that the questions were standard. But again, until she pulled that badge out, she wouldn't do it.

"I mean," she said, trying to sound causal, "if you were worried, wouldn't you have reached out and asked her to text you back or something?"

Darcelle replied, "Of course I did. We have heard no response. We cannot find her cell phone. We have no idea where she is."

"Who is we?" Eleri asked, though she had a sneaking suspicion. Darcelle gave only the names *Lafae* and *Gisele*. Not Cabot or Carson, or either of the other two Salzanis, though Eleri suspected they were in this up to their eyeballs as well. She asked the next phrase as a question, "I'm assuming you've reached out to your friends?"

Darcelle paused, going still for just a moment. Not as though the question had caught her, but as though it had made her realize something. She looked Eleri dead in the eyes before inquiring, "Who would I ask?"

Eleri frowned, and Darcelle clarified, "I have no friends. I have only my home and the shop. I have only my sisters, when they deign to interact with me."

"But you live with them," Eleri pointed out, knowing full well that siblings didn't always get along. Not every set of sisters was as close as Echo and Ember had been. She shuddered at the thought and pushed her focus back to the present.

"Well, *live* is a strong term," Darcelle conceded. Her arms were still crossed, and she didn't elaborate any further. Instead, she pushed. "I *need* my oldest sister back."

Eleri found that interesting. Darcelle seemed to feel no love for the other women in her life, and by her own words, she had no friends. Yet she claimed she needed her sister. Eleri wanted to push that envelope further, but she was afraid to give herself away. She was doing well right now, making slow advances, getting Darcelle to speak.

Just as Eleri was getting ready to open her mouth, Darcelle turned the table again, putting herself in the driver's seat and asking the next question. "Why do you believe your sister lived so long after she disappeared? Did you see her? Do you know where she went?"

Eleri shook her head. "Not at the time, no." And she wondered why she was giving this information over freely, but for whatever reason, her instincts told her that bargaining with Darcelle was the right thing to do now.

"So why do you believe she lived?" Darcelle pressed, as though she knew Eleri was going to give an answer she couldn't defend.

It rubbed Eleri the wrong way, the suggestion that her knowledge was belief and not fact. Darcelle had neatly pushed her into wanting to give up her information.

Yet given that she was standing in a shop called Mystic Vudu ... and that the bone-handled knife had been here and subsequently disappeared ... and given what she knew of the sisters Dauphine, Eleri decided to tell her. "Because I saw her, and I spoke to her in my dreams. I had no idea where she was, but I knew she was alive and that she was relatively safe." And then she said, "That was aside from the few times I saw her bleeding. And now, I think you know something."

Darcelle's face stayed flat, but her eyebrows rose as she asked Eleri, "Was your sister Mackenzie? Helena? Emmaline? Esther? Sarah? Rebecca? Or Misty?"

57

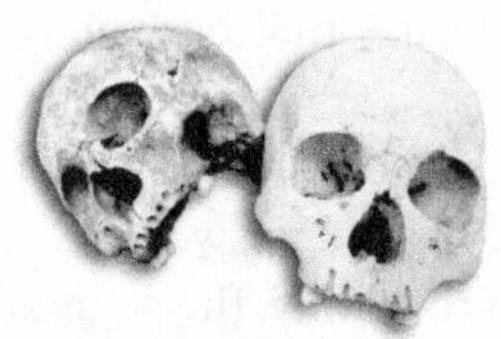

Darcelle walked home, her thoughts tumbling. She wasn't sure what kind of tacit agreement she had just entered into—but at least knew who it was with.

She had made a deal with her own personal devil.

She had watched Eleri Eames go sheet-white as she had listed the names of the little girls that Eleri's sister might be. Even Donovan had looked shocked. She smelled the wolf on him, though he wasn't one of their own. There were so many around the city who worked with Cabot and with her sisters, and Darcelle didn't know them all, but she could smell them. This man was ... well, he was different.

One thing she knew, though—and she knew it without the use of any special powers—was that he was loyal as a dog to the Eames woman.

She'd had no doubt from the first time she met Eleri that Eleri had some power of her own. She also had no doubt that Eleri was not confident of that power. Unlike Darcelle, she'd not been raised in it, not been trained and honed it from Day One. So Eleri Eames was a bit of a wild card; however, Darcelle was done dicking around.

She left the shop sign turned to "Closed," gathered a few more supplies, and headed home. She had decided it was better to collect things bit by bit rather than raiding the shelves all at once. If her sisters were keeping an eye on her, she didn't want to come home with a big bag from the shop. It was better to walk in the door with a few items in her purse and sneak them in, one by one. Even so, she was overstocking, but she felt the need.

When she found Alesse—or *if* she found Alesse, or when Alesse just came home of her own accord—Darcelle would need spells, either to bind her sister or to collect blood from her sisters. Regardless of how it might play out, if she were going to cast the final spell to break out of here, she would need an arsenal.

There was something going on between her and Eleri. She noticed the way the air crackled between them. It was almost as if they knew each other from more than just the girl's infrequent visits into the shop and the time that Eleri had come to her home.

Given what Eleri Eames had said, Darcelle had a feeling the redhead and her partner were on the right track to find the missing sister. And she now believed Eleri had gotten much, much closer to finding her sister's remains than she was aware of.

She was still uncertain about how the whole thing had gone down, but Darcelle understood that she and Eleri had done a tug of war, back and forth, each pulling on the chains. Donovan had stood by, watching and staying out of it, for the most part. In the end, they'd compromised. Eleri would help her find Alesse, and Darcelle would help Eleri find Emmaline.

Though Eleri had not given the name, she had flinched ever so slightly as Darcelle had rattled off her list. It was *Emmaline.* That was the one, Darcelle was sure.

In a bone-deep way, Darcelle saw that it made sense. Eleri sparked when she got too close or when she was angry. Darcelle wondered if other people could see it, or if it was merely a product of her own upbringing that she spotted it so easily. She suspected it was a little bit of both. If the missing sister was, in fact, Emmaline, then Darcelle knew something else Eleri didn't. Emmaline's blood had been the most powerful the family had ever had.

Emmaline's death had been an accident. Were it not for Tempeste going off the rails one night, Emmaline would likely still be alive—and though Darcelle had not been fully grown, she and her sisters had been old enough to see that, once Emmaline was gone, Tempeste's best bloodline was missing from her spells. And then Tempeste had begun to age dramatically.

Darcelle had been young when her grandparents had died, and she'd never paid attention to *how* they had died. She never noticed that the dates on the tombstones were far—too far—into the past, much further back than an adult would have expected. Her grandparents had each lived to be well over one hundred years old.

Her mother would have probably followed suit, given that she had died late into her seventies and had looked to be merely in her thirties for most of her life. No one had even believed she had daughters approaching adulthood when Darcelle was a young woman. It was funny, because Tempeste had not given birth to her first baby until she was well into her forties.

However, it had been Emmaline's passing that changed Tempeste. Apparently, as Tempeste had aged naturally, Emmaline's blood had been more and more necessary to maintain her health. When Emmaline died, Tempeste began to go downhill. So while Darcelle had not realized the dates on her grandparents' headstones were highly significant, she did realize then that her mother was much, much older than she, or truly anyone around her, had suspected. It was only in that last decade, without Emmaline to prop her up, that Tempeste had begun to show her true chronological age.

There had been others that followed Emmaline, as Tempeste had tried to recreate the magic that she had found. None had ever worked as well, and Darcelle and her sisters had watched as their mother slowly slid into madness—or perhaps, she had finally embraced it. Tempeste Dauphine had never been stable.

It had been during those years toward the very end that she had tied Darcelle to the store. Even wild and crazy and mentally ill, she'd been a force to reckon with.

Darcelle remembered well the time, ten years ago, when they had lost Emmaline, and subsequently lost the force that made them powerful. Her sisters were still trying to recreate it.

Darcelle held a lot of information, and she was going to keep it close. Her sisters knew how powerful Emmaline had been and what the family had accomplished with her. But they thought she was dead and gone. And she was. What her sisters didn't know was that Emmaline's blood had walked into her store.

58

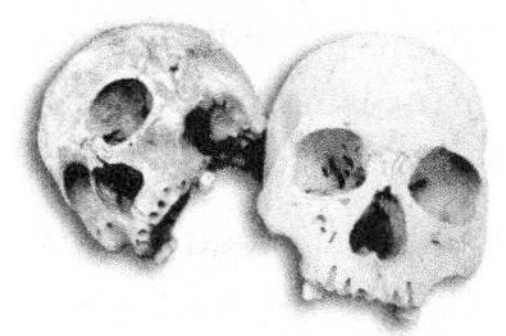

Donovan had driven them home. Even though it was Eleri's rental, he had slipped the keys from her loose fingers when they arrived at the car and shuttled her around to the passenger side. He changed his initial diagnosis. She wasn't just shocked by Darcelle's announcement. She appeared to actually be in medical shock.

He hoped she was merely paying zero attention to the outside world while she thought things through. He hoped she was still reacting to the conversation that had just happened in the store, and not some spell—or worse, some *curse*— that Darcelle Dauphine had placed on her. But Eleri looked so pale and unresponsive, he was amazed when she fastened her own seatbelt.

Donovan no longer doubted the other woman's ability to do such things as cursing someone. He'd tried to hide his own shock. Knowing Eleri as well as he did, he was still surprised that even she did not manage to hide her reaction when Darcelle mentioned her sister's name. He'd expected a better poker face—but Eleri had not seen that coming.

There were so many problems with the whole scene, he thought as he started the car and turned, heading down the street and back toward Grandmere's. He wasn't really in a position to talk, so he let Eleri have her silence while he stole his.

It wasn't just that Darcelle knew Emmaline's name, but that the name—the whole list of names—had come to her so readily. Something in the way she said "Emmaline" made Donovan think she had a suspicion which girl was Eleri's sister. It was entirely possible, given Eleri's unusual coloring, that Darcelle had recognized some similarity between the two Eames girls and figured out that she had known the sister of the woman standing before her.

Still, Donovan had seen pictures of Emmaline. Though she also had unique coloring, she had blonder hair and bluer eyes. It wouldn't necessarily be obvious that the two girls were sisters. Then again, if Darcelle had been around Emmaline as long as Emmaline had supposedly been alive after she was kidnapped, it was more than possible that she recognized the connection.

He took the next turn and crossed the bridge back into the Lower Ninth Ward, grateful to be leaving the French Quarter behind him.

No. The problem wasn't just that Emmaline's name rolled so easily off of Darcelle's tongue. It was that the other names did, too. She didn't simply ask, "Is your sister Emmaline?" Instead she had listed seven names, rattling them off easily.

It was stunning. As an FBI agent, he'd wanted to slam her to the counter and pull his cuffs and arrest her there on the spot. She knew the names of at least seven missing children.

But he didn't have his cuffs, and he wasn't an active agent right now. They had not yet heard back from Agent Almasi about the bones Eleri had not-so-anonymously handed in, but Donovan suspected that at least one of the names that Darcelle had listed would match to at least one of the skeletons, if not more.

When Darcelle recited the list of names, it had made his heart beat faster. Blood had left his head and pooled in his feet. *How many children were missing in total?* he wondered. And even as he thought it, he realized this crime was worse than he'd initially imagined.

Darcelle had listed only the names of *female* children. Eleri asked after a *sister,* and so Darcelle didn't list any male names at all. She had listed the name Mackenzie, and though common now, it hadn't been a common first name when Mackenzie Burke had disappeared. He suspected the Mackenzie that Darcelle referenced was the same one that had begun this case. He had more than suspicion. He was starting to develop Eleri's gut sense. He *believed.*

Mackenzie Burke's bones had led them here and led them to their conversations with Darcelle in the first place. While all the names she had listed had been female, some of the bones they had dug up in the graveyard that Cabot frequented had been male, which meant the names she listed were only half of the missing children—or maybe less.

Donovan stopped himself from speculating. Perhaps they had stolen mostly female children and only dabbled with a few males. However, as he thought about it, the likelihood of that happening was slim. It would mean that they had dug up one of the only male victims in their random, three-grave search. That math didn't add up. So chances were, whoever was stealing children had stolen both males and females for whatever rituals they were casting.

His breathing became shallow, and his heart beat faster to make up for the drop in his blood pressure. Physiologically, he knew what was going on in his system. He was in the early stages of shock himself. *Maybe he shouldn't be driving,* he thought, but he pressed the gas pedal a little harder and made another turn for Grandmere's.

He looked toward Eleri sitting next to him and realized that she wasn't coming around as he'd hoped. He hadn't been watching, mostly thinking and sliding under his own dark suspicions. Perhaps she had put the same pieces together as he did.

They had been very concerned with their three excavated skeletons and ten turned graves—but now that Darcelle had rattled off seven names, he suspected the problem was much larger than they had thought. It was entirely possible that he and his partner had turned over a leaf on one of the largest child trafficking rings in the nation.

He was curious what names Agent Almasi might come back with for the bones from the cemetery. Mackenzie Burke had a Dauphine family name in her past. Eleri Eames was a Remy and a Hale. Would the other names trace back to prominent families of power in the occult and underworld? He suspected they would. The kidnappings did not seem random.

Reaching across the center console of the car, he picked up Eleri's wrist. She turned it over as though he was reaching to hold her hand and comfort her, but that's not what he was going for. He placed two fingers against her pulse and felt it flutter. It was too low, too inconsistent. Luckily, they were home.

He pulled into the driveway, opened his door, and stood up. Forcing himself through breath-holding and tension exercises, he tried to push blood through his system via his muscles, almost the way an astronaut would to keep his blood pressure up. Donovan needed his to stay awake long enough to get around the car.

As he came to the other side, Eleri was slowly emerging, her eyes still not quite focusing, her pupils still a bit dilated. While she might have put together the same things he had, she had one other problem. She had just made a deal with the devil herself.

Grandmere opened the door to greet them. As she looked between the two of them, she asked only one question. *"What did you just do?"*

59

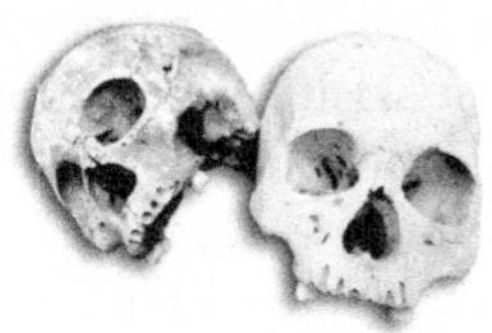

Eleri had held up fairly well under Grandmère's stern eye and harsh questions, or so she wanted to believe. Grandmère had basically told her she'd made a deal with the devil. Eleri knew her Grandmère was right, but she was also certain that, if asked, she would do the same thing again.

Darcelle Dauphine had listed Emmaline's name. She had also said she would help Eleri find her sister. Eleri didn't believe Darcelle would *help* her, but she figured Darcelle would point her in the right direction. She was more than confident that Darcelle didn't have to *find* Emmaline—she *already knew* where Eleri's sister was. The trick would be getting her to tell.

By the time Grandmère had finished questioning her and Eleri had gotten done answering, both of them were angry. She didn't like Grandmère coming at her, and to be fair, she'd wondered something all along. Now she had to ask it.

"Grandmère, why didn't *you* find Emmaline? You have the power to do this. You had to have had an idea of where she was."

Grandmère merely glanced down and to the side, as though ashamed. Eleri's anger grew bigger in response. She hated being angry at Grandmère, as much as she hated what Grandmère had done or hadn't done.

"*Why didn't you look?*"

"*I did,*" her Grandmère yelled back at her.

She didn't think Grandmère had ever yelled at her. In fact, she didn't think she'd ever heard that tone in the woman's voice, nor felt the air hit her, almost like a sonic boom, with the force of her great-grandmother's anger.

"I did look," Grandmère repeated in a much softer tone this time.

"Did you not suspect that she was here?" Eleri motioned her hand beyond the window, as though to encompass all of New Orleans. "She was *inches* away from you the whole time!"

Eleri knew from the look on her Grandmère's face that the old woman felt guilty about what had happened. Eleri was angry at herself, for never finding out more, never gathering enough clues to figure out where Emmaline was being held. She bore that guilt, but she was also angry that Grandmère hadn't been able to find her sister. Even though it might not be Grandmère's fault, the rage simmered in her.

Again, her demand put a sour, shamed expression on Grandmère's face. Eleri had never seen her great-grandmother with that face before. Still, her anger kept her pushing forward.

Donovan held back. He stayed at the corner of the room, once again watching the two women go at it, and either deciding that it was not his place to get involved or perhaps that it wasn't safe for him. Maybe he was just watching and thinking he could keep the two of them in check. Eleri wasn't certain that he could.

"I had my suspicions," Grandmère said. "I knew what you two girls were."

Eleri nodded. She'd been far too young at the time, a mere ten years old. She'd had no clue what was running in her veins, no clue the power that came through each branch of her family. But Grandmère had known. Grandmère had been an adult, old before Eleri was born, and supposedly wise.

"I told you, child. I did look. I hit a brick wall."

"You could have pushed it down."

"At what cost?" Grandmere seemed sad about this.

"What do you mean, *what cost?*" Eleri demanded, the tail end of the tone of her question rising. "The cost was Emmaline's life. Did you know she was still alive?"

Grandmère nodded, and Eleri felt the shock hit her, starting in the center at her heart and radiating out through the tips of her fingers, her toes, and the top of her head. She had sustained too many shocks today. Would she even survive the next one? She might join Emmaline. Something about that thought was peaceful and welcoming.

She hadn't known for several years that her sister was still alive. She'd initially wanted to believe, because her mother insisted it was true. Nathalie had told her every night that Emmaline would come home. Safe. Soon.

Now, of course, Eleri knew her mother had been telling herself that. But even at ten, eleven, and twelve, Eleri had been skeptical. She'd known her mother had no proof, only hopes and dreams. And she herself didn't fully accept any of it—until she started seeing Emmaline in her dreams. Even then, she hadn't truly *believed* until she realized that Emmaline was older. Only then did she think that she might actually be seeing her sister, and not some manifestation of wishful thinking. But Grandmere had known all along.

"If you knew," Eleri growled, "why didn't you get her?"

"Do you not understand what I came up against, child?"

"No. Clearly, I don't," Eleri said.

"Well, you felt it when you tried to check out Darcelle Dauphine."

Eleri thought back. It had been like smacking a wall that went into the sky. It had seemed insurmountable. It had seemed electrified—it didn't just block her by standing in her way, but that each time she came up to it, it actively pushed her back. Eleri's anger started to dissipate a little bit.

"I understand you hit a wall—but it was Emmaline's *life,* Grandmère."

"It wasn't supposed to be!"

"What?" Eleri asked, startled.

"Yes, I knew Emmaline was alive. I also knew that she wasn't truly being harmed. She wasn't with your family, and that was awful. I knew she'd been kidnapped. I knew she was being held against her will. I knew she was sad, and I knew she should be returned to her home. But I also knew she *couldn't* be."

Eleri grew more and more confused. Grandmère spoke in a frantic state, as though she was trying to purge herself of information she had carried as a heavy burden for years. This was not the calm, collected, wise woman Eleri had known all her life.

"She wasn't supposed to die!" Grandmere whispered, almost in tears. She spat the words as though she too was angry about the decision of the past. "I thought, when she got older, we would be able to reach out to her. If she reached out to us—and I knew she would, I *knew* she would!—then the two of us might have overcome the wall, or the three of us together."

She paused as Eleri absorbed what had been her great-grandmother's cherished dream—that Emmaline would somehow find her own way home. Eleri had been a child. Emmaline had been younger.

Grandmere continued. "Her death was an *accident,* Eleri. I thought she was going to live to eighteen, to adulthood. She was getting stronger. Then she could have reached out to us."

Eleri blinked. "You were just going to leave her there for a decade? They cut her, Grandmère."

"And I cut you, child, and I cut myself. I've done it. Emmaline was okay."

"She wasn't *okay,* Grandmère. She was a child. She was eight years old when they took her. She had to be petrified."

"Did she seem petrified when you saw her?" Grandmère asked.

Eleri stopped. It wasn't anything she'd ever really considered, but when she'd seen Emmaline in her dreams, her little sister had seemed serene.

She had to give Grandmere an honest answer. She shook her head no, though she didn't say the word.

Emmaline had always reached out to her. They had gone running through the woods. Emmaline had told her secrets, and she'd smiled. In the beginning, they had played dolls. Later, Emmaline had occasionally talked about a boy, and as they had become adults—or at least, as Eleri had—Emmaline had told her about the things she saw. But she'd never supplied enough solid information for Eleri to find her.

Eleri had often asked, "Where are you?" But Emmaline had kept her mouth shut, as though she did not wish to be found. She would only press her lips together and shake her head when Eleri asked.

It was only after Emmaline died that she began to help Eleri with her work. It was only then that Emmaline seemed to know things, like where Eleri could find a clue, a criminal, or a missing child. Emmaline told her secrets.

Grandmère was watching as many expressions crossed Eleri's face.

"She didn't, did she?" Grandmère asked again, making her great granddaughter face the truth.

And this time, Eleri said the word: "No. But I didn't see her for several years. She had time to get used to it and to acclimate."

"I'm sure that she did," Grandmère said. "But I can tell you, I saw her right away, and they made sure she was not terrified. They made sure that she was as happy as she could possibly be, although she was away from her family."

"Why would they do that, Grandmère? It doesn't make any sense. They kidnapped a child. They used her for her blood."

"That they did," Grandmère replied. "You, of all people—with all your degrees and studying—do they not teach you that everything affects the blood?"

Interestingly enough, science did find that. Immunology rode heavily alongside mood. The strength of the immune system and even the kinds of hormonal support a body had often depended whether you were an alpha or a beta in your situation. Health depended, in large part, on whether you were happy. While there were many, many other factors, the frame of mind definitely affected the body. Eleri only blinked again.

"Emmaline wasn't supposed to die," Grandmère said again. This time her voice was soft, and she sounded sure of herself. Eleri still could not accept what her sister had endured.

"Why, Grandmère?" she asked. "Why did you not go find her anyway?"

"Because if I had done that," Grandmère said, "they would have come back. Only they would have come back for you."

60

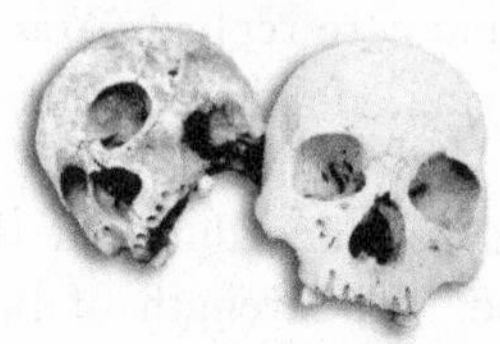

Eleri stared at Donovan, trying hard to listen to his words as he argued against her.

She had not expected this.

"We don't know that the Dauphine family is behind all of this," he told her.

"We don't know that they *aren't*," she countered, her voice rising.

They both knew there was plenty of circumstantial connecting evidence, including the family's relationship to Cabot, Cabot's frequent trips to the graveyards, and more.

Eleri had been working all day, frantically trying to connect whatever dots she could. She felt she had enough. Donovan didn't.

She'd managed to get copies of the dental X-rays from the bodies she and Donovan had dug up. Though she'd taken her own photos of the skull, and particularly the teeth, she needed the radiographs to do a comprehensive forensic match. She'd talked Agent Almasi into sharing what had been taken at the lab from the bones she'd turned in. He had emailed them to her on the sly, in exchange for her helping him, she guessed—but she used what she knew and her backdoor access to several operations for missing children to do her own IDs. She was a forensic scientist listed with both NamUs and DoeNetwork.org. Thus, she had more information than the casual site visitor.

As a scientist, she often did identifications for the volunteer groups. She helped family members find lost loved ones, since she knew what that was like. Volunteer work was something she had always done—and, now, suddenly, she felt grateful to have that access, to be able to call up copies of dental records the families had filed.

She still remembered the names that Darcelle had rattled off. They were burned in her brain now, and Eleri suspected she'd still be able to recite the list on her deathbed. So she started pulling old records by those names, rather than any of the other features she might have sorted for. The names were the most definitive information she had; she didn't know when they'd disappeared or how old they'd been at the time, but she knew some possible names.

As soon as she found a missing child named Helena—and there were, sadly, several—she started checking the dental records the families had left in the online files, hoping for someone like her to come along and let them know what had happened to their child. She didn't have to check far. The first two Helenas were ruled out quickly, but it took only a moment to see that the third one matched. The dental records were nearly identical in certain features that would have lasted from the youth of her disappearance until five years later.

Helena Dawson had disappeared four years after Emmaline. Apparently, she had not made it a full decade after being stolen and had died at a much younger age. According to what Eleri could glean from her bones, Helena probably only lived three to five years in captivity.

She'd set Donovan to researching the girl's name and family history. She wanted him confident that she had done a thorough job, and not think she'd short-changed her investigation because she wanted so desperately to come up with a match. But she'd done the work. She knew that although baby teeth fell out and adult teeth came in, certain features were unchangeable. If she could find them, she could make a match, and she had.

In addition to giving Donovan everything she'd found, she sent that information back to Agent Almasi, receiving another thank you for the furtive exchange of information between them.

Though it took Donovan a while, he produced a relatively extensive family history on the girl. Eleri wasn't sure she liked where Helena's case was going, but she had to admit, she needed the information it was generating. Helena Dawson was also a distant relative of the Dauphine family.

That was information that Eleri had not shared with Agent Almasi. She wasn't sure yet how it pertained to the kidnappings. She had an idea, but she was still a way off from proving it, and Donovan was urging her to wait.

Eleri, on the other hand, was considering several options for moving forward. One was going on their own. They had enough information to move in and confront either Darcelle or all the sisters, or even Cabot. The problem with that strategy was that the only Dauphine sister Eleri reasonably thought she could find was Darcelle. As of yet, she could only connect Darcelle to her own family—which was pointless and proof of nothing. It was the family that she connected to both Cabot Salzani and evidence of ongoing crimes. Thus, Darcelle was the least of the people they needed. The only solid thing she had on Darcelle was the woman's own admission of knowing where the missing children were.

Eleri's other option was going to the Bureau and handing over everything she knew. That would mean literally "making a federal case" out of it. It meant handing over control of her past. She would become a witness rather than an agent. But it also meant the case most likely would be handed to Almasi. It might mean going in with Almasi and bringing in the SWAT team. That held a certain appeal that Eleri couldn't deny.

Almasi's crew, which now included several forensic scientists, had dug up four more skeletons from the cemetery. She had asked him about it, and though he hadn't supplied the full details, he'd given her just enough to make her beg for more.

They'd identified that they had two young males and two females, all below the age of maturity, but all old enough to identify by gender. When she'd spoken to him, he had information that the team was still working and that another skeleton was partially removed, and it appeared to be too young to determine gender. It would require DNA testing to determine XX or XY chromosomes.

Eleri had begged him again for X-rays of the dental work on those skeletons, but Almasi had not yet sent it. She didn't know if this meant he simply had not gotten around to it or if it meant that the dental X-rays had not been taken and the work simply didn't exist yet for her to match it. It also was possible that he'd simply grown tired of their tit-for-tat arrangement and would never send them.

Though she'd mulled pinning her badge on, calling Westerfield, and asking if he could make this a NightShade case, she wasn't quite there yet either. Each time she thought it through, she figured that was how it would end up. But right now, there was one more thing to do.

"Donovan, we have to go. We have to get Darcelle."

"I don't think that's wise, Eleri."

She raised an eyebrow at him, as though to ask why he thought not, and he brought out the big guns first. "You understand that's a federal case of kidnapping. By *us*."

"She'll never press charges. We can link her to dozens of dead children."

This time, he'd raised his eyebrow at her. "Not dozens," he murmured.

Even with what Agent Almasi's team had dug up, they still hadn't amassed ten full skeletons. Of course, finding the skeleton of even one missing child was significant. Any missing child was far too much, and she knew that deep in every bone in her body. But Donovan was right. She was over-exaggerating the case based on how she believed it would pan out. And she had to be sure they caught the perpetrator.

Emmaline had gone missing twenty years ago. Eleri had no reason to believe either that her sister was the first or that whoever was doing it had stopped.

"It could be Cabot's family and the Lobomau," Donovan offered up. "If we go after the Dauphine sisters, we could wind up in more trouble than we can handle."

Eleri pondered that for a moment. He wasn't talking about legal trouble. Still, she couldn't make that scenario play out in her mind. "What would the Lobomau do with all those children?"

As she watched, Donovan's features turned dark, his eyes going almost black with the thought of that.

"No, Donovan." Eleri offered it in harsh words as a command. "Don't go there. That's not what this is. The children all have the scars on their forearms. They've all been in bloodletting rituals. We know this. We can see it on my own arms. The Lobomau don't do that. It has to be the Darcelle sisters."

Donovan had popped back at her faster than she could think. "How do you know the Lobomau don't do that? *I* don't know the

Lobomau don't do that. I don't think Wade knows. Clearly, Cabot and the other Salzanis are working with the Dauphines," he said.

"Exactly," Eleri commented. "And that's why we need to get Darcelle. She has the answers to these questions."

The argument had gone back and forth, and in the end, both of them were right. Darcelle was the key that would crack the case. She had already said she would tell them where Emmaline was in exchange for Eleri's help finding Alesse.

Donovan knew they didn't have enough information, but he wasn't sure about Eleri's next decision.

"It's time to be the federal agents that we are, Donovan."

"We are federal agents on leave—not working an official case."

"Darcelle doesn't know that. She doesn't know what we are. I'm ready to tell her."

In the end, Eleri had simply left, going outside to get in the car. Donovan had no choice but to follow her.

Eleri knew her partner would not leave her to do this on her own. He was too afraid she wouldn't come back at all. *Truthfully,* she thought, *it was an option, but she had to try.*

Darcelle Dauphine had said she knew where Emmaline could be found. Now Eleri needed that information, and she would get it in whatever way she could.

Donovan opened the door to the passenger seat as Eleri shoved the car into reverse.

Grandmere had lingered in the back of the house. She seemed weary, as though she had had enough of Eleri and her ideas, enough of punishing questions, enough of dredging up a history she had barely learned to live with.

Eleri knew she'd put the old woman through an emotional ordeal, but she had no time to regret it. She was in a position to make things right, at least the best she was able. So she sped across the bridge into the French Quarter, nearly squealing the car into a parking spot they finally found a block and a half from the Mystic Vudu store. Eleri wished at once for a spell that made parking easier. It seemed if she were actually a powerful witch and could push people down stairs or spark off a voodoo shop owner, she should be able to find better parking than this.

Her energy increased as they walked, until steam was nearly coming off her as she got closer. Again, Donovan followed her, though it was more like he tumbled along in her wake as she marched angrily toward the front door of Mystic Vudu, throwing it wide as she stormed in.

She was glad to find there were no customers. She didn't know what it would be like if she had to throw people out. People had cell phones everywhere these days. Who knew what they would see or record?

She had brought handcuffs with her, one of the few items from her kit. She knew they might be utterly useless, but at least now they served as part of her uniform. When

she pulled out her badge, she saw the shock register in Darcelle's wide, deep brown eyes.

"Darcelle Dauphine, you are under arrest on multiple counts of kidnapping. This is a federal case. Place your hands behind your back." Eleri almost barked the words.

She cuffed Darcelle easily and led her out the front door. The woman left calmly, and Eleri almost laughed as Donovan flipped the shop sign to *Closed*.

They got into the car, tucking Darcelle into the backseat, the way one would a prisoner—a hand on her head, pushing her low and making sure she didn't bump herself on the doorframe, so she wouldn't have a reason to file a lawsuit later—although if Darcelle wished to file a lawsuit, she would have so many reasons.

This was the action that started the clock. Eleri knew she now had a limited time to prove that Darcelle and the Dauphine sisters were what she thought they were. Otherwise, she would be the one who wound up behind bars. Her heart sank at the thought that—if that happened—she still wouldn't have her sister. She had to succeed at this.

Donovan sat in the backseat as Eleri headed toward Grandmere's house. It was not where one should question a witness, not in any actual federal investigation, but he believed it would keep things calm. However, as Eleri pulled out of the French Quarter, Darcelle Dauphine's eyes rolled back in her head, and she began to moan. Halfway across the bridge, blood began coming out of her ears and her eyes.

61

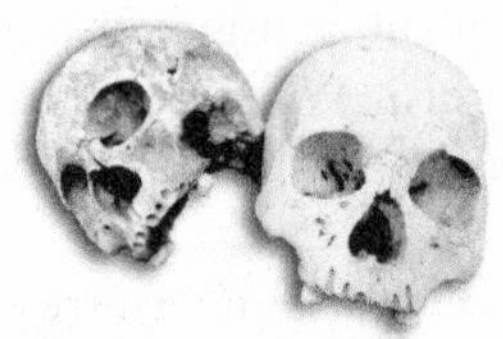

Donovan sat in the back seat of the rental car, next to Darcelle. He watched in shock as blood had slowly formed and run in tiny rivulets that pooled in the pinnae of her ears.

He'd watched, but didn't speak, wondering if it was some kind of spell Darcelle had cast on herself, a parlor trick to get out of a situation she didn't want to be in. So at first, he hadn't said anything to Eleri. Then, when Darcelle's eyes rolled back into her head, he saw that Eleri had witnessed the reaction in the rearview mirror.

Eleri kept driving and Donovan remained silent, letting Eleri make that decision. But slowly things changed. Blood began seeping out the edges of his prisoner's eyes, and she moaned and writhed about. Her hands, tied behind her back, made her squirm because of the spasms in her shoulders. To him, it looked like pain—real, deep, and system-wide pain.

Donovan was no longer able to think of the woman as his prisoner and now had to treat her as his patient.

"Eleri," he shouted, banging on the back of her seat. "Eleri, turn around. Something is very wrong. Stop the car."

As they were in the middle of the bridge between the French Quarter and Lower Ninth Ward, Eleri had to keep going. Luckily, the bridge was short and on other side, she pulled over and parked on the side of the road.

"Shit. Donovan! Cell phones." She was looking left and right and

Donovan followed her gaze. Though he didn't see anyone recording, people were watching. He didn't know why they would record a car pulling over on the side of the road, but if someone decided to, or if this car was randomly in the background of a recording for an entirely different reason, it could get ugly.

A few of the people on the side of the street moved toward the car as if they wanted to help. Another car slowed and rolled down the passenger window. Donovan did not want Eleri to flash her badge. As soon as that showed up on any kind of social media, somebody would be telling Westerfield about this. Neither of them could afford it.

"Donovan, we can't stay here. We have to go somewhere else. I don't know where, though."

He looked frantically back and forth between his partner and the woman next to him. Darcelle had not stopped moving. Her hands twisted in the cuffs that Eleri had put on her. Slight clinks from the lightweight metal maintained that they held, but she was in such an odd position. Normally, when transporting a person in handcuffs, there would be a well in the seat and a place to link the cuffs, so that the prisoner could not escape. That set-up at least had some level of comfort for the prisoner. Rental cars offered no such thing.

Darcelle moaned louder and rapidly leaned over, placing her head between her knees. The sounds grew worse as Eleri put the car in gear and continued on.

"El, you have to stop. I don't know what this is." Donovan was waiting for his prisoner to vomit up blood. Though he didn't doubt the blood itself, he wondered still, in his rational mind, how she might have created this. What kind of witchcraft—or even magic shop trickery—might make it appear that she was bleeding? How would she have known to be prepared for this? Eleri had slammed into the shop like a Valkyrie and had Darcelle's hands behind her in moments.

As he thought back, Darcelle had worn the slightest smirk as Eleri cuffed her. Darcelle had willingly placed her hands behind her back, and said, "You don't know what you're doing." Perhaps it referred to this. He frowned at her, tugging on her shoulder, lifting her face up. As her mouth opened, he saw blood along her teeth, in the edges where the enamel met gum line.

It looked almost like sudden-onset Ebola virus. It couldn't be. He wasn't worried about the CDC this time, though he had been several times in the past in his career. No. This was not biological. It was witchcraft.

However, it did not look like it was witchcraft that Darcelle was causing.

"Eleri," he cried, pounding on the seat again. "I think she's actually in pain."

This time when Darcelle moaned, he heard two sounds. She had leaned over again and he was still waiting for bloody vomit or red-tinged saliva to hit the floor.

He then took the only breath he'd taken since he began to panic, and he smelled it. "Eleri! Eleri, stop. We can't keep going. She's actually afraid."

Now he was not looking with his physician's mind. He had opened his wolf's nose—just a little—and now it was so obvious. Darcelle, who had smirked when they put her in the car, was now petrified. The pain coming off of her was such a sharp stench, he wondered how he'd missed it before.

"Eleri, Eleri!" He demanded she stop, and even though she didn't, he could see she was looking for a place. It was just that nowhere good existed. As he spoke, he heard again as Darcelle moaned, two sounds.

"Again," he demanded of her, leaning down, his head aimed toward hers, his features shifting to let his ears open up and catch all the sounds. He didn't worry about what the woman might see. Darcelle knew what he was, so this would be no surprise. She was in too much pain to be dangerous.

This time he heard the words, "Go back."

He lifted up, trying to keep his face low, lest anyone on the sidewalk be able to see into the car and observe a man with a protruding snout and a single, large ear.

"Eleri," he growled. "Go back!"

The snout made it hard for him to speak. He twisted his face. Normally, when he changed, it was piece by piece, methodical and relatively slow compared to what he'd done today. This, this fast snapping of tendons and ligaments to put pieces into the right place —to put only one side of his head this way—was excruciating. It hurt going in, and it hurt coming back out. He cracked his neck, his hands still on Darcelle's shoulder, and she didn't fight it as he held her down.

Even now, with all of his human features—his nose small and his ear back in human shape—he heard it clearly, and he smelled everything on her.

"We have to go back. There's a weird smell. I don't know what it is. It's not what's making her bleed though. I can't ..."

Eleri glanced up at him in the rearview mirror and sensed that he, too, had begun to panic. It wasn't just Darcelle that made her turn around, but Donovan's reaction to what was happening. He was grateful that, despite her ability to stomp off and leave him in the dust, letting him run to catch up, she was still willing to listen when it really mattered. She was on a mission, and the mission was decades old. He understood that.

"Eleri, go back. Turn around. She said go back." He breathed the words in and out, not able to make full sentences as he fought his own harsh breathing and his fear over what might be happening in the seat beside him.

Eleri did not wish to follow Darcelle's orders. He knew that. However, she was willing to take a chance on him.

It took another four minutes. Darcelle was almost screaming now as Eleri made a series of right hand turns, and headed back across the bridge.

By the time they landed on the side of the French Quarter, Darcelle had noticeably calmed down, though she was still writhing, moaning, and dripping red spittle from her mouth. Honestly, as Donovan looked at her, he wasn't sure how she would survive this. For a brief, twisted moment, he even thought of what it was going to take to clean the rental car's carpet. But then he forced his attention back to the present and away from the strain, from another shock, another hit, another strange happening, and from the past few days.

Eleri pulled up in front of Mystic Vudu, but then changed her mind. She circled the block, taking the partially obscured alleyway around to the back. It was a good choice, Donovan thought. But he didn't get to linger on Eleri's decisions as Darcelle sat upright again. Her head tipped back. Though there was blood marking the curves and wells of her ear—and though it had dripped from her eyes, like deep red tears, and still tinged the edges of her lips and gums—she was breathing deeply. She swallowed. She rubbed her ears with her shoulders, using her sweater to wipe away some of what had dripped out. He noticed, at least, no new blood was coming.

Darcelle's head lolled against the backseat. Her breathing labored for a moment, as she took one deep breath, and then a second and a third. When she seemed to finally get enough oxygen, she rolled her head toward Donovan, and said something he didn't expect. "Thank you. I cannot leave the Quarter."

Eleri frowned. "Your home is outside the Quarter."

"Barely," said Darcelle. "I can go home and I can go to the store. What you just saw is what happens if I leave my path." Tipping her head back, she stared at the car ceiling. She seemed to have regained herself, because she laughed, and as she looked at Donovan, she said, "You can take me home, or you can kill me."

62

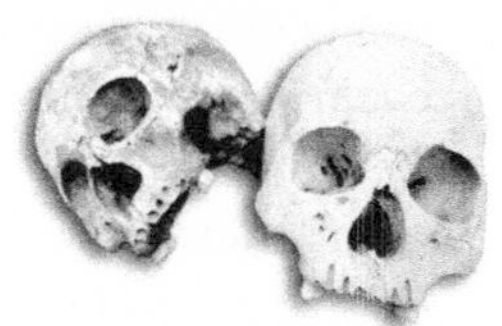

Eleri turned around in the driver's seat, stunned, as she stared into the backseat. Though she'd gotten glimpses while driving and had seen that it was bad, she hadn't been able to truly look. She did now.

Darcelle had blood running down her face from her eyes. It left red trails down her neck from the bleeding in her ears. And, in her mouth, it outlined her teeth in a wickedly evil grin, which Eleri somehow found fitting. She still hadn't been able to decide if the woman had done it on purpose, or if it truly was some effect that was happening *to* her, rather than *by* her. She thought for a moment about putting the car into drive and heading off in a different direction to see if it happened again. But, unfortunately, that would prove nothing.

If Darcelle was a decent actress, all she would have to do is lean over and moan. Bite her tongue. Let some blood drip from her mouth, and it would appear the same thing was happening all over again. In fact, Eleri did not have hard evidence that that wasn't what happened this time. But whatever Darcelle had done, she had convinced Donovan that she was having an actual medical emergency.

As they parked in the alley behind the store, Darcelle's head leaned back, and Eleri was suddenly grateful for the tint on the back windows of the car. The alley wasn't as private as Eleri would have liked. People walked through here, and cars used it as a shortcut regularly. If anyone looked in and saw Darcelle's bloody face, she and Donovan would have their hands on the hood while a cop searched them for weapons, which they were both carrying. Luckily, they carried federal badges as well—but no matter how it went down, and no matter how they walked out, it would not look good.

It probably didn't help that Darcelle was a hometown girl. They'd found strong evidence that someone inside the city was in the pockets of the Dauphine family, or at least the Salzanis. Eleri knew anything they did to Darcelle now would not play out well for them in the end.

Eleri's plan had just crashed and burned. She had flashed her badge. She had issued an arrest that, technically, she was allowed to make, but that would seem sketchy if it was ever brought to court.

Thankfully, this change in plans meant she hadn't dragged Darcelle back to Grandmere's house. Eleri was grateful for that one thing—that no Dauphine had ever been in Grandmere's place, and that Darcelle would not have visual knowledge of where Grandmere lived. Still, the whole plan was royally screwed.

In the back seat, Darcelle laughed a few times. It was a bitter, harsh sound. To Eleri's ears, it sounded like the other woman was no happier about this situation than she was.

Donovan was still staring hard at her by way of the rear view mirror, as if to ask, "What do we do now?"

For that, Eleri had no real answer. Her mind raced through options. One plan was to blindfold Darcelle. Drive again, far away from where they now sat. Then she could see if the woman doubled over and bled at the right time. Would she have these troubles if she couldn't see herself leaving the city? Could Eleri take various routes with false turns and get her to fake it, even if they stayed in the area? It seemed more than a bit time-consuming and excessive, and only would prove what Eleri already suspected—that Darcelle was either a good actress, or that there really was some reason they couldn't leave the limits. Eleri and Donovan were still federal officers, but if they did something to actually harm this woman, they would be the ones going to jail.

There was another option. And she didn't like it.

Smacking her hands on the steering wheel, Eleri listened as Darcelle laughed a little harder at her frustration. Eleri almost barked an order, but she realized that was not the way to treat Donovan. He didn't deserve her irritation and was probably feeling a lot of it himself. He was probably mad at her, rather than just the situation. She had dragged him into this, hoping he wouldn't let her go off on her own half-cocked.

She realized now, that was exactly what she had done.

She looked over her shoulder and asked, as politely as she could, "Is there any way you can clean her up? I don't like the option of going to her house, which means we have to use the shop. But see what you can do right here?"

She would have to go back to where she started. She almost started talking through a plan with Donovan, but she didn't want to say anything in front of Darcelle. And inside the confines of the small rental car, every place was in front of the woman.

Honestly, Eleri didn't even know what she should say. Would they interrogate Darcelle, as she had originally intended? She hoped so. She thought they should try—but they would be sitting on Darcelle's home turf. In fact, the only places they knew Darcelle would be safe were places she not only frequented, but owned. Eleri's hands were tied, and tied tightly, by federal law.

She found it interesting that Westerfield managed to get around most of the laws that might have restricted them, but *she* couldn't. Though there was a good chance he would get them out of it later—if it came down to that—there were still no promises of help. There was no proof Westerfield could make it happen, so Eleri and Donovan would be working on assumptions. What could Nightshade do for them? What could they do for Nightshade? How might it end up playing out?

Westerfield had once told them that in Nightshade, "There were no rules, because none existed." It wasn't because her boss wasn't willing to make rules and stand behind them. Eleri had always thought the nature of Nightshade left her with uncertain guidelines, and never more so than right now.

She watched as Donovan bent over, reaching for one of the kits at his feet. They had plenty of supplies now: first aid kits, digging kits, bone-cleaning kits, and various pieces of equipment in the trunk. They were a regular mobile pharmacy and forensic center.

She watched in the tiny mirror as he poured liquid onto a piece of gauze and began wiping at Darcelle's face and down her neck, trying to remove the blood, so they could walk her into her shop without arousing suspicion. It was a full five minutes before he declared the woman ready to leave the car. Eleri looked back, still seeing red blood on the Darcelle's shirt. The patterns were unmistakable, but there wasn't anything they could do about it. It just figured that Darcelle had worn a white Tshirt today …

Eleri came around and helped lift her prisoner out of the car, using the woman's shoulder and arm for leverage. She walked alongside her, arms linked. Darcelle had no choice, but Eleri was trying to make it look more casual and less like she was steering a prisoner. She didn't want anyone who lived or worked around here—maybe someone who knew Darcelle personally—to call the police on them. It would not do to have anyone coming into the middle of the interrogation she was about to start.

She was glad they were behind the store, where fewer people might see them, even though other doors opened onto the street back here. They led to the backs of other shops, and thus to the people Darcelle was most likely to interact with, Eleri suspected.

They quickly shuffled her inside and closed the door. Eleri headed to the front of the store and closed the wooden blinds, the dark teak-looking wood shutting everything out and lending an eerie silence to the place, as the little dolls stared at her from their perches on the shelf.

The three of them stayed out of the front room. Even though the blinds were closed, Eleri didn't want anyone on the street to see shadows moving. They searched the back for an office and found it, but since it was the size of a coat closet, they didn't all fit. Eleri wound up dragging the chair from behind the cash register into the open space of the back room. Darcelle would be interrogated amongst her poppets.

They settled her into the chair, letting her bound hands stick between the wooden slats that made the back of the seat. Darcelle had not protested, nor said anything since she had finished laughing in the back seat of the car.

As Eleri stood in front of her, and was opening her mouth to speak, Darcelle beat her to it.

"So, you're a fed." Darcelle smirked as though the information were funny. Then she mused, "What an interesting combination you two are."

She turned to look at Donovan then, her eyes squinting, "You, too?"

Donovan didn't speak, only reached into his back pocket and, with a practiced wrist, opened the wallet to display the glinting badge. Darcelle didn't know it, but the line under the letters F B I had little diamonds on the end, indicating that, not only was he a federal agent, but he also belonged to the Nightshade division.

That, Eleri thought, as Donovan tucked the wallet back away, just as smoothly as he'd pulled it out, *was something to use in their favor.*

Darcelle might think they were feds, and they were—but they weren't quite limited the way most federal agents were. Westerfield knew what they could do, and if something happened with Darcelle, they would not have to fight to normalize it. They had followed as much protocol as they could. She had decided against driving Darcelle around, testing the spell damage she received. Aside from not being officially on this case, Eleri was now back within her rights. She hoped.

Looking at Darcelle, she said, "You know where Emmaline is. Tell me."

Darcelle shook her head and shrugged as best she could with her hands bound.

"Tell me," Eleri repeated. "This is now a federal interrogation. You will be brought up on charges of kidnapping at least eight children across the US."

Darcelle shrugged again as though none of this mattered to her and she shook her head again, as though shaking off the charges. "But I didn't kidnap them."

"You knew of them. You did not help with federal investigations."

"I didn't know they were missing," Darcelle said. The words were stated in a cadence not her own.

It was a lie, clearly, rolling off her tongue, and not cleanly. If she was a good liar, she'd not done her job at it this time.

Darcelle sounded more like herself when she said, "I only asked which one was your sister. I don't know, exactly, where Emmaline is ..."

63

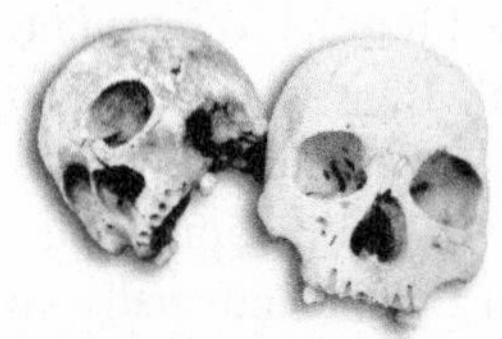

Eleri sighed, the sound long and weary even to her own ears.

"So you know, but you *don't* know?" she asked Darcelle, letting her irritation show.

The other woman shrugged yet again and Eleri became afraid that was all this interrogation would yield.

"I know where most of the bodies are buried." Darcelle smiled as she said it, using the standard phrase as though it were funny. At that moment, Eleri could not think of any situation less funny than so many missing children.

She stared hard at Darcelle and played another card. "Three of the bodies have been positively identified now. Two by me."

"Well, aren't you just a little Jack of all trades?" Darcelle smiled wider this time, and Eleri noticed some of the blood still showed between her teeth, giving her a macabre look that seemed fitting for this macabre interview.

"There's a full team digging up that cemetery where Cabot's been hiding the bodies."

That small flinch in Darcelle's eyes again let Eleri know she'd hit a mark. "The more they identify, the less useful you become. You want to be useful to us. It's your only way out."

Darcelle didn't react to that and Eleri stepped forward. Still, she was careful not to get close enough to be susceptible to a stunning head-butt, should Darcelle burst up and forward. Not close enough, she hoped, to spark the air between them or give Darcelle any ideas. She also wondered what Darcelle might be doing with those hands behind her back.

Donovan stood behind her, watchful, making sure the woman was caged in, even as she sat tied to the chair. But the chair was wood, and the things in the shop were more than Eleri wanted to deal with. She wouldn't have been surprised if the poppets started flying off the shelves to attack her. But she stayed the course and continued.

"Every moment that you don't tell us what you know, we figure out more of it for ourselves. Every moment you don't tell us makes it more likely that you wind up in jail."

Once again, Darcelle only laughed in response, her head tilting back, her mouth open. The sound was hearty, as though she was genuinely amused. "I would not survive jail," she said.

Eleri shrugged. "That's okay. You'll suffer while you're there."

"No," Darcelle replied, calm, cool, and firm. "I won't make it to jail. You saw what happened. I don't believe there's a penitentiary in the area I'm allowed to go to."

There wasn't, Eleri knew—not within the city limits. A county jail, yes, but it was a little farther away than where they'd driven Darcelle before she began moaning and bleeding.

Eleri had suddenly had enough of the shit. "What is that? You have to explain that, or I'm going to drive you out of the city again."

"What do you think it is, little witch?" Darcelle spat the words, and Eleri found it funny. She and Darcelle were of an age. Darcelle was actually a few years younger, but the tall, willowy woman kept referring to her as "little witch." It was meant to be an insult, although Eleri couldn't tell if it was a reference to her stature or her powers.

When Eleri remained silent, Darcelle began to speak. Something in the tone of the words made Eleri believe that Darcelle had wanted to get this off her chest for a while. And wasn't that the art of interrogation—to make the suspect feel a need to tell you what you wanted to hear?

"It's my mother," she said. "My mother cursed me."

"Your mother is dead."

Darcelle ignored Eleri's interruption, as though her mother being dead was of no issue in the story. "She needed someone to run the shop, and I was the stubborn one, always at odds. She often put spells on me as a child to keep me in line. Honestly, they never really worked. But this last time, she used all the magic she could find. And now I cannot leave the line between my shop and the home—on most days."

Eleri latched onto that one little piece. "What do you mean 'most days'?"

Darcelle offered only that maddening shrug again. But at least she kept talking. "Maybe it was out of kindness or sheer evilness. My mother gave me one day a week where I can roam the city for a few hours in the evening, after the shop closes."

Eleri frowned. That didn't make any sense to any of them. "Maybe it was to keep me from going mad, because if I'm mad, the shop goes under, and the legal family income disappears."

Eleri latched onto that, too, but she put this one in her back pocket for later. If someone mentioned *legal* family income, there was surely also *illegal* family income to be accounted for.

"I never know which day it will be, so each night, I try to step off of my path and see if the pounding headache hits. If it doesn't, I go another step, and another. And sometimes I can go to the restaurant three blocks over and get some lobster bisque," she said. "Sometimes I can get some *etouffee* or a good burger. One week, I made it to a theater to see a movie. Once, I got close enough that I watched a street fair down on the South Side. I was two blocks away, and my head hurt like a motherfucker the whole time, but I watched."

The anger came through in her words, and Eleri had a moment where she almost felt sorry for the bitch, but she couldn't quite muster it. "So, if you know these places where the children's bodies are buried," she asked, circling back, "then tell us."

Darcelle shook her head, and Eleri tried another tack. "What's holding you back Darcelle?"

"*Seriously?*" Darcelle asked, as though Eleri were stupid beyond measure. "I want out! I'm ready. I've been trying to break this spell for fucking months!" She ground the curse word through her teeth, and Eleri could almost imagine an actual curse had been cast with it.

She looked Eleri in the eyes. "You and I need each other, little witch. You can help me break this, and I can help you lay your sister's bones to rest."

Eleri felt her eyes narrow and her nostrils flare. "How?" She was interested in hearing this theory.

Darcelle turned then, awkwardly, her hands still jutting out behind the chair. She looked over her shoulder to see if Donovan was still there. He didn't move. Eleri had been watching his face in her peripheral vision and she'd seen the expressions cross his face as Darcelle spoke. Eleri could tell he had been alternately confused, angry, irritated, and surprised. But he now held a single, steely glare, not letting Darcelle read anything from him.

Eleri had no idea what Darcelle got from looking, other than knowing that he still stood back there. But it seemed to be enough to convince her of something. She turned forward to face Eleri again. "My mother's blood made this curse. I need her blood to break it."

Eleri glanced at Donovan, and back at Darcelle. "How do you get that if she's dead?... Do you have some saved?" she asked, thinking how disgusting that might be. And then, her thoughts walked sideways, and she wondered if they had saved Emmaline's blood in any manner—and how disturbing it would be to find that.

Darcelle shook her head, "No, and that's the problem. To get my mother's blood back, I need all four. I need Lafae, Gisele, myself, and Alesse."

Eleri was starting to catch on. Alesse was missing. Darcelle could not break her own spell without her sister, and her sister was nowhere to be found. Darcelle wanted the federal agents help to find her sister, and she would then use her sister to break the spell.

Eleri frowned. "You're suggesting you blood-let on three women who are not consenting?"

Darcelle laughed again. "Who consented to any of this shit?" she barked. "I didn't consent! My mother used my blood for spells all the time. She used all of us girls, so don't talk to me about consent." She watched Eleri, all laughter gone from her expression. "I need to find Alesse—and I need your blood to do it."

There was a pause and she spoke, softer this time. "My mother used Emmaline's blood all the time. She was strong on Emmaline's power. It was your sister's blood that cast the base spells for this one. So to break it, I need her blood."

She paused, and Eleri felt her heart clench.

"I can't get Emmaline's blood. Which means ..." Darcelle let the words trail off as she looked down at Eleri's arm. "I need your blood, too."

64

"You have got to be fucking kidding me."

Eleri fumed as she stared at Darcelle, still sitting in the chair, wearing her calm expression as though everything she'd said had made sense.

"I get this little chain reaction you've set up," Eleri said again, jabbing her finger at the floor to make her point as she paced back and forth. "But *why*? Why do you need my blood to get Alesse? You need Alesse to get free. That's not on *me*." She was trying to put all the pieces together, but she still couldn't understand how her blood would bring Alesse back.

"You have the same blood as your sister," Darcelle said. "Exactly the same blood."

Eleri thought otherwise. Perhaps they'd had different blood types, or antibodies. Genetics was like that. Siblings were only fifty percent alike genetically. But Darcelle was shaking her head, maybe seeing the scientist at work and understanding what Eleri was thinking.

"No," she said. "You are from the same bloodlines. You have the same blood. What we could do with Emmaline, we can do with you."

"Fine. You can cast cool spells with my blood." Eleri stopped pacing as though that would help her brain wrap around it. "How does that bring Alesse back?"

"As soon as I cast a spell with *that*," Darcelle said, nodding toward Eleri's arm, "she will feel it."

"Why can't you cast a different spell she would feel?" Eleri protested, even as she wondered why she was having this conversation. The dark-skinned woman looked at her through white eyes, with little bits of blood scabbing in the corners. Her mouth still had traces of red that Donovan hadn't been able to clean. Nothing about her said "rational person," and none of this made sense to Eleri's rational mind—although much of her life had never made sense to her rational mind.

Darcelle turned away. "Alesse has blocked me." It seemed like a tough admission.

"So? Unblock her." Eleri thought there must be a spell that would work. The FBI could get around blocks and encryptions on computers and cell phones. Surely, Darcelle had witchcraft powers equivalent to that.

Darcelle shook her head. "No. She has blocked Gisele and Lafae as well." Still looking to the side, Darcelle wore a pained expression that made it seem as though she was upset by this fact, but Eleri couldn't be sure the reaction was genuine.

There was always the possibility that Darcelle was simply playing them like violins. Eleri looked to Donovan, who was still standing behind the woman in the chair, still making expressions that Eleri could see. He was helping to guide her, but staying silent. Now, Donovan only shrugged.

No advice there, Eleri thought. Perhaps she should ask Grandmere —but what would she do with Darcelle while she headed home? She couldn't leave Donovan here alone with this woman. Darcelle was a powerful witch, and Donovan—wolf though he may be—had no skills to counteract that. Even Eleri truly didn't; she had only the hope that if she got angry enough, more skills might emerge. She might save them. Something might work out. She truly didn't know what she could and couldn't do. Perhaps Darcelle's nickname for her was correct.

"Surely there's some other spell you can cast that will be a beacon, some kind of bait, to draw Alesse home."

Darcelle nodded. "I'm sure there is, but I have been looking since Alesse left. I have been casting spells every night. How much longer do you want to wait, little witch?"

Eleri shook her head at Darcelle this time. "You call me that. You call me *little witch*, but you're the one who can't find your sister."

"You can't find yours either," Darcelle snarked, biting off the words even as they flew from her lips.

For a moment, Eleri seethed—but only until she realized her anger was what Darcelle wanted. She wanted Eleri and Donovan making snap decisions, and that was something they absolutely could not afford to do.

"What?" Darcelle asked. "The feds don't let you do what you want?"

Another tease, another poke, another taunt. Eleri stood firm this time, her head slightly tilted, her gaze square on the other woman. "I'll make my own decisions, thank you. I appreciate what you're trying to do here, but you're going to have to back the fuck off for a second."

Her voice had gotten harsher as the sentence carried on. She needed to talk to Donovan, someplace where Darcelle couldn't hear.

"Give us a minute," she said, and motioned to her partner.

Behind Darcelle, he waved his hands, pointing to the woman in the chair, and then aiming his palms up, as though to ask, what would they do? Eleri still motioned him forward. They would leave her here. She didn't want to have that conversation in front of Darcelle, so that Darcelle wouldn't know that they were, in fact, simply leaving her unattended in the other room. Let Darcelle believe they had something up their sleeve, some FBI trick.

Only nodding as he passed in front of the woman still sitting in the chair, her hands in cuffs, Donovan followed Eleri into the other room. They spoke in hushed tones. Eleri's voice was barely a whisper, but Donovan he could hear her. If Darcelle was not a wolf, and if she hadn't cast some spell to hear them, both believed they wouldn't be overheard.

"What do I do, Donovan?" She practically mouthed the words, not offering any sound, and yet Donovan still seemed to pick it up.

He looked at her and came in very close. He didn't whisper, knowing as Eleri had learned at Quantico that whispers carried farther than voice. "It's up to you, Eleri," was all he offered. "It's your sister, your case, and your blood. It's not my choice."

She put her hands up in frustration. "I don't know! I don't know what to do."

His hand motioned in front of her, telling her to tone it down, and she did, but she didn't stop ranting.

"If I give her my blood, what will she do with it?"

He said, "Well, we make her cast the spell here. I don't know enough to know what she'll be casting, but at least we'll watch. At least she won't get to carry your blood away and do something *else* with it." His face scrunched up, and he looked like he was struggling. Eleri understood. It was a surreal conversation.

Eleri nodded, liking his plan to keep some semblance of control. She added a contingency of her own. "Okay. Let's also give her a timeframe in which to get her sister here."

Donovan nodded. "Let's ask her how fast she thinks this beacon will work. Hopefully, she will give us a time that's her best estimate."

"Why would she do that?" Eleri said.

"Because hopefully, she'll brag a little bit—and then we'll demand that exact time. It should make her have to work harder."

Eleri nodded. "You'll be here. You'll be watching, right? I might need your medical expertise if she tries something, or if something goes wrong ..." She let the words trail off.

"I want to have my kit handy before we start."

"Good idea," Eleri said. She wanted him to have access to everything: EpiPens, sterile gauze, Steri-Strips, even extra saline. Some were things she wouldn't have expected in a first-aid kit, but Donovan had known to include them—as though he had intuited he would be watching a bizarre ritual involving Eleri's blood.

This was what her whole search had come down to. Almost twenty years ago, her sister had been kidnapped—and eventually killed—for her blood.

Now Eleri was going to buy her back with her own.

65

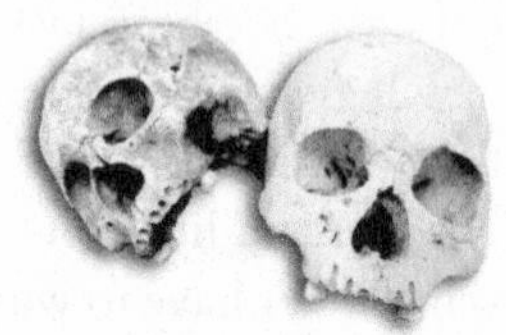

Eleri stood with her arm held out in front of her. Darcelle had reached out in silent request. Her hand hovered over the altar, palm up, as she waited for Eleri to lay her wrist into Darcelle's grip. Eleri figured she would hand over the same arm that Grandmere had drawn her blood from.

She'd figured that part out even as Donovan had suggested it to her. She would not give Darcelle the choice. If she had to bear a scar, she would bear two, close enough to each other to look like one. If she suffered any damage, she would still have one completely usable arm.

After they had undone the handcuffs, they allowed Darcelle to stand and walk around the shop, gathering her things. Eleri and Donovan had followed her closely. Even when she had given them little tasks to set up the altar, they simply refused to do her bidding, telling her that she had to do all of this herself.

"Well, you want me to get my sister here inside of four hours," she snapped. "How am I supposed to do that if you won't help?"

Eleri had just looked at her and made a questioning face and followed her around the store as Darcelle picked out an herb, and then a black candle, and then a binding ribbon.

"That's what you said: four hours," Eleri told her, rubbing it in the wound a little bit, knowing that she was going to get a wound of her own.

So Darcelle set up the altar. It took almost thirty minutes and had included her pulling out a bone-handled knife from behind the desk. Eleri had seen it lying on the table, but hadn't contemplated it until Darcelle set the knife on the altar.

For a moment, Eleri had thought it might be another resin-handled one, but very quickly, she saw that it wasn't. For a moment, she didn't dare put her fingers on it—and then she did. Again, she saw flashes of images, different from the ones she had seen the first time. These were of girls in white dresses, boys in white drawstring pants and cotton tee-shirts. They held toys in their grip and went running through the woods. They were happy and playing and then ... they weren't. They stood solemnly in a line, hands clasped, blood dripping, much the way she had seen Emmaline in the past.

Yanking her fingers back, Eleri had glared at Darcelle. "Is this my sister?"

She had not seen Emmaline in the images, but if she had been seeing through her sister's eyes, she would not have seen her face.

Darcelle almost smiled. "Is that what you wondered? Is that what you wondered the first day in the shop?"

"No," Eleri admitted. She spoke before she thought better of deciding what to share and what not to share, and so it was out there. "No," she repeated. "I didn't know that first day in the shop. I truly did come in here on a whim."

Darcelle shook her head. "There are no whims, little witch," she muttered as she continued arranging the altar. "No," she offered finally. "It is not your sister. I do have things of your sister's, but not her bones. My mother would not allow it."

Eleri could not hide her look of surprise. Perhaps she was grateful her sister had not been made into a knife and carved into tools in her afterlife, but it seemed strange that Tempeste Dauphine, who had abused her sister so much, respected her corpse.

Darcelle shrugged. "Mama was batshit," she said, but didn't elaborate. She simply stood on the other side of the table, a table Eleri saw was made of wood, and she imagined without screws, staples, or any other metal hardware, such as brackets or braces. Though, she reminded herself, that idea came from witchcraft. While Grandmere used a liberal dose of the craft, she had no idea what Darcelle might use. She watched carefully.

When Darcelle held out her hand, Eleri offered her right arm, wrist first. Darcelle noticed the gauze bandage. "You did some on your own," she said, and Eleri only nodded in response this time, thinking before she spoke, not wanting to give away too much information. Let Darcelle think she knew enough to do these spells. She would not tell that it had been her Grandmere, and Grandmere alone —who had cast this one.

Darcelle pulled out the knife, the blade of which was the same half-moon shape as the first knife Eleri had spotted in the store, symbols or sigils had been carved into the bone handle, but these were different. She wondered what they were about. Instead of asking, she pretended it didn't matter. Perhaps she didn't care, or perhaps she could read them and understood them. Let Darcelle figure that one out.

Using the knife, Darcelle slit the gauze neatly. It sliced cleaner than Eleri would have expected, without the zipping sound of the threads being cut. And even Donovan, standing to the side, had watched it with surprise, as though some magic was already afoot.

When Darcelle's hand found Eleri's skin, she ran her finger down the faint, thin scar there. Even Donovan appeared surprised, though he didn't say anything. Eleri knew it was healing much too fast.

She said to Darcelle, "If you cut me, you heal me, bitch."

Darcelle nodded. "Healing is simple magic, little one. Not a problem." Then, turning the blade over, she fit the hook into the top end of Eleri's scar and drew it deep.

It should hurt more than it did, Eleri thought, as she watched the blade sink into her own skin. She was glad she wasn't squeamish about her own blood. *Lord knew, she might be, after this.*

Instead of being afraid, Eleri imagined she was Emmaline. She imagined this was her life, and that she did this periodically to give these women the spells they craved to fulfill their greed. Emmaline had been the source that drove them. Eleri stood here now, in her thirties, but standing as though she was an eight-year-old girl, perhaps being bled for the first time and not knowing what would happen.

Darcelle drew the knife to the end, pulling it slowly out of the flesh and leaving the cut standing open. It bled profusely.

Didn't spurt, though, Eleri told herself. Darcelle had cut masterfully and had not hit an artery. Blood welled into the slice, and Darcelle held the cup underneath it, somehow managing not to spill. She worked with exquisite care. It was almost as though the blood itself knew it was precious.

At last, when it seemed she had enough—and when Eleri thought she should have lost enough to be lightheaded—Darcelle pulled a piece of white cotton from the table and ran it down Eleri's arm. The soft cloth pulled the blood along with it, getting her arm remarkably clean. She watched as Darcelle threw the fabric scrap into the chalice. The bleeding on her arm seemed to have stopped.

Was there something on the fabric? Was it another spell? she wondered.

For a moment, her head swam with questions—and then, it just swam. But she took a short, sharp breath through her nose and focused on her arm. Still holding her wrist firmly, Darcelle handed Eleri's arm to Donovan. With whispered words, she said, "Patch her up, Doctor."

Eleri frowned. Had they ever told Darcelle that Donovan was a doctor? Had she simply picked it up because Donovan was the one with the medical kit? Perhaps it was a nickname. Eleri didn't know, and it took her a moment to realize she had been distracted from the spell that was being cast behind her.

Donovan was watching over her shoulder, though, so nothing was going wrong while her thoughts meandered. She heard low chants from Darcelle, and she heard pleas to Gods whose names she recognized from Grandmere's vocabulary.

Sparkles formed in the room, but Eleri couldn't tell if it was Darcelle's magic or blood loss. Darcelle seemed not to notice, and Donovan was monitoring her arm carefully, checking her cut, wiping it down with alcohol again. The cut stung slightly—but, just like last time, not as much as it should.

He'd begun to wipe it dry and put little sterile strips across it. Eleri watched in fascination as he made neat rows binding her wound. She knew she should paying attention to the spell, but somehow, she simply couldn't force herself to do it. It was though her attention had been stolen.

Suddenly, she realized, perhaps it had. Her head turned, and she felt Donovan's fingers catch on her wrist as she seemingly tried to jerk it away. But she hadn't. She'd simply been distracted, and Donovan was holding her in place.

"Eleri," he said. "Eleri, I need you facing this way."

But she couldn't comply. She had to watch Darcelle. The woman dragged her fingers through the chalice of blood and drew two lines down the front of her face. She was using only Eleri's donation and none of her own, Eleri realized suddenly. Darcelle was casting, and the blood she was using was only Eleri's.

She became angry. Why was she the sole source for this spell? Why did Darcelle not use her own blood? She snarled, and Darcelle glanced up at her and then at Donovan. "Hold the little witch, Doctor. She cannot interfere."

With no further commands, she resumed her chanting. Her eyes grew dark even as the shop dimmed in the fading light of day. Eleri watched as the woman became completely oblivious to her and Donovan. Darcelle was tuned into her spell, working her prayers, and calling whatever she was calling, to create a beacon to her sister.

More sparkles filled the air, stronger now, and Eleri realized they were stronger at the edges of her vision.

Shit, she thought. *Not magic.*

She was going to pass out. It felt like someone had grabbed her feet and swung her around, and as she headed toward the floor, she heard voices overhead.

"Dammit!" she heard Donovan yell. "She's having a seizure. You fix this, Darcelle. You fix this!"

But when Eleri looked up, she saw only the ceiling. She heard footsteps around her. As the sparkles closed in, faces leaned over her, and at last, one face became clear.

Emmaline reached down, offering her hand to help Eleri up.

66

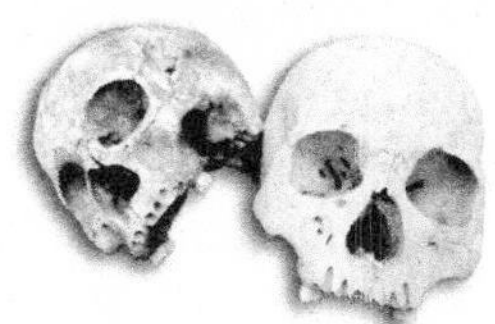

The doctor was yelling at her, but Darcelle continued chanting, focused on the spell before her. They had given her only four hours to bring Alesse home, and she'd already spent forty-five minutes gathering the crap she needed, getting the blood from the little witch, and saying the spell.

She had three more rounds to chant before she reached the nine total that she needed. And so, she recited the words again and again, blocking out everything around her.

The little witch had gone down, and that was not supposed to happen. But Darcelle couldn't let her attention be pulled away. She would deal with the two of them in a few minutes.

Unfortunately, the doctor continued yelling at her. He would have grabbed for her, but Darcelle had deftly stepped away, feinting to one side and then another, moving her body while her focus stayed on the spell in front of her.

She had to reach Alesse. She had to get her sister to come home. If she didn't, the two feds would take her to the prison, and she would die. As she had thought before, there was a very good possibility that if she died, she would be stuck on this same path for all of eternity. How could she ever undo the spell if she didn't have a corporeal form to do it? So she kept chanting.

No matter how he grabbed at her ankles, no matter how he cursed her, Darcelle ignored the doctor and kept at her work. Her life depended on it. When at last she reached the final round, she let her voice build to a crescendo. She was certain the neighboring shop owners could hear her, as they were not yet fully closed up for the night. But none of that mattered as she finished it off and lifted her hands. She called the gods—the light and the dark—and she watched as all the small lights that had gathered in the room formed up and becoming a single, glaring glow that shot out the top of the shop.

There, she thought, falling into a heap on the floor. *It is done*.

Alesse would see it. She could not miss it. Now, Darcelle need only wait to see if her sister came.

There was a problem she had not mentioned to either of the two feds. She could do the spell, she could call her sister, and she could put out the appropriate bait with Eleri's blood.

But the gods knew, she'd tried before. Perhaps some of her previous spells had worked. She was strong. They should have worked, and Alesse must have seen them. But she hadn't come home. So there was every possibility that Alesse might not come this time, either.

Darcelle considered briefly the possibility that Alesse might not be able to return. Perhaps she had gotten herself into something far too deep. Darcelle hoped not. She would not survive life in prison, and she would not survive an afterlife chained to this stupid, fucking shop.

She crumpled, rolling the best she could to ease the brunt of it, but still she felt her head snap against the hardwood floor. She lay there for a moment, breathing as though she had been underwater for a long time, as though she had been thrown to the floor and had the wind knocked out of her. She gasped for air.

The doctor was still shouting at her. And as Darcelle lolled her head to the side, she saw the little witch on the ground, shaking in a seizure.

Shit, she thought. She should let the witch just go. They had no great ties, except for the fact that whatever Eleri had in her blood, it was powerful.

Darcelle had felt the kick from it while she worked. She wore the little witch's blood on her face. *Perhaps I shouldn't let the woman go*, she thought. *Perhaps I should save the witch, if only for myself*. Even if she couldn't get her sisters here, Eleri's blood might be strong enough to break the spell that bound her to the store. That had been the hope all along. Eleri might make that spell better.

Darcelle was a Dauphine, but Eleri was a Remy—and so much more.

She rolled to her side and stretched her hand out. She had nothing left to give, but she had to find something.

She realized she needed these two on her side. She needed them to help her get Alesse in line—and they would, because she had promised them Emmaline in return. She had made a promise that perhaps she couldn't keep, but she would not tell them that yet.

She held her palm out, aimed toward the little witch, but nothing happened. Not until she dragged her hand to her own face and rubbed the blood that was there onto the palm of her hand, and then held it out again, did any of her magic work.

Slowly, Eleri's body stopped shaking. The doctor, kneeling next to her, holding her head and her shoulder, and ignoring the cut on her arm—now bleeding again—looked up at Darcelle. Perhaps it was a thank you—she didn't think she would ever know, but let him believe that she had saved the little witch.

Then, her own eyes rolled back and she passed out. But somewhere in the void, she heard the voices.

"Fuck you, little sister. Fuck you."

She almost laughed. Yes, she had found Alesse. However, she frowned, wondering if her face was actually frowning as her body lay on the floor of the shop. Darcelle was somewhere else, and she didn't know where, and she didn't know how—but she was free for the first time.

She saw Alesse and she saw that her sister had a small boy with her.

Fuck, she thought. This was going to be a shit show.

And then, with a jolt, she snapped back into her body, opened her eyes, and saw the same damn, fucking ceiling of her shop that she always did.

67

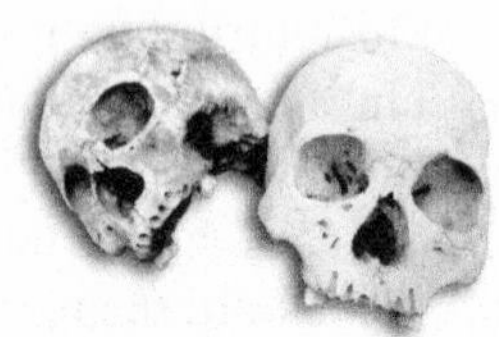

When Donovan finally got Eleri upright and into the one chair they had, his breathing began to slow, just a little.

Darcelle was still lying on the floor, almost as though the spell had stripped the oxygen and bones from her body. She rolled a little bit and met his gaze, almost as though asking, *Are you going to help me?*

No. He wasn't. In fact, he tried to ignore her, although he was certain she could still be dangerous. She looked to be almost completely incapacitated—but he didn't put anything past her.

He stood across the table from Eleri and, using one arm, he swept everything to the side. He'd probably just ruined a very specific altar arrangement, and maybe even damaged what was left of the spell. He gave zero fucks. Eleri had been seizing, and he had almost had a heart attack as he watched her.

"Eleri," he said. "Look at me."

Holding one finger upright in front of his own nose, he waited for her eyes to show he'd come into focus. Luckily, they did, clearly and quickly. He moved his finger back and forth. Eleri didn't even ask what he was doing. She could tell that things had gone wrong. If he was testing her, she would trust that he had good reason to.

She nodded at him and he nodded back at her. Her eyes had traced perfectly. Good news. Another breath came out of his lungs, another weight lifted off of his shoulders. He looked at her pupils then. He had no flashlight, but the pupils seemed to be equal and, as best he could tell, reactive.

That seizure had scared the ever-loving crap out of him. The memory of it, infused with adrenaline, was unclear now in his mind. Though he felt he could still see her falling in slow motion, he didn't know if the seizure had been the thing that had made her tumble, or if she'd passed out and hit her head first and *that* had triggered the seizure. There was also the possibility that the seizure was nothing physical and was entirely the result of Darcelle Dauphine's little spell. If that were the case, everything he'd done had been pointless. But he'd not been able to wait and run the risk of Eleri sustaining some kind of damage.

Donovan glanced down at the floor again, at the woman sprawled there, her dark skin glowing in the dim light coming through the few windows between the slats of the blinds. They'd left a lamp on in the office, and a little bit of that light filtered in, too, as the sunlight faded.

He checked his watch. Three more hours. Jesus, how had it only been an hour? It felt like they'd been here for days. But he didn't say that.

He didn't dare leave Darcelle behind him. He didn't trust her enough to ever let her pass behind him again. But, she was down on the ground and to his side, where she stayed in his peripheral vision. She might still be dangerous, but he definitely needed to take care of Eleri.

Eleri had jerked away and begun convulsing when he was only halfway finished placing the Steri-Strips on her arm. Now he pulled at her wrist again, and she easily gave it over.

The top half of the long cut, the part toward the elbow, had neat strips. The bottom half had been tugged open again and blood was beginning to well along the seam. The wound itself puzzled him. As deep as it was—and he had seen the tip of the blade go into her skin at least half an inch, if not more—it should have been bleeding much more than it was. It had bled profusely when Darcelle had first cut it. But something about the knife, the cut, the spell work, the sparkles, or the magic in the air—he didn't know—made the wound bleed when blood was needed and stop when they were done.

He wanted to start over, but that wasn't an option with Steri-Strips. For a moment, he was grateful that he hadn't been stitching her and she hadn't had a thread with a small needle attached to the end flailing around and causing further damage during her seizure. Still, he couldn't undo the strips that he had done, even though the last few had threatened to pull apart. Taking them off required a special medical solvent that the regular stores didn't carry. Without the solvent, the strips would rip out chunks of skin if he tried to remove them. He'd have to leave them in place. He lifted his kit off of the ground and up onto the tabletop, all while still keeping an eye on Darcelle. He re-cleaned the wound and went back to work pulling it together as Eleri watched.

Moment by moment, Eleri seemed to be regaining her strength, and that made him happy. Unfortunately, Darcelle also seemed to be recovering. By the time he had Eleri's wound completely closed in neat, marching, tiny beige strips, Darcelle was sitting up, her arms wrapped around her knees, her head still hanging down.

Eleri looked over. "Okay," she said. "Where is my sister?"

A harsh, bitter chuckle emanated from the woman on the floor. "Not yet, little witch. Mine isn't here. And you two have to help me get what I need from her first."

Donovan watched as Eleri's eyes narrowed. He assumed she was thinking the same thing he was. It was absolutely not in their jurisdiction to hold someone down while someone else collected blood.

Darcelle lifted her head and frowned at them. "Not like that."

She'd muttered it as though she could read his mind. He wondered if she could, and he didn't like it.

Eleri tried a different tack, one that made Donovan startle, but he hoped he hid it well. He kept his mouth shut and continued working. Though the Steri-Strips were in place, he still needed to wrap the wound in gauze, a bandage, and tape. He held her arm with one hand, the warmth of her skin reassuring him that her heart was beating regularly and she wasn't about to pass out again.

"Darcelle," Eleri said, her voice calm but menacing. "Tell me about my sister."

Darcelle eyes flickered off to the side as though she were remembering. "Blond hair, blue eyes," she said.

Eleri nodded, as though the two had needed this confirmation to make sure they were speaking of the same story.

Darcelle talked freely, surprising Donovan. She told Eleri how she and Emmaline had played together as children. It turned Donovan's stomach just to listen. Eleri had lost her sister, and Darcelle had gotten her. She had gotten the dolls, the running through the woods, and the late-night discussions about boys.

But Darcelle and Emmaline had *not* been sisters—Darcelle made that clear. So not only had Eleri not gotten her sister—Emmaline had lost her sister, too.

Eleri frowned, obviously hating both sides of that. Had Emmaline had anyone to love her as family? Donovan hoped so.

"She had a good life," Darcelle said.

Eleri snorted. Donovan had, too. Shockingly, as they glanced up at each other, they almost laughed.

Emmaline had had a good life, he thought. She'd been kidnapped. Just because she hadn't been horribly abused or sold into slavery, that did not mean she'd had a good life. He'd worked missing children's cases and he'd seen bodies, identified them. Sometimes families had kidnapped a child merely because they wanted a child of their own. It never worked out well.

Darcelle insisted the children they kept had played together and lived together. Their farm was big, and though the children weren't allowed to leave, there was plenty of room. She insisted they were well educated. Darcelle and her sisters had not attended public school, her mother claiming she homeschooled them. There was something about the way Darcelle said it that caught Donovan's ear. The fact that she used the word "claim" made him wonder. She had not seemed uneducated in any way—but, he figured, that might be a product of her own doing rather than her family's.

Then the conversation petered out. It felt far too short to Donovan, as if the ten years Emmaline had been missing from her family could be summed up in just a few sentences.

But Eleri turned the topic, once again surprising him. He had her arm wrapped now. She was alert, bandaged, and safe, so he ducked into the back office and pulled a second chair out. But he sat on it himself, still not giving one to Darcelle, who remained on the floor, still sneering at him.

"So you had Emmaline," Eleri started. "And her blood was some kind of all-powerful elixir."

He heard the sarcasm come through. Seeing where she was going, he asked the question himself. "So, when Emmaline died, why didn't you come for Eleri?"

They would have solved this case a decade ago, he thought. Eleri would not have been taken.

Interestingly enough, Darcelle seemed to have similar ideas. "She was almost twenty years old," Darcelle said. "She had already been accepted to college. We stole children—not adult witches we couldn't control."

As the words left her lips, a strong wind seemed to blow open the back door. In the doorway stood a woman, her eyes sweeping the room and glowing with anger.

68

Eleri sat at the table, feeling the gust of air blow her hair back. Donovan had been a rock, but now it felt as though she stood there alone in the room. She knew without asking. This was Alesse Dauphine.

Alesse's eyes darted left and right, checking out the strange and probably unexpected scene before her. Her skin, not nearly as dark as Darcelle's, was offset by wide brown eyes and lush lips. Her sneer matched her sister's. It almost appeared as though the wind she'd created with her entry had blown her own hair back as well.

"What have you done, little sister?"

The tone of her demand was harsher in Eleri's mind than in her ear.

She watched as Darcelle got to her feet, and though Eleri had expected the movement to be wobbly, Darcelle stood strong.

"What do you mean 'what have I done'?" she volleyed back with the same strength the demand had warranted. She waved her hands around the room. "I called you back. I called you back when you blocked all of us. Bully for you. You blocked us, and I found you anyway," she taunted.

Alesse spun around, seeming ready to leave, before Darcelle said, "Do you not see who sits at my table?" Her hands stopped waving around this time and centered on Eleri.

Eleri froze. She was being held up as a specimen for inspection, and she wasn't sure what she should do. Should she act like she was here at Darcelle's request—as though the reason they had drawn Alesse back was legitimate? Eleri stayed still, figuring that if she made a move now, she wouldn't be able to take it back.

Alesse's intense gaze scanned her up and down. "Remy!" she whispered, as her eyes lit up.

Darcelle nodded. "I found Emmaline's blood." Her fingertips still pointed Eleri's way, and Eleri sat unmoving.

The conversation was not one she wished to be in the middle of, but the first part of her mission had been accomplished. Alesse had arrived. Only then did she realize that Alesse had one hand tucked behind her back. She tugged it now and pulled forward a child who appeared to be about ten years old.

He cowered, barely managing to stay upright and stepping in front of Alesse only as she motioned him forward. "I, too, found a Remy", she said.

Darcelle waited for further clarification, and Eleri followed their lead. Beside her, Donovan stood up, now the tallest of the four of them. For that, she was grateful. Though they faced Alesse and Darcelle Dauphine, at least their numbers were matched.

Eleri found her eyes darting to the little boy's face. If he was a Remy, he must be some kind of cousin of hers. She looked him over for familiar features. His pale skin didn't resemble any relative of the Remy clan, but she did find a few similarities.

She almost held out her hand and said, "I'm a Remy, too"—but she didn't think that would accomplish anything. It certainly wouldn't soothe a child who'd been dragged away from home and into a voodoo shop.

Instead, Eleri looked to Alesse, and making a bold gambit, she entered the conversation, "Where did you find him?" she asked.

Alesse laughed. "California."

It wasn't much, but it would be enough. Eleri turned next to the boy, "What is your name?"

"Brandon," he managed to reply before Alesse smacked the side of his head.

Bitch! Eleri thought. Beside her, she felt Donovan jolt, but there was nothing they could do right now. Facing these two women was something like confronting drug-crazed burglars with loaded guns.

Darcelle was standing tall, staring her sister down, looking as though she had never cast a spell that left her boneless and on the ground for half an hour. "We need Gisele and Lafae," she said.

Alesse laughed again, sounding crazier than she looked. "They are already on their way. I think his is the best blood yet." She dropped the little boy's hand and he skittered into the nearest corner.

He stayed on his feet, as though watching for a chance to run away. He pressed himself into one of the shelves, though he acted terrified of the poppets lining the walls behind him.

The back door, still open, now became crowded with two more Dauphine sisters.

"Oooh," Gisele said. "You brought the boy."

Eleri was going to crush them. She had his name and his state of origin. She had a relative timeframe for his disappearance. The Dauphine sisters were going down, and little Brandon was going home. This might be the worst experience of his entire life, but he would go home safe and—at least from today forward—unharmed. Eleri made that vow to herself. She wished she could make it to him. She hadn't saved her own sister, but she would save him.

Donovan shifted a little, and he leaned over, looking at her and then he pointedly looked down at his own hand. The two of them stood slightly behind the table, allowing his fingertips to stay just out of view. Eleri could see he had made the letter L with his thumb and forefinger.

Fuck, she thought. It wasn't just the sisters they had to worry about. The Lobomau were arriving, too. Donovan smelled them coming.

Alesse was explaining, "Look what's in our shop! We have Emmaline's sister."

Giselle's eyes went round, as did Lafae's. The two looked at each other and almost cackled and clapped their hands with glee. Eleri felt her blood run cold. She had done this. She had agreed to bring Alesse home. She knew that Darcelle would use her blood to cast a spell—but she had promised it was a spell to set herself free.

Now Eleri doubted the plan. She doubted Darcelle's ability to or even intention to carry through. Could she even cast a spell and set herself free, with all three sisters standing there watching her? What if they took Eleri and Donovan hostage?

Eleri knew they wanted her blood. They all had reason to never let her go. Hell, they'd held her sister for almost a decade. They were kidnapping children from all over the US in an attempt to replace the blood they'd lost with Emmaline. There was nothing that she wouldn't put past these women.

Eleri thought quickly, as they were now vastly outnumbered, and soon they would be outnumbered further. Lobomau loyal to the Dauphine family would come through the door at any moment. *Should she offer her blood, and hope that's enough? Could they try just walking out the door?*

The chalice of blood still sat on the altar, strangely not coagulating. There wasn't time to dwell on that. Eleri and Donovan needed to get out of here, and she need to take the boy. Though he cowered at the edges of the room and was no longer in Alesse's hands, the sisters stood between her and Donovan and the boy.

She was starting to open her mouth to announce that she was leaving, to force their hand, when she caught Darcelle's eye.

Darcelle's gaze narrowed at her, and it told her something that struck Eleri with horror. This was not going to go down the way Darcelle had promised it would.

Alesse leaped forward, her hands reaching out for Eleri as she rallied to a battle cry her sisters would die for.

"Bind her!"

69

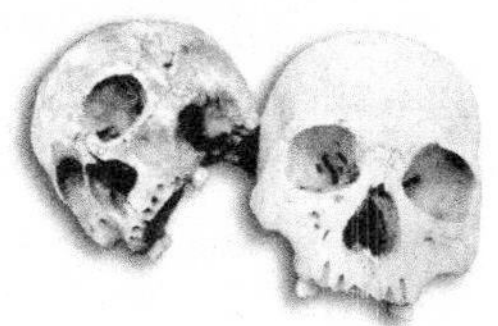

Eleri stood frozen for a moment, much like the little boy did.

She'd thought they were going to grab her and physically bind her, but instead, they seemed to be referring to a spell. As she watched, the sisters spoke to each other through some language that didn't involve words. They exchanged looks and seemed to know suddenly it was time. Each had a position, and they moved in concert.

Just starting to move her feet, Eleri found herself instead knocked out of the way. She and Donovan were jostled aside as dark hands reached for the materials on the table and began rearranging them back into almost the original layout Darcelle had used.

Donovan tried to reach in as they moved the chalice of Eleri's blood to the center of the space, but as his hand tried to pass between the sisters, he stopped suddenly and cried out in pain. Eleri could see his hand had bounced off an invisible wall that knocked him back. He shook his fingers the way he would if he had run into something physical, although there was nothing she could see.

The sisters paid no heed to them now, and she was afraid that they had gotten what they wanted. She had no power in this situation. Suddenly, she felt incredibly foolish. She'd donated blood on the word of a witch she knew she could not trust. She donated the most powerful blood the witch's family had ever seen—and now they were here, gathering around it in a circle. As she watched, they all joined hands in one smooth motion, right over left, locking together as though they were a single unit. She thought that, right now, they probably were.

Eleri's eyes met Donovan's. The expression on his face said he had no more idea what to do here than she did. Together they took a step back. Eleri's heart raced and she tried to think. Darcelle had said she would call Alesse back and that she needed her sisters' blood to break the spell on her.

Now it sounded like Alesse had entirely different ideas for what to do with the blood. Eleri had thought the sisters would donate their own for a spell so Darcelle could set herself free.

Suddenly, she saw the error in her reasoning. Why would the sisters donate? Why would they help Darcelle break the spell? If they would do such a thing, surely they would have done it years ago. Darcelle had seemed bitter about her position in the family, as though her sisters were taking full advantage of her being stuck between the house and the shop. Eleri had no doubt of that. Just the few interactions she'd had with Lafae and Gisele had led her to believe that they were the kind of women who would happily let their sister suffer for their own freedoms.

Should she let this family drama play out? Should she try to fight it? Eleri felt terrified and exhausted, caught in indecision.

As she watched, all four sisters put their right arms into the circle. Each sister handled the knife for a moment and then passed it to the next until four arms were cut and bleeding freely. So far it matched what Darcelle said, but what did they intend to do with that blood? Eleri knew nothing of spells, aside from what she'd seen. They might be releasing Darcelle, but could just as easily be binding Eleri.

She didn't recognize the words. The language was not English, nor was it French. A moment later, she felt small tremors coming up through the base of the floor. At first, she thought it might be just her imagination—but across the way, she watched as the little boy suddenly splayed his hands out, reaching for purchase on the shelves behind him as the little poppets swayed.

Again, she glanced at Donovan and when she looked back, all four sisters had added their own blood to the chalice that held hers. She was revolted by the sight. She could smell the copper and iron on the air, and almost taste a tinge of it on her tongue. She thought of Darcelle bleeding from the eyes as they drove across the bridge into the French quarter.

Eleri wondered which urge would be stronger for Darcelle: binding Eleri and having Remy/Eames blood for all the spells she wished to cast into the future, or setting herself free.

There was no way to guess the woman's true motivation. Eleri was furious with herself for letting it get this far.

Donovan surprised her by taking action. She watched as he slowly approached behind Alesse, no longer jamming his hand between the women as if trying to reach for something on the table.

This time he slowly pushed at the space and tested it. She saw it then, the way his fingers flattened, the mild blue in the air as though he was pushing on something that gave only slightly with his touch. The invisible barrier was too strong for him to push through. A moment later, he was leaning his whole body against the barrier, even though Eleri couldn't see it.

It scared her that the sisters could create a force strong enough to support a grown man without seeming to notice. Donovan stepped back, still silent. He looked at her as though to say, "What do we do now?"

The chanting continued. The wall would only get stronger. Eleri watched as Darcelle's face split in a wicked grin.

Eleri could not read the expression. Had Darcelle just tried to damn her? Had she succeeded? Had she instead set herself free? Eleri couldn't tell, but whatever it was she had done, it made Darcelle so happy, her eyes glowed.

At that moment, the other sisters' heads snapped toward Darcelle in startled amazement. Eleri realized whatever had gone down wasn't what they expected.

Whether or not it was what Darcelle had told her would happen, she still did not know, but Eleri had to take advantage. Her heart was pounding. Her anger raged at the thought that they would bind her the way they had bound Emmaline—the idea that they could use her as they had used an eight-year-old child. They thought her powers weren't strong enough, or that she had no control of them. All of these feelings built up as rage inside her.

With a shrill, primal scream, Eleri raced forward. Unlike Donovan, she did not go at the sisters' backs.

Instead, she dove between their feet, imagining she opened a hole in the wall they had made.

She slid smoothly under the table—although she had no idea

whether that was because she'd found an unprotected pocket of their magic or because she'd opened the barricade with power of her own.

Under the table, the air zinged and buzzed. She saw only their feet and couldn't tell what was going on over her head, but she knew what she had to do. She had to disrupt the spell. She could not let them bind her. What would Grandmere say?

From under the table, Eleri watched as Donovan's feet turned. Then she saw a set of dark, bare feet in the corner near the boy.

Holy shit, Eleri thought. Grandmere had arrived.

She did not see the little boy's head or the top half of her great-grandmother, but she saw the older woman grasp his hand and hold him tightly.

In her peripheral vision, she watched Grandmere move the child behind her, much the way Alesse had done when they entered, but for entirely different purposes.

All at once, the four sisters seemed to realize something was going wrong. Donovan's shout alerted her to the fact that the door had opened again and Eleri watched as Grandmere placed herself directly between the boy and the opening door. Wolves burst in, more of them than Eleri could count from the feet alone. More than just the Salzani brothers.

Now, even she could smell the wolf on them, but she was under the table and she remembered why she was there. Slamming her hands upward, she rocked the table. She tried rock it toward Donovan, but she had no idea if she succeeded.

She watched as the sisters jumped back and she felt the air clear a little, as if perhaps their bubble had burst.

Donovan shouted, and she saw feet turn toward him. Even as she crawled out the other side, toward Grandmere and the child, she came upright to standing. In a flash, she turned back and saw the table rock twice, settling flat onto its feet. But Donovan had already reached into the middle and grabbed something.

It took a moment to recognize that he held the chalice of all the blood—hers mixed with the Dauphine sisters. The four of them screamed at him. Eleri wasn't sure the exact words they yelled. She couldn't tell if it was French, English, incantation, or something else —but none of it stopped Donovan.

Eleri held her hands out toward him as though she could protect him and watched as he spun and flung the blood across the shelves. It dripped in red spatters along the walls and down the faces of the poppets. As she listened, Alesse looked up to the ceiling and screamed a rage that turned the air red.

Eleri felt the oldest sister's voice course through her. It felt as though the blood in her veins was freezing and cracking. Pain shot in bolts along every limb and into her heart. She felt the beating slow … two … three … and then her heart stopped.

Her muscles felt like sludge and she knew she was dying. She noticed Darcelle flash a wicked smile and then turn to one of the wolves. Only he wasn't a wolf. As Eleri's vision went dark, she heard Darcelle tell Caspian Salzani, "You owe me."

Then Caspian stood as a guard in the door while Darcelle ran past him and out gleefully into the night. Eleri blinked again, her chest heavy, her vision fading.

Caspian held them as long as he could, but it was only three more blinks by Eleri's count. Then the wolves tore at him and ran out the door after Darcelle.

70

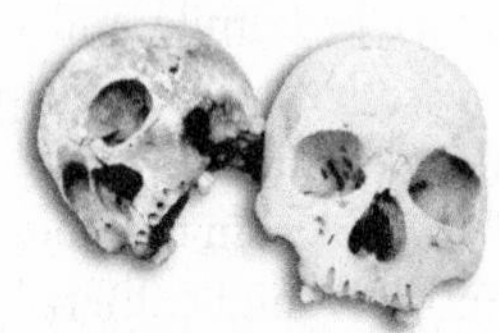

Eleri stood in the corner of the shop, stunned and unmoving. Though she felt as though she couldn't breathe or move, she'd not yet fallen. She watched as Donovan's fingers went lax and dropped the chalice, letting the very last of the red blood spatter and then run into the boards of the floor, seeping into the long cracks in the wood.

She watched the three sisters register shock and confusion as they began to understand that Darcelle had run off. It took only a moment for Gisele and Lafae to let their confusion turn to anger. But, for Alesse it turned to pure rage.

"*What did you do?*" she yelled at Eleri.

Her hands were out in front of her, pulses of energy flying from the oldest sister's palms. Though Eleri didn't see them, she saw the chairs rock with the blasts. She saw Donovan stumble backward as one of the blasts hit him. Even the other Dauphine sisters reacted to the waves Alesse was putting out.

In her anger, she spun around the room, coming to Eleri last. But Eleri found Grandmere stood beside her, the little boy still tucked behind her skirts and cowering. For the briefest of moments, Eleri wondered what he would do in the years to come with what he had seen here today.

Unable to even lift her arms as a shield, Eleri was unsure if she would survive this—and if she didn't, Grandmere would have to be the one to save the boy.

Grandmere moved slowly, calmly—ice in contrast to Alesse's fire —and raised her hand as the shock wave came around. It bounced off Eleri. She saw it but did not feel it. Instead, she felt warmth, and the cold fear that had cracked in her veins slowly thawed. She felt stronger, and her hands clenched into fists.

"*My sister is gone!*" Alesse's anger seemed uncontainable now that she realized she had been thwarted—by an inexperienced witch and an old woman.

Eleri found her own rage in return. "*So is mine!* Yours ran away because of the way you treated her. Mine was *stolen*."

Where was Darcelle? Eleri wondered. Even as her anger was directed at Alesse, she knew she was not being a good witch because she couldn't seem to focus. Focus was required for spells. It was one of the few things all the witchcraft sources agreed upon. She didn't have focus right now because she couldn't help wondering: *Where was Darcelle?*.

As Alesse charged at her, Eleri knew she needed Darcelle. Darcelle would tell her where Emmaline was buried. *That was our deal!* This angry beast of a sister would not. Alesse's lip curled up as she spat at Eleri.

"Fuck you! You set my sister free."

Eleri had not been sure until now that Darcelle was truly free. She had seen that Darcelle had left the door wide open and disappeared, but that didn't mean that she had been able to escape the narrow path she was cursed to walk. Only Alesse's words let Eleri believe Darcelle had achieved her goal.

Eleri wanted to scream, *What about our deal?* Darcelle had promised to tell Eleri where to find Emmaline. But something pushed her useless anger aside and she felt a renewed strength. It had to be coming from Grandmere. Standing like a solid mountain behind her now, Grandmere let Eleri move forward and control the scene. She did not see it, but she felt Grandmere's hand reaching out toward her, giving her strength to her great-granddaughter even as she sheltered the boy.

Eleri turned and looked at each sister in turn as she decided to play the one card she had that was superior to theirs. There was every possibility they would laugh her out of the room, but she was going to try it.

Alesse moved her hands in a threatening gesture, and she seemed confused as nothing happened. Eleri reasoned that must be due to Grandmere. Gisele and Lafae closely watched the older woman, as though wondering how she had accomplished this.

But it didn't really matter how. It only mattered that they—at least temporarily—seemed powerless.

Eleri took advantage. Reaching into her back pocket, she pulled out her badge.

"Federal Bureau of Investigations," she said. "You're all under arrest."

Donovan, too, whipped out his badge, a slow grin forming on his face as he moved about and seemed to see that, finally, the witches held no power over them.

He was not gentle. He grabbed Gisele's hands, though she fought him, and this time his physical prowess worked. Gisele's witchcraft seeming to have been halted by Grandmere's presence. The old woman stood silent and still, almost as though she wasn't really there. She let everyone else control what happened, though Eleri guessed Grandmere was truly the most powerful presence in the room. Through all of it, and without moving, she kept the boy tucked safely behind her, her hand still raised, palm out, toward the sisters, apparently rendering them powerless. Eleri had never been more grateful in her life.

Lafae fought until Donovan pushed her head toward the table, yanking her hands up behind her. It was a move that nearly pulled the shoulders out of their sockets, and it made the perpetrator want to comply. Donovan had no compunction about using it on the youngest and smallest sister.

When she was on the ground, he tucked Lafae aside and went after Gisele. She had tried to run out the door while Eleri manhandled Alesse. Despite her larger size, Eleri managed it, though eventually she had to push the woman face down on the floor, with a knee in her back to get the job done.

Behind her, Gisele was struggling with the door, as it seemed to be locked, and she—for once—seemed unable to work the knob.

Grandmere again, Eleri thought, as she and Donovan stood up and went after Gisele in tandem. Once they were on her, she went quickly, snapping her jaws together and refusing to make any noise. She acted as though this was an interrogation and she was a hostile witness. Only they hadn't asked her anything.

Darcelle was nowhere to be seen. In fact, Eleri didn't even remember anyone shutting the door behind her, but right now, everything was closed and bolted. *Must have been Grandmere,* she thought.

At last, all three sisters were cuffed, and Donovan looked to Eleri first, but issued the command. "Let's take them outside. They have way too much power in here. We need them on the street, even across the street. I don't know how much distance will do, but we have to try."

Eleri nodded, once again thinking of people outside with cell phones and such. It was dark, and that would work in their favor. But still, the idea of being so conspicuous made her shudder.

"Back door," she said in response—the same direction that Gisele had been running when she'd tried to escape, and the same direction that Darcelle had seemingly fled into the night. One by one, they led the sisters out, parking them behind the shops across the way, sitting them on the curb.

Donovan was calling Westerfield as he stood watching over them, and Eleri went back inside for Grandmere and the boy. She found only the little boy who sat, tucked into a small ball, by the bookshelf.

Eleri frowned. "Where's the old woman?" she asked.

When he only stared in response, she remembered his name.

"Brandon?" she said, reaching out her hands, and waiting a slow eternity while he finally found the trust to put his in hers. "We're going to get you home," she said.

She spent a good three minutes talking to him in soft tones until he stopped shaking so hard his teeth rattled. She thought about those teeth, and his little skull, and the fact that they would remain in his body. His arms would remain uncut. Only when she had him by the hand and she had looked around the remainder of the shop did she again ask him, "Brandon, did you see where the old woman went?"

He shook his head, and then he whispered, "She disappeared."

71

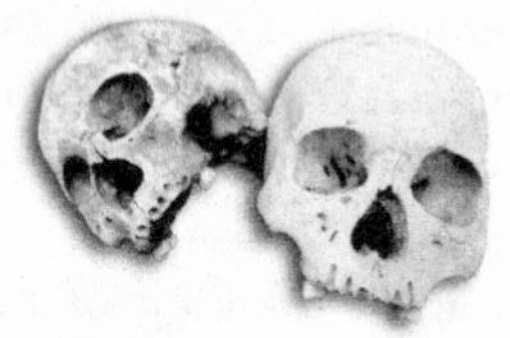

Donovan was exhausted. It was not Agent Westerfield who had appeared in the alley at the back of the shop, but Agent Almasi.

Eleri recognized him on sight, which at least made Donovan feel better. They wouldn't be working with just anyone in the New Orleans branch office. This was the man who had been on the case of the missing children.

Donovan kept his eyes roving up and down the street for the eternity that they waited for the other agents to show up. He'd been searching for Grandmere, whom Eleri said had disappeared.

She'd brought the little boy out to him, and he'd worked as best he could to keep the boy in his sight, at his side and away from the sisters. It was problematic though, watching the boy and the women. Donovan was guarding the Dauphine sisters with his gun drawn. He wondered if their witchcraft was good enough to stop a bullet and hoped he didn't have to find out. But while watching them, he'd not been able to spot Grandmere.

Eleri had searched the shop thoroughly and had not found her great-grandmother there, either. Donovan had also been keeping an eye out for Darcelle. In fact, when he spoke to branch office on the phone, one of the first things he requested was that they check the Dauphine home. Donovan rattled off the address, saying he had three of the sisters in custody, but the fourth had fled. It was the first place they should look for her.

Five agents eventually showed up. They could not have looked more like feds if they had been wearing mirrored sunglasses. Donovan almost laughed. Their suits and their telltale gaits gave them away.

He was more than grateful to hand over his prisoners, and he wondered what would happen next. Would the sisters regain their powers when they were put into interrogation? Would they walk out? What would happen? He had no idea.

He shook hands with Almasi and got the names of the other four agents. Eleri asked them, "Did you find Darcelle?"

Almasi shook his head. "The agents who checked said the house was empty. It didn't look like anyone had been there."

"Are they tracing the roads between the house and here?" she asked. They didn't know the exact path that Darcelle took. Donovan shook his head.

Almasi reassured them. "I do have an agent driving it. He should be here any moment."

The other agents were busy reading the sisters their rights and ducking them into the backs of cars. Luckily, they had as many cars as there were sisters, so they could separate their new prisoners.

Donovan felt his exhaustion come over him in a wave, and Eleri once again took the little boy's hand and introduced him. "This is Brandon. He's from California. Alesse showed up with him tonight."

Almasi took it all in stride, and for that, Donovan was grateful. It was obvious to the feds that he and his partner had been neck-deep in what should have been a federal investigation, and that they'd been running it on their own.

"Show me the inside," Almasi suggested. Eleri nodded toward Donovan, as though to ask, *Can you take point on this?* He supposed he could. His was the only blood *not* spattered on the walls. Well, his and the boy's.

Almasi whistled as he stepped into the large back room.

The walls were still lined with trinkets for sale, spells, and candles. Donovan looked around, following Almasi's gaze, trying to see it with fresh eyes, but he found he couldn't. It was impossible to erase his memories of what had happened in this room.

Almasi rubbed the short hair on his head and said, "Well, this is a shit show."

Donovan could only agree. Almasi pointed. "Is this the normal state of the shop? Do you know?"

Donovan told him, "I've only been coming here for about a week, but as far as I can tell. I mean the dolls and the items and the quantity of stock, yes. The blood on the walls is from tonight."

Almasi stared at him. "They were doing some blood shit when you two arrived?"

Donovan nodded and let it stand at that. There was every possibility the Dauphine sisters would tell a different tale when they were questioned. There was also the possibility they would disappear from custody before they were questioned. Donovan was not going to write his own ticket on this one. Silence was the better part of any valor he could find.

"That's creepy as fuck," Almasi muttered, rubbing his hand across his head again.

Donovan tried then to be helpful, pointing to the table, the contents of which had scattered when Eleri tipped it. It took a moment to see that the knife was on the floor.

"That knife," he said. "Don't touch it."

Almasi was reaching for it, but Donovan's words stopped the man from even using his gloved hands. Instead, Almasi squatted and shone his light on it.

Donovan couldn't quite bring himself to get that close. "That handle," he said, "is made from a human bone."

Almasi raised his eyebrows, and Donovan continued. "Eleri identified it."

That should be good enough, he thought, and Almasi seemed to agree. "It's possible," Donovan added, "that there are several more on the shelves, though I know for a fact that at least one is just a resin cast, so the knife itself doesn't contain any real bone."

He watched as Almasi frowned, and he explained their theory that it was placed on the shelves to discredit what they'd seen before.

"You'll want to check behind the cash register and in the back office," Donovan mentioned—though to be fair, Almasi would have probably done those things out of rote inspection, anyway.

He let Almasi walk to the edges of the room and shine his flashlight on the blood that was now congealing in spots on the walls. Some had been thick enough to drip. Most hadn't. It looked like a murder scene, and Donovan was grateful, at least, that it wasn't. He'd seen plenty of those, too.

He wondered how to phrase this and whether or not he should, but in the end, he decided to go for it. "I know you're from around here," he said, "so you may know more of this than I do. The Dauphine sisters were in the middle of some kind of spell work tonight. I don't know exactly what kind of spell they were casting."

It wasn't really a lie.

Almasi nodded, apparently not having been put off by the scattered and abandoned altar in front of them.

"What are you saying?" Almasi asked. His hands were on his hips, and with the lights now fully on, the shop had at least a slightly less evil cast.

"I'm saying, they believe they can cast serious spells. You might want to watch out for them at the station."

Almasi chuckled. "You think their spells are going to get them past me and my guys?"

Donovan also laughed, trying to pretend he didn't believe what he had seen with his own eyes. "I'm saying that *they* believe they can, and it might make them try things you would never expect."

Almasi nodded, seeming to accept that definition. "I don't know what's going to happen with you and your partner," he told Donovan. "That's between you and your SAC. But you should be aware that I have to contact him and file this."

"No hard feelings," Donovan said. "I expected nothing less."

Almasi nodded once again and then he looked over his shoulder and said, only, "You're dismissed."

Donovan left the shop via the back door and found Eleri in the alleyway, alone. "Where's the boy?"

"Someone from child services took him. She seemed really nice, and he liked her. His family has been notified." Her voice sounded far away, as though those were the best things she could conjure to say about the night, and they probably were.

"We have to get back to Grandmere," she told him. "Are we free to go?"

He nodded at her and started feeling in his pockets for car keys, as though they were an ancient item that he had long forgotten about. She, too, searched her pockets. Eventually, she produced them, and he remembered he was not the one who had driven here. It felt like years ago.

Slowly, they walked through the dark alley toward the rental car. She backed out, turned around, and drove away. Donovan was grateful no one followed them.

In the mirror, he saw the two remaining agents standing sentry at the back door. They disappeared into the darkness behind him and he looked at his partner next to him.

He wasn't sure if Eleri should be driving right now—but then again, he wasn't sure that he should either. Though it was tempting to tip his head back against the seat and let exhaustion overtake him, to let sleep drag him under, he felt he had to watch over Eleri. She, too, was crashing, and they were in control of a vehicle. He forced his eyes to stay awake and let the small buzz of knowing that they had not yet located Grandmere keep him awake and running.

As they pulled into the narrow drive, he noted that his rental car remained, but there was no sign one way or another of Grandmere. An empty driveway didn't mean much for a woman who didn't have a car.

The lights were not on in the house. He and Eleri flipped them on as they opened the door.

"Grandmere," Eleri hollered, walking through the house and heading down the hall.

Donovan was looking in the kitchen, seeing no trace of the woman aside from the rag left on the kitchen counter, as though she had been interrupted while cleaning.

Then he heard Eleri gasp from down the hall. Turning, Donovan followed the one sound. Eleri had made no more.

He found her, standing in the hallway as though she couldn't set foot across the threshold, though she had reached in and flipped on the light. In the harsh glare of the bulb cutting through the darkness of the night, he saw Grandmere lying on her bed, her eyes open, motionless.

72

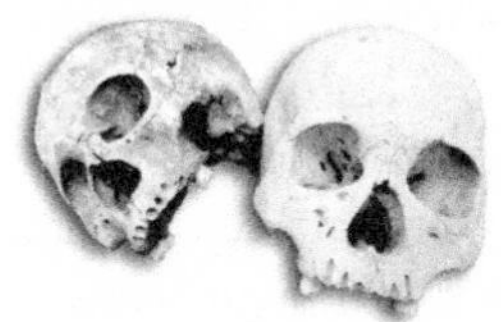

Eleri felt the pressure at the back of her eyes as she saw Donovan standing over Grandmere's body.

Donovan looked up from where he held two fingers to the old woman's neck, his expression sober and sad. He shook his head at her. But she hadn't needed him to tell her Grandmere was gone.

In fact, as she looked around, it seemed Grandmere had never left the house tonight. Her feet were bare and she wore her house dress. Perhaps Grandmere had never actually been at the store, though she and Donovan and the little boy and even the sisters had all seen the older woman.

Eleri pressed her lips together to keep them from quivering. What on earth would she ever do without Grandmere? She tried to be logical about it. Grandmere was well over ninety, possibly even a hundred. She'd had a good long life. Eleri tried to console herself that she'd had her great-grandmother for a longer time than most. But it didn't make the loss any easier.

Searching for sanity, her brain turned to the logistics. She would need to call her parents and tell them Grandmere had passed. Someone would need to sell the tiny house. Eleri thought she herself should clean it out. Lord knows she didn't want Nathalie Beaumont Eames finding the human bones Grandmere kept in the closet.

It occurred to her then that Frederick would know what to do. She almost picked up her phone to call him, but then thought better of it. She felt hands reaching for her shoulders, and only as Donovan grabbed her did she realize her knees had buckled and she'd started to go down.

"What do we do?" she whispered.

"Well, we need to call someone. We need to have the body interred. She should be taken to the morgue."

Those were all reasonable things, but Eleri didn't know if "reasonable" applied to her great-grandmother. She shook her head and held her phone up to Donovan. "Frederick," she whispered. "Call Frederick."

The Dauphine sisters had buried their dead in the back of their yard—and some in the courtyard of the home. Perhaps she should do the same for Grandmere. Though being interred at the majestic Dauphine house on the outskirts of the French Quarter hardly seemed the same as a makeshift cemetery on Grandmere's small lot in the Lower Ninth Ward.

Donovan guided her out to the front of the house and sat her on the couch. He pulled out his phone to call, but instead it rang. While he spoke in low tones to Frederic, she looked around the room.

She looked to the coffee table, which again appeared more like a regular coffee table and less like an altar. She looked to the shelves, seeing that the knickknacks were not knickknacks, but spell items. Tiny bowls of salt, feathers and fur, tiny poppets waiting for their day.

The table in the dining room looked very different to her. Where, when Grandmere had run the place, it had been covered in her scraps of fabric and her spellcraft supplies, it was now dominated by towels that Donovan had rolled up where Eleri had laid out her bodies, and by computers where they had set up their own mobile center. And as Eleri looked at the table, she realized that everything was wrong.

Three of the Dauphine sisters were in custody now, though she had no idea how long that would last. Darcelle had completely gone missing. To top it all off, not only was Grandmere gone, but she still hadn't found Emmaline.

When Frederick arrived, she felt Donovan shaking her shoulder, and she realized she'd fallen asleep on the couch. As she sat up, she moved her face to try to smile at her cousin, and she felt the skin crack with salt. She'd been crying, even as she slept.

When Emmaline disappeared, her life had gone on without her

sister, even though at the time, she'd felt that was impossible. She told herself she was a child. She told herself her mother was right, and Emmaline would come home. Nathalie Beaumont Eames still seemed to believe that. Eleri was going to shatter her mother's world more than once, because even if she didn't find Emmaline's remains, she had spoken to a person who told her Emmaline had died and confirmed what Eleri had known intuitively all these years.

When Frederick refused the hand she offered to help him, he merely put his own hand on her shoulder, holding her down on the couch. As he did, she felt the warmth infuse her. She felt, suddenly, at least a little bit better.

She whispered, "Grandmere?"

He smiled. "She's still here."

Somehow, it was enough to make Eleri feel better. No matter what she believed, no matter what she thought, somehow, someone believed. And Grandmere would still stay alive in that way. Eleri felt the back of her vocal chords shaking and tightening, and she was unable to speak in response.

Frederick seemed to understand, and he leaned in as he whispered. "She wasn't able to save your sister. But she saved you. That's what she wanted."

Her throat ratcheted down again, and Eleri felt fresh tears start as her cousin turned away.

It was Donovan who asked, "How should we handle this? I would call an ambulance and send her to the morgue, but I don't know if that's what you want."

Frederick shook his head. "No. That was not what Grandmere had planned." And Eleri laughed that Frederick also called her the same thing. But of course he would. He was of the same generation as she, and they all called her that. Every time she was here, she always felt as though she had the old woman to herself. She liked to forget that she wasn't the only remaining great-grandchild.

At last, Frederick and Donovan came out and asked for her help. She'd watched as Donovan acted as assistant once more, doing as her cousin told him. They'd wrapped the body in a fabric that Frederick brought with him and carried her with great dignity through the house. Though she had no energy left, Eleri followed Frederick's instructions and helped them load Grandmere's body into his car.

Grandmere had made her plans, he said. She'd left careful instructions for him. Eleri frowned. She believed him, of course—but she had no idea what he might do. Perhaps he would sink her into the swamp with flowers, or put her on a Viking pyre and light it aflame. She only knew that, despite her worry and her doubt, she had to trust him.

At last she found her voice. "Is there somewhere I'll be able to go, to visit her?"

"Of course," he said. "There's a family lot just out of town."

Eleri frowned harder. "I didn't know that."

"Why would you? The family has long lives, and it has been quite a while since we buried anyone. Grandmere's older sister was the last."

Eleri hadn't even known that Grandmere had an older sister. Her face must have shown that. Frederick smiled in response. "That's exactly why I am now in charge of this family, and not you."

That, at least, made her laugh.

Donovan asked, "How will you do this? Will you file this with the city? They'll notice a missing person."

Frederick shook his head. "No, they won't."

"What about her Social Security?" Donovan said.

Frederick laughed openly this time. "Grandmere collected no government checks and had very few government records, aside from the deed to the house, which she put into my name almost five years ago."

Eleri felt her head snap back. Though she didn't regret that, and she thought Frederick *should* own the house, she just found it odd that Grandmere had planned so far ahead. She had known she wasn't much longer for this world; she must have.

"But she was so healthy," Eleri protested. "I thought she'd be here another ten years."

It was Frederick who clucked his tongue and said, "Grandmere was already one hundred and seventeen."

73

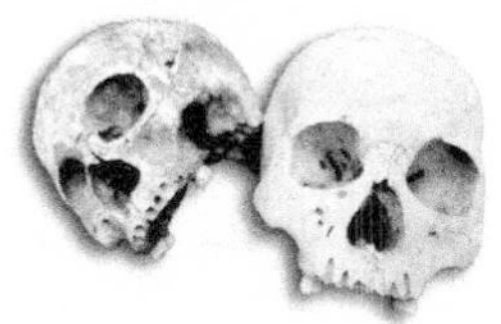

Eleri sat at the small kitchen table, eating a breakfast she had made herself. It was nowhere near as good as the ones Grandmere had made. The house felt flat, two-dimensional instead of three-dimensional. She wondered if her brain would ever get right again.

Donovan headed down the hallway, having slept late, though Eleri had been unable to. She didn't begrudge him that. One of them needed to be sane, and it wasn't going to be her. She pushed a plate toward him, having set it on the other side of the table, hoping the smell of bacon would wake him. It was the last of the food in the refrigerator, as she had discovered Grandmere only bought for the day or two ahead, walking to the store frequently, as though it was a social outing instead of stockpiling supplies and staying in.

So far, no one had showed up knocking at the door, wanting Grandmere to grant them a spell or a potion of some kind. Eleri wondered if her great-grandmother had sent some kind of cosmic warning out into the ether. Maybe a ricochet or a ripple had happened through space, letting everyone know she was gone. She was still stunned by Frederick's words. She had thought Grandmere was well into her nineties, but one hundred and seventeen?

How old was my mother? she wondered. *Was Nathalie one of these seemingly immortal women, too? Was she?*

Donovan was eating his breakfast, inhaling the eggs while Eleri picked at hers, when his phone rang. Swallowing the bite he was on, he showed the screen to Eleri. Agent Almasi was calling him.

She gleaned from Donovan's side of the conversation that they were expected out somewhere, and she wondered if she should tell Agent Almasi that her great-grandmother had passed. When Donovan hung up, she asked exactly that.

Shaking his head, Donovan asked, "What would you tell him? That she showed up at the shop and then we found her at home, deceased?"

Eleri shrugged. "There was enough time for her to come back."

"You and I both know she never left this house. Frederick is burying her body. If we say that she's gone, there's every possibility that Almasi won't trust us, or that he'll just get curious and look up the records."

Eleri nodded. "He'll see that she was never declared dead. Won't somebody eventually get suspicious?"

"Possibly, but it's unlikely, if nobody has any reason to go looking for the records." He paused, thinking. "You know, at one hundred and seventeen years old—and given the family history—it's entirely plausible she doesn't have a birth certificate, either. With no Social Security, it means, *no.* No one will go looking for her."

Eleri decided that, until something went wrong, she would let Frederick handle it. It might not be entirely legal, but it wasn't entirely illegal, either. Eleri had plenty on her plate without dealing with the rest of this.

"Almasi wants us?" she asked, turning her attention to the present.

Donovan, whose plate was now clean, stood. "Yes, he wants us at the courtyard house."

"Did they find Darcelle?" Eleri stood, suddenly excited, but Donovan shook his head and she felt like sinking back into her chair.

Forty minutes later, they were across town in the French Quarter. The house was swarming with agents. Yellow tape crisscrossed the front balconies, though people walking on the sidewalk could reach out and pluck it away. Inside the courtyard, and all over the back yard, Eleri could see agents were digging.

Almasi greeted them as he opened the wrought iron gate into the courtyard, allowing them entry. He looked back and forth between them. "I don't know what kind of voodoo you two have, but your SAC told me to put you on this investigation. I thought for sure you would get reprimanded—and instead, I now have to put you on my team."

He didn't seem horribly upset about it, so Eleri merely smiled and asked, "Why are we here?"

"You're a forensic scientist, and we need more knowledgeable hands," he said. Then he turned to Donovan. "Former M.E., correct?"

Donovan nodded. That was when Almasi's expression turned serious. "We have more here than we can handle. I don't have enough agents to cover the number of bodies coming up." He waved to the gate and the people ogling the scene from the other side of the street. "We need to do this quickly."

"Isn't someone tarping the fence?" Eleri asked.

"It's on its way, but the tarps we brought initially weren't big enough," he said. "People were looking around the edges. We've only been here for a few hours, though we taped up the house last night." He rattled off information as he walked into the house, expecting them to keep up, both physically and mentally.

"Darcelle?" Eleri asked.

The agent shook his head. "No sign of her. No use of credit cards, no tracing to bank accounts."

A thought ran through Eleri's head again. Darcelle had said, *There was legal money in the family*, and that implied there was also illegal money. There were Lobomau all over the streets in New Orleans. Though they had disappeared from the shop as quickly as they had come, she wondered where the wolves were now. Would any of them shelter a missing Dauphine sister? She'd heard what Darcelle said to Caspian. And though it looked like the youngest Salzani had been ripped apart by the wolves, there had been no evidence of him at all when the place cleared.

Donovan looked out into the crowd, and Almasi asked, "What are you looking for?"

"I thought the Salzanis or some of their associates might be watching the wreckage."

Almasi nodded in understanding. "Give me the names. We'll pull IDs and get agents on it."

Eleri tapped Donovan's back. "Better to let Almasi and his people look for them. Cabot and his crew are watching for us, but maybe not for the rest of the feds."

Slowly, they turned to the yard and got to work.

It was two days later that Eleri was on her knees under the tree that grew in the corner of the courtyard. They had pulled up approximately seven bodies from the ground, though they didn't have complete skeletons for all of them yet. Some of the bones appeared to match to the original finger bone she'd tried to bring home in her pocket that first day.

The agents now took the bones freely from the house, so there was no remaining trace of whatever had held the bone there the first day Eleri had come.

In the soil under the tree, there had been more bones woven in between the roots. But then Eleri found a body that was free of entanglements, as though the tree had grown around it, rather than through it.

As she carefully extracted this delicate skull from the earth, she knew she was looking at Emmaline.

74

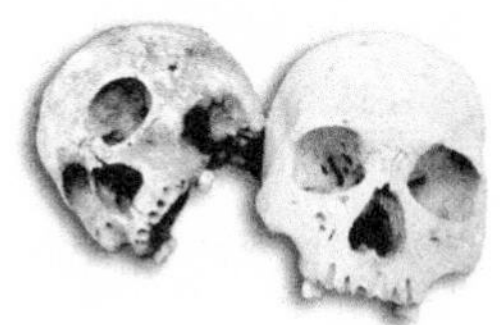

Eleri drove the rental car up the freeway. The road stayed mostly clear, making the drive easy. The hot summer sun left the day a pretty blue, if not a pleasant temperature. But the air conditioning in the car helped make up for it.

Eleri's bags were secured in the trunk, and a wooden box was strapped into the passenger seat next to her, almost as though it were a person. To a certain extent, it was. Although Eleri breathed deeply and, for the first time, with a freedom she had not known in almost twenty years, a weight still sat heavy on her chest. She wondered if she'd ever shake it.

She'd spoken to her mother and father, telling them what she had done. She had told them about Grandmere several days earlier, but she waited until she had everything in place to tell them about finding Emmaline. It had come as a second blow to them, much harder than the loss of Grandmere.

Nathalie had been raised by Grandmere. Her own mother had been absent since Nathalie was an infant. The first Emmaline had been dead since Nathalie was a toddler. Given that relationship between Nathalie and her grandmother, it had only occurred to Eleri *after* she'd delivered the news, that her mother had lost both her mother and her daughter with the span of a few days.

The two cases could not have been more different. If Nathalie knew how old Grandmere was, then she must've thought, as Eleri had, that Grandmere was likely immortal. That had proven not to be the case. While her death wasn't a surprise, it seemed a shock to everyone's system that Grandmere was gone.

Emmaline had likely seemed immortal to her mother, although in an entirely different way. Emmaline was forever frozen in their household at eight years old. The pictures were everywhere. The pictures of Eleri showed her growing up and moving on and becoming an adult. But Emmaline, equally represented in photos on the walls, was forever eight—not gone, not dead, but not found, either.

Eleri had completed a task she'd begun within hours of Emmaline's disappearance. Emmaline's bones now nestled in a piece of linen she had pulled from Grandmere's closet, inside a box that she had also pulled from storage.

Grandmere's home had yielded a wealth of things that Eleri had not known about. Frederick had pulled up a trap door in the kitchen that her grandmother kept hidden under a rug. He led Eleri down into what had once been a root cellar, but now was Grandmere's storage.

On a roughly hewn shelf was a decorated box that had been made for Emmaline. As Eleri stared at Frederick in wonder, he'd only said, "She knew—as well as you did, and as well as I did—that Emmaline has been gone for a while. She also knew that you would find her."

He had left her there after saying his piece, probably expecting her to bring the box up on her own. He seemed to have known she would need a few minutes to throw her arms over the beautiful wood piece and once again cry for the loss.

Unlike her mother, Eleri had believed that Emmaline was dead. But much like her mother, she had harbored a tiny thread of hope. She so wanted to be wrong. She wanted to find her sister alive, though she'd never been able to fathom a story that would have allowed Emmaline to live well into her late twenties yet not come to find her family.

Eleri had tried so many times to imagine scenarios in which Emmaline was still alive. Part of her had believed that, if she was creative enough to come up with a story, then it might be true. Still, the majority of her had always known that this was what she would find. Now, having it done, there was no longer a path before her. It was harder than she could have imagined.

Surprisingly, her father had been heartbroken by the loss of Grandmere as well. Despite his harsh feelings about how Grandmere had let his daughters run free, he'd loved the old woman deeply. Then it was devastating for him to hear about his daughter.

Eleri did not believe he'd ever thought as Nathalie did. He had seemed more accepting of the fact that he would never see his youngest child again. But now, knowing that it was final, Eleri understood that was different.

It didn't make it any better or worse, knowing that her family was one of twenty getting the same notifications this week. The FBI had identified most of the bodies. Seven had come out of the courtyard, and ten more out of the graveyard in the back. Five had proved to be missing children. The others were deceased Dauphine family members.

Darcelle's grandparents had turned up, as well as Tempeste Dauphine, along with another aunt and an uncle who had been buried on the property as well.

Almasi's team had found no more than the ten turned pieces of earth in the cemetery that Donovan had found that first night the two of them had checked. Though the FBI team had gone over the whole place with ground penetrating radar, and an expert to read it, there were no additional bodies there.

How Cabot had managed to go in, dig up graves, and bury new bodies on top of them without anyone finding out, no one knew. That was a question only the witchcraft of the Dauphine sisters would likely ever answer.

Once the bodies were in the branch office and identification had started, Donovan had left town. Both of them decided he needed to get home and back into Westerfield's good graces as quickly as possible. Even though they'd officially been on the clock these past few days, it was best to be Westerfield's agents again—at least for the sake of the job.

Donovan let Eleri drive him to the airport. She'd insisted, dropping him off and turning right back around. She wanted to go back to Grandmere's house and have one last night alone, before the house became Frederick's—before she left, possibly never to return.

She packed up everything. All of her bags were ready to leave the home, but not her memories of Grandmere. Though Frederick had said she could come back anytime she wanted, Eleri wasn't sure she saw that happening.

The day before, she'd driven to the branch office where agent Almasi had remanded the care of Emmaline's bones to Eleri, entrusting her to return them to her home.

They'd pushed through the official ID as fast as possible, as a courtesy to another agent. Because of this, her family was given custody of Emmaline's remains, and Nathalie was planning a service. Eleri had carefully transferred the bones into the box Grandmere left for her, packed her sister into the car, and headed north for Patton Hall.

75

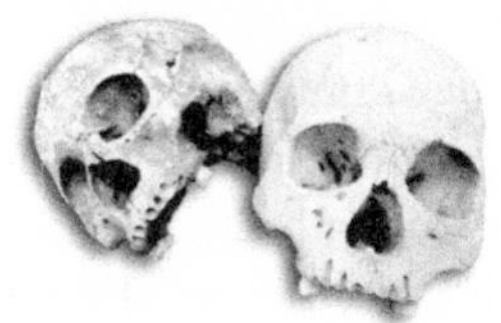

Eleri was an hour away from home when her phone rang. Donovan had called frequently to make sure the trip was going okay. He was worried about her—not enough to insist that he come along, but enough to insist that she check in periodically. Avery had done the same, and she had enjoyed long talks with him that alternately let her cry and helped her take her mind off the issues at hand. She had planned several days to see him while he had a break. He was going to come to Patton Hall to meet her parents. Despite it already being an incredibly tough week, she thought maybe this was the time to do it. Maybe it would make Nathalie Beaumont Eames happy to know that at least her one remaining child had someone in her life.

She and Avery had decided they should stay together, and that this was likely what their life would be like—mostly on the road, mostly away, and catching whatever time they could. Eleri, for a while, had thought she wouldn't be able to live like that. Now she realized she had no other options.

This was the life she had chosen for herself. She had become an FBI agent because of her missing sister, because of the agents who had talked to her and questioned her in the days immediately following Emmaline's disappearance. She had wanted to be like them. She had gone into the Bureau, and later been promoted into the Behavioral Analysis Unit.

She remembered her first days and her first partner, J. Binkley

Raymer, the good old cowboy who helped usher her along and taught her everything he thought he knew about being an agent.

She'd spent later years in the "basement" of the BAU, analyzing files and helping to catch killers, all the while thinking that one day, she would find her sister. And now, Emmaline sat in the box on the seat next to her as her phone rang.

Eleri flipped the phone over and saw that it was neither Donovan nor Avery, nor anyone in her family. It was Agent Westerfield. She thought about not answering it. Her job as an agent was done, wasn't it? Wasn't this what she had come for?

But it wasn't. Donovan had finally told her the man he'd smelled in the alleyway was possibly a brother. Dr. Marks was still missing. And GJ would definitely need a hand forensically with what her grandfather had left her.

No. Her work was far from done.

Her hand rested lightly on the box in the seat beside her. She had found her sister, and she was bringing Emmaline home, for whatever it might be worth at this late date. The thought of not answering the call—of not working with Donovan, of not being what she was—wasn't anything she could fathom. So she picked the phone up, and she answered, "Eames."

Westerfield didn't bother with pleasantries. She knew him well enough now to understand that he'd offered his condolences once, and that would be it. So she wasn't surprised when he rattled off an assignment.

"Can you make it to Nebraska in four days?" he asked. That was the longest he'd ever given her to get on the road. That was his only nod to the family tragedy she was currently suffering.

Mentally, she did the math and shuffled her time. It would only cost one day off her trip with Avery.

"Heath?" she asked. Whether or not Donovan would be there would make a difference. She was going to have to pull her shit together to do this, but there were more people who needed what she and Donovan could do.

She didn't kid herself. She wasn't the only FBI agent out there. She wasn't even the only NightShade agent, but what she had was something special. Selfishly, with everything she'd lost this week, she wasn't willing to give up anything more.

"Yes, the two of you are going in undercover," he said, and then amended it with, "Kind of…" and she listened while he explained. A small town in Nebraska. A dead body, and so on. She would get the details later. She had four days.

He hung up, and she turned the corner onto the small country freeway that led to Patton Hall. She was so close, but as the speed limit dropped, the time got longer. She felt perhaps this time, instead of letting it frustrate her, she would use the extra minutes to prepare.

The trees were lush and green overhead. As the roads got more familiar, her heart settled into her chest. She thought of the dreams she'd had the night before.

Emmaline had been running through the woods. This time, she no longer wore a white cotton dress or chambray. She was in jeans. Jeans with metal rivets, snaps, and zippers, like the girls had sometimes worn when they were children, when Mama didn't have any special event for them to dress up like pretty little ladies for. Eleri smiled.

Emmaline had on a T-shirt with a snarky saying on it. And Eleri had laughed at her, thinking yes, that was how Emmaline would have turned out. Emmaline, forever seventeen, had run through the woods, begging Eleri to follow her. They had come to the clearing with the small square house with the white siding. The porch cut in to the front corner, and the door set at a strange, forty-five-degree angle.

Emmaline pushed open the door and stepped inside. Again, Eleri followed, laughing the whole time.

Inside, the house was quiet. She had seen this house before and had found so many things and so many clues in it. In fact, she thought that once she might have seen the goddess Aida Weddo here.

But this time, she heard a whisper from around the corner. "Makinde." And, as she came to the back room and the rocking chair, she found Grandmere.

ABOUT THE AUTHOR

AJ holds an MS in Human Forensic Identification as well as another in Neuroscience/Human Physiology. AJ's works have garnered Audie nominations, options for tv and film, as well as over twenty Best Suspense/Best Fiction of the Year awards.

A.J.'s world is strange place where patterns jump out and catch the eye, little is missed, and most of it can be recalled with a deep breath. In this world, the smell of Florida takes three weeks to fully leave the senses and the air in Dallas is so thick that the planes "sink" to the runways rather than actually landing.

For A.J., reality is always a little bit off from the norm and something usually lurks right under the surface. As a storyteller, A.J. loves irony, the unexpected, and a puzzle where all the pieces fit and make sense. Originally a scientist and a teacher, the writer says research is always a key player in the stories. AJ's motto is "It could happen. It wouldn't. But it could."

A.J. has lived in Florida and Los Angeles among a handful of other places. Recent whims have brought the dark writer to Tennessee, where home is a deceptively normal-looking neighborhood just outside Nashville.

For more information:
www.ReadAJS.com
AJ@ReadAJS.com

Made in the USA
Las Vegas, NV
16 July 2022

51677737R00215